SADDLED IN SECRETS

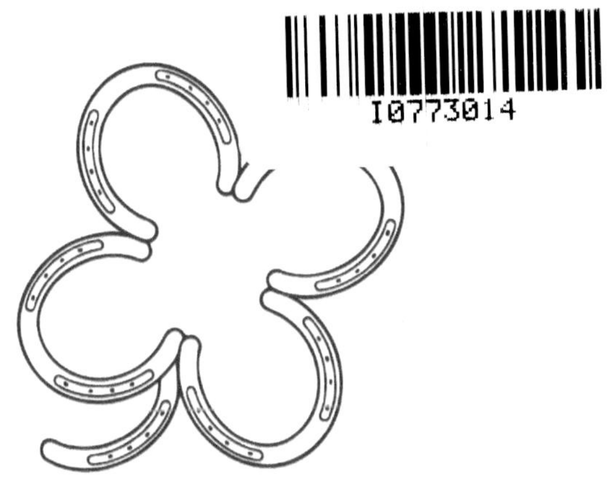

USA TODAY BESTSELLING AUTHOR

HARLOE RAE

NOVELS BY HARLOE RAE

Reclusive Standalones
Redefining Us
Forget You Not

#BitterSweetHeat Standalones
Gent
Miss
Lass

Silo Springs Standalones
Breaker
Keeper
Loner

Quad Pod Babe Squad Standalones
Leave Him Loved
Something Like Hate
There's Always Someday
Doing It Right

I'd Tap That (Knox Creek Standalones)
Wrong for You
Yours to Catch
Score on You
Headed for Home

Cloverleaf Meadows (The Benson Family)
Buckled in Barbwire
Saddled in Secrets
Tangled in Trouble

Total Standalones
Watch Me Follow
Ask Me Why
Left for Wild
Lost in Him
Mine For Yours

Screwed Up (part of the Bayside Heroes standalones)

This book is dedicated to throwing caution to the wind and letting the morally gray stalker bodyguard have his way with you.

A note from the author...

Thanks for choosing to read *Saddled in Secrets*. This is one of my favorites, but don't tell the others. You're in for one heck of a ride.

This novel is a standalone set in the fictional town of Cloverleaf Meadows. If you haven't read Buckled in Barbwire, this book might contain minor spoilers for Brody and Paisley.

I also wanted to warn you about potential triggers. At its core, Saddled in Secrets is the same feel-good story you'd expect from a typical Harloe Rae romance. That being said, Colton Keller—the main male character—is raised by a criminal organization and his past plays a role throughout the story. There are a few violent scenes and mention/use of guns. His upbringing gives him permission to do some not-so-legal things to Bianca—the main female character. (It's just some light stalking and abduction in the name of love.) Colton is desperate to protect the woman he's obsessed with. We love that about him.

Happy reading!
xx
Harloe

PLAYLIST

A Lot More Free | Max McNown
Necklace | Gabriella Rose
Drunk Love | Ty Myers
Options | Cameron Whitcomb
Girl on Fire | Alicia Keys
Weren't for the Wind | Ella Langley
I Got a New One | Elizabeth Nichols
Hate Me | Blue October
Don't Give Up on Me | Andy Grammer
You Need to Calm Down | Taylor Swift
Roar | Katy Perry
You Can't Stop This | Alex Warren
Run It | Jelly Roll
Fall into Me | Forest Blakk
Back of My Truck | Steve Ray Ladson
From Austin | Zach Bryan

Listen on Spotify!

"I've discovered that limits don't exist when Colton Keller is involved."—Bianca Benson

SADDLED IN SECRETS

PROLOGUE

Cotton

Seven years ago…

THE CROWD ROARS WHEN MY OPPONENT CRUMPLES onto the stained concrete. Their rowdy applause is meant to congratulate me, but the noise just spears at my temples like a drill. I don't feel victorious. Everything hurts, especially my pride. It's been three years since I left my father's crew and this is all I have to show for it.

That weighs me down more than the heavy ache in my muscles. I stumble to my corner of the makeshift ring and collapse onto the folding chair. It barely holds me upright. The metal legs wobble under the force of my desolate reality. I'm not sure how much longer I can do this. But what choice do I have?

A glance around the dingy basement proves just how far my ambition has taken me. I fought to escape a life of crime… only to fight for food and a roof over my head.

Maybe this is where I belong—in a windowless room that smells like piss and sweat.

"Great job, kid." A meaty palm claps my bare shoulder.

I'm off the chair and rounding on him in the next breath, all signs of exhaustion forgotten. The man's low chuckle mocks me over the dying cheers of my win. I clench my bruised knuckles and he lifts his hands in surrender. Once the red haze clears from my vision, recognition takes hold. Even a gutter rat like me knows Jimmy Benson.

His family—mostly his older brother—practically owns the entire town of Cloverleaf Meadows. They're millionaires, local celebrities, and legitimate. The cash they rake in through their multiple businesses is squeaky clean. My father's wildest dreams couldn't reach their level, no matter how many laws he broke to get there.

But this Benson in front of me isn't strait-laced like the rest of them. Dad used to brag about Jimmy sniffing around his games every now and then. I can only imagine what this rich asshole wants with me.

"You just made me a lot of money." He rocks back and forth on the soles of his expensive cowboy boots. "And I think there's potential to make a lot more."

Ah, there it is. I narrow my eyes, silently telling him to fuck off. There's not a damn thing he could say that would interest me.

Jimmy bobs his head and raises his palms again. "Okay, I get it. Just something to think about."

And then he's blending into the crowd like a poisonous snake. My upper lip curls, the fire in my gut rekindling. Fucking criminals. They're all the same.

I'm about to reclaim my seat when another man

approaches. His stride is poised and relaxed, labeling him as not a threat. This Benson deserves my attention, unlike his uncle.

My chin lifts in greeting. "What're you doing here?"

An underground fighting match doesn't seem like Brody's scene. We're from complete opposite sides of the tracks, but that hasn't kept us from crossing paths. He's older than me, but not by much. Rumor has it that he's about to take on more responsibilities at Benson Farmstead. Must be rough having unlimited wealth and power at the age of twenty-five.

"I could ask you the same question," Brody drawls.

Which is odd until I recall how I started our conversation. "Something I can do for you?"

"Well, that depends."

My sigh is losing interest with this exchange. "On what?"

"Whenever I've followed my uncle to these matches, you're in the ring."

"And?"

"You're damn good. Drop 'em like flies."

A prickling sensation spreads along my nape and I step back. "I don't need you to stroke my ego… or anything else."

His glare warns me to watch what I'm implying. "You're not my type."

"Hey, man. No offense."

"None taken and for the record, I couldn't care less about what direction your dick swings."

"Uh, right. My bad."

"Do you like doing this, Colton?" He motions from the bookies dolling out filthy cash to the blood stains on the floor.

I shrug. "It pays the bills."

"How about I offer you an alternative?"

My hackles rise. Assumption is quick to tell me that he's just like the rest. But there's no greed in his gaze. I don't see disgust or pity either.

"Let's hear it," I say.

Brody widens his stance. "Now that we've settled I'm not hitting on you, I wanted to offer you a job. There are a few options. Security mostly."

I could almost smirk at his cavalier, don't-give-a-fuck attitude. "Okay, I'm listening."

"Our auction barns and trailer lots need to be guarded. You've proven to be more than capable of defending yourself. My property can use that protection."

Bile rises in my empty gut, but the question needs to be asked. "How's the pay?"

"Better than this."

"What's the catch?"

"There isn't one. I can tell you're fighting as a last resort. It's probably killing you to feel trapped in these conditions. Your drive and determination deserve more than"—he gestures at our surroundings again—"this."

My sore muscles flex, suddenly itching for another round. "Don't act like you know me."

"Tell me I'm wrong." He whips out a business card and tucks it between my scarred fingers.

Against my better judgment, I thumb over the embossed script. Dirt immediately smudges the white paper. How fitting.

"That's my personal cell," Brody continues. "Use it or not. The choice is yours."

Five years ago…

It's damn ridiculous that my fingers tremble while I enter the numbers into the keypad. Almost embarrassing, really. The pressure is getting to me in this moment, but I've been working toward this move for a lot longer.

Brody has rewarded my loyalty countless times over the last two years. Just yesterday, he gave me a personalized code to the locked gates of Benson Manor. That grants me access to his private estate and inner circle. This is the first time I'm entering the promised land unaccompanied, and the sense of trust is more uplifting than a bonus payday.

My truck sputters something fierce as I pull forward along the curved driveway. The 1979 F-350 is in bad shape and needs to be restored, but she's all mine. I bought her as a project to keep me busy, but the list of parts is endless. Not to mention expensive. That process might be able to start soon thanks to the promotion and salary increase. I'm officially at the top-tier of Brody's security team. Maybe I'll be the lead someday.

He's hinted that the position could be available soon if my dedication to the company continues. What's crazy is this has become so much more than a job for me. It changed my life. Brody scooped me off the bloody pavement and gave me an opportunity to succeed. So, yeah… I'll keep busting my ass to follow his orders. The perks aren't too shabby either.

Through the windshield, acres of manicured lawns

stretch in front of me. The Benson mansion and connected offices are on the left. Three large barns and numerous other farm buildings are on the right.

That's where I first see her.

Tires squeal when I slam on the brakes too hard. I barely register the racket, too focused on spotting Bianca Benson in the flesh. Until now, Brody's younger sister was basically a rumor I've heard about. I've watched random clips of her at a competition, enough to prove she's real. Stumbling upon her during practice is another thing entirely.

Not only do seven years separate us, but her barrel racing career requires constant travel. She's the real deal, a professional athlete, winning championship buckles and big checks all across the Midwest. Broader than that, I'm sure. Her mom started her young and they drive wherever the rodeo circuit takes them. Bianca will never have to work beyond her passion—rich in her own right, just from doing what she loves. If that's not inspiring, I don't know what is.

Which is why I find myself hopping out of the truck and cutting across the grass toward the outdoor arena rather than meeting Brody in his office. Bianca is running a brown horse through the pattern. The pair moves seamlessly as one unit around the sharp turns, but the rider steals the show for me. Her braid whips behind her like a lasso. She sure caught my attention with an invisible rope. I have an unexplainable urge to snatch the elastic from her hair and set the dark waves free. That seems more her style, or how she should be. Wild and reckless… flowing with the wind.

After crossing the imaginary timer, Bianca pulls the horse to a stop and her eyes immediately find mine. My lungs seize at the impact. Fuck, she caught me. I drop my gaze, glaring at my worn boots that need to be replaced.

"I like your truck," Bianca calls over the distance.

Heat crawls up my neck. She's making fun of me, pointing out where I stand, as if I'm not painfully aware of how far apart we truly are. I scold myself for getting off track and wandering over here. This is my first day on the new job. Brody is waiting on me. But instead of working, I'm drooling over his younger sister. She's only eighteen, which dumps on another load of shame.

But then Bianca adds, "It has great character. Looks rough and sounds angry, but I bet it's super reliable. You'll never have to question if you'll make it to where you're going. Maybe that's symbolic, hmm?"

All I manage to do is blink in rapid succession. My palm blindly reaches out for support on the nearest fence post. This woman has rendered me speechless, not that I'm much of a talker on a good day.

Bianca giggles at my stunned stupor. "Do you ride?"

I shake my head, still at a loss for words.

Her smile widens. "Might have to change that if you wanna keep up, Cowboy."

Before I can pick my jaw up off the ground, she's trotting off. My stare latches onto the graceful sway of her hips in the Western saddle. That's why I don't notice Brody is standing next to me until it's too late. I freeze at his unexpected presence. The air turns thick, heavy with uncertainty. Guilt sweeps in next and reprimands me for being sloppy. Dammit, he's probably gonna send me packing. It's what I deserve for allowing myself to get distracted.

"I see you met Bianca," Brody muses.

My gulp is thick and can be heard over the pounding in my chest. I'd like to consider us friends, not that I have any others for comparison. Brody has never treated me as anything other than an equal. We respect each other even though he's seen me at my worst. This might finally change his mind.

"Not really," I say after a long pause. "Just stopped to watch her run the barrels."

His glare burns into the side of my face. "Don't make me regret this, Colton."

Resolve washes over me, along with an unavoidable sense of duty. "I'll never give you a reason to doubt me, boss."

"C'mon then." Brody tips his head toward the part of the estate that houses the business offices. "We've got work to do."

And with that, I turn away from the temptation that is Bianca Benson.

Two months ago…

I rip off my baseball hat to rake a hand through my hair. Brody's most recent request hangs between us like a tipping point. Unease slithers into my stomach while I consider the options, but there's only one choice.

"You want me to guard Bianca?" My voice is gritty, as if I just walked into a cloud of dust. I just can't believe he asked *me*.

Brody nods. "But for the sake of her feelings, let's refer to your position as a travel companion. Just for this trip."

"Why do you want me to go?" It seems too convenient seeing as I'd find a way to join her regardless.

His flat stare calls me an idiot. "I'm not letting her fly off to Europe on her own. Usual safety precautions aside, Bianca is upset about our mother's death and wants to escape. She's more reckless than usual."

"Can you blame her?"

He scowls. "She can act like an adult and not abandon her family."

"I don't think that's what she's doing," I mutter.

Bianca is hurting and has every right to grieve in her own way. From what I've seen, her typical outlet would be to hit the road for a rodeo. Those trips were something she did with her mom. It's not my place to express too much of my opinion, but she hasn't left town since Marion passed. This escape overseas might be exactly what she needs. While her brother's intentions might be decent, he's asking me to intrude. She's going to buck this idea harder than a wild filly. If I were to go about it on my own, she wouldn't be aware of my presence.

As if hearing my resistance, Brody grunts. "That's not your problem to worry about. Just watch out for her. You're the only one I trust."

"As her companion," I repeat. Clarification is key.

"Think you can handle it?"

Fuck, talk about a loaded question. Brody warned me to keep my distance and I've listened. Mostly. That first glance haunted me. I had to get another, which quickly spiraled into an addiction. Her comments about my truck stuck with me too, even after all these years. I've made sure to be a reliable presence if she ever needed me. The urge to protect her kicked off from there.

Whenever Bianca was in town, I wasn't far from her side. She doesn't know about my obsession since I've always kept to the shadows, and I plan to keep it that way.

If asked, she would say we're practically strangers. Meanwhile, I probably know her better than myself. Five years of stolen moments add up to an unrequited love worthy of some Shakespearian shit.

I've tried to fight this infatuation, but Bianca is some sort of a magnet. She makes the days brighter and the lonely nights shorter. Her smile cures the darkness I still harbor. Whenever I'm near her, my troubles fade into a muted hum. I no longer care about where I came from or smothering my demons. The past doesn't feel so heavy and there's a future worth striving for.

That doesn't mean I deserve her. Nobody does, which is why she's still single. Bianca doesn't date, at least not seriously. The only guy I've overheard her mention is Scout. He's just a faceless name, but I'll admit to picturing his demise. Such a waste of effort. I'm better off trying to convince myself that Bianca is secretly crazy about me and can't get attached to anyone else. A smirk almost makes an appearance. Just fantasizing about it is delusional enough.

I can count on one hand how many times we've spoken. And now her older brother is hiring me to follow her. I have his permission to finally step out of the shadows.

Bianca is going to hate me for this.

The elastic hair tie around my wrist snags my focus. I snap the worn band against my skin, my head bobbing along before I realize it. "It won't be a problem, boss."

Bianca

The next day…

The plane reaches cruising altitude, but leveling out does little to untangle the knots in my stomach. I haven't been able to relax since the behemoth of a man plopped his sculpted ass on the leather sofa across from mine. Colton's presence spreads across the private jet's cabin like a virus. It's suffocating and reminds me why I wanted to do this alone.

A disgruntled huff escapes me while I slump lower in my seat. "I still can't believe you're crashing my vacation. This was meant to be a solo excursion."

Colton just grunts. That's it. No actual words to engage in a respectful conversation.

Good thing I can talk for both of us.

"Once we land, feel free to go your own way. I don't need you following me around."

The flat look he shoots at me disagrees.

"Brody wouldn't know, if that's what you're worried about," I try. "It can be our secret."

The mention of my older brother doesn't make an impact on his stony features. I would've been surprised if it did, but it was worth a shot. Colton is extremely loyal to his best friend. When Brody hired him to escort me, there was zero resistance. He owes him much more than babysitting duty. Whatever insane amount he's getting paid doesn't help my case either.

Defeat rests on my chest like a sack of bricks. It adds to the grief and stress and exhaustion already piled on me.

My breathing kicks up. I count to three, slowly exhaling the pressure from my lungs. I miss my mom. What I wouldn't give for just one more hug. The harsh truth that I'll never get one is devastating.

All I have pushing me forward is the determination to fly free for once. But the ginormous dream killer across from me wants to clip my wings—just like Brody and Dad.

"Please, Colton. The entire point is to go off on my own. It's really important to me."

He doesn't so much as blink. His lack of compassion is concerning. It troubles me more than it should. I suddenly feel too exposed and avert my gaze to the nearest window. It's dark beyond the glass, which offers zero comfort. Maybe this is a mistake.

I hang my head, allowing the pain to wash over me. Mom's death is still fresh like a festering wound. She left us so suddenly. My emotions have been rubbed raw over the past two months. Sorrow sunk its claws deep and I desperately needed a reprieve.

As if the agony of losing my mother wasn't enough, the entire town has placed bets for when I'll crumble. Odds were sooner than later if I'd stuck around.

I told my brother I needed to do some soul searching and find myself. It might seem strange and probably selfish, but I couldn't stay at the manor for another minute. The walls started closing in on me, regardless of the mansion's size. Our family estate is too empty without Mom. Her absence is a gaping hole at every turn. I had to get out of there, just for a reset. No matter how brief.

This trip was my mom's idea. She'd dreamed of touring Europe when she was younger. Since she never got the chance,

I decided to do it for both of us. Once the idea formed, I couldn't stop thinking about it. I didn't make plans beyond getting to Germany. That's where she mentioned wanting to start once. My uninvited guest doesn't fit into the itinerary.

Colton continues to stare straight ahead as I pull myself from those thoughts. His expression is stoic and impassive, revealing just how happy he is to be here. We have that in common, which might make it easier to get rid of him.

With nothing else to look at, my gaze takes a leisurely stroll across his face. Tan skin emphasizes rugged features. That stubbled jaw could cut steel. Muscles are stacked on muscles underneath his snug shirt. I'd appreciate it if he didn't look so damn hot on the clock. The grumpy attitude really does it for me too.

A long-winded sigh breezes from my pursed lips. At least I have decent scenery for the duration of the flight. Once we land, I'll find someone more personable to scratch this itch he's inflicted with his broody bossiness. Either that or I'll sleep for an entire day. The latter is more likely.

Weariness settles in my bones and I sigh. I'm just so fucking tired of pretending. I wanted to go somewhere to escape the reputation of our last name for a while. Where nobody knows me. It's not too much to ask.

But now, I'm trapped on a plane with my brother's best friend and he won't even speak to me.

I don't know what it is about Colton that grates on my nerves. Maybe it's the fact I can never get a reaction from him. At this point, I just want to see him falter.

"I'm horny." My voice is a purr as I sprawl out on the couch. "Let's have sex."

Colton's blue eyes clash into mine. Static crackles between

us as he watches me. He's completely still. I'm not sure if he's even breathing.

Laughter bursts free from my successful strategy. "Oh, that's what it takes? You're totally busted, Cowboy."

The heat in his smolder fizzles into a glare. "Brat."

I recoil. "Excuse you?"

Colton's nostrils flare from a heavy exhale. "You're a spoiled brat, Princess."

Fire smacks my cheeks. "And you're a rude asshole."

He shrugs. "Just doin' my job."

My jaw drops. This is the most he's talked to me in the five years I've known him. I'm not sure where to go from here.

"You could be a bit more understanding," I mutter.

"That's not what I'm getting paid for."

"Ohhhhh," I breathe. "This is all about money. Got it."

His jaw clenches. "No, this is about keeping you safe."

"I don't need you to protect me."

"That's not your decision." His smug expression sends a hot spike of irritation through me.

My eyes abandon his unwavering focus for the sake of my pride. "It's probably best if we don't talk anymore."

Colton braces his inked arms along the back of the sofa. "I give it two minutes. Max."

I clamp my lips tight to prove him wrong, but the tickle in my throat is prepared to do the opposite.

This is going to be a long-ass trip.

Colton

Once again, I find myself sitting outside of Bianca's bedroom in our suite. It's become a habit since we arrived in Germany last week. She fucks herself frequently and I'm stuck in the same space with her insatiable appetite. I didn't expect her to constantly dangle forbidden fruit in my face. It's almost as if she's torturing me for denying her a quick fuck on the plane. But something tells me she doesn't know I'm listening like a creep.

A prickly awareness spreads across my nape when she moans from behind the closed door. She releases another throaty noise, making my cock twitch. It's an instinctual response at this point. Her show is about to begin, and my dick wants a starring role.

"I'm ready," Bianca's breathy tone beckons.

My head thumps against the wood separating us. She whimpers and rustling follows. I bet she's ramping up for the next level. Her vocals are enthusiastic. Even the toy she uses is loud and unapologetic. If I didn't know better, I'd think she wants me to hear her.

"Yes, yes!" Her voice teases me through the barrier between us. "That feels so good."

Arousal pumps hot through my veins. Physical desire is a weakness. A distraction. I don't allow myself to fall victim to these urges, but Bianca Benson is my exception.

Typically, I can maintain a tight grip on my control even when she's around. The hair band on my wrist nears its breaking point when I snap it against my skin. The sting is useless against her pull. This situation has proven to turn me into a simpering fool. I find myself in this exact spot night after night, waiting for her performance to hit the climatic peak. Bianca is unraveling my composure and I'm unable to stop it. Much like now.

My hand rips at my belt, fumbling to undo my jeans

in a hurry. I'm not sure I've ever been this hard. My cock hurts, and not because I've been jerking off more than usual.

Images assault me while I gather precum from the tip, stroking the moisture over myself. I picture her sprawled out in bed, bare pussy on display. The vibrator sinks into her easily. There's minimal resistance. She's that turned on. I'm right there with her, pausing only to spit in my palm to glide faster. It would take a few pumps from her hand to make me blow my load. A throb pulses through my dick while Bianca mewls. I envision her thrusting the toy deeper.

Fantasy and reality merge when she whimpers. "Ohhhh, don't stop. More. Please."

Desperation coils in my gut, ready to burst. My dream girl is just beyond reach. How easy it would be to reveal my position and join her.

A recognizable buzz tells me she's upped the speed, getting herself closer. Fuck, she's testing my limits.

As if hearing my control fraying, her sweet seduction calls out. "I need you."

That command snaps me out of it.

"Bianca," I growl.

The vibrations cut off immediately. Silence descends and stretches. It's quiet enough that I can hear fabric rustling. She's probably going to bed. That means I should too.

But she pushed me tonight. I need relief or my brain won't rest. Sleep still won't come easy, but I'm about to.

My palm resumes pumping a steady pace. The throb in my cock spurs me faster as I stare into the darkness. I picture Bianca sitting in the oversized armchair facing me. She watches as I stroke myself, leaning forward to get a better view. Her big tits nearly spill out of her shirt. My balls tighten when I imagine tugging a pebbled nipple be-tween my teeth.

Warm tingles spread across my lower back in warning. I'm close. Bianca's lush lips pull up in a coy grin. She wants to see me lose it. That rips a garbled rumble from me, along with spurts of cum. I bite down on my knuckles as my re-lease coats the other hand. The third pulse hits my lower stomach and I jolt from the force.

"Fuck, fuck," I groan into my fist.

"Colton?" Her soft voice slaps me from the fantasy.

My high from the burst of pleasure evaporates instantly, replaced by the shame of being caught. Bianca's face would be scrunched in disgust to find me in this position. The sticky fluid covering my abs feels dirty. It burns like acid—a careless mistake.

I scramble to my feet, rushing across the living room to my door. This is what I get for surrendering to temptation. The lock clicks shut just as I hear hers open, but she won't find me loitering again.

Not until Bianca is ready to take all of me.

Bianca

A fast techno mix blends seamlessly into the final beats of the one currently playing. The heavy notes pulse into my chest like a living thing. Shouts roar across the crowd and people begin jumping. Their excitement is infectious, pumping me full of renewed energy. This is exactly what I needed. Stress and grief melt away as the electric tempo blasts from the speakers.

The nightlife in Germany doesn't sleep. Everyone other

than Colton has been dancing nonstop for hours. I've lost track of time in this windowless room, which is most definitely on purpose. It's safe to assume the sun will be rising when we leave. Unless the party runs on an endless loop, which is highly possible. There's no sign of stopping in this club.

I thrust my arms into the air while swiveling my hips. Sweat drips down my back from the effort. It's sweltering with so many bodies crammed into such a small space. We're constantly bouncing off each other like a friendly mosh pit.

A guy leaps in front of me and I stumble backward on my Jimmy Choo wedges. He reaches for my arm to steady me. His touch is gentle, dropping away once I'm stable. Smoke and strobe lights distort my vision, but there's no denying the man is hot.

There's a silent apology on his lips while he stops to stare. I accept his gesture with a grin. His responding smile is paired with a smolder meant to incinerate panties. My knees get a bit weak. His dark eyes study my face before taking a noticeable dip to admire the rest, but then a massive cockblocker steps between us.

Colton glares at me. He ditched his Stetson for the evening. His light brown hair is tucked under a backward baseball hat. I'm not sure which variety I prefer. Either way, he looks menacing.

I wiggle my fingers, attempting to charm Colton's surly attitude into submission. His scowl only deepens. Same cycle, different place. It's laughable.

My humor fades when he swoops in, his exhale breezing across my sweaty skin.

"Don't even think about it," he rasps. "You're not going home with anyone, Princess."

"Other than you, right?"

His nod is slow and steady. "You won't leave my sight."

I fight to trap a whimper after that gravelly command. Instinct suggests I give him sass and ask what happens if I do. His guttural voice sounds like a promise of much more than sharing a suite. Goose bumps break out despite the feverish temperature surrounding us.

My lips brush his ear when I whisper, "I'll do whatever I want, Cowboy."

He straightens to give me the full intensity of his stare. I can read his expression like an instruction manual. Just yesterday, he listened to me get myself off. I haven't told him I know. Was I being loud on purpose? Yes. But then I got embarrassed.

It's not like I actually want to sleep with him. Another glance at his towering frame has me reconsidering. A rough and dirty roll in the hay wouldn't be bad. Well, it probably would. I laugh at my own twisted solution of fighting this attraction. Colton glowers in return. Ugh, forget it. He'd probably be a snooze in the sack.

As if hearing my prediction, his eyes meet mine in a heated exchange. It feels like a tease caressing my skin and I shiver despite the sweat clinging to me. More prickles break out along my arms when his gaze dips to trail a droplet of sweat trickling between my breasts. This skimpy dress is definitely a winner. Power surges in my veins. I want him to crack.

But Colton's focus returns to my face. "Ready to leave?"

I laugh, the tune raspy from yelling over the music. "And do what?"

"Rest your back."

"It's fine. My scoliosis doesn't mind dancing." I roll my lips between my teeth, fighting a smile over the fact that he seems to care about my condition.

"It wouldn't hurt to get some extra sleep," he presses.

"Or we could have sex."

His jaw grinds. "No."

"Bummer," I sigh and cast my sights across the crowd. "Guess I'll have to find someone else to do the deed."

His blue eyes light on fire. "Go ahead and try. He won't be walking out of here with his dick attached."

"How attractive," I mutter.

Colton towers over me until he's all I see. "Fuck around and find out, baby girl. You have no idea what I'll do to protect you."

Colton

"Another glorious day." Bianca hums as we browse the first aisle of the outdoor market.

I inhale, trying to catch a whiff of her perfume. "Mhmm."

"Are we lucky or what? The weather is crisp but not too chilly." Her attention is quick to spot a tiny horse figurine that's for sale at the next booth. "Gosh, I love this town."

"And their handmade crafts," I mumble.

Trips to these local events fit into our regular routine. She's in her element and radiating happiness. The glow in her expression matches the sparkle in her eye. It's incredibly endearing, spreading warmth through my blackened heart.

"I do love my crafts." A grin lights up her features even more while she spins in a slow circle. "Look at all this stuff. We'll never get bored."

Yearning spreads through me while my focus devours her joy. I discreetly pay the vendor for the small horse statue and tuck it into my pocket. "This is where we'll stay until you decide otherwise."

"I can't imagine anywhere better. It's cozy and peaceful and exactly where I imagine my mom visiting."

"You chose well," I praise while sliding into stride next to her.

Bianca tips her head to the sunny sky. A dark braid hangs over her shoulder. My fingers itch to discover if her hair is as silky as it looks. I clench my hand into a fist and fight the urge as usual. Her smile widens while she soaks in the moment.

"Essen feels like the place I've been missing," Bianca sighs to break apart the silence. "I was meant to be here."

"Your mom would agree," I murmur.

"She put the idea in my head for a reason. There's such rich history." Her arm flings toward a block of nearby buildings that are older than Minnesota. "Just look at that, Cowboy. The architecture is freaking impressive."

"Sure is," I agree. "Not to mention the endless festivals and parties."

"This is the best." She grants me another wide smile. The carefree expressions are frequently aimed at me lately, but I'm always eager for more.

I get caught staring and lower my gaze. "It's strange that you've never been to Europe until now."

"Why's that?"

"You're rich beyond reason. If you snapped your manicured fingers, a private plane would appear and jet us off to another location."

She wrinkles her nose. "Don't make me sound so… spoiled."

"Well," I chuckle. "That's the truth. It's refreshing that you don't take it for granted."

I'm expecting a rebuttal, but Bianca is quiet. My gaze slides over to find her eyes already on me. A blush colors her cheeks and she averts her stare.

"You have a nice smile," she murmurs. "It's an underrated trait for men. Really sells me."

I hadn't even realized I was smiling. The expression was almost nonexistent until she started dragging them out of me. My lips quirk higher under her admiration.

Bianca sighs. "Too bad my brother hired you to follow me around."

"Why's that?"

She hops on the balls of her feet to get closer to my ear. "You're growing on me."

Desire floods my bloodstream like a drug, but I force myself to appear unaffected. We've fallen into a cooperative pattern of sorts that I refuse to ruin. She's finally accepted my company without a fuss. I appreciate walking beside her rather than behind. The lines are still drawn between us, but they're getting weaker. An opportunity to blur them isn't hard to come by.

Like now, our hands almost touch with every step. How easy it would be to clasp her palm in mine. Would she allow it? We still haven't discussed how I stood and listened to her fuck a dildo. Maybe she doesn't know I was there. Or it might be a mistake she'd prefer to forget. I can settle for her friendship. That's more than I deserve.

My phone buzzes with an incoming text. I pause next to

an artist's booth and dig it out of my pocket. Bianca purses her lips, already assuming it's from her brother. She's not wrong.

> Brody: Need you to do something for me.

> Me: Name it.

What he sends next puts a blade in my grip.

> Brody: Take Bianca's phone. Block her from social media. Make sure she can't communicate with Paisley. I need this wedding to go through without a hitch.

My gut plummets. It will sever the delicate understanding I've achieved with his sister. There isn't a choice when it comes to Brody's demands. The loss is already spreading through my chest, leaving me cold. Just like the unfeeling pawn I was raised to be.

We might've had something. How foolish. Why did I let myself believe she could see me as anything but her brother's enforcer? When I dare to look at her, there's a frown twisting her beauty.

"What is it?"

"Nothing for you to worry about, Princess."

Not until I follow through.

Bianca

Another week, or maybe even two, has dragged by. It's difficult to tell when time blends together in a monotonous blob. Colton reverted to a stone pillar after Brody bossed him around about something. The wall between us is taller than ever and I'm too stubborn to climb it. Not after he's refused to budge on almost everything I request.

Instead, I'm back to entertaining myself. The hook pulls the yarn through the loop to finish my last stitch of this row. I exhale and hold up my work in progress. It's about halfway there, if my makeshift pattern is anything to go by.

My eyes flick to the screen just as the Quickfire Challenge is starting on this episode of *Top Chef*. The contestants race around the kitchen to gather supplies. Captions scroll to tell me that they're responsible for creating innovative versions of cheese curds. I can almost smell the fried goodness from here.

Meanwhile, a masculine voice whispers sexy somethings directly into my ear and I shiver. The romance I'm listening to on my Kindle is cranking up the heat. At least someone is getting fucked properly. My ass slouches deeper into the velvety cushions as I resume crocheting.

Movement on my right catches my focus but I don't turn. It's just Colton doing whatever the hell he wants. Several choice words curl on my tongue, ready to fling at him. But he doesn't deserve my insults.

"Possessive jerk. Never has any fun. Spiteful prick. Wouldn't know how to treat a lady if chivalry hit his stupid sexy face," I mutter at his reflection in the bay window.

A smile lifts my lips and spirits. What can I say? It's difficult to keep my mouth shut, especially when it comes to that man and his controlling tactics.

The brooding slab of destruction paces into the living room. Colton stops in front of the television and turns to where I'm parked on the sofa. His hulking form is completely blocking my view. Rather than stoop to his level, I turn up the volume on my spicy audiobook and focus on yarning over like a pro.

He steps closer, giving me a whiff of his spicy cologne. I breathe through my mouth to avoid inhaling him. His cowboy boots enter my lowered field of vision. The brute is baiting me on purpose. Why he insists on doing so is beyond my comprehension of this sideways situation.

I glare at him, but remain silent. This is our new normal. We almost turned a corner after strolling through outdoor markets for days on end, but then my brother texted him. Maybe Brody thought we were getting too close, which seems odd. Not that I can ask him.

My phone is missing, which prompted Brother Dearest to cancel my credit cards and lock me out of all my accounts. Colton is being a real dick about letting me talk to anyone. The potential for a truce between us went up in smoke after that.

These days, after recent developments, we're back to barely tolerating each other. It bothers him that I don't sass him at every opportunity. I doubt he'll ever admit it. His mouth presses into a pissed-off line while mine curves upward. I silently celebrate these small reactions.

Unfortunately for me, this man isn't a quitter. His sinfully full lips are moving but I can't hear him. I find myself wondering if I'll see him smile again. But then I reprimand myself. *Why do I want to see him do anything but take me home?*

He's still blabbing on about something. I tap my

headphones and shrug. At inhumane speed, he snatches the Bose off my ears.

"Hey!"

Colton crosses his arms, dangling my escape from reality like a carrot. "I asked you a question."

My eyes narrow into slits. "And I chose not to answer."

Fury burns in his blue gaze and he inhales a deep breath. "What are you making?"

"Why do you care?"

"Bianca," he growls.

"Ear muffs." I roll my eyes at this sorry excuse for a conversation.

A furrow dents the space between his brows. "They're not round."

"Thanks, Captain Obvious." Frustration huffs from me as I examine the triangular shape. "These are for Luna. I'm making a pair for Bandit next."

"Your horses?"

"Their ears get cold in the winter."

"That's the most ridiculous thing I've ever heard," he grumbles.

"Shouldn't have asked." I stab the hook through a loop for the next stitch.

Colton doesn't move from ruining my view. It's clear he isn't done being a pain in my ass, but I don't have to entertain him. Animosity rolls off him in furious waves. The crash against his shallow tolerance makes me edgy. If he doesn't leave, I'm likely to crawl out of my skin.

"Do you have something else to say, Cowboy?" I force a sweet smile. "Or can I return to pretending you're not here?"

"How can you do"—he waves from my crochet heap

to the television before lifting my headphones—"all of this at once?"

"That's not for you to worry about. It's my bubble of chaos and you're intruding."

"Don't you want to go somewhere?" He motions to the splendor of Essen, Germany that waits just beyond the glass.

But I've lost interest with him breathing down my neck. "I want to call Paisley."

"What's her number?"

My upper lip curls at his smug tone. Such a fucker. I can't remember my best friend's digits and he's rubbing it in my face.

"Ask Brody." This isn't the first time I've suggested the easy solution.

"He's busy." And that's the typical response I receive in return.

"Can I check my socials?"

"Those accounts are compromised."

Irritation grates on my last nerve. That's been his robotic reply whenever I've asked. I examine his features for any hint of deception. It seems strange that my entire digital footprint would be impacted after my phone was stolen. Not that I can confirm or deny the claim. Even the Wi-Fi on my Kindle is limited.

"How do you know?"

"Brody told me to keep you offline."

"And you do whatever he says."

His nostrils flare. "Yes."

"Loyal lapdog," I sigh.

"Just doing my job."

"Yeah, yeah." A flick of my wrist dismisses his excuse. "When can we go home? I'm ready for this technology lockdown to be over."

"Soon."

"That's what you always say."

Colton's shuttered gaze drifts to the front door. "And eventually, the answer will change."

My fingers strangle the ball of yarn to resist throttling him. "I thought if I snapped my fingers, a plane would appear in the sky?"

"As it turns out," he drawls. "Even you have limitations."

"Go figure. I'm a hostage on my own vacation," I mumble absently. "Trapped in a gilded cage with my bodyguard. How romantic."

This trip lost its purpose before it truly began. My stomach sinks while I mourn the wasted opportunity. Mom would be very disappointed.

"Don't fret, Princess. You'll be breaking hearts and wreaking havoc on your home turf by the end of the month." The tattooed grump's expression sours into a tight pucker. He probably ate a lemon to perfect the look.

I toss my unfinished ear muffs beside me. "That's still two weeks away."

"Could be faster." Another evasive response.

The urge to snap at him gnashes my teeth. I hate how much power he holds. It's only gotten worse since I lost my phone. Maybe I should try masturbating my brains out again. At least I was blissed out then.

But Colton might hear me if I do. The reminder heats my cheeks. That won't fly, especially when we're barely on speaking terms.

Whatever. I stare at him while he glowers in return. A sigh buzzes my lips. Such an attractive grouch. My gaze swoops lower, appreciating the full package. His shirts are unnecessarily tight. It's like he can't find any that properly contain his oversized ego. Or he's purposely putting himself on display. If that's for my benefit, it's another missed opportunity. There's no sex in our future.

Colton's mouth opens but then his phone chimes. He digs it out of his pocket and glances at the screen. Tension solidifies his muscles into a statue.

"Duty calls," I grumble at his reaction.

"We'll finish this discussion later."

"I'd rather not." My fingers beckon for him to return my precious headphones. "Just leave me alone, m'kay?"

Colton's flinch is slight, but I notice. Guilt threatens to retract my statement. Pride raises her head and flips him off.

Just a bit longer. Once we're back in Cloverleaf Meadows, we'll go our separate ways and I'll put this disaster behind me.

CHAPTER ONE

Present day…

I'M NOT SURE WHERE TO BEGIN, BUT MY CURRENT pickle of a predicament seems adequate. My morning started off with a ransom call. And for the record, receiving threats of bodily harm before sunrise is a rude awakening.

Do what we say and nobody gets hurt.

The cagey voice haunts me as I blindly follow the directions.

If your dad and brother show up, the mare pays the price.

A shudder racks my limbs and I grip the steering wheel tighter. As it turns out, Uncle Jimmy decided to steal my late mother's favorite horse to pay off a debt to this shady crew of cowboy criminals. I'm not sure how he got onto our property and snatched Echo without anyone noticing, but the fact that he's my dad's brother must've lent a hand.

Maybe Colton will get fired. The thought almost makes me smile until the GPS tells me to turn right.

All these people want from me in exchange is a conversation. Or so they claim. That's how I find myself pulling up to what appears to be an abandoned building on the outskirts of town.

Paisley is practically trembling in the passenger seat as I shift the truck into park. My best friend is the only person these crooks approved to join me on this rescue mission. Based on the ashen hue to her complexion, I should've left her sleeping in my brother's bed.

But it's too late now.

I cut the engine when an older man appears in front of the steel structure. From the corner of my eye, I notice Paisley typing on her phone. She's more than likely texting Brody, choosing to ignore my warning. The instructions I received were very specific about not telling anybody else or they'd hurt Echo. That means I better haul ass before reinforcements arrive.

Hinges creak when I open the door and jump out. My bestie follows my lead, sticking to me like glue while we approach the guy shrouded in shadows. I ignore the tension knotting my stomach into a tighter tangle with each step.

"You made the right choice, Bianca Benson."

My heart lurches even though it's not surprising he knows my full name. Uncle Jimmy obviously gave this man every bit of information he needed to contact me. What's shocking is the guy's appearance. I'm instantly creeped out when his dead eyes settle on me, shivering from the impact. My body naturally sways closer to Paisley for moral support.

"Where's Echo?" It's a small victory that my voice doesn't shake.

He lifts his chin to where some goon is loading the buckskin mare into my trailer. "This won't take long. I just needed to get your attention."

"By stealing my horse?"

His shrug indicates he couldn't care less. "Jimmy owed me money. I have something we need to discuss. The opportunity fell into my lap."

"Okay, so…?" I roll my wrist to move this along, emboldened by his nonchalance.

He stays silent while keeping that flat stare fixed on me. I get the hint that this portion of the program doesn't require an audience. With a beaming grin that belongs in a beauty pageant, I turn to my friend and try to remain calm.

"Will you go check on Echo while I finish this… friendly chat?"

Paisley remains rooted to the spot. "Are you sure?"

My nod is automatic. "I'm fine. Echo needs you more than me."

After a parting glance at the scary dude, and against her better judgment, she does as requested. The stranger's emotionless gaze watches her walk away, allowing me to openly study him. He looks like a moldy sack of expired produce. There might be muscles underneath his Western shirt, but what remains of his bulk can't hide the rot taking over. I swallow when bile tries to climb up my throat.

His disturbing eyes return to me. "Do you know who I am, Bianca?"

My hip cocks to the side, feigning nonchalance. There's no reason to expose the tremble in my fingers.

"Other than the guy who accepts stolen horses as payment?" I glance at the sky, avoiding his creepy focus. "Not a clue."

The man's flat expression remains devoid of any feeling. "I can see why he likes you."

It's obvious he expects a response from me. Too bad my stubborn streak is longer than the Kentucky Derby. I lift my brows, unwilling to eagerly grab for the carrot.

"Gonna need a favor," he states.

"And I'm gonna need to get gone before you ask." I kick it in reverse, keeping him in my sights.

A muscle jumps in his clenched jaw. "I'd wait if I were you."

My boots pause in the gravel. "And why is that?"

"I'd hate to make your life difficult."

"More threats? How innovative." Not sure where this death-defying attitude is coming from, but I hope it sticks around.

"Just need you to pass along a message. That's all," he states.

"Why don't you do it yourself?"

"He won't listen to me, but I have a feeling you'll get a different result."

"Not sure how that's possible." Any acquaintance of this man's is now an enemy of mine.

"My son is quite taken with you," he mutters.

"I also find that extremely hard to believe."

Something unsettling glints in his eyes. "Colton hasn't mentioned me?"

That blow almost tips me sideways. "Colton is your son?"

"Indeed. We're estranged, but I'm hoping to fix that. With your help." That last part isn't a request.

"What do you want him to know?" I hate that my voice shakes.

"The family business needs him. Daddy wants him to come home."

My lips part on a traumatized breath. But then, by some miracle, a loud commotion distracts me from the disturbing news he just threw at me. I whip around to my trailer before he can land another blow.

"This conversation isn't over," he bellows.

I don't spare him a backward glance. "It is for me."

"He's worse than I thought," I mutter to myself while making a hasty retreat from the front yard.

Paisley and Brody probably want answers, but I'm not ready to go there yet. They don't have much room to argue either. My best friend married my brother strictly for his convenience. It's a bizarre twist of fate I'm still wrapping my head around. But that's a puzzle I'll attempt to solve a different day. Right now, I need to figure out what to do about my so-called bodyguard and the truth bomb that his father just dropped on me. Maybe I'll get to fire him myself.

"Can't freaking believe it." Grass is crushed under my boots as I stomp across the lawn to the beat of my frustration.

I didn't plan on speaking to Colton Keller ever again after the disaster in Germany. That assumption has turned out to be foolish, much like his offenses against me. The worst of his crimes wasn't even revealed until we got home a few weeks ago. The phone he took—but had me believing was stolen—is tucked safely in my back pocket. After my brother and his fake-but-now-real wife made nice, my former jailer was permitted to return my precious device. As a shock to nobody, he swept his behavior under the *just did what I was told* rug. I called him a twat waffle and we've barely spoken since.

He's crossed more lines than a dark romance that's heavy on the trigger warnings.

I'm pissed at Brody too. He put the deception into motion, but Colton was the one to drive the damn bus over me. Besides, Paisley already gave my brother hell for the whole ordeal. She's dealing with him accordingly. That makes Colton my problem, but I want nothing to do with him. Unfortunately for me, after the events from this morning, he seems to be an unavoidable issue.

A sweet crispness drifts on the autumn breeze and I inhale slowly. I need to decompress before doing anything else. My mind isn't quite right after the stress from this morning. At least those cowboy criminals kept their word and let me bring Echo home. A shudder ripples through me while I recall my conversation with the leader. It's not one I'll ever forget.

Here's to hoping my current crochet project and a cooking show will distract me for a bit.

Just as I'm about to hang a hard left into the house, I spot Dad in his favorite Adirondack chair. The one beside him is empty. That was where Mom used to sit. Gosh, I miss her something fierce. A pang ricochets through my heart and I change course, striding over to him.

"Hey, Dad. Want some company?"

His unfocused stare is wandering across the sprawling acres of Benson Farmstead. I follow his gaze to appreciate the view.

White fencing leads to our three main barns. Horses roam in the pasture closest to us. The cattle are corralled on the opposite side. Numerous storage buildings are visible in the distance. Apple orchards and organic produce fields are planted beyond that. There's plenty more where all that came from around the compound.

It's paradise. Plain and simple. This property has been in our family for generations. That's why I'll never choose to live elsewhere, even though most would've already fled the nest by twenty-three.

Dad blinks from wherever his thoughts had wandered and offers me a weak smile.

"You've had quite the start to your day, kiddo. Take a load off."

I plop down when he pats the space next to him. My mom's presence instantly wraps around me like a warm hug. Her memory is here with us, which takes a bit of the edge off. It allows me to relax in the chair, breathing deeply for the first time since I received that phone call.

My palm pats his. "How are you holding up?"

"Me?" He scoffs. "I'm not the one who had to rescue our missing horse. When your brother called to tell me, I couldn't believe it."

"That was an unexpected twist."

"Jimmy really buried himself in the shit this time." He scrubs a hand along his weathered face.

"Any idea where he went?"

Dad shrugs. "Off the grid. He'll resurface once he's run out of money or ran up another tab with the wrong people."

"I assume he's done this before."

A slow nod confirms my hunch. "It's gotten worse since the divorce. Donna was smart to leave when she did, but Jimmy is unraveling without her. It's become an addiction. I should've been paying more attention."

"Is that how he got through security?"

He nods. "The guards had no reason to question him. Jimmy hasn't done anything to raise that type of suspicion. He's usually in and outta here with a trailer to take horses or cattle to the auction barn. I didn't think he'd ever stoop low enough to steal one of ours. It's my fault for not flagging him."

The somber note in his tone cuts me deep. "Give yourself a break, Dad. You're dealing with enough as it is. Jimmy is his own person. Not to mention a grown-ass adult. He can take care of the mess he's made."

"But he still dragged us into it."

I blow out a thick exhale, tempted to suggest we fire Colton. That's not the support Dad needs right now. "What can we do?"

"Remind the folks who took Echo that we aren't interested in cleaning up after Jimmy and his selfish decisions." Dad's shoulders hunch more than usual under the weight of these recent events.

"Do you know them?"

"Unfortunately."

A wince pinches my features. "Are they dangerous?"

Dad takes entirely too long to think about it. "From my understanding, they prefer to stay under the radar. Their organization gets by on low-level deals. Mostly," he tacks on absently.

Too many possibilities whip through my mind. "Am I supposed to know what that means?"

"No, Bee. Don't you worry." He gives me a grin that's meant to be reassuring. "This is for me and your brother to handle. I'll probably get your cousins involved too. But you stay out of it, okay?"

Easy for him to say. I bounce my knee as indecision plagues me. The jostling motion tweaks my hip and a cramp spreads from the joint. I hiss while rotating my leg, attempting to stretch away the burning pain.

A comforting palm lands on my arm. "You okay, kiddo?"

"Just the usual," is my sputtered response.

Except this feels like a charley horse on steroids. Driving under duress put more strain on my muscles. Heat stings my eyes while I try to breathe through the debilitating spasm. There might be a knife stabbing into my thigh at this point.

After a solid minute of trying not to cry, the agony recedes into a dull throb. I massage the area to keep the relief coming. Dad is silent beside me, unsure what to do. The only option is to wait until it stops. It's normally not this bad, but these random onsets are somewhat expected.

I'm out of alignment due to the severe curvature of my spine. There's a lot going wrong back there. My skeletal structure as a whole is impacted—such as one shoulder is slightly higher than the other and the right side of my torso dips in while the left bumps out. Sometimes I worry about my ribcage collapsing, but that's mostly a nightmare. I have muscular imbalances too. That doesn't mean I'm restricted to certain activities. It's just something I've dealt with since getting diagnosed with scoliosis in fourth grade.

"Should've kept that brace on," Dad mutters.

"Mom wouldn't hear it."

Natural development and growth in my early teens took priority. Once my mom realized the pressure it put on my chest and lower stomach, I was freed from that torture device. That meant I leaned heavily on other treatment options. Yoga, physical therapy, and regular massages are vital. Can't say I'm upset about the choice. I'd make the same one for my daughter.

The parent that doesn't have to deal with menstrual cramps and boobs grunts his contention. "But now you're more crooked than a dirt road through the woods."

"Jeez, thanks a lot." I roll my eyes. "It corrected my curve two whole degrees in the years I wore it. Not worth the hassle. Hasn't gotten much worse as I've gotten older either."

"Yeah, yeah. Your mother knew best." He chuckles, which is a joy to hear. "There's always surgery."

Unease worms through me like a cold dose of reality. "That seems like a last resort. Not to mention it's a very invasive procedure. The soreness and aches are manageable for now. If it gets to a point where I can't move or function normally, I'll look into other treatments."

"Just worry about you."

"Right back at ya, Pops."

He scoffs. "I'm healthy as a horse. Straight as an arrow too. Not sure where you got that curvy nonsense from."

"That's one way of describing my scoliosis." I shift my pelvis, rolling in small circles until my hip is quiet again. "See? Good to go."

But Dad's shrewd gaze doesn't appear convinced. "Maybe you should call Dr. Powell for an emergency session."

I wave off the suggestion of extra physical therapy. "A spin on Bandit will do the trick."

Some might think my pain would get worse from horseback riding, but it's actually beneficial for me. I'm aware that's not the norm, which goes to show how extra twisted scoliosis is. It impacts everyone differently. What helps some might hurt others. I just stick to what makes me feel better and horses do that for me—in more ways than one. My worries melt away when I'm in the saddle. Crochet and channel surfing can fix the rest later.

But just as I'm about to stand, our conversation from before this detour prods at me. I'm still not sure how to broach the subject. "Weren't we talking about something important?"

Dad hangs his head as humor shakes through him. "You're asking the old fart with a poor memory?"

"At least you're aware of your downfalls," I tease.

He makes a shooing motion. "Go ride your horse and leave me in peace. It's time for my mid-morning nap."

But I stay rooted to the chair. "Dad?"

"Bianca?"

"How much do you know about Colton's past?" I blurt the question even though it's been perched on my tongue for hours.

Brody could give me an answer, but my brother is on my shit list. I'd rather avoid him for the time being. Besides, my father has to know. He's the most reliable source as far as I'm concerned.

His keen stare narrows on me. "Whatever you're about to say is better off being spoken to the man himself."

A pit forms in my stomach while the unavoidable route to the truth presents itself. "That's exactly what I'm afraid of."

"He ain't gonna bite ya."

Warmth spreads through me like a lethal infection. "I wouldn't be too sure."

"Something I should be concerned about?" Dad's voice carries a protective edge.

If only I could pass off my problems that easily. "I can handle him myself."

"Mhmm, that's my brave girl." He beams with pride. "Didn't raise you to shy away from the tough stuff."

"Kinda wish you had."

"Gonna make me dizzy goin' 'round in circles, kiddo."

"Welcome to the circus." I bobble my head back and forth.

"Just call me the ring master. But hey, I'll tell you this much." Dad leans closer as if he's about to spill very expensive tea. "Colton will do just about anything for you."

My lungs quit functioning until I consider his conspiratorial tone. "Ohhh, no you don't. You already played blackmail matchmaker with Paisley and Brody. I'm not falling into this trap."

He folds his hands over his middle, reclining deeper into the sloped seat. "Suit yourself."

All I can do is laugh while knowing full well Dad is far from done sharing his opinion on the matter.

CHAPTER TWO

Cotton

MY GAZE HAUNTS BIANCA'S RUSHED STRIDE TOWARD the horse barn. I haven't taken my eyes off her since she returned from that unexpected disappearance. She left too abruptly for me to tag along, but I tracked her location to an unfortunately familiar area. There's been a sinking feeling in my gut ever since.

I adjust the brim of my hat and consider the repercussions. Bianca hates me enough as it is. If the truth of my past comes out, she'll never speak to me again. Can't see much of a future if that happens.

Damn, I'm in too deep. What started as a forbidden attraction to my best friend's younger sister became a full-blown obsession when she blossomed into an undeniable need. Toss in the protective instincts I gained along the way and here we are. The intensity borders on panic at times, which is why I don't let her roam too far.

I almost lost my mind after she left unannounced this

morning. Darkness threatened to consume me, along with the demand to chase her. Those urges were about to take the wheel, even just to follow her home, but then she pulled into the driveway.

My thoughts are still in tatters as I watch her from the shadows behind the tool shed. I'll be on her ass for the rest of the day. It's not rational or normal and I've learned to accept that.

These stalker tendencies didn't exist until I met Bianca Benson. If she knew the lengths I've gone to in recent years, she'd probably run or have me arrested. I'd almost like to see her try to get rid of me. The tightness in my chest only eases when I have her in my sight. She's awoken parts of me that were better left sleeping, but there's no shaking me loose now. Satisfaction carves my lips into a smirk.

As if determined to push me from hiding, Bianca bends to pet a dog that's run up to her. She gushes all over the pampered pit bull while sticking her ass in the air. Lucky pup. Not sure which one this is. There are too many to count. Her bleeding heart rescues the lost causes from shelters and rehabilitates them into faithful companions. Maybe that's why I'm drawn to her—in hopes she'll give me a life worth living. But I'll never let myself have her. It's not like she'd argue.

That doesn't stop me from stepping onto the gravel path behind her. Bianca turns at the sound of my approach. Her friendly smile slips into a scowl when she realizes it's just me.

"Colton." She mutters my name like a curse.

I walk forward until her bewitching scent fills my lungs and calms me. "Hey, Princess."

Bianca's eyes flick from my baseball hat to the ink

covering my arms, trailing lower over my shirt and belt buckle that leads to the bulge beneath my zipper. She sputters as the denim stretches tighter under her admiration. I should be ashamed of my body's reaction, but the blush staining her cheeks is far from offended. Her gaze remains on my swelling cock and she traps her bottom lip between her teeth. The urge to thrust my hips forward to give her a better view flexes my muscles.

After a thick pause, her gemstone green eyes lift to the sky while she mutters something that sounds like a prayer for patience. "Why are you following me?"

It's almost comical that she believes this is a rare occurrence, but my expression remains neutral.

"I wanted to make sure you're okay." My gaze drops to her right hip to avoid confusion.

When the joint seized and she crumpled in pain, it felt like a whip lashing across my skin. Failure drilled into my bones while I watched her suffer. There wasn't anything I could do. Not that I'm in a position to extend open arms for support. Any attempt wouldn't be welcome.

Which Bianca confirms by crossing her arms in a defensive pose. "I'm fine."

"Looked like a bad one."

Her sigh is a blatant dismissal. "You're off the clock, Cowboy. Time to find a new victim to harass."

I almost smirk in the face of her sass. As if I care about anyone but her. Well, that's not entirely true. Brody is my best friend. More like a brother. He found me at my worst and gave me a purpose. If I'd stayed on my own any longer... I grimace at that alternative. It would've destroyed me. But thanks to him, I don't have to worry about succumbing to the past. That's why I've kept my distance from his sister—out of respect—but then he went and hired me to guard her. It's almost like he knew I was already doing the deed for free.

Another annoyed huff escapes the woman in front of me. Our gazes collide. There's something churning in hers. That intuition from earlier has me widening my stance, preparing for the firing squad. But Bianca stays quiet. I'm more than familiar with this attitude she insists on serving me. Her stubborn silence chaps my ass and she knows it. My irritation spikes when she presses her lips into a firm line, making me do the honors.

"Say it," I rasp.

Her chin lifts. "What makes you think I have anything to say to you?"

I know you better than you think, Princess. But I don't reveal that. It won't earn me any favors after the mess I made in Germany. There's just so much left unsaid between us. A new complication is the last thing I need in this uphill battle.

The tension between us strangles me until it's difficult to drag in a full breath. "There's something on your mind. Let me have it."

Bianca's pause is heavy as she considers how hard to jab. "Where did you grow up?"

"Outskirts of Cloverleaf Meadows." Which is the middle of fucking nowhere.

"Is your family still there?"

It's a struggle to keep my expression devoid of emotion. "Not sure."

Her brows pinch inward. "You don't talk to them?"

The thought alone sours my stomach. "Haven't kept in touch."

"Why not?"

"How about you tell me why you're asking instead," I drawl.

"I met your dad." She thinks on that for a beat before adding, "Or that's who he claims to be."

Fuck, it's worse than I thought. "And?"

She falters, clearly expecting a different response. "He wants me to pass along a message."

"I'm not interested in hearing it."

"Okay." Bianca averts her stare. "Guess I'll deal with him on my own."

Fury blisters under my skin and I bristle. "What's that supposed to mean?"

"Why do you think he accepted Echo as payment from Uncle Jimmy?" Her deadpan tone isn't appreciated. "It got my attention. Now Daddy Dearest wants to use me to get to you."

I lunge forward until we're almost touching. "Did he threaten you?"

To her credit, she barely bats an eyelash at my proximity. "Not really, but I'd prefer if it doesn't reach that point."

Old wounds rip open in a painful slash that curls my hands into fists. "I'm gonna kill him for roping you into his illegal shit."

"Let's not be extreme."

"You're right," I mutter. "He deserves worse."

Her eyes bulge. "What's worse than death?"

"That's for me to worry about."

"Uh-huh, sounds familiar. I'm just supposed to pretend everything is sunshine and rainbows."

"It's dangerous, Princess. You need to stay far away from him."

Bianca scoffs. "Too late."

The uncertainty of this situation makes me itchy. I hate that we're miles apart while standing so close. It's my fault but I can't convince her to trust me when she knows better. Not until I take out the trash.

"I'll handle him from here, okay?"

"Just like that?" She snaps her fingers.

That lack of faith offers me a challenge. It's a chance to prove myself and protect her in one swoop. I shift closer until my height towers over hers. Bianca just shoots me an annoyed glare. My lips almost twitch. So damn sassy.

"You think I won't?"

Her laughter lacks any trace of humor. "Oh, I'm well aware of your dedication to a task. You're still hounding me even though I'm home safe and sound. The job is done, Cowboy. I'm not your problem anymore."

"That's what you think," I rasp.

"Very funny. If I'm such a pain in your ass, allow me to quit for both of us." Bianca spins on her heel and resumes stomping to the barn. Her glare skewers me over her shoul-der. "And stop following me."

I give it approximately five seconds before going directly against her wishes. My steps shadow her fuming silence until we're almost at the door.

"Seriously?" She whirls back around, hands parked on her curvy hips. "I'm going for a quick ride. There's no harm in that."

"Then you shouldn't care if I watch."

"Fine, have it your way." No sweeter words have been spoken. But then she adds, "Nobody ever listens to me."

That stops me short—false as it is—but she doesn't get too far ahead. One problem at a time. Eventually, I'll reveal just how much control Bianca Benson has over me.

CHAPTER THREE

Bianca

"Okay, let me get this straight." Paisley's forehead is creased into deep lines. "Colton is still acting like your bodyguard?"

"Yep," I confirm with a pop of my lips. "If Brody wasn't following us, his best friend would be."

She shields her eyes from the sun while glancing at her husband. "Is that true?"

My brother's perma-scowl locks onto her. "Shouldn't have run off on a rescue mission without telling me."

She slams to a halt on the sidewalk. "Is this a punishment?"

"Safety precaution," he corrects. "More for her than you."

Frustration rises when his head tips at me like I put myself in this position. "Nobody is coming after me."

"There's always a risk," he says smoothly.

"But we're just going shopping at Life's a Stitch." Paisley points at the brick building on the next block.

"The craft store is extremely dangerous." A dramatic eye roll pairs well with my sarcasm.

My bestie glances between me and Brody. "Then why do we need a chaperone?"

"They're paranoid," I mutter.

She grips my arm. "What aren't you telling me?"

I inhale a lungful of fresh air, but it doesn't offer clarity. "According to the overbearing men in our lives, it's not for us to worry about. Isn't that right, brother?"

He grunts, but doesn't dispute the explanation regurgitated by Dad and Colton.

Paisley tugs me off to the side, avoiding fellow pedestrians. "Is this about that creepy guy we had to meet to get Echo back?"

"Yes."

"Did you find out who he is when you talked to him alone?"

"Yes," I repeat.

"And?"

"It's probably better if you don't know." I'd kept her in the dark on purpose, but that makes me somewhat of a hypocrite.

Her blue eyes narrow in agreement. "Tell me, Bee."

"He's…" I blow out a heavy breath. "Colton's father."

Paisley's jaw drops. "No way."

"Mhmm, caught me by surprise too. I wasn't sure if I should believe him, but why would he lie? Anyway, that whole ordeal caused Colton to double down. It's worse than before, which was already suffocating. He's following me ev-er-y-where," I drag the word out for emphasis. "Even to the arena on my own property. I can't ride my horse without a shadow."

"But he isn't here now," she notes absently.

"Only because this one is," I remind her with a stab of my thumb at the glowering grump. As if we could forget my brother's intrusion.

"Seems strange if Colton has been hounding your ass harder than ever."

"Thanks for that visual." I clench involuntarily, but then a realization strikes. My stare whips to my brother. "Where is he?"

The intensity in my voice catches me off guard. It's not that I care. Nope. Not even a little bit.

"Gave him the night off," Brody drawls.

A prickling sensation sneaks along my nape. "Is he confronting his father?"

"Don't know what you're talking about."

"Cut the shit. You know by now that he wanted me to pass along a message to Colton."

"Which is…" Paisley interjects.

"Shit, sorry." After sending a scathing glare to my brother, I turn back to my friend to fill in the rest of the details. "Turns out that scary dude runs illegal operations in these parts. Whatever that means."

"It's not your business," Brody grunts.

"But it's Colton's to inherit."

Paisley huffs. "I'm lost. Again."

"That's the message," I clarify. "His dad is ready to retire or whatever criminals do in their golden years."

"What's Colton going to do?"

I shrug. "Beats me."

We turn the force of our joined attention onto my brother. He pinches the bridge of his nose. "Just drop it, yeah?"

"Unlikely." I tap the toe of my boot into the concrete.

"He's tying up loose ends," my brother shares almost unwillingly.

My curled upper lip isn't impressed. "How ominous."

Brody pulls at the cuffs of his shirt, looking ready to throttle me. "Are you going shopping or what? I have work to do."

"Feel free to go do it. We can take care of ourselves."

"Gave Colton my word that you wouldn't leave my sight while he handles things."

"Uh-huh, how precious. Remind me," I coo and tap my chin. "Who's in charge?"

His annoyance skewers me. "Not you."

"We'll see about that." I loop my arm through Paisley's and drag her forward. "Let's ditch him."

"I don't think that's a good idea." But a backward glance makes her shiver. "Oh, maybe it is. He looks positively feral."

"Is he following us?" My gaze remains fixed forward.

"And then some. Me likey his sex face." Her throaty tone makes me gag.

"Gross. Not sure I'll ever get used to the two of you together."

"Give it time. We're still new." She blows him a kiss.

"And extremely affectionate." I turn to see Brody hot on our heels. "You're making it harder to get rid of him."

"Like he'll ever lose track of us in this town. People will snitch instantly."

My fingers curl around the door handle of Life's a Stitch.

A warm burst of heat and the overpowering fragrance from scented candles welcomes us. "I'll crochet a blindfold for him unless you'd prefer to do the honors."

Paisley scans the large store stocked with potential. "You know buying a boatload of crafts and not doing a damn thing with them is more my thing."

"And not leaving you two unsupervised is mine." Brody appears like a pest I've tried and failed to exterminate, looping his arm around his wife's shoulders.

"Impossible," I groan while fetching a cart. "How can I get a moment's peace?"

"Quit putting yourself in dangerous situations," my brother suggests unhelpfully.

"Dad said these people weren't necessarily dangerous."

He snorts. "That's a pacifying statement if I ever heard one. He avoids upsetting you whenever possible."

My stomach drops. "Is Colton in trouble?"

Brody chuckles, but the mocking sound tapers off when he notices I'm not amused. "Don't underestimate him, Bee."

"I have no idea what he's up against."

"There's not much that can stop him." His glare drills into me.

An icy shiver creeps down my spine. "And why is that?"

"Ask him tomorrow."

"He won't tell me anything. The guy is a vault of secrets."

Which is the way it should be. Whatever Colton is hiding doesn't involve me, much like he said. I'm determined to keep my distance.

"You'll be surprised what you can drag out of him." My brother's muttered tone suggests that's upsetting for him to admit.

"Puh-lease," My hand blindly grabs a bag of cotton stuffing, squeezing harder than necessary. "He'll do whatever you tell him, as I've unfortunately experienced."

"Mhmm," Paisley mutters absently while dumping an armful of glitter jars and rhinestones into the cart.

When Brody smiles at his wife and her selection, I almost topple sideways. "Whatcha making, Twinkles?"

"Not sure yet." She boops him on the nose. "But we can never have too much sparkle."

He makes a rumbling noise in his chest and hauls her against him for an indecent hug. "You can decorate me again."

My best friend melts into his embrace. "Deal, husband."

As a hopeless romantic, their obvious love and near constant displays of affection fill me with giddiness. I could kick my feet and giggle at their combined happiness. But as Brody's younger sister, I've got the serious ick. My focus averts with purpose while they continue discussing creative uses for Paisley's purchases.

A shudder rolls through me and I swerve into the next aisle. Footsteps don't follow. A peek over my shoulder finds them in the exact same position. I could probably slip away from these two lovebirds without notice.

The cart squeals when I slam to a halt. An idea forms in my mind like a complicated crochet pattern. My smile stretches as the details solidify and a feasible plan of escape stitches together. Just for a few days to be free of my last name. The microscope this town puts me under has gotten too focused over the past several months. After Mom passed, I realized she shielded me from more than bad boys and speeding tickets. Although, I bet she'd be tickled pink to know how close Colton is guarding me in her absence. But that's not the point.

Privacy and autonomy are taken for granted. I'm desperate for a small slice right now. That's all I need. The urgency that constantly claws at my chest goes quiet and I can breathe.

"What's that look for?" Paisley is suddenly in front of me, blessedly detached from Brody.

I blink from the daze, but my grin remains. "A design just spoke to me."

"Love when that happens. The project actually gets done," she sighs.

A renewed sense of excitement puts a spring in my step. "It's the best."

CHAPTER FOUR

Cotton

I CREEP ALONG THE SIDE OF THE BUILDING, AVOIDING the cameras docked overhead. Shadows conceal me as I approach a past I never planned to revisit. I'd prefer this stain on society disappeared entirely. Voices from inside the warehouse disturb the silence and prove they're still going strong.

Gravel crunches beneath my boots like broken memories. As predicted, Walker is guarding the main entrance alone. It's almost like a decade hasn't passed. My cousin got assigned that post when he turned eighteen and finally earned some responsibility. His lack of ambition must've kept him from climbing higher in the ranks.

I find myself wondering if his sister is nearby, but dismiss the thought immediately. Frankie was a scrawny teen when I left. I'd hate to see what this life turned her into.

Walker is standing under the single spotlight with his back to me. Plumes of cigarette smoke curl above him and stretch toward me in a toxic cloud. His addiction is more important than paying attention to the threat closing in behind him.

Old habits of my own slip on like well-worn jeans. My knife is pressed against Walker's throat before he can take another drag. "Don't move."

This is how my father trained me to be. Ruthless. Cold. Effective.

My cousin's Adam's apple bobs with a gulp. "Welcome home, Colt."

"Not staying long. Just need to re-establish the boundaries."

Walker snorts and makes sure I can see his eyes roll. "Still a traitor then?"

"Yup." But only to those who betrayed me first.

"Such bullshit," he spits. "We're family, Colt. Blood bonds us. Gonna shred me to pieces over some rich bitch?"

I dig the steel into his skin until a trickle of blood drips over my knuckles. "Don't talk about her."

Walker doesn't listen, which hasn't changed either. "She's got you all wrapped up, huh? Just like the boss said. He's got you pegged."

"Get him out here." My voice is deadly calm.

"How do you expect me to do that while you're holding a blade to my neck?"

"Not my problem. Just make it happen."

He tosses his cigarette before digging out his phone. The screen is bright in the darkness, even with the spotlight over us. I squint while he types. His message provides minimal context, just stating someone is out front to see him. Probably did me a favor not mentioning my name. It won't grant him leniency.

But he doesn't know that.

My weapon lifts off Walker's throat in a false surrender. He doesn't get the chance to move. After raising a bent arm, I jab my elbow between his shoulder blades. He spins toward me, allowing my cocked fist to clock him twice in the jaw hard enough to send him reeling. I stretch out the burn in my knuckles. Damn, that feels good.

Walker stumbles to the side and clutches the injury. "What the fuck?"

"Told you not to talk about her."

"Does she—?"

That's all he gets out before I'm lunging forward. My knee rams into his gut while I get another punch to his face. He sputters, spitting out blood as his head snaps back. The sight feeds my instincts that I usually keep on a tight leash. Power surges through my veins and the demand for violence roars. I stalk him like easy prey, ready to strike again.

"Colton."

The sharp tone cracks through the ferocity like thunder. I halt in my tracks even though I quit obeying that voice's orders a decade ago. But this is his turf and I'm outnumbered.

My boots grind into the rocks—envisioning the much more satisfying crunch of bone fracturing beyond repair—as I turn to the man in charge. James Keller is an imposing force, but I feel nothing when our eyes meet. Emptiness is my comfort zone when it comes to this shitty excuse for a parent.

I've seen him around town since I left the crew. This is the closest I've been. He's older—deep into his sixties—and it shows. More weathered than an abandoned shack left to rot. Time hasn't been kind to him, but he still oozes dominance.

Shame threatens to surface. I try to push it back down, but the contempt swallows me. The fact that I allowed him to control me for all those years shrivels my pride. Dark memories haunt the edges of my vision, beckoning me to get lost in the pain. But then I absently snap the elastic on my wrist. The slight sting settles me.

Chocolate brown hair and forest-green eyes replace the void. Her smile is radiant, cracking through the murky depths. Bianca is my tether—the stars in the night when I'm lost. The reminder almost brings me to my knees. I'd crawl over broken glass for that woman.

And skewer my father if he ever puts her in harm's way again. He glares when I refuse to cower. His authority doesn't rule over me. Not anymore.

Rough hacking interrupts our hostile reunion. Walker is still recovering from my assault and not being quiet about it.

"Get yourself cleaned up." My father dismisses him with a flick of his wrist.

I stay quiet, assessing him. His attention roves over me in return. Crickets serenade our standoff.

My dad clears his throat. "Well, you're here faster than I predicted."

"Rather get this over with." I cross my arms and continue glaring him down, urging him to spew whatever bullshit spiel he planned.

"That girlfriend of yours is an effective pawn."

Anger surges in my veins, flexing every muscle to pounce. "Stay away from her."

His eyes gleam after I gave him the desired reaction. "I might dangle her in front of your nose until you listen."

The insinuation almost makes me launch at him. "If you try to contact her again, we'll bury you."

"We?"

"You know who I'm friends with."

"Friends," he laughs but the sound is a taunt. "Don't fool yourself into thinking you're one of them, kid. You'll never truly fit in. They'll always see you as an outsider."

I force myself to appear unaffected, but my blood is boiling inside. "The roads we've traveled don't mean shit. When it comes to Bianca's safety and well-being, we're on even ground. The entire Benson family will destroy you if she gets hurt. That's a war you won't win. I'll be at the front of the line to watch you fall."

"Damn," he chuckles again. "Quite a speech. They've really turned you against me."

"You did that on your own." The damage he caused would cost a fortune to fix, and that's just the psychological aspects.

"What's it going to take for you to come home? Claim your rightful place at the top. That's where you belong." He beckons me forward. "Don't settle for the scraps they're tossing at you. All of this can be yours."

My boots remain firmly planted on the other side of this imaginary line he's drawn. "Not interested."

"No? Does your precious treasure know about your past? Or is she under the illusion you were trained to fight in a prestigious academy?"

"Not sure what that has to do with anything." I'm under no illusion that Bianca thinks of me beyond being a pain in her ass.

My father scoffs. "You're a gutter rat like the rest of us,

Colton. The sooner you remember that, the faster we can get back on track."

There's some truth to his words, but I don't want to hear it. Brody saved me. I ran from my father's crew when I was twenty. It wasn't easy to leave, living on my own. The last seven years have been a breeze in comparison to the first few thanks to him taking me in. The trust and responsibility he's handed over is worth far more than anything this crook is trying to swindle.

I'd love to punch the smug grin off his wrinkled face. He won't let me walk out of here as easily if I do. It might be a battle already depending on his mood. Fine by me. Walker's bruises were just a warning. I stretch my knuckles again. As if my father could forget what he created.

But this isn't about swinging our dicks. It's best to reserve the violence for if he contacts Bianca again.

My flat expression reflects boredom. "We done?"

"What do you think?"

That this was an enormous waste of my time and patience. "Was there a plan beyond pissing me off?"

He shrugs. "Just hoping to have a conversation, which is what I told Bianca. Be sure to pass along my gratitude."

My vision narrows into a point where he's the target. "If you're smart, you'll forget she exists. You don't want Dennis and Brody as enemies."

He waves off the barely retrained fury in my voice. "She served her purpose. I just needed to get your attention."

"You got it." But not for much longer. My skin is starting to itch. I need to get back to the manor.

His sigh almost sounds resigned, but that can't be right. "The truth is that I'm sick."

"Tell me something I don't know."

"It's cancer," he clarifies. "Stage Four."

That gives me pause, but little else. If he's expecting sympathy, he should've thought twice about beating it out of me. The disease will make him suffer a worse fate than any torture he dealt. Maybe there's a semblance of reckoning in that. But I still feel nothing. He doesn't deserve an ounce of pity.

When I don't respond, he fills in the lull. "I don't trust anyone else to run the business."

It's comical that he believes I'll eagerly jump into his leadership position like I didn't leave on purpose. This delightful meet and greet was meant to remind him of where we stand—on opposite sides of the fence. That's how it will remain.

"You won't see me again unless you force the issue, and then you won't like the outcome."

My father squints at the overhead light where bugs are swarming. "I'm dying anyway. How much worse could it be?"

I grunt. "Of all people, you should know the answer."

His attempt at coaxing me back into the fold misfires like a shoddy pistol. My father must read the decision in my blank stare. He nods and steps back.

"I'll be seeing you, son."

"Not your son."

Amusement brightens his gnarled features. "Disowning me officially?"

I turn away, but give him the answer as my parting gift. "Did that when I walked out the first time. Hammer this reminder into your thick skull. There won't be a third one."

CHAPTER FIVE

Bianca

KNOTS TIGHTEN IN MY STOMACH AS I TIPTOE ACROSS the yard. I stick to the shadows, avoiding spots that will trigger the motion detectors. Just a few more feet until I reach my car. After that, I can go wherever I want and stay gone until my moral compass drags me home. There isn't much of a plan beyond getting past these walls caging me in.

"I can do this." The whispered encouragement is purely for me and the nerves trying to lock my legs. "Stay sleuthy, Bee."

Tonight unfolded into opportunity. Dad has bingo, which keeps him occupied until nine o'clock. Brody decided to take his wife out for dinner. Colton was the last to leave, trailing after my brother and Paisley as if I went along with them. My phone that's secretly tucked into her purse strongly suggests that's the case. Following a false scent serves him right. I had my suspicions about him tracking and that confirmed it.

The window for escape is slim. I'm moments away from finally running wild. My muscles flex in preparation and I dash to the large boulder that hides me from the last sensor. It will really suck if my brother or Colton get alerted to me creeping across the lawn. Black leggings and a hooded pullover only hide me to a certain extent.

The cool metal of my sleek Audi meets my back once I cover the remaining distance. My door opens with a whoosh. A smile curls my lips when the overhead lights stay off. That was smart thinking, but I don't have much time to gloat. I slip onto the leather seat like a stain. My index finger shakes as I push the ignition button. The quiet purr from the engine resembles a stampede trampling on the silence.

Terror freezes me for several seconds. My wide eyes scan from left to right, triple-checking that the coast is clear. Paranoia has its claws in me, but there's no sign of anyone. Sweat slicks my palms when I grip the wheel and pull forward onto the driveway.

I use my brother's code at the gate just for shits. It's the same reason I made a fake body lump under my covers before fleeing the scene. Colton will curse me for that extra detail. Too bad I won't be there to see it.

The road to freedom appears in front of me like a miracle. Tingles race up my spine as I stare straight ahead. There's nothing except darkness, but it's never looked more inviting. My foot meets the accelerator and I'm gone.

"Holy shit," I breathe. "I did it. I actually freaking did it!"

Thunder crashes in my pulse and can probably be heard from a mile away. Nobody is here to listen. The street is blissfully empty. My high beams blaze across familiar landscape that will lead me to nowhere in particular. *Paradise.* Flutters replace the tightness in my gut and I press harder on the gas.

"See ya, Colton." My laughter is manic as I celebrate this small victory. "Good luck explaining my disappearance to the boss."

The thrill of pulling this off shimmies my hips. That's when I realize what's missing. I created a playlist full of women power anthems just for this occasion. "Girl on Fire" by Alicia Keys is the first song to blast through the speakers. Positive energy radiates from the tempo. I start singing like I'm on stage, putting on the performance of a lifetime. As I'm belting out the lyrics, stress flakes off my shoulders like burnt skin.

I'm about to really let loose on the chorus when movement in the backseat strangles my vocal cords. A shadowy figure appears in the rearview mirror, noticeably sitting upright. My scream hits an octave that might shatter the windows. The intruder doesn't appear fazed by my shrieking.

"Holy shit!"

This time, the expletive is paired with a sharp swerve. The tires squeal as I struggle to regain control. A muscular, tattooed arm shoots forward to stabilize the wheel.

I recognize the ink first. His woodsy scent is a close second. Somehow, the telltale cologne didn't register while I was focused on making a run for it. The weight of a shackle returns to my ankle as if it never left. What a damn tease.

My palm blindly smacks at the volume button in an attempt to hear myself think. The quiet does little to comfort me. Fringes of fear still shadow the edges of my vision. I try to slow my breathing and soothe this frantic response. It fails, much like this attempt at freedom. So much for leaving my troubles behind. The road in front of me now leads to a dead end.

Heat pricks at my eyes, but I choke down the threat of tears. I won't cry. Not in front of him.

"Are you fucking serious, Colton?" I grit out between clenched teeth.

"Princess." The nickname is a scold. "Did you really think it would be that easy?"

His tone is calm as he casually props an elbow on the center console. Meanwhile, I'm fighting to keep my heart from beating out of my chest. I focus on the bold yellow lines that disappear into pitch black.

"Why are you lurking in my backseat?"

He climbs into the front with the grace of a ballerina rather than a six-foot-five buzzkill built like a linebacker. His stare burns into my profile. "Dramatic impact?"

I glare straight ahead. "Very funny."

"It fit the vibe. You were sneaking across the lawn like the star in an action movie."

The fact he's making fun of me after cancelling my plans is salt in a very raw wound. I need to pull over. Immediately.

A darkened building appears on the left. After a quick scan of our location on Chestnut Avenue, I realize it's the feed store. At this hour, the parking lot will be blissfully empty and ideal for ditching unwanted cargo. I crank the wheel hard. The sharp turn sends Colton crashing into the window.

Thick fingers prod at a spot on his forehead. That's probably going to bruise. "The fuck?"

"Whoops." I lift a shoulder. "This situation has me edgy."

He glances at Cloverleaf Cooperative, which is obviously closed. "What are you doing?"

"Well, I almost had a panic attack thanks to you." My Audi screeches to a halt near the plant nursery. "And now, I'm dropping you off. Get out."

"After you, Princess."

I shoo him like a nosy stud colt crowding my space. "Go away."

"No."

Something cracks inside me. This shouldn't be a battle. I shift into park and turn to face him. Our gazes lock. A spark travels between us and I shiver.

"Please, Colton. Let me do this."

He winces, but the crack in his stony mask is gone in an instant. "I'll go with you."

"That defeats the purpose," I say dejectedly. "How did you know?"

"I saw Brody and Paisley leave. You weren't with them, regardless of what your phone's tracking suggested."

Damn this man and his bombproof work ethic.

"Why didn't you just wait by my car and catch me before I got in?"

"That would've ruined the surprise."

"I'm so glad my misery is amusing. You gave me false hope."

"You gave that to yourself. Nice pipes by the way."

My cheeks burn at the reminder of what he witnessed. "I hate you so much."

"Doubt it."

"Why do you insist on torturing me?"

He snorts. "You don't know what torture is."

"It's relative," I deadpan. "For me, it's when you break into my car and ruin my attempt at solitude. Again."

His shrug gives zero fucks. "You can't escape me. When are you gonna learn?"

"Probably when you start to listen. I want to be alone."

"Too bad."

My chest rises and falls as I resist the impulse to throttle him. That probably wouldn't end well for me. Instead, our stubborn streaks glare at each other. It doesn't take long for me to admit a silent standoff is another fight I won't win.

"I'm still really mad at you, Colton. This stalker behavior isn't helping. Please just go."

"Not happening, Princess."

"Why?"

"My father can't be trusted. I'm worried he's going to come after you again. You need protection."

"I can take care of myself."

Colton's flat look begs to differ. "He isn't a nice man. There's no telling what he's planning next."

That gives me pause. "You really think he'll come after me?"

"If he's that desperate to get me back." He flexes his hands, curling his fingers into tight fists.

That's when I notice the mottled patches and scrapes. "What happened to your knuckles?"

"Punched my cousin in the face."

"Your cousin?" I sputter.

"He deserved it."

I study him and his nonchalant tone for a moment. There's so much I don't know about him, but I'm not diving into that bottomless pit. He's a mystery and can stay that way.

"So," I sigh. "You're going to follow me around until your father is no longer a threat?"

"Yes."

"And Brody approved this?"

"Obviously," he drawls.

"Do I get a say?"

"No."

I don't know why I bothered to ask. My safety is more important than free will according to the men in my life. A familiar sense of hopelessness settles on my shoulders. But this surrender isn't permanent. I just need to regroup and think of a plan that will satisfy the brutes.

"How long will this confinement last?"

"Not sure. He has cancer. It's gonna kill him sooner or later."

A painful ache spreads through my chest. "Oh, how awful. I'm so sorry to hear that."

"I'm not." But there's a gruff edge to his voice. "Between the cigarettes and drugs, it was only a matter of time."

"Ohhh-kayyy." Just one more piece to the incomplete puzzle that is Colton Keller.

"Don't feel bad for him. He doesn't deserve your kindness."

"If you say so," I mumble.

"I do."

"But can't you just…" I stall and twirl my wrist. "Strike a deal with him or something? You know… before he goes."

Colton grunts. "He's not much for negotiating."

"Must run in the family."

His sharp glare cuts into me. The sneer twisting his features is pure menace. "I'm nothing like him."

"Whoa!" I hold up my hands in surrender. "Didn't mean to offend you."

Untamed fury crackles in the air. I can practically taste the animosity rolling off him. This is the first time he's revealed his scary side to me. It's a far cry from the subtle cues of annoyance I'm used to pulling from him. I don't like it. Not one bit.

As if hearing my concern, the tension bleeds from his stiff posture. He slumps against the seat, scrubbing a palm over his face.

"Shit. Sorry," he mumbles. "I shouldn't have snapped at you."

My lashes flutter at the abrupt change in his personality. "Want to make it up to me?"

"I'm not letting you go off on your own."

My groan is pitiful. "I'm so tired."

"Let's turn back and you can sleep this off."

A fierce scowl berates him. "Quit treating me like a child made of glass. I'm twenty-three, not thirteen."

"Thank fate for that," he mumbles.

That comment doesn't make sense and I choose to ignore it. "I don't want to go home."

"Afraid to sleep next to that pile of pillows impersonating you?"

My mind whirls. "How did you see that and still make it to my car before me?"

"I'm very good."

"Unfortunately." I shift into drive, admitting defeat. "Any requests?"

"I liked the song you were singing. Turn it back on."

The urge to smack his smug tone clenches my hands on the wheel. "I meant about where we're going."

"You pick. I'm just along for the ride."

"Paddock it is," I chirp.

His jaw tightens. "Great."

A slow grin spreads across my lips. That reaction is what I prefer to drag out of him. Small, but telling.

"Gonna be a long night, Cowboy. Buckle up."

CHAPTER SIX

T HE PADDOCK IS PACKED WHEN WE WALK IN. ONE thing the folks of Cloverleaf Meadows can agree on is supporting their local community and small businesses. Alongside whatever the Benson name touches, this place is a cherished staple in town. From satisfying hunger without breaking the bank to scratching the gambling itch at the pull tabs counter, they've got it covered.

And the crowd agrees. Everybody is damn glad to be here. Decked out to resemble an old-fashioned saloon, the Paddock has country charm and a cozy vibe. A server buzzes by with a tray full of food to feed a family. Several others weave around in a practiced formation to gather orders. It's a random Wednesday night, but every table is occupied. More people stand in clusters at the back where there's shit to do like throw darts and ride the mechanical bull.

The bar sits in the center, occupying a majority of the real estate in this large room. Bianca strides straight for a stool. It's the only one available at the rail. Anyone in her path quickly moves as if they sense the significance approaching them. I'm very familiar with the effect she has on others. Her sassy ass parks on the seat and I hover from behind like usual.

A bartender with a towel slung over his shoulder leans too close to her for my comfort. I move until her back is almost touching me and the guy gets the message. His eyes widen at my towering presence before he takes off to fetch Bianca's cocktail. She swivels on the stool to confront my waiting gaze.

Her glare is ready to slice me in half. "I could use some space, Cowboy. Nobody is gonna try snatching me outta here."

As if she can guarantee that, but I'm not a total dick. My boots inch backward to give her an arm's length of freedom. That's all she gets after the stunt she pulled earlier. Last thing I need is to lose her in this sea of bodies.

Her dissatisfaction huffs loudly above the music before she whips back around. There's already a dull ache stabbing into my skull from the noise, but this is Bianca's element. Sugary sweet words of gratitude signal the arrival of her martini. I'm forgotten as she gets lost in the feel-good energy. Her shoe taps along to the popular Riley Green song that's playing. She smiles at fellow patrons while sipping on her drink. Men openly admire her lush curves in the stretchy material she's wearing. Her outfit is entirely black and looks painted on.

They probably don't notice how her right side dips in deeper. Or that she's perched herself slightly off-center to alleviate the uneven pressure from her hips and pelvis.

Whenever she stretches slightly, it's to ease a discomfort that's blooming somewhere. There's probably a dull ache spreading from the muscles around her crooked spine right now. Seats with a backrest are much better for her condition. Massages are very beneficial as well. The list goes on—all factors of her scoliosis. What she considers a major imperfection is a piece that makes her even more special. I worship every part—even those she considers flaws.

One dude is willing to risk his life, turning until their legs brush. Red tints the edges of my vision. I'm about to intervene again when someone clamps a hand on my shoulder.

"You owe me fifty bucks."

My attention shifts from Bianca to her brother beside me. "Why's that?"

"The wife bet that we'd find you here. I was certain Bianca stayed home tonight. Couldn't give me a heads-up to stack the odds in my favor?"

"She tried to run off," I tell him. "This was a last-minute decision. Really more of a compromise."

Brody almost smirks, but then he notices Paisley doesn't have a chair. It takes a single glare to change that. The guy responsible for testing my limits moments ago wisely surrenders his stool to her. It's the Benson impact. She offers her gratitude before sliding in beside Bianca.

"I think this is yours." Paisley sets a recognizable phone on the counter.

Emerald eyes roll at the failed tactic. "Thought I was being so clever. Let him track a decoy instead of me for a change."

Brody's wife glances at me. Whatever she sees on my

face has her laughing. "Never gonna happen, sis. That man is hooked on you like a trailer hitch."

"More like an incurable disease." She winces and hangs her head. "Shit, that's super insensitive after what he shared."

"Which is?" Paisley rolls her wrist.

"That's his story to tell." Bianca buttons her lips.

Affection warms my chest and spurs my heart into a gallop. Fuck, this woman gets to me even when she's not trying. She's considerate of my feelings whether she realizes it or not. I couldn't care less if she blabs about my father's illness, but she didn't and that means something.

"You need a drink before we dive into the latest shit storm Colton created." Bianca signals for the bartender.

With them taken care of, Brody gets our conversation back on track. "Where was she going?"

I shrug. "Didn't get that far."

He bobs his head. "It's not as easy as it used to be. She'll get away eventually."

"Not if I can help it."

"Taking this new role seriously. I respect that." The admiration reflects in his tone.

A grunt is my only response. Bianca is much more than a job. He probably already knows, but that doesn't mean I'll admit it. A confession like that could cost me everything.

Or Brody could surprise me again. I stare at the thick braid hanging down Bianca's back and consider that possibility. His sister is a delicate subject. One of his only weaknesses. We have that in common. The rest is up for debate.

But that doesn't sit well. Even at the beginning, Brody didn't treat me as less than. My father likes to assume the Bensons aren't decent people. The truth is that they're far more. Their entire family—excluding that bastard Jimmy—are the superior sort everyone else should aspire to be.

I'd been barely scraping by after leaving my father's crew. Brody gave me a job when I needed it most. Down to my last dollar and zero luck. A punk from the wrong side of town didn't deserve his trust, but I worked hard to earn it. After two years of proving myself, he granted me access to his inner circle. That's when I met my biggest downfall. The rest is fucking irrelevant.

Bianca was only eighteen when I first saw her. Barely legal—definitely too young to pique my interest—but I couldn't fight the obsessive need to stay close. That's why I settled for watching over her in secret.

Only seven years separate us but our life experiences put us on opposite sides of the scale. She's too innocent and soft. A princess. I'd ruin her. More than I already have.

The day will come where she meets a man actually worthy of her. I'll have to let her go. It'll cleave me in two—the thought alone is painful—but she's not mine. Not how it truly matters. I swallow thickly and avert my gaze. Just so long as he treats her right, unlike the mysterious Scout. That coward has yet to show his face.

I haven't pried about the dude's identity, but I haven't forgotten either. He's probably a troll from the internet. They probably had an online relationship of some sort and kept in contact. That's the only explanation I can manage. The alternative flexes my hands into fists.

"Be honest with me." Brody's voice slaps me out of the violent thoughts.

"Always," I say without hesitation.

"Do you love her?" He lifts his chin at Bianca, as if there's any confusion.

I almost swallow my damn tongue and shoot a glance at the woman of my dreams. She's too preoccupied with her own conversation to overhear ours. Thank fuck for small miracles.

"Not sure how to answer that," I mutter.

His gaze slides to me. "I asked for the truth."

My stare lifts to the wood beams on the ceiling. "I know my place, boss."

"That wasn't my question."

It's seems like such a simple thing to admit, but there's nothing simple about my feelings for Bianca. This obsession consumes every part of me. It can't be summed up in a single word. The constant burn in my chest lurks just beneath the surface. I'm a bomb waiting to explode, releasing the savage destruction.

But I tell him the short version that he expects to hear. "Yes."

Brody's nod is sharp and concise. "Good."

I find myself faltering again. "Good?"

"That's why I trust you to guard her. This isn't just another job for you."

Which echoes my sole purpose. "Her safety is what matters most. Always."

"I believe that. With your heart involved, you'll do whatever it takes to protect her."

"I'll never act on my feelings." It seems important to admit that.

A crease appears between his eyebrows. "Why not?"

The reasons pile up like a multi-vehicle collision. "Won't let it cloud my judgment."

"Only adds to your dedication," he counters.

"Don't deserve her, boss. You know what I've done. What I'm capable of doing again." The scabs on my knuckles suddenly feel like stains on my soul.

His loud scoff gathers the attention from several nearby tables. He ignores their curious looks. "She could do a lot worse than you, Colt. And I doubt there's anyone better."

Any lingering doubt that he views us on uneven ground vanishes. In this moment, we're equal. His vocal acceptance heals something that I assumed was beyond repair. It must show on my face and Brody chuckles.

"Don't get ahead of yourself, big guy. Just because I approve doesn't mean she will. My sister is pissed at you."

"I was following orders."

"Which I appreciate."

"Bianca doesn't," I grumble.

He peers at his sister while she flails her arms to animate a point. "She can be a tad… unreasonable. Stubborn too. Her grudges have the tendency to last longer than a summer drought."

"I don't mind."

His eyes widen. "Damn, you're really fucked."

"What else is new?" Never stood a chance after the way I was raised.

Brody scrubs over his mouth before asking, "How's your dad?"

"Dying."

He blanches at my tone that's noticeably absent of emotion. "No shit?"

My gaze feasts on Bianca to fight off the claws of the past. "If I believe what he told me."

"Well, damn. That's why he wants you back."

"He can find someone else." Even my dumbass cousin can fill the role.

"Think he'll accept that?"

"Has to eventually, right?" Maybe I'm being callous, but that cruel bastard doesn't deserve anything else from me.

Brody bobs his head. "And in the meantime, we'll be extra cautious."

"Told her as much already." I glare at a guy across the bar when his interest narrows in on what's mine. He sees me towering behind her and wisely looks elsewhere.

"How'd she take it?"

"She didn't knee me in the balls."

"Eh, the night is still young." Brody flags down the bartender to order a beer.

I accept his offer to add one for me. "Might as well. She's promised it'll be a long one."

CHAPTER SEVEN

Bianca

"**O**h, my heart. Just look at her. Jamie hasn't been this happy in ages." Amber glances up at where her daughter is riding the horse I'm leading around the small corral. "This place is even better than I'd heard. A true miracle center." She sniffles and wipes at her eyes before adding, "You're doing so much for these kids. Thank you."

Emotion clogs my throat as if I haven't heard a similar speech countless times. I'm a sap, especially when it comes to children. That's precisely why I turn into a blubbering mess whenever I volunteer at Camp Cloverleaf. The therapeutic youth program is a blessing, much like Amber said.

"That's very sweet, but I'm not responsible for much more than this." I drift a palm along the sorrel mare's neck for emphasis. "The owners and managers are the real saints, along with the founder."

Who was my mom.

This camp was one of her many charitable endeavors.

Whenever she would visit, the sparkle in her gaze was extra bright. That's another reason I get choked up from being here. Her presence is reflected in each smile and laugh. Mom was always moved to see how many benefited from the free services. I blink away the threat of tears. Her spirit lives on and I'm so grateful.

"You're doing your part," Amber counters. "There are many other places you could be instead. I wouldn't have willingly offered to be here when I was your age. Trust me, your goodness is showing through."

A sting attacks the bridge of my nose. This kind woman is determined to make me cry.

"That means a lot. I appreciate it," I murmur.

My fingers comb through Toffee's brown mane while I try to rein in my feelings. The trusty horse dutifully walks on, picking up the slack for me. She's extremely reliable and doesn't need me to guide her, but it's required for novice students. Since this is Jamie's first lesson, her mom joins the session too. Her comfort and well-being are why we're all here.

My grin lifts to the little girl sitting in the saddle. Jamie is quiet, but there's a serene expression on her face. Like she's at peace. It's a common occurrence for the kids that enroll in services here. Instinct tells me that this one will become a regular.

After guiding Toffee to the center of the pen, I signal her to stop. I turn to Jamie and smile again. "All done, kiddo. You did awesome."

She blinks at me and remains silent.

Amber moves to stand next to her, patting her bent leg. "What do you think, sweetie? Was it fun to ride a horse?"

The little girl rests her hand on Toffee's neck, stroking her glossy coat slowly. A few seconds pass. Her mom doesn't move or speak, just waits for a response. I almost hold my breath in anticipation.

After what feels like a full minute, Jamie nods. The motion is slight, but visible. If that's not enough, Amber's wide grin snuffs out any doubt that this was a major success.

I mentally pump my fist. That's what we're aiming to achieve.

"And this was just your first stop," I chirp. "Next on your schedule is the petting zoo."

After helping Jamie dismount, we exit the corral and I point to the trail they need to take. It can be a bit confusing to navigate for first-timers. Camp Cloverleaf is set on thirty-five acres of repurposed farmland at the edge of town. The property was donated to Youth First—a local organization—after Mom got the initial plans in motion. From tending the vegetable gardens to molding clay in pottery class, the list of therapeutic services is extensive. Call me biased but the horse stables are my favorite.

"Hopefully I'll see you again soon." I wave to Amber and Jamie when they begin walking away.

The gracious mom beams at me over her shoulder. "You can count on it. Thanks again, Bianca."

With my heart full and a pep in my step, I stride toward the barn with Toffee in tow. The distance allows me to get lost in my thoughts for a moment. I tip my face to the sky and exhale. This is what I needed after the past several days trapped under Colton's overbearing reign.

Camp Cloverleaf is one of the few spots that he relents slightly. He's probably wearing a path into the grass over at the picnic tables. That's his usual place to pace obsessively until I'm done with my shift. Jamie was my final student for the afternoon, which doesn't give me long to enjoy the peace.

I can't complain too much. Aside from my mom leaving us far too soon and potential danger lying in wait, I've been very fortunate. There's just this urge to break free from the judgment Dad and Brody still hold over me. I had a rebellious and reckless phase, like any teenager fighting for independence. It's not as if I did anything that bad. But here I am, struggling to be treated like a responsible adult.

These restrictions are meant to protect me, but I feel smothered. I can't even remember the last time I went on a date. Not that I've been in the mood for romance since losing Mom. Lust is one thing, and I can feed that beast on my own, but it takes effort to build a real connection with someone. Maybe I should try. It could be fun, comforting even.

While I'm considering the possibility, a woman materializes from the shadows of a horse stall. The sight of her startles me and I yelp, freezing on the spot. She prowls forward in a predatory motion that raises my hackles higher. Her strapless leather bodysuit might as well be gasoline on the fire.

"You're a tough woman to get alone," the redhead purrs.

I tie Toffee to a hitching post while squinting at this stranger, searching my memory for recognition. "Do we know each other?"

"Colton hasn't mentioned me?" She pouts her ruby-stained lips in an exaggerated manner. "I'm offended."

A spike of terribly misplaced jealousy tries to rattle me. "I don't think he'd care."

Her head dips in acknowledgment. "Some things never change. That's why the boss sent me. He figured his son wouldn't pass along his appreciation."

"And you're here to do the honors. How completely unnecessary."

Her shrug is graceful. "You'll want to hear what I have to say."

Disbelief snorts from me. "I don't see how that's possible."

"A little birdie told us that you're having trouble leaving town on your own. We can help you escape."

"Ohhhh," I laugh while wondering which gossip is responsible for outing me. "The cowboy criminals want to make me disappear. Convenient."

"Is that what you're calling us?" She flips red hair over her bare shoulder. "I'll have shirts made."

"That'll have you dressed more appropriately at a family-friendly facility," I mutter.

Her glare is sharper than her stiletto nails. "Bitchy, huh? Makes sense."

"Excuse me?" I bristle and straighten to my full five-foot-three height. If she wants to talk shit, I'll gladly bring out my own claws.

"Don't get your thong in a twist," she huffs. "That's just what Colton sees in you."

"Guess he has a type," I fire in return.

Flames dance in her eyes and she steps closer. The air shifts, swirling with hostility. Those self-defense classes are about to finally pay off. I grin while bracing for her next barb.

But just as she's about to pounce, a blur of motion races

into the barn. The adorable bundle of energy launches herself at the redhead's legs, cinching them in a fierce hug. It must be a very happy day. Those have been rare for Ronnie lately. Maybe this stranger is good for something after all.

I realize the villainess is frozen in place. She stares at the little girl and her demeanor instantly changes from the child's onslaught. Gone is the badass bombshell. In her place is a subdued version, unaware of where to put her hands. She lifts them like this is a hostage situation and nobody has to get hurt.

Ronnie's father arrives a moment later. My oldest cousin bends at the waist to catch his breath. "Gosh, she's fast."

"Found someone of interest." I nod at the two still locked in an embrace.

Byron's lips part at the sight. "What's happening?"

"She's a superhero, Daddy." Ronnie snuggles the unresponsive woman as if she's her new favorite stuffy.

Byron admires the skintight outfit in a very different light. "She's something."

The little girl parks her chin on the redhead's thigh, gazing up at her with blatant adoration. "Will you be my mommy?"

My heart clenches. She looks so hopeful. Meanwhile, the spandex seductress appears horrified.

Her dagger nails pry off Ronnie's arms, allowing her to stumble backward and away from the clutches of affection. She glances at the little girl before whirling on her biker boots and running off.

Ronnie sighs, a goofy grin painting her lips. "I like her."

"Why's that?" I can't help wondering.

Her slim shoulders bounce while she stares off in the

direction the stranger went. The peaceful gleam in her eyes is almost adorable. "Dunno, but she's super pretty."

"Sure is." My cousin is wearing a similar expression. "Who is she?"

"Don't even think about it," I scold. "She works for Colton's dad."

Byron's eyes snap to mine just as my devoted bodyguard appears out of thin air. It must be a trick of the trade.

Colton stands entirely too close to me. "Who works for him?"

"Your lover," I croon.

Ronnie clasps her palms to her chest. "She's gonna be my mommy."

"Is this a regular thing?" I ask her dad from the corner of my mouth.

Byron looks lost. "No, she's never done this."

"Could've picked a more likely candidate," I mumble.

Ronnie shakes her head. "She's gonna take away my sadness."

I share a look with Byron. The sweet girl lost her mama at the start. Nina died during childbirth. She didn't even get to hold her precious angel. That tragedy has stuck with my cousin all these years, but Ronnie didn't seem to feel her mother's absence. Not until recently, right after her fifth birthday. Her abrupt attitude shift is what initiated her frequent visits to Camp Cloverleaf.

My cousin whips off his hat, dragging an agitated hand through his hair. "What should I do?"

"Tell me her name," Colton interjects, his gaze heavy on me.

"Don't know, but she was stunning. You know how to pick 'em, Cowboy." I bat my lashes at him.

"You dated her?" There's an accusation in Byron's voice.

"I don't have an ex," he spits at my cousin before returning his glare to me. "What did she say to you?"

I inspect my manicure that's crusted with dirt. "Just some stuff."

"Be specific."

"Ask me nicely," I clap back.

His jaw clenches. "Don't be a brat, Princess."

"That's like asking me not to breathe."

Byron clears his throat and turns Ronnie in the direction of the playground. "We'll just leave you two alone."

I watch them go as Colton fumes next to me. He's absently snapping something on his wrist. My eyes narrow on what looks like an elastic band. It's pink and braided, fraying from age. Weird. But his strange habits aren't my biggest issue at the moment.

"You're ruining my good mood," I tell him.

"Bianca," he growls. "Cut the shit."

"You first."

"Just tell me what that woman said to you."

My exhale is done with his bossy attitude. "She offered to whisk me away for a few days or longer. The timeline was a bit fuzzy."

"You better be fucking joking."

"Seemed pretty serious to me." Not that I'd ever agree to go along with them, but he doesn't need to know that.

"Stay away from her."

"Ditto."

"Don't even know who she is."

"The notches on your bedpost are that insignificant, hmm?"

Colton moves with lethal speed, trapping me against the stall at my back. His breath mingles with mine when he leans in. "None of them are worth counting."

My chest bumps his with my next labored breath. "Why not?"

"They aren't you."

CHAPTER EIGHT

Cotton

Me: You sure about this?

Brody: Do what you gotta do.

Me: She's gonna be pissed.

Brody: Since when has that stopped you?

THE SINKING SENSATION IN MY GUT DIPS LOWER while I read over our recent text exchange. Bianca might actually end my life after I pull this stunt, but it's necessary. My father didn't bother to wait a week before sending someone else to hassle her.

That bad choice forces me to take more extreme measures.

I lift my gaze from the phone screen. Bianca is leaning against one of the many trucks her family owns. The tight jeans she's wearing are meant to test my control, especially when her left hip is cocked in defiance. Pieces of her brown hair lightly flutter in the breeze like a contradiction. My confession at Camp Cloverleaf teases the distance between us, daring me to cross the line with more than flimsy words. Her eyes narrow into fiery slits as I continue to stare.

"Let me guess," she mutters. "My brother put his foot down."

I nod. It isn't a question that needs verbal confirmation.

Her pert nose crinkles. "Why can't Paisley come instead? We've hauled our horses all across the Midwest and didn't need a chaperone."

My flat stare provides a thorough explanation. "You're stuck with me, Princess."

She tucks her arms tight across her chest. "Fantastic."

"And I'll drive."

"Fine by me."

That surprises me and it must show on my face. She huffs, looking anywhere but at me. Several of her dogs provide an adequate distraction. A full minute passes as she pets them and avoids me.

"I'll own that I'm a passenger princess at heart," she grumbles eventually.

"Nobody would assume otherwise."

Bianca reaches for the pickup's door handle, but pauses when I grab her bag and head toward the barn. "Where are you going?"

"We're taking mine." The fully restored 1979 F-350 gleams under the morning sun like a beacon.

Her eyes bulge at the glorious sight. "You're going to pull

my trailer with your relic? I figured you were just testing the wiring."

"Horses are already loaded." Which could be considered a warning sign, but she's too caught up on my choice of vehicle.

"Doesn't that go against a collector code or something?"

My boots crunch over gravel, which mimics the sound of me stomping on her argument. "A truck is meant to haul. That doesn't change with age. Reliable, remember?"

Bianca's lips part, the memory washing over her shocked expression. "Wait, this is the same truck?"

And that goes to show how little we've interacted over the years. It's been mostly me sticking to the shadows to keep an eye on her. If not for that pesky habit, we'd be strangers.

"Doesn't look as rough, huh?"

Her gaze wanders over the green custom paint with new appreciation. "Uh-huh, sure doesn't. That makes this even worse. I'm not responsible for any damages. It's your risk to take."

"Don't sell Fern short. She'll take us wherever we wanna go and won't put up a fuss."

Bianca slams to a stop beside me. "Fern?"

A sweeping motion acknowledges the vintage beauty in front of us in case there's any confusion. "You're about to get officially acquainted."

She blinks at me slowly, as if this news is difficult to process. "You named your truck?"

"Of course."

A smile crawls across her lips until she's full-on beaming. "That's almost cute, Cowboy. Who knew you had it in ya?"

"Cute?"

"Do you prefer adorable?"

That doesn't deserve a response. Instead, I dump her bag in the living quarters portion of the horse trailer. Mine is already in there, along with everything else we'll need. Bianca is quiet and doesn't question me again. She's too busy gawking at Fern's custom cowhide upholstery from the open passenger door. Two dogs flank her, whining for permission to hop in.

"There isn't room for them," I say while rounding the hood.

"I noticed." She remains still, staring at the solo bench that stretches across the cab.

"They sure as shit don't make 'em like they used to, huh?"

"It's beautiful." Her breathy voice is like a light switch, turning me on with a quick flick.

"She," I croak.

"Oh, right." There's a hint of pink coloring her cheeks when she glances at me. "I love what you've done with her."

"We've been through a lot together."

"Gettin' sentimental on me too? Jeez, I better be careful or you'll grow on me."

My gaze feasts on hers, blue searching green for a truth she probably won't admit. "Would that be so terrible?"

Not that she has much of a choice. The hitch in her breath sounds like surrender. "We should go."

I couldn't agree more. It's about damn time Bianca's fine

ass breaks in the spot next to mine. My gaze moves from her to the truck. "What're you waiting for, Princess?"

Her legs shift awkwardly. "Where's the foot thingie?"

"There aren't any."

"How do you expect me to get in? We aren't all built like Viking giants." Her eyes rove over our drastic difference in height. "I'll pop my hip out of the socket trying."

A chuckle threatens to rattle me. The visual of her scrambling to climb in is entertaining. Add in the fact that she's too proud to ask for a lift and I damn near double over. But I'd never put her in a situation to get hurt.

In a fluid motion, I scoop Bianca off her feet. She's buckled in right where she belongs before a complaint can escape her mouth. A smirk tugs at my own while I return to my side and get behind the wheel.

A crank of the key in the ignition has Fern rumbling to life. That purr is such a sexy sound, only overshadowed by any noise the woman next to me makes.

"Hear that?" I glance at her while shifting into drive.

"She doesn't sound angry anymore."

"You remember." Fuck, that does something to me. I focus on the minimal effort it takes my truck to pull ahead with her loaded trailer attached. "And you were worried. Never doubt classic American muscle."

"Do trucks fall under that category?" She taps her chin, lips puckered to one side.

If I didn't know better, I'd think she was teasing me. "Google it."

"Maybe I will since I actually have the option." She whips the device from her pocket like it's a weapon to use against me.

Which is true in a sense. The reminder that Brody gave me an order to confiscate her phone in Germany—allowing her to believe it was stolen—is a dark cloud above me. I might never escape the gloom. Bianca notices the clench in my jaw.

"Awwww," she croons. "Did I ruin the moment?"

I tighten my hand on the steering wheel. Such a brat. But it'll be me destroying what little peace there is between us.

The pickup rolls to a stop at the main gate. "Ready to leave?"

"Almost," she chirps.

And then the rodeo princess proceeds to build her bubble of chaos. A hands-free phone mount gets stuck to the dash. There's already a cooking show playing on the screen. Subtitles scroll along at a rate I couldn't follow if I used my full concentration.

With that step complete, Bianca taps at her iPad and slides AirPods into her ears. There's undoubtedly a romance audiobook picked and prepped to turn her on. Last, but certainly not least, is the yarn bag. Whatever crochet project she's currently working on is now bundled on her lap. It's probably another set of horse earmuffs. Winter is coming after all.

Bianca's fingers begin moving at lightning speed while I try to process this madness. I've observed her multitasking methods on countless occasions over the years and it still fascinates me. My brain just doesn't work like that. It's only when she motions for me to get a move on that I realize we're still idling in the driveway. Go fucking figure—she caught me staring again.

I shake off the stupor and ease on the gas. Fern glides forward, rumbling her enthusiasm. At least this journey will be smooth for one of us. The road ahead is paved, but it's about to get rocky.

That kicks my pulse into a trot, mimicking the thump from the tires eating miles. It's too damn quiet. My thoughts are spinning in a whirlwind faster than the overstimulating mayhem beside me. I turn on the radio to fill the void.

"A Lot More Free" by Max McNown streams from the speakers. It's one of Bianca's favorite songs. I almost tap her on the shoulder, but then notice her head is bobbing to the beat. She's mouthing the words too. This woman's attention span doesn't have a limit.

Which is why she doesn't miss what happens next. Her narrowed gaze scans the landscape. She turns in her seat to get the full picture and then rips the pods from her ears.

"You missed the exit, Cowboy."

"Did I?"

"Yes," she confirms while gesturing at the window. "Zumbrota is that way."

I force my eyes to remain fixed ahead. "We aren't going to Zumbrota."

In my peripheral, Bianca goes very still. "Where are you taking me?"

"To a different barrel race."

"Where, Colton?"

"Somewhere safe."

"Why?" Her voice is too calm, ready to raise hell or an alarm depending on my answer.

"My father proved he can't listen. He won't stop harassing you until I surrender or end what's left of his miserable life. Rather than do him a favor, I decided to remove you from his reach."

Her breathing grows shallow. "Would you actually do that?"

"Do what?"

She huffs. "Don't act innocent now. Have you hurt people?"

"Yes."

Her posture stiffens. "Did you kill any of them?"

"Haven't been pushed that far, but I'd do it for you."

"That's concerning." But the raspy edge in her voice suggests she's more worried about her reaction.

I wonder what was swirling through her mind when I said my father deserved worse than death for involving her in his criminal business. "Does it scare you?"

"Probably should," she mumbles.

"But?"

"You've never given me a reason to fear you. The worst you've done is act as a massive obstacle to block my freedom." She makes me sound like a construction cone.

"I'd hate for you to see what I'm actually capable of."

Bianca is studying me, trying to peel away my protective layers. "Who are you?"

"Those secrets aren't free."

"Are you gonna blackmail me?" She huffs. "Brody probably gave you tips."

"No," I grunt in response. "I'd prefer if my past stayed buried."

"But you'll tell me if…" She trails off, expecting me to fill in the blank.

The truth is, Bianca doesn't realize what she's asking.

The answers will cost her a lot more than a polite conversation. Probably more than she's willing to give. Not that I'd ever push her. What happens between us romantically will always be her choice.

"I'm willing to negotiate," I say.

"What do you want?"

"For now, I'd like you to go along for the ride and not kick up a fuss."

That triggers her memory of our situation. Fire burns in her glare, searing my averted gaze. "Stop the truck."

"Not gonna happen."

"Pull over, Colton."

I shake my head. "Just try to relax. You'll like where we'd headed. Get back in your bubble of chaos until we arrive."

Bianca whacks me across the chest with her iPad. "Listen to me! You can't do this."

"Knock it off, Princess." My voice is the crack of a whip against her bundle of fury. "I'm driving. Think about your horses in the back."

Her exhale sounds like a pissed off dragon. "You can't abduct me against my will."

"I can and your brother approved it."

"He's not the boss of me."

"That makes one of us." But this was my idea, not his.

"You don't have to do everything he says just because he's paying your bills."

"This isn't just a job for me," I bellow. Regret tries to snatch the words back, but it's too late. "I'd protect you regardless."

"As a favor to Brody."

"No, for me. The thought of you getting hurt…" I let

that statement hang in the balance for a moment, strangling the steering wheel like it's a threat against her. "Fuck, never mind. It's unacceptable."

"Um, okay? That's borderline possessive."

My nod agrees wholeheartedly. "I need to keep you safe."

"Well, I don't need a repeat of Germany. Please take me home."

"Can't do that."

"Please," she repeats.

My resolve almost wavers at the whine in her tone. But then I imagine her begging me for something else. "This trip is gonna be different."

"How so?"

"I won't steal your phone."

Her gaze flings to her beloved device that I snatched at Brody's request. She didn't know the thief was me until I returned it. One more mistake I won't live down.

As if on cue, she mutters, "I'm still mad about that."

"Have I apologized lately?"

"No, and don't bother. It won't solve anything." Her hollow tone carves into my chest.

The urge to cradle her hand in mine drops my right arm onto the space between us. "Well, for what it's worth, I'm sorry. I felt really shitty taking it, but your brother gave me an order. He didn't want anyone to interfere with his plans."

"Yeah, yeah. Your loyalty to him is most important."

"That's not true."

"Then what is?"

I chew on the answer I want to reveal, but she's not ready yet. "Your safety."

"Saw that coming from a mile away in the wrong

direction." She tucks her arms across her chest and glares straight ahead. "Your white knight hero complex doesn't fix what you continue to break, Cowboy."

"Just trust me, okay? It'll get better once this shit with my father is handled."

"I won't hold my breath."

"Complain to whoever you want." I jerk my chin at her phone that's still mounted on the dash.

"How generous." Her scoff is thick with sarcasm. "Won't do me any good."

"How about if I try to give you some space?" Just spitting that out is a challenge.

Bianca eyes me suspiciously. "Starting when?"

"You'll just have to wait and see."

CHAPTER NINE

Bianca

"**S**TAY PUT." COLTON'S GRUFF COMMAND PUSHES MY brattiest buttons.

I pop open the passenger door, swinging my legs over the bench seat. My boots hit the dirt and I breathe a sigh of relief. The drop from the truck is no joke, especially for lil' ol' me. It's like sliding off a very tall horse.

My jailer's grunt reaches me on the ground. "Can't listen, huh?"

"Just following the trend." And with that free fall out of the way, I get a good look at the scenery. "This isn't a barrel race."

Unless the property owner has an arena hidden behind the quaint little farmhouse or equally charming barn. There isn't any noise either. It's quiet and peaceful. I can hear birds in the large oak trees to the right. A rope swing hangs down from a thick branch. The wooden seat sways in the breeze as if beckoning me.

I get a similar vibe from the oversized windmill, squeaking slightly as the blades pick up speed. Ripe apples perfume the autumn season. The cluster of trees is on the left near a pasture gate. Rows of lilac bushes are planted along the fence, ready to perfume the air in spring. Flower gardens frame stone paths that cut across the lawn. Upon closer inspection, these colorful blooms are a variety of daisies. They're my favorite—Mom's too—and I'm struck by the sight.

The whole package is endearing. I find myself being pulled in as if I'm home. It's a natural comfort welcoming me, like I've been here before. This is the type of place where a young couple plants roots and watches their love expand over the years.

Colton appears at my side. Bandit and Luna flank him, their lead ropes looped in his hands. He must've unloaded them while I was admiring the view.

"Figured we'd unpack and get settled before you decide what to do," he drawls.

I peek up at him, finding his gaze already on me. "Why would we do that?"

"You can stretch your back. Two hours in the same position can lock up even the most pliant muscles. I don't want you to get sore."

A furrow creases my forehead while I study his expression. That's another thoughtful gesture. A dull ache had started brewing in my hips and lower back, but it wasn't anything I couldn't handle. That doesn't mean the break isn't appreciated.

Colton would make a considerate boyfriend—minus the light stalking and abduction. For days, I've been chewing on that heated comment he breathed across my lips at Camp Cloverleaf. *They're not you.* The raw passion in his voice had curled my toes and spiked a fever. It's almost like he's caught feelings, which sounds crazy to my own ears. I didn't get a chance to pry before he backed off. Now we're at odds again.

Do I think the grumpy jerk is attractive? Sure. Did I suggest we sleep together on more than one occasion? Shamelessly guilty. Does that mean I forgive him for his many offenses against me? Not a chance and I'm getting off track.

I rip my gaze from his backward baseball cap, shifting my sights to the large shed in front of us. "Where are we?"

He took us west rather than south. I stopped paying attention to the map after we blew past New Ulm. It was all unrecognizable country fields beyond that.

His gaze roams over the grassy land that extends in every direction. "Middle of nowhere."

"Care to be more specific?"

"Morgan is the closest town, if you can even call it that."

"And we just stopped for a quick reprieve or…?" I lift my brows, willing him to chat me up for a change.

"There are several competitions in this part of the state until mid-November. The Redwood Rodeo starts tomorrow if you're interested. Or you can relax until next weekend." That's a decent string of sentences for the man of few words, but it doesn't make sense.

"You're planning on us staying here?" I gesture to the rustic paradise surrounding us to avoid confusion.

"Would you prefer camping in the trailer? I thought you wanted space."

"That's not what I meant and you know it."

Colton narrows his eyes, the blue appearing lighter in the afternoon sun. "Where were you headed when you tried to skip town?"

The shift in topic gives me pause. "Didn't have a specific location in mind."

"You did," he insists.

"No, I didn't. I just wanted to go… somewhere else." I toss my hands up, exhaling heavily. "Away from Cloverleaf Meadows and the expectations of my last name. The rodeo circuit can be suffocating too. It's a rich person problem and I know that, but the pressure of being a Benson is exhausting. Especially after my mom died. I wanted a break. It actually felt like a need. That's why I decided to take that trip to Europe on a whim, which didn't go as planned. The next time, I figured I'd just drive and see where the road took me."

It probably would've led me to a spot exactly like this if I'm being honest.

His nod acts like he heard me. "Does your restless spirit approve?"

"Restless spirit," I scoff. "That's what you got out of my speech?"

"Do you prefer a different term?" He grunts when I don't answer. "That's what I thought. Nobody knows you out here. You can even pretend to be someone else."

"But there's no hiding from you," I retort.

"Am I that bad?"

"You represent what I'm trying to escape. I don't actually get peace while you're hovering over me."

"It's not safe for you to be alone." He stands with the

horses on either side of him, forming a defensive guard against any attack.

"What's going to get me?" I spin in a slow circle. "There's probably nothing for miles."

Colton dips his head. "The property sits on four hundred acres of land. Only eighty are fenced in. That's as much space as you're going to get."

Fire burns in my veins. "I hate you."

"And I deserve it. Doesn't change the facts. This is the best I can do. Run free. Go buck wild. Ditch your elite reputation. Blend in and be normal." He's really expanding his vocal cords today.

"Fine. Whatever." Another argument lost—go figure. My attention wanders to the house, wondering what's waiting inside. "Did the owners owe you one or is this a random rental?"

"I bought it." Colton states that as if he's telling me the sky is blue.

My lips part on a shocked exhale. "When?"

His voice is unusually soft when he says, "Middle of July."

A lump instantly clogs my throat. Mom passed earlier that month. The timing seems too purposeful. I search his bottomless ocean stare for answers that never surface.

"Why?" It's more of a croak than a question.

"Figured I should get my own house. It was long overdue."

"And you chose somewhere hours away from the office?"

"Consider it more of a vacation home."

My brows leap to the barn roof. "Is that a joke?"

"If you want it to be."

"What's the real reason?"

Colton stares deep into my soul, trying to convey a message. "Maybe I was planning ahead."

"For what?"

"The urge to skip town." His casual tone suggests he's repeating the obvious.

"Do you have a restless spirit too? Or did you do this for mine?" Just asking makes me sound like a presumptuous brat.

But then he dips his chin. "It's for us. We can come out here whenever the mood strikes."

Hysterical laughter bubbles from the depths of my shock. "Take it easy, Cowboy. This is a temporary arrangement. Gosh, you make it sound like we're permanently attached at the hip."

"However long it takes." The words are uttered under his breath, but I hear the desire in them.

"Ah, right." My humor simmers to a breathy exhale. "You're hiding me from your father."

Colton glares into the distance. "Until Brody and your dad deal with him."

"What're they gonna do? Flex their dominance?" I snort at the visual.

"Essentially."

"They aren't violent people."

"They don't have to be," he argues. "Dealing with a threat doesn't have to involve pain. There are more creative ways to make a man back off. Your brother has every resource available. He'll use them as necessary."

The dots aren't connecting. "So, why are we hiding?"

"My father's crew is a speck of dirt compared to your

family. He doesn't stand a chance and he knows it. That could push him to do something really drastic. I won't risk your safety." That reason is beginning to sound like an excuse.

Which leads me to regurgitate an overused line of my own. "This is just a job. Why do you care so much?"

"Princess," Colton sighs. "Do I really need to answer that?"

"I wouldn't have asked otherwise."

His eyes burn into mine, hot coals on a smoldering fire. "You're not ready."

I blink to escape the snare of his intensity. "More secrets?"

"Always."

A sigh wheezes from me when I bump into another blockade. He's calm and relatively chatty. Meanwhile, my emotions are running on high alert. His father is a bad man. There's dangerous drama surrounding me. Colton is talking in riddles. I'm clueless as to what's happening behind the scenes.

"Just for the record, I don't appreciate being left in the dark."

"I'll share any updates I receive."

"And keep me trapped here until the coast is clear." Frustration threatens to rise again, but I swallow the urge to scream.

"You're not a prisoner. We can leave whenever you want," my jailer reassures.

"But we can't go home."

"Not until my father fucks off for good. Whoever replaces him won't try to drag me back into the fold."

My stomach squeezes at the finality in his tone. "You're not planning to see him before he…?"

"Already did. Made my peace with our situation long before now. There's nothing left to say."

"Um, okay." I allow a lull to slip between us while I ponder the vast differences in our family dynamics.

The way he speaks about his father reveals a detachment. His childhood probably lacked everything I received in abundance. Heat pricks my eyes as I imagine young Colton in desperate need of a hug, but getting ignored instead. There's no warmth or fond memories. Grief won't hold him hostage. Maybe it's better that way.

My lashes bat away the unshed tears. "Will you let me stay here on my own?"

His extended pause reveals the truth. "Maybe."

"Liar." But it's a step in the right direction.

"Invite Paisley or some other friend if you need better company." Colton's hand roams the length of Bandit's glossy neck.

My heart absolutely doesn't soften to him petting my horse with affection. "I already told her that you changed course and took me in the opposite direction against my will. She didn't seem all that surprised."

"You didn't either. I was expecting more of a fight."

"After the initial burst of shock, I realized this"—I wave at the makeshift safe house—"should be expected. Why waste my energy trying to escape? Short of smothering you with a pillow, I'm not getting away."

"Glad to hear you're finally seeing reason."

My eyes narrow at his smug tone. I should probably be more upset, but it won't do me any favors. If he wants to pretend this situation is normal, I can play along. That doesn't mean I accept it. I'm just trying to rationalize his extreme protective instincts while waiting for the storm to pass. Otherwise, I will actually lose it.

"I'm going to let Bandit and Luna graze for a bit before finding a trail to explore." My fingers reach for the lead ropes.

But Colton doesn't give. "I've got 'em. You can check out the house. It's a keypad entry. The code is zero-four-two-seven. Master bedroom is all yours. Unpack and change. Then we'll go for a ride."

"That's my birthday," I whisper.

"I'm aware."

"Why is the code my birthday?"

He chews on his answer for a moment. "It's a combination neither of us will forget."

Which sounds more like a meaningful decision rather than strictly for convenience.

My head is spinning again, but I focus on the other part of his statement. "*We're* going for a ride?"

"If that's all right with you."

I squint at his nonchalance. "Are you planning on hoofin' it?"

"Sure, Princess." Colton's stubbled cheek twitches as if he's about to smirk. "I'll eat your dust and enjoy the view."

CHAPTER TEN

Cotton

FORTY-FIVE MINUTES LATER, WE'RE WALKING IN A single file line across a sloping field. I have the best damn seat in the land thanks to Bandit's don't-give-a-shit disposition. The gelding allows us to trail behind at our leisure. Maybe he enjoys ogling the mare's ass the same way I'm staring straight ahead at Bianca's curves.

The stretchy shirt she's wearing accentuates every supple inch in a tight caress. Whoever designed that garment is a genius. I'm lost in the slow sway of her hips when she turns in the saddle.

Bianca smiles, looking pleased to catch me drooling over her. "How you doin', Cowboy?"

I tip the brim of my Stetson. "Just fine, Princess."

"How's the view?" She motions to the rural landscape enveloping us.

But I couldn't care less about prairie grass or willow

trees whipping in the breeze. My focus doesn't stray from her lush hindquarters. "Won't hear me complain."

A blush paints her pretty cheeks. "I'm beginning to think you're flirting with me."

"It's about time." For me to admit it too.

She laughs and shakes her head, allowing the sun to turn her brown hair into melted chocolate. "Too many secrets. Just like showing off your riding skills. Why didn't you tell me you learned how?"

I shrug. "Topic never came up."

If it had, I would've missed out on Bianca's stunned expression when she stumbled to a halt at the hitching post. Her wide eyes couldn't believe I'd properly tacked both horses while she explored the house. That shock doubled when I gripped the saddle horn and swung onto Bandit in a fluid motion. She's been peeking back at me frequently ever since. Probably to make sure I'm not full of shit and still astride my mount.

Like now, her eyes narrow on me and my natural seat. "Who taught you?"

"YouTube mostly," I admit.

Her laughter increases in volume. "No way."

"Any professional horse person worth their credentials has a channel. Damn good tips on there."

She sobers, nibbling on her bottom lip. "Have you watched any of mine?"

I nod automatically. "Been a subscriber for five years."

Her eyes bulge again. "That's basically when I started posting."

My chest puffs up a bit. "I was your first follower."

"How is that possible? I had a flood of hits the minute

my account went live. To be the first, you would've needed to be watching the second I activated it."

"I'm well aware." In more ways than one.

Her gasp electrifies the distance separating us. "That's… stalkerish."

Our gazes clash in a heated exchange. "Does it bother you?"

"Maybe." But there's a telltale grin curving her lips, revealing the truth.

Bianca likes the idea of my obsession. I wonder if she realizes how far that fixation goes. A house stocked with her favorite things should be a big fucking hint. There was no missing how her gaze stuck to the flowerbeds packed with daisies. Her serene smile in that moment was a precious gift. If only she looked at me with the same fondness. Maybe she'll learn to appreciate my protective habits and forgive me for the deceptions along the way.

Right now, the sparkle in her features is piqued in interest. "Why didn't you just ask me for lessons?"

"That wasn't an option."

She assesses me in silence, staring deep until I can practically hear her pulling at my protective layers. "Is that why you didn't talk to me for all those years?"

My chin dips in acknowledgment. "There wasn't much to say."

Not while Brody's warning constantly taunted me.

"You don't seem to be at a loss for words anymore," Bianca muses.

"Our change in circumstance helps."

Her exhale drowns out the trickle from the creek we're

passing. "That's one way to describe my brother hiring you to guard me."

"Just for Europe."

"Which expanded into a promotion of lockdown proportions thanks to your dad." She rolls her eyes, not appreciating the position I'm in.

That's why I find myself admitting, "You're not a job to me, Princess."

"Yeah, yeah. My safety is most important. You'd probably volunteer to protect me just to stay on Brody's good side."

My molars grind under the force of her assumption. I don't think she's ready—and I've said as much—but she'll discover the depths of my infatuation eventually. Might as well rip off the damn blinders.

It starts with a chuckle, which startles Bianca. I stare at her, not afraid to expose what she does to me. Her lips part while mine slant into a smirk. She's the only one who gets to witness such jovial expressions from me.

"You think it started when your brother hired me? Nah, that was him granting me easy access. Not that I need it. I've been watching you for five years, Princess." My voice is a blade that slices through the divide separating us. "And I'm not just talking about online. You've been under my protection since I got permission to enter Benson Farmstead. This job promotion—if that's what you insist on calling it—makes stalking you much more convenient. I'll never quit either. Consider my position permanent."

Dumping that off my chest releases the shackles, but waiting for her reaction still suspends me. I glance at the faded elastic band on my wrist. The urge to snap it hasn't plagued me since she got buckled into my truck. Those restless nerves are at rest. Maybe I will be too. *Soon.*

Her lashes flutter as she recovers from my truth bomb. I expect disgust to curl her upper lip next. But rather than cringing or appearing disturbed, she bursts into loud laughter.

"Oooooh, are you trying to scare me again?" Another shrill giggle bursts free.

Now my jaw drops. Most would view this situation as a concern. Meanwhile, Bianca is treating it like a joke.

"I'm serious." But my stern retaliation doesn't hold an edge over her humor.

"Oh, I believe you. It makes total sense."

Disbelief renders me speechless for several moments. "You're not upset?"

"Been there. Done that. Didn't change the outcome." She shrugs, gathering her composure with a deep inhale. "If I'm going to have a stalker, it might as well be you."

I damn near fall off my horse. "Why?"

"You're not a threat to me, Cowboy." And then she clears her throat, dropping her voice to mimic a lower octave like mine. "I need to keep you safe. This isn't just a job for me. You have no idea what I'll do to protect you, Princess."

My nostrils flare as I listen to her impersonation. I don't want her to fear me, but this response is something else entirely. "Are you mocking me?"

She shakes her head, biting her bottom lip. "I wouldn't dare."

But her theatrical performance strongly suggests otherwise.

"Try again," I grunt.

"Oh, Colton. You're my hero. How can I repay you for chasing away the bad guys?" Her breathy tone strokes me from root to tip.

I'm half hard in the saddle while she's putting on a show. "Such a fucking brat," I growl.

She bats her dark lashes. "What're you gonna do about it?"

And now she's taunting me. I tighten my hand on the reins, imagining her will bending to mine. The surrender would be very sweet—and fleeting. She might agree for a night, but I want forever.

"You couldn't handle it," I warn.

"Other way around, Stalker," she coos.

"Say it again," I blurt. What I'm specifically demanding must show on my face.

"Stalker," Bianca exhales automatically. "Do you want me to be submissive?"

I barely manage to trap a groan. Fuck, this woman drives me to the brink of madness. Visions of her begging for relief assault me. She's on her hands and knees, bare ass thrust in the air. Whimpered pleas drip from her pouty lips as I prepare to slam into her from behind.

Harder. Faster. Please.

Bianca's amused hum cuts into the fantasy. "Mhmm, I think you'd like to dominate me. Does that involve teaching me a lesson when I'm naughty? Maybe a spanking? I've always been curious how that would feel in the heat of the moment."

A quake rocks my equilibrium as her temptation hits me. The semi-polite restraint keeping us apart just snapped. It's as if her fingers are dancing along my spine while my cock plunges deep into her cunt. She'd be slick and warm, like melted honey dripping on my tongue.

This afternoon has taken a promising turn and I'm along for the ride. Bianca is right there with me, squirming in her saddle. Our conversation just kicked open a door we've barely cracked before. There's no going back once we cross the threshold.

I've given her space, whether she believes it or not. The distance I've kept didn't get me anywhere for years, but now we're sharing a home for the foreseeable future. This could be the beginning of us if I can convince her to take a chance on forever with me.

Bandit snorts and I jolt from those wishful thoughts. Bianca is studying me too closely again. Her lips curl seductively once she has my full attention.

"Wanna play a game?"

My mouth goes dry. "Probably not."

She pouts. "I could make your life much more exciting."

"Ditto, baby girl."

Her eyes flash, the challenge sparking into flames. "We should race. Whoever wins gets to choose a prize."

I snort. "The odds are heavily in your favor."

"Are you gonna let that stop you?"

"I don't make a habit of fighting to lose."

"That's a shame. I thought you'd never quit following me." She's pulling the strings and I'm all too aware.

"Go on then." I lift my chin. "Take the lead."

She tosses her long hair. "Finally gonna eat my dust, Cowboy."

"Just the way I like it." Although, I'd prefer if she stuck to the Stalker endearment.

When she turns to face forward, my gut clenches in preparation. Luna begins to prance and I imagine Bianca gave her some sort of cue. In the next instant, they take off at a fast pace. She doesn't glance backward to see if we're catching up. That gives me ample opportunity to plan an attack of my own.

"You can run and try to hide, Princess," I call to her quickly retreating form. "But I'll always find you."

CHAPTER ELEVEN

WIND HOWLS IN MY EARS FROM LUNA'S SPEED, MAKING it impossible to hear the thunder of hoofbeats. The beautiful scenery is a blur through my watery vision. I tip my head to the sky, soaking in the blissful freedom. There's nothing quite like running full speed on a horse.

We race for about a minute and it's obvious our competition is no match for us. It was risky to leave Colton behind, but I trust Bandit to take care of his rider. They're probably loping along at a cautious pace. I wouldn't expect anything faster from the safety police.

Luna begins to slow when I sit back in the saddle. A smile naturally appears—from the thrill of the ride and our win. I twist around to spout about our victory, but the boasting dies on my lips. They aren't behind us.

"Shit," I breathe.

The liberating vindication sours as concern twists my stomach into a pretzel. I turn Luna to retrace our path, my pulse kicking into a trot to match the mare's bouncy stride. The land in this section is flat and open. Only a few trees interrupt the grassy expanse. It should be incredibly easy to spot them, but they're nowhere in sight. That doesn't stop me from scouring the field as if they'll magically appear.

"Colton?" My voice is loud, but doesn't carry. I cup a hand around my mouth and try again. "Colton!"

Only the squawk from an agitated bird replies. Not a peep from my so-called stalker. It's quiet and still and alarming. My heart thumps wildly to drown out the silence. Luna's ears flick back and forth, which has me searching for the noise I can't hear. She flinches a second before I'm yanked out of the saddle from behind. The world spins as I'm clutched and spun in a pair of strong arms. My back gently meets the ground in the next ragged breath.

Luna takes the opportunity to bolt, abandoning me to fend for myself. Meanwhile, I'm stunned motionless. My shocked state allows Colton to effectively pin me beneath him.

"Gotcha," he rasps.

This mountain of a man lowers, covering me like an avalanche. He blocks out the sun and my ability to comprehend how I got into this position. I should be crushed under his weight, but he props himself on a bent arm to avoid annihilating me completely. His upper body hovers above mine while our lower halves press tightly together. That allows me to feel how much bigger he is.

My eyes go wide when an unmistakable bulge pushes into my pelvis. Holy shit, Colton is hard and definitely not hiding it. The solid ridge is just as impressive as his ability to sneak up behind me. It's only logical that his dick is huge to match the rest of his imposing size. I bet he fucks like a maniac on a mission. Images assault me and I squirm against the unfortunate pressure that throbs between my legs. He grunts and gives me more of his weight to fully trap my hips.

"Well," I huff. "I'm not going anywhere."

"Not until I allow it." The gravel in his voice scrapes over me and I shiver.

Colton tilts slightly to block the autumn chill, but I'm not cold. Heat rolls off him to blanket me through our layers of clothes. It's almost comfortable except for the fact that I'm held captive between two unforgiving surfaces.

My heaving chest meets his with each labored inhale. It's difficult to breathe with him so close. All I smell is him invading me. It's smoky and thick—a forest of dense pines that's impossible to escape. I drag in another lungful of the addictive scent before refocusing on my predicament.

"You planned this."

It's not a question, but he nods. "Did I scare you?"

"No, I'm getting used to you sneaking up on me." The memory of him materializing in my backseat will haunt me for years to come. "But the horses are probably halfway back to Cloverleaf Meadows by now."

Now he shakes his head. "I tied Bandit to a tree. Luna won't ditch her boyfriend."

"How do you know?"

"They're herd mates and she's loyal."

My brown quirks. "Are you trying to imply something?"

"Wouldn't mind if you came running to me."

"Sorta did before you pounced from who knows where. Were you watching me look for you?" Not that I'll admit to being worried.

"I'm very good at my job." Colton grits out that last word like it tastes foul.

"Those talents don't extend to games," I chide. "You misunderstood the point, Cowboy."

"Stalker," he rasps.

I smile at his demand. "Such a stalker."

He glares down at me. This close, I can see dark specks trying to invade his blue eyes. It reminds me of danger smothering light in shadows. How fitting.

But I'm beginning to suspect this tough guy has a gooey center. That's totally my type, or who I picture myself truly falling for. My gaze sweeps across his features curiously. He's still tan despite the cooler season, which isn't fair. The attraction tugging at me isn't either. Maybe if Colton's nose wasn't shoved so far up Brody's ass, there could be more than stolen moments between us.

I settle for admiring him while he shamelessly stares at me in return. His cowboy hat is missing, exposing light brown hair that's disheveled in a sexy style. I'm tempting to run my fingers through the short length and determine if there's something soft about him. The scruff on his face looks coarse, much like the clench in his jaw. My palms choose that moment to wander. Chiseled slabs of muscle flex under my exploration. I trace the toned definition along his torso until he makes a strained noise as if he's the one trapped. My hands drop flat to the grass.

"What's my prize, Princess?" His voice is even gruffer than before.

I squish my lips to one side. "When did we decide you're the winner?"

"From my perspective, it looks like I ended on top."

Colton glances down at me and a much more pleased sound rumbles from him.

"You're really dominant, huh?"

"Would you prefer if I'm the one to surrender?"

The visual alone is comical, especially since he doesn't budge. "Is that another joke?"

"Guess you bring out the funny side of me." Yet his tone is completely deadpan. "Tell me what I win."

I pull in another stilted breath. "What do you want?"

His stare burns into mine like a brand. "You."

"Well, in case you didn't notice, you've got me covered. I'm your helpless captive."

"We both know that isn't true."

"Would you like me to pretend?" I bat my lashes, slipping into the role of a damsel in distress. "Oh, no. You caught me. How will I escape? It seems impossible."

His answering groan is guttural and he shifts against me. "That's right, Princess. I've got you right where I want you."

It's not far-fetched—I'm completely at his mercy. "Will you let me go if I surrender?"

"No."

My bottom lip pops out in a dramatic pout. "What're you going to do to me, Stalker?"

"Keep you."

I walk my fingers up his strained arm. "Forever?"

"Yes." Now his tone is smoother than melted butter.

I'm not sure if we're still playing this new game. He sounds serious. A thrill tickles my lower belly. One night of passion might dissolve this pesky chemistry sizzling between us.

"Are you gonna strip me bare and have your way with me?" I try to wiggle with zero luck.

"Not yet." But the promise of when hangs in the air.

"What's your plan then?"

"Trying to figure that out." Colton dips his head until our noses brush. "Just like having you close."

"I think you're a romantic." My chin tips up to bring our mouths within kissing range.

His lips caress mine in the faintest touch. "Would that please you?"

That gritty rasp intoxicates me. A burst of desire has me arching into him. Our chests meet and I rub against him like a mare in heat. My nipples pebble in the restrictive confines of my sports bra, the friction sending sparks to my core. When I mewl, he sips on the sound but doesn't kiss me.

Masculine energy ripples off him in seductive waves. After a slow inhale, I'm nearly dizzy on the power he's holding over me. His musky scent might as well be initiating sex.

"Yes," I sigh. I'm agreeing to everything at this point.

But Colton still suspends himself just out of reach. His stubble scratches my skin. It's a tease more than anything.

"Do you understand that I'd do anything for you?"

My brain is hazy, wrapped up in the fantasy. "Uh-huh."

His blue stare travels beyond the fog and protective layers to cradle my deepest yearning. "And in exchange, you'll be mine."

Warm fuzzies swaddle me in a cozy embrace. "Okay, Stalker. Do your worst."

He chuckles and I almost pass out. "You're in a very agreeable mood."

My nod bumps his forehead. "I want the sex."

That flips some sort of switch. Colton stiffens and the heat in his gaze cools. "Is that all you want?"

"Foreplay wouldn't hurt." My focus drifts to what I can see of our surroundings. "Doubt anyone will stumble upon us out here."

"We're not having sex."

The lust clouding my judgment wafts away with a gust of wind. "Don't you want me?"

"With every beat of my heart."

Warmth returns to my limbs and I slump against the ground. "So, what's the problem?"

"I'm gonna be your first."

Shock steals my voice seconds before laughter bursts free. "That card has been punched, Cowboy."

"Let me finish," he growls.

My eyes narrow into slits. "Yes, sir."

"Your first love." Colton leans in until his breath mingles with mine. "You'll love me like you've never allowed yourself to love another."

Understanding dawns like a long-awaited sunrise after an especially dark night. "This isn't just about you protecting me."

"Haven't I made that obvious?"

My mouth works silently as I try to process his intentions. "I honestly thought we were just gonna have sex quick."

"Which is why we aren't. Not until you're ready."

"Ugh, this speech again." The slight whine in my voice is definitely called for.

"I'll repeat myself until it sticks."

"And I'll take your dick for now." I manage to rock my hips into his.

"That's part of the package deal. You don't get this"—he grinds that impressive length into my pelvis—"until you're hopelessly in love with me. Until I'm buried so deep, you can't get rid of me. Even if you try."

Now isn't the time to unpack those loaded statements and the attached relationship requirements.

"But you're hard."

"You're near me." He states that as a logical fact, as if those two things coincide.

I pause to collect my scattered wits, fully aware we're not on the same page. That leads me to wonder just how far ahead he is.

"Why is the keypad code my birthday?"

"It's an easy date to remember. I don't want you to get locked out." Which mirrors his earlier answer.

"But this is your house."

"It's yours too."

Confusion wars against the sweet sentiments. "Is that why you gave me the master bedroom?"

"You deserve only the best."

"Did you plant the daisies?"

"I want this to feel like home."

"That's why the cupboards and fridge are stuffed full of my favorite foods." I didn't take a full tour of the inside, but a brief glance in the kitchen revealed everything I like to eat. Same goes for the products in the bathroom.

"Think of this place as your escape." He'd said something similar when we first arrived, but it hasn't truly sunk in.

I search his unwavering stare, finding the answer but confirmation is crucial. "Do you love me, Colton?"

His jaw ticks as if the truth is stuck. "Yes."

"Since when?"

"The beginning."

My breath escapes on a whoosh. "Five years?"

His head dips. "Is that hard to believe?"

"Extremely," I blurt. "We barely saw each other."

"That's not true."

"Fine, I didn't see you."

The stalker on top of me ghosts his lips along my cheek, drifting to my ear. "Which is why this is one-sided."

"You…?" The rest of the words catch in my throat. I clear the disbelief and try again. "You love me?"

There's not an ounce of hesitation when he says, "Unconditionally."

My mind goes blank in these uncharted waters. I would've guessed the attraction was mutual. That's simple enough. What Colton just declared is the opposite.

Love.

It's basically a foreign concept aside from my handful of sexual partners. Those were one and done and forgettable. Something tells me Colton is looking to leave a permanent mark.

Confusion keeps me mute. How am I supposed to react? I'm not in the market for a relationship, let alone whatever he's proposing. This man has acted as my jailer for the better part of three months. He's been stalking me for much longer. Nothing about this situation is normal.

"I don't expect you to ever love me, but that's the only way we'll be more than this."

"Damn," I breathe. "Is that meant to be a kinky ultimatum?"

A snort scolds me. "No pressure."

"Sure about that?"

He nods again. "It's no secret that I don't deserve you."

"But you brought me to the middle of nowhere in hopes I'd fall for you." Not to mention against my will.

"Brody encouraged me to shoot my shot. He knows how I feel."

And just like that, I'm reminded where his allegiance actually rests. "Would you have admitted all this if he didn't approve?"

His gaze averts. "Eventually."

I cluck my tongue. "Doubt it. You can't go against his wishes and I totally get it. He earned your loyalty."

This isn't me being petulant or insensitive. I just know where I stand when it comes to him and my brother. Mom's voice chooses that moment to pop into my head, reminding me of her suspicions. She was certain Colton stuck so close to the farmstead for me. The theory seemed highly unlikely, but it's obvious I wasn't paying enough attention.

A crease carves into the space between his brows. "You'll always come first, Princess."

I pat his shoulder. "Maybe you'll prove it someday. Better hurry if you're planning to use our forced proximity to your advantage."

"Am I supposed to know what that means?"

"It's a book trope. One of my favorites," I admit on an exhale. "Which fits right into the unrequited romance you've whipped up."

Colton blinks. "Is that a good thing?"

My palms shove at his chest and he finally relents, rising to his knees. "Depends on what you decide to do next."

CHAPTER TWELVE

BIANCA'S MEANING BECOMES CLEAR LATER THAT evening. I thump my head against her bedroom door when a low buzz kicks on. This scene is painfully familiar.

My cock throbs, demanding I change the script. As tempting as it was, I never barged in on her while we were in Germany. At the time, I assumed those were meant to be private moments. It's becoming clear now—as I hear her moans rise in volume—that Bianca is doing this on purpose.

The doorknob gets hot under my hand while I stay still. If I storm in there, our dynamic will shift. But isn't that the point? There's more to our story than unrequited love. That term burns in my gut until it festers. I've used it before, but that was back when I chose to deny myself. It's different now. I want her to become just as obsessed.

Bianca moans as if agreeing to my terms. But then she voices her actual desire. "Ohhhh, Scout. I've missed you."

That damn name stops me cold. Something dark and

ugly twists inside me. If she's fantasizing about another man in there…

Nope, fuck it. I'm crashing into her room before logic can stop me. My knees threaten to buckle as lust clouds my vision. I've pictured this moment countless times and the vision in front of me puts my wildest dreams to shame.

Bianca doesn't flinch—or pause—when I halt at the foot of her bed. "Hey, Stalker."

But her greeting doesn't penetrate. I'm too distracted by her naked body sprawled out on the pink sheets I bought. The soft glow in the room allows me to see every exposed inch of her. My concentration bounces over bare flesh and unbridled passion, unsure where to focus first. As if that's not enough, her lilac perfume works quickly to intoxicate my willpower. The delicate scent blends flawlessly with wanton seduction, lulling me into a trance. It's an overload of sexual stimulation.

Bianca whimpers while sliding the purple vibrator along her slick center. The thrusting mode is turned on low, just as a slow tease. That lazy motion paired with the quiet humming snatches my attention. I stare, completely captivated, as the silicone dildo glides forward in a smooth sweep. Her wrist rotates in a circle, adding pressure. A pitiful noise escapes me when she taps the head to the top of her mound. She doesn't use the attached vibrator meant for her clit—not yet. This is just a rehearsal and I'm the lucky bastard with a front row seat.

All I can do is gawk at her presentation. That's precisely what Bianca is doing in this explicit position. Just as I envisioned, her legs are bent and stretched wide. That puts her pussy on display for me. Her arousal glistens in the dim lighting. She's already so damn wet. My mouth opens, jaw hanging slack, in desperate need for a taste.

"Just gonna stand there?" Her smoky tone curls around me like temptation.

I nod dumbly. That's the extent of my capabilities at the moment.

"Pity." The bold seductress pouts. "I've been waiting for you to finally join me."

That jostles me from the clutches of dumbstruck awe. Her meaning punches through the lust, but doesn't make sense. She's just getting started. Unless…

Bianca grins when I widen my eyes. "That's right, Cowboy. I heard you jerking off to me all the way back in Germany. You're less subtle than you think."

Words continue to fail me. My brain hurts along with my balls, but shame holds no space in this scenario. It's not a secret that I want her with every fiber of my being. She's perfect. Mesmerizing. The type of beauty that can make me crawl across the floor and beg. I allow my stare to roam along her generous curves. Her tan skin looks softer than satin. My empty palms clench at nothing, wishing her supple breasts were filling my grasp. She's thick in all the right places and can take every inch that I want to give her. The sight of her is too much. Fuck, I could come from just looking at her.

And she knows it. Bianca arches her back, putting her pointy nipples on better display. "Why don't you come closer?"

That would be the end of this charade. I force my feet to remain planted on the floor. A challenge sparks in her hooded gaze. She lifts a hand to cup her tit while dragging the vibrator through her slippery slit. The toy is lubed in her desire, proving she's practically weeping for me.

My cock complains again, an ache spreading through the hard length. I'd whip it out but that would require me to use energy on something other than drooling over her. As if hearing my dick cry out for mercy, Bianca lowers her eyes to the bulge in my jeans. When she licks her lips, I damn near faint.

"Does that hurt?" The concern in her voice tries to lure me.

I grunt when my cock twitches. "Nah, I'm used to it."

"Why torture yourself?" A quiver works through her from toes to tits when she hits a good spot. "Just go with the flow."

My scowl is aimed at the shit decision to deprive myself. Surrender would be very sweet. But Bianca isn't just a random girl. I refuse to treat her like one. She doesn't get to pretend this is meaningless either. The reinforced resolve must show on my face.

"C'mon, Stalker. Play with me," she croons and rolls her hips.

"You haven't agreed to be mine."

"Just once," she whines.

"Real cute," I chuckle, the gritty noise a stark contrast to her breathy moans. "If we head down this road, there's no stopping."

"Does that include a mutual masturbation session?"

My restraint wavers, but I smother the weakness. "Can't cross this line."

"Until I'm committed to hopelessly falling in love with you?"

"Yes," I grind out. I'm nothing if not dedicated to what I want.

But Bianca is more willful than a wild mustang. Her

stubborn streak won't let her bend to my demands. The gleam in her green eyes confirms as much.

"What if that doesn't happen?"

"Then we pretend this didn't either." I gesture at her bare body.

Bianca blinks innocently. "Does that mean you'll quit stalking me?"

Never. But I probably shouldn't admit that freely.

"I won't stop protecting you regardless of your feelings toward me."

Her eyes narrow like a whip lashing out to reprimand me. "That's not what I asked."

The truth climbs up my throat, but I've already spilled enough secrets for one day. "I should leave."

"You should stroke your cock for me."

My pants remain firmly fastened. "Are you gonna be mine?"

"Maybe for tonight."

"Not good enough. It feels wrong seeing you like this unless there's more to us." But my protest is barely a grumble.

"You're getting paid to watch me. Might as well get a private view." Her husky tone fondles my balls until I'm ready to blow. "This fake dick is gonna stuff me to the brim."

Bianca begins pushing the dildo shaft into her sex. I grind my molars, trying to rip my stare off her temptation. It's useless. My resolve is no match for her bold fuckery. She's brazen and eager and stripping away my resistance with each seductive whisper.

My full concentration feasts on her pussy stretching around the plastic girth. The toy hums, pumping into her gently. She grinds into the motion and mewls loudly. This rodeo princess is a natural exhibitionist in the arena, but I didn't realize that trait extended to the bedroom. Murky shadows tint the edges of my vision. No, I can't accept that. Not unless it's a brand-new habit to rile me.

While grasping at the remaining tatters of my control, I'm reminded that she had someone else on her mind not too long ago. "Who the fuck is Scout?"

Her pouty lips curl into a seductive grin. "Jealous?"

"Yes."

"Good," she purrs. "Maybe that'll spur you in the right direction."

"Dammit, Bianca."

She laughs, the syrupy tune pumping my arousal. "I can always rely on Scout to handle my needs."

With the vibrator shoved to the hilt, she bucks her hips at a sultry tempo. Her eyes slide shut as if her imagination will do the honors of conjuring better company. That won't do. I'm the only man she thinks about while that pretty pussy drips.

"Keep 'em open," I bark.

Her lips curve as she disobeys. "Or what?"

"Princess." My voice is rough, on the edge of breaking.

She flutters her lashes to taunt me. "Am I being a brat?"

"Yes."

"Are you gonna punish me?"

I shake my head, trying to clear the lust. "Can't."

"Should I punish myself?" Her painted toes curl into the blankets when she slowly withdraws the toy.

"How…?" My voice cracks and I clear my throat. "How might you do that?"

"I won't come unless you do." The soft thrum from the vibrator cuts off.

"That's not fair." We both don't need to suffer.

Bianca shrugs, totally unbothered. "Then do something about it."

"Not until you're mine."

"Kinky ultimatum." She huffs and squirms on the mattress. "Why can't we just get off together? There's no harm in that."

"It's all or nothing for me, Princess." But I'm already too invested to turn away.

"Is that why you barged in here? You assumed I'd give in," she accuses without malice.

"If I did, you'd be in a much more agreeable mood." And she wouldn't mention Scout ever again.

Bianca holds up the purple wand that's coated in her desire. "Recognize this beauty?"

It's a rhetorical question. There's no mistaking the Kaya Thrusting G-Spot Heating Rabbit that I slid into her drawer. My vision distorts when she resumes fucking herself with the dildo, filling her pussy in a fluid motion. The quiet hum of the thrust setting kicks on and she swivels to hit that secret spot deep inside. I swallow roughly, but it's impossible to speak.

She grins. "Mhmm, me too. Some might find it odd to discover their favorite type of sex toy in the nightstand of a bedroom that doesn't belong to them. I'm choosing to be grateful since I forgot mine at home. The clit stimulator is top notch."

And that's when she flips on the vibration feature. Her breath hitches when the smaller tip finds its mark. She arches off the bed, the delicate curve meant to entice. My gaze devours the spectacle while I fight with the last of my resolve. The dildo remains fully seated inside her while she begins to rub the stimulator over her clit. From where I stand, she's the definition of an erotic illusion. The alluring spectacle will vanish if I blink.

Indecision is a breeze disrupting the careful balance I've maintained for five years. Bianca is my best friend's younger sister. She's also the love of my life. It goes against my moral code to shackle her to me, but I'm relieved we've finally reached this point.

The conflict makes my head spin. I need to get ahold of myself. But my leer is roaming over her bare curves again in the next instant. She's lush and warm and begging for relief. Bianca's heavy-lidded gaze admires me in return. Those green eyes rove across my heaving chest, trailing lower while she pumps the toy in and out at a leisurely pace.

Why is she torturing me? She knows that I'm crazy about her. The truth has been spilling out of me like a broken pipe. Is this a test? I'm going to fail. This is how she wins. It's only a matter of time until she claims victory in this battle of wills. The sparkle in her eyes is already accepting my defeat.

"What do you want from me?" The hitch in my voice might as well be a white flag.

She curls her index finger, beckoning me. "Your surrender."

My gulp is thick. I promised myself I'd never let anyone control me again, but this is different. Bianca isn't using her power over me to inflict harm. Her body craves pleasure and passion. I can give that to her without abandoning my plans.

"Can I touch you?"

"Only if I get to touch you," she murmurs.

I shake my head immediately. "That's not an option."

"Then touch yourself. I want to watch you for a change." Her hips roll forward, desperate for relief.

My cock leaks in response. I'm already so close. Bianca stretches her legs, splitting her naked thighs wider. The stark difference in our state of undress isn't lost on me. I need the clothes as a defense. If I shuck the layers, nothing will stop me from hauling her against me. And then I'll forget why I'm withholding sex.

The quiet buzz of her toy accompanies our labored exhales. We stare in silence. Three more seconds tick by. In the end, my obsession demands I claim her. Once and for all.

All she has to do is compromise.

"Tell me you'll at least consider it," I rasp.

"And if I do?"

"You'll earn a reward." I take a step closer to the bed, widening my stance. Renewed confidence puffs my chest when her gaze roves me. The desire in those green eyes isn't misplaced. "I can make you come harder than you ever have before."

A bright flush races up her slender throat, painting her cheeks red. "I like the sound of that."

"Have you ever squirted, baby girl?"

She sucks in a sharp breath. "I don't think so."

"You'd know if you have. I can do that for you." The bulge straining against the front of my jeans is very confident.

Bianca licks her lips. "Prove it."

"Only if you agree to give me a chance."

CHAPTER THIRTEEN

Bianca

THE FIRE IN MY VEINS FIZZLES AS COLTON'S negotiation registers. He earns a glare for that. My frustration is beyond sexual at this point.

This fucking guy.

I'm naked, playing with myself, and practically begging for sex. Meanwhile, he's fully dressed and refusing to give into what we both so obviously need.

This is the same man who has no issue capturing me against my will. He doesn't think stalking crosses the line. Buying an escape house and filling it with my favorite things doesn't either. But casual sex? Well, that's a punishable crime unless I accept the whole package. All in the name of love.

The temperature in this pressure cooker rises to meet his demands. Can I see myself falling for Colton? A glance at his devastatingly sexy face gives me butterflies and I have my answer. But will I actually open myself up to the possibility of love? That's an entirely different section of the book. The fact that he's the one pushing for a commitment makes this a fairytale from Neverland.

"You're a mythical creature," I muse absently.

His stoic expression doesn't crack. "If that's what you need me to be."

He's definitely something else. The proof is towering at the end of my bed. Colton's blue smolder has rarely left me since he walked in. The way he stares at me is such a turn on. Not sure how I didn't notice sooner, but it's like I'm the sole purpose for his existence. That's an intense power to hold over someone. As I watch him watch me, the flames reignite in my belly. A girl could get used to this undivided attention that's bordering on obsession. I've never felt more desirable, which probably reveals something about me.

When Colton chuckles randomly, my vagina clenches very much on purpose. It's an instinctual response to the rusty melody. Colton rarely laughs, which makes the few he's given me special. I want to hear it while he calls me a brat and thrusts balls deep. That's my only excuse for moaning like a horny goat.

"Need something, baby girl?"

And now I'm wetter than a paddock in spring. Why does that name do it for me? He's creating fantasies left and right and I can't hold back much longer. My stubborn pride raises her head, stomping a foot at this unbelievable situation.

Rather than give in easily—I've already served myself on a damn platter—I snap my legs shut and prop upright on the pillows. "Do men regularly pass up a sure thing?"

"You shouldn't talk about other men." His authoritative tone rushes over me in a harsh jolt.

It makes me think of him bending me over a table and spanking my ass until I can't sit comfortably. I squirm on the mattress. A cool breeze tickles my slick arousal, reminding me how eager my body is for his. And then I recall his resistance to my efforts.

"What do you suggest I do to them?"

His broad build seems to double in size as he radiates fury. "Not a damn thing if you care about their survival."

"That's no fun. Maybe I'll skip straight to the sex. I'm not getting any 'round here." Am I goading him? Yes. Do I feel good about it? Yes again.

And Colton doesn't disappoint. He prowls forward, stopping just short of crawling onto the bed. "Nobody else touches you."

"Says who?" I wag my finger and cover my nakedness with the blanket. "I'm not agreeing to be anything other than your reluctant roommate, and that's already a stretch. You're not getting a chance at more from me until I sample the goods. What if we're sexually incompatible? That would be—"

"Impossible," he finishes for me.

"How do you plan on proving that without fucking me senseless?"

Colton gets to work unbuckling his belt. A thrill shoots through me and I sit up straighter. When his jeans are undone and sagging around his hips, I'm propped at crotch-level for an optimal view. He lowers the waistband of his boxers at a pace meant to torture me. Mattress springs squeak when impatience urges me to yank the stretchy material down myself. But then his cock is set free.

And I'm dick-notized at first sight. "Uhhh…"

Yep, I've been reduced to a mindless puddle. My jaw drops in the same instant my brain shuts off. A soft whimper slips free as I float on this lusty high. There's just so much to see. I wipe the drool off my chin and gather enough sense to focus on the most shocking revelation.

"You're pierced?"

And not just a little bit. Five horizontal posts decorate the underside of his shaft. The embellishments are notched in an even row to climb his entire length like a ribbed texture. That leads my appreciation to a thick loop speared into the center of his flared head. The silver glistens in the dim lighting, demanding my attention. It's quite an overwhelming display.

Well, damn. Colton is more studded than a leather jacket at a rock concert.

There's another clench in my pussy, but this time it's from doubt. His dick has to be at least nine inches long. The bedazzled beast will split me in half. I might be bold and putting on a show that'll make cam girls blush, but I'm not experienced enough to fit that inside me.

But that's a concern for a different day. Right now, I'm going to enjoy the view.

"How fascinating." There's no disguising the awe in my voice. "What do you, um… call all that?"

"Most refer to this as a Jacob's Ladder. But the whole section here"—he traces a path down the midline of his dick—"is called the frenum."

"A Frenum Ladder," I breathe.

"Mhmm." His hand gestures at the hoop notched into his tip. "And this is a Reverse Prince Albert."

"Aren't barbells supposed to have balls on the ends?" I

study the modest gauges that have flat pieces on both sides to hold them in place.

"It was recommended to start with this style of jewelry until we're sure you can handle more."

"That's… considerate." But then I gawk at the thicker ring hooked into his tip. "What about this one?"

"Meant to stimulate your G-spot. This design"—he flicks the round connector in the center—"is highly recommended to do just that. If it's too much or not enough, I can easily swap it out."

My eyes are dry from lack of blinking, but I can't force myself to miss any action. "Now I *really* want the sex."

"That can be arranged," he taunts.

I yank myself from the pinnacle of peens and glare at him. "Clever strategy."

Colton flexes his hips. "Agree to be mine."

It takes great effort to ignore the rod bobbing for attention. "You're crazy."

"About you."

"Good grief. Somehow you manage to make that sound romantic." I mutter under my breath about deranged stalkers wanting to settle down, but then the glimmer from his dick distracts me. It's a shock to my system all over again. "How did this happen?"

"Professionally," he drawls. "In a tattoo parlor."

I roll my eyes at his sassy ass. "You sure are full of surprises. Did it hurt?"

A pearl of precum appears during my careful inspection and Colton swipes at the moisture, spreading it to lube his cock. "Totally worth the pain."

My exhale sputters. "I bet the ladies appreciate your dedication to their pleasure."

"This is only meant to service one woman in particular, if she'll have me."

I freeze. "You didn't do that for me."

But he nods. "Overheard you mention penis piercings once and decided to go for it. If you were gonna try a flashy cock, it sure as shit was gonna be mine."

"You went through all this"—I motion wildly at the metal stabbing through his sensitive flesh in several areas—"just because I made an off-handed comment?"

"Willing to do whatever it takes to swing the odds in my favor."

"Oh-kayyyy," I expel a lungful of flabbergasted shock. "That's next-level, Stalker."

"Does that mean you'll let me satisfy your curiosity?"

He fists his studded length, rolling upward to thumb the hoop at the tip. My eyes track the lazy motion, lulling me into another trance. But then a pesky detail wiggles its way to the surface.

"Hold on," I blurt. "That pierced penis conversation happened like… Gosh, I don't even remember."

"Two years ago." A muscle twitches in his stubbled cheek, almost revealing a dimple. "I was there."

"Clearly," I mutter. "But that's not the point. You haven't been with a woman since then?"

"It's been much longer."

"Before you first saw me." The guess is more of a statement based on every other outrageous thing he's admitted.

His head bobs to cement my assumption. Damn, I'm tempted. Call me delulu, and I'll admit to stanning for slightly unhinged behavior. This man is proving to be somewhat of a morally gray marvel.

"What if I change my mind?"

Colton's hand stills on his shaft. "I'll make sure you won't. Once you're mine, my every breath will be dedicated to making you happy."

He sounds so positive that we'll just ride off into the sunset without a care in the world. Meanwhile, I'm still concerned about fitting his monster cock into my very average-sized vagina. Just thinking about taking his whole length riles me up, shooting warmth into my lower belly. My breathing picks up and I'm at risk of spontaneously climaxing. I spotted a bottle of lube in the nightstand drawer. My lips curl at the reminder. It might be tight, but we'll fit.

Challenge accepted, big guy.

But this is wild, even for me. I'm not ready to dive in head over heels. I've never had a serious boyfriend. Any man that's showed interest quickly proved to have shallow and selfish intentions. It tarnished my faith in happily ever after. If it weren't for growing up around my parents and their blissful marriage, I might've written off the concept much sooner.

As if reading my hesitation, Colton releases the choke-hold on his dick. "I'll take good care of you, Princess."

My gaze is still latched on the pierced prize jutting up like a beacon. "Mhmm, I can see that."

"You can trust me with your heart." The sincerity in his voice lifts my gaze.

I get caught in the emotion swirling in his expression. He wants me to leap. The devotion in his stare promises to catch me.

The mood calms when he relaxes his stance, taking away the strain between us too. I'm guarded and jaded, but Colton is determined to break through my walls.

Words are glue in my throat. "Can I think about it?"

"Of course." He shrugs like my delay doesn't hurt, but trying to shove his rock-solid erection back into his pants definitely will.

"Don't," I rasp.

His fingers pause as he studies me. That allows me to keep ogling his cock. A rumble that sounds like pure male satisfaction rises off his chest.

"Tell me what you need to give this a chance."

I shiver at his soft command. "A test ride might do the trick."

"No." Colton resumes the painful process of stealing his dick from view.

"Can I at least watch you take care of that?" My open palm rises toward his swollen tip that's steadily leaking for me.

"No," he repeats.

"But you said—"

"It's yours," he confirms. "Which is true. My dick has belonged to you since that first glance, but that doesn't mean I'll fuck you."

I pop out my bottom lip. "What does it mean?"

"We're gonna do this when you're ready."

My lashes bat at him as if his iron will can be so easily swayed. "I don't get to touch you until then?"

"Not without the magic words."

"I'm beginning to really despise your kinky ultimatum."

"No pressure," he reminds.

"What if I'm not interested in getting attached?"

"Too late and too bad." He finishes buttoning his jeans. "I'm interested in forever. That's not up for negotiation."

Meanwhile, my bare ass is still very much in the air—not that he seems to notice. Whatever cracks I'd chiseled into his stony resistance have been fully repaired. Colton backs away from the bed slowly, giving me plenty of time to stop him. A disgruntled huff flops me flat onto the mattress. The urge to scream flexes my throat, but I swallow the insolence.

He pauses before stepping into the hallway. "Is that your final answer, Princess?"

"For now," I mutter.

"Sweet dreams," he croons and crosses over the threshold.

As if that will save him. I grab the gifted dildo and chuck it at the closing door, narrowly missing his head. Colton's chuckle fades as he walks away and leaves me to handle my own release. That's just fine.

I get myself situated on the mountain of pillows. With a deep inhale, the agitation fizzles. After exhaling, I'm ready to finish what I started. And thanks to my obsessive jailer, I have new inspiration to get me there faster.

A crisp visual of Colton climbing toward me forms quickly. Rather than abandon me in my time of orgasmic need, he covers my body with his like a protective shield. His intensity and temptation threaten to smother me. Much like in the field, he consumes my senses. I breathe deep to inhale him. That musky masculinity is delicious.

Pretend Colton isn't shy about eliminating sexual boundaries. When I arch into him, he puts more weight on me. The pinned force is gentle but strong. He uses his control to spread my legs wider and align our hips. His cock pulses in a desperation I can feel inside of me.

And then the ribbed texture on his shaft glides along my slick center. I tremble against the cool sheets when he repeats the motion. His pierced tip teases my entrance. I clench against nothing, but it's easy to imagine the burning stretch as he fills me. He's going to wreck me for all others. That sends a burst of heat through me and I'm already nearing the peak.

An insistent throb spreads from my core. I drift a palm down my torso as the fantasy continues to play. Sparks shoot from my clit the instant I make contact. So. Damn. Sensitive. I'm not sure I've ever been this turned on.

My thighs quiver while I set a frantic pace. Pressure builds at record speed. A few swipes and I'm thrust over the edge into climatic bliss. Tingles erupt in an explosion that steals my breath. I smile at the empty room, letting my eyes slide shut as pleasure takes control.

Muscles twitch as sensation returns to my limbs. As the rush slows to a comforting ripple, I almost laugh. Colton provides very titillating material.

Challenge most definitely accepted, Stalker.

CHAPTER FOURTEEN

Cotton

MY BARE FEET SLAP AGAINST THE FLOOR AS I PACE the length of the kitchen again. The wood is going to groove at this rate. I can't be bothered to care, not when the clock is mocking me.

It's almost ten o'clock in the morning and there's still no sign of Bianca. Force of habit had me checking on her once or twice, just to make sure she wasn't tying her bedsheets together or anything. Her bubble of chaos was activated on the last peek to give proof of normalcy. The shower turned on an hour ago, but she stayed upstairs.

Panic gnaws at me while I wait for her appearance. Yesterday changed our status, which was very much on purpose. Last night, on the other hand… Fuck, that was an unexpected twist. Sweat instantly slicks my palms while I recall the sultry grind of Bianca's naked hips. She wanted me to soothe that desperate ache and I rejected her like some sort of lovesick saint. I hang my head, cursing my own name.

The uncertainty of where we stand now is a toxic puddle I'm stuck in. Bianca is probably fuming. I can withstand almost anything except her silence. That's a torture I can't endure again. She can poke fun at my one-sided feelings. Tease me for protecting her. Force us to remain platonic. Ridicule me for abstaining from sex regardless. It doesn't matter what she says. She just can't ignore my existence.

Silence surrounds me in response. The knot in my gut grows until I'm forced to stop pacing. Rather than break down her door and demand she speak to me, I grab my phone to text Brody.

Me: What's the latest?

Brody: The wife demanded we stop by for a visit. Bianca put it in her head.

My stomach drops. Not the update I was looking for.

Me: Whenever you want. There's plenty of space.

Brody: I'll keep you posted. Too much shit to do around here.

Me: Any trouble?

Brody: Nah, town is quiet.

Which is good, but suspicious. I scrub at the thick stubble on my jaw.

Me: Any rumors?

There's a long pause. Probably pissed him off right along with his sister. It's not like he gives a shit about gossip. But thanks to me, his family is involved too.

Brody: Paisley just told me a woman was asking about you at the farmer's market.

Me: What woman?

Brody: How the fuck should I know?

The creak of hinges followed by footsteps distracts me. Bianca descends the stairs in a skip that I feel in my chest. The energy instantly lifts with her chipper approach. Her lilac scent is fresh, wafting over to me like a peace offering. When she smiles at me, every worry washes away and I can breathe.

"Rise and shine," she chirps.

I sag into the oversized kitchen island. "Hi."

"Holy shit." Bianca slams to a halt near the fridge. "Are we expecting company?"

My mouth slides into a frown. "Brody didn't say when they're coming."

Her forehead creases before she waves at the large surface currently keeping me upright. "That's a feast for a whole family."

It's only then I remember there's an assortment of food cluttering the counter. "Thought you'd be hungry."

She creeps forward to inspect the options. That gives me a moment to openly study her. A thick braid hangs over one shoulder, still damp from the shower. Another burst of lilac greets my deep inhale and I'm intoxicated all over again.

After a pleased rumble, my hooded gaze sweeps over her face. She doesn't have a stitch of makeup on. I stare at her flawless skin, itching to feel the satin on my calloused palm. Her tight jeans and pink shirt are last for me to admire, but definitely not least. The standard riding outfit tells me that we'll be headed to the barn after breakfast.

"Hello?" Bianca waves a hand between us.

I'm slapped back to reality as if I snapped the elastic on my wrist. "Huh?"

"Did you get all this delivered somehow? Or did you leave me unguarded"—she gasps dramatically on that word—"to grab takeout?"

"I cooked."

"No way," she blurts.

The urge to grin twitches my lips. "Want to check the dishwasher? I can pause the cycle."

"You know how to make"—her gaze scours over the brunch items—"Eggs Benedict?"

My shoulders straighten at the awe in her voice. "There are fluffy biscuits with extra creamy gravy too."

Her jaw drops. "Who are you?"

"Yours," I answer automatically.

Bianca studies me for several seconds. "Quite impressive, Stalker. I'll need to confirm it's edible before making a final judgment on this grand gesture."

"Can I fix you a plate?"

"I can do it."

"So can I," I insist.

"Okayyyy." She gives me a strange look as if I'm not making sense.

"Take a seat." I lift my chin at the table surrounded by six chairs.

When she chooses to sit next to the window, I almost smile again. I arranged it this way very specifically and she just rewarded my efforts. Bianca loves a spot with a view. The seat she picked offers an unobstructed shot of the daisy gardens I planted for her.

Instead of getting caught gawking, I get busy piling all of her favorite breakfast foods onto one plate. It's complete chaos—just the way she loves it. The dish is almost over-flowing when I set it down in front of her. Bianca breathes in the unmistakable aroma of bacon and savory satisfaction. I retrace my steps to fill a mug with hazelnut coffee, grabbing a glass of sparkling orange juice in the other hand.

She blinks at the full picture. "This might be the most delicious sight I've ever seen."

I scoff. "No need to lie."

It's not a secret she was raised in luxury. She probably has a list of personal chefs on speed dial. I can't even imagine the gourmet meals she's had.

But Bianca huffs right back at me. "I can smell the care that went into every morsel. That makes all the difference."

There's a clench in my heart and I spin around before saying something sappy. After grabbing myself a cup of coffee, I sit a few chairs away from her. It's where I get my favorite view.

"Why are you so distant, Stalker?" Her stare targets me like heat-seeking missile.

"Wasn't sure I'd be welcomed closer."

When she smiles, her eyes twinkle. "Why wouldn't you be? I'm surprised you aren't parading around like a proud peacock."

"Not my style."

"Should be," she argues. "You're somewhat responsible for the multiple orgasms I gave myself."

"Fuck," I grunt through clenched teeth.

She preens after getting the desired reaction from me. "And if that's not enough, you're definitely responsible for this spread about to fill my belly."

"You haven't tried it yet." My tone is slightly perturbed.

She glares at my absent plate. "Did you eat already?"

"This isn't about me."

"You're just going to sit there?"

My heart beats wildly, desperate to connect with hers. "And watch you."

"Mhmm, sounds familiar. If you're trying to butter me up, this is the way to do it." Which could stroke my ego to distraction, but then her stomach grumbles.

"Eat," I command.

"Yes, sir."

And just like that, my cock raises to half mast. The throb pulses stronger when she spears a piece of French Toast. I'm transfixed by the simple motion of her lifting the fork to her mouth. When her lips part, I have the irrational instinct to snatch the utensil from her grip and feed her myself.

"Ohhhhhhh." Her lashes flutter and she slumps deeper into the chair. "Yummmm."

I relax in my own seat. "You like it?"

She chews slowly as if savoring the bite. "Gosh, yes. Passes the inspection with flying colors."

"Thank fuck for that."

Her giggle tapers off into snort. "What would you do if I hated it?"

"Start from scratch."

A forkful of eggs hovers in midair. "You wouldn't."

"Don't underestimate my desire to please you."

A muffled moan slips free when she shoves the bite into her mouth. "Keep this up and I might marry you by the end of the year."

I freeze, not even daring to breathe. "Don't say shit like that unless you mean it."

She huffs and rolls her eyes. "I wouldn't say shit like that unless I meant it."

"Careful what you say next, Princess." My body is tense and ready to launch across the space between us.

"Unless I flash a green light, you're not going to maul me. Unfortunately," she grumbles.

"Don't tempt me." After a warning rumble, I force myself to stay seated.

Bianca winks like a sassy brat. "Do you know your love language?"

"Not a damn clue."

"I'm not sure which one this covers, but I think it checks all the boxes." She hovers her fork over the plate before settling on more hash browns.

"Would've cooked for you a lot sooner," I rasp.

"It's not just the food. You're very…" She purses her lips while searching for the right word.

Meanwhile, I scoot to the edge of my chair. A silent plea moves my lips as she finds it.

"Convincing."

"Is that all?" I'm desperate for more.

"No, I'm beginning to realize you're very complex. Much like my developing feelings for you."

My dick is ready to punch through my zipper to reach her. "Gonna give me a chance, Princess?"

"Close to considering it." She tips her head sideways. "What's your favorite thing to eat for breakfast?"

"I'm not picky."

"That wasn't the question."

My eyes lower to the mug in my grasp. "Toast and coffee."

She laughs. "Easy enough. You can have tomorrow morning off."

"You're going to cook for me?"

"Let's not get ahead of ourselves. Toast is very basic and requires zero skill."

"Might burn the bread," I mumble.

"Thanks for the vote of confidence." Bianca squirms, but abruptly stops. A wince pinches her features.

I'm on my feet in the next second. "What's wrong?"

She startles at my extreme reaction. "It's just my back. Nothing major."

My gaze scours over her, looking for visible injuries. "You're sore?"

Her hip rotates in circles on the chair. "I'll be fine."

"Did you sleep okay?"

She shrugs. "Not really. I actually woke up really early. The mattress is softer than I'm used to. My lower back locked up. Did some yoga to loosen the strain. That helped, but a few specific exercises from physical therapy really eased the ache. After that, I texted Paisley and gave her the address. Listened to a chapter of my audiobook. Worked on the ear muffs for Luna. Then I called my dad. He wasn't at all surprised to hear you snatched me against my will."

I'm nodding along, but one part of her rambled recollection strikes deeper. "That's unacceptable."

"Which part?"

"The shitty bed."

She waves that off as I grab my phone. "It's okay. I've had much worse in very fancy hotels."

"You shouldn't have to deal with that here."

"I'll get used to it."

Like hell she will. My bratty princess doesn't suffer for a second if I can help it. She'll be in better shape tonight, but that doesn't fix the immediate problem.

"What can I do for you?" Or to her, if she'll allow it.

The smile she gives me is soft. "I'm really okay."

"Can I give you a massage?"

"Is that a serious question?" Bianca is already turning around, giving me access to her crooked spine.

My palms loom for a moment, deciding where to land. I choose to focus on the lower section. When my fingers dig in, she trembles and rewards me with a loud whine.

"Yessss, right there." Her body goes lax, slouching against the chair for support.

My hands wander lower, rubbing into the tough spots at the base of her spine. The noise she expels lets me know I've hit the spot. Bianca is limper than a cooked noodle, allowing me to have my way with her.

"Don't stop," she groans.

"Never," I murmur under my breath.

"Seriously," her voice is hoarse. "How are you an expert at everything?"

"I'm very determined." Which I prove by changing tactics, kneading into her muscles.

"Harder," she demands.

My fingers are quick to comply. It would be better with oil against bare skin, but this is progress regardless. She's letting me care for her. Willingly. That's a privilege I'll gladly accept.

Bianca shudders in my grip, prompting me to keep going. Arousal flushes my skin the longer I work her over. There's no hiding what her sounds are doing to my dick. And then she wiggles her ass as if that's going to offer relief. When she releases an especially sultry wheeze, I rip my hands off her shoulders as if she burned me. It's not far from the truth. Her throaty moans are trying to incinerate my willpower.

"Don't you dare." She shoves backward, nudging my cock in the process.

"You're doing this on purpose," I rasp.

As if proving a point, she grinds into me again. "I'm just trying to get at the kinks."

"More like expose mine."

Bianca glances at me over her shoulder. "Give it to me, big guy."

"You're not ready." But I resume massaging her pain away.

She watches me as I focus on her needs. "You're doing most of the right things, but it needs to be my choice."

"I'm a patient man." My palms drift lazily along her back. "I'll wait for you to choose me. No matter how long it takes."

Bianca opens her mouth to reply, but a loud bark interrupts her.

I'm moving before I even realize it. My long stride carries me to the hallway hutch where I stashed a Glock. I didn't get an alert about a perimeter breach from the high-tech security system I installed in this place. That doesn't mean shit when dealing with my father's minions, though. They can easily avoid the invisible shield.

Bianca gasps when I load a fresh magazine into the gun. The chamber is empty as I stalk toward the front door, but that can change quickly. A glance out the small window reveals no immediate threats.

"What are you doing?" She whisper-shouts from several feet behind me.

I thrust my arm out behind me. "Stay put."

"You're not going out there."

"Don't follow me." And then I'm stepping onto the porch.

Muscle memory takes control. I'm on guard, prepared to shoot any intruders. The familiar role slips over me like a comfortable shirt. With the Glock pointed in front of me, I scan the area. No fresh tracks mark the dirt. There aren't any glints from scopes. It's quiet and still, but I can't be too cautious. Not when Bianca's safety is at risk.

I'm not sure why my father would go to such trouble to hunt me down, but I wouldn't put it past him. A dying man is known to be careless is his final days. If they found us, there's no telling how this might play out.

That's when a bush rustles. I whip the barrel of the gun at the twitching leaves. My heart thunders as I click off the safety, bringing my finger to the trigger. A dog leaps from the shrub and runs straight at me.

It's a scraggly thing—more bones than meat. I lower my weapon, but keep it ready. The pup takes that as a sign to join me on the stoop. A startled cry turns my blood to ice. But when I spin toward the sound, Bianca is staring at the mutt next to my feet.

I gulp when she hesitates to cross the threshold. My gut clenches as I wait for her to look at me. If there's fear in her eyes—aimed at me—I'm not sure what I'll do. But when those green depths crash into me, only concern is glimmering on the surface. For me? That can't be right.

"Is it safe to come out?"

My gaze does another visual sweep of the property, finding no signs for concern. I nod in confirmation. "False alarm."

She slinks forward, still unsure. "Did you think it was him?"

"Won't take any chances." Which reminds me. "I told you to stay put."

Bianca swats my ass as if I'm a naughty submissive. "Since when do I listen?"

My body goes rigid. The spanking does something to me on an elemental level. A quake rolls through me, hardening my dick into solid steel before I can register a sting. It's an odd sensation that immediately sprouts a hunger for more. What the actual fuck? But now isn't the time to evaluate the simpering response. I rip myself from the fantasy about to take shape and glare at the woman responsible.

"It could be dangerous," I growl.

"He looks harmless," she coos at the scruffy dog. "Or are you a lady?"

The ball of brown fur and dirt thumps its tail on the wood. That invites Bianca to lower into a crouch, extending her hand for the mutt to sniff. With zero hesitation, the stray licks her fingers. She giggles and begins petting its matted fur in exchange. I'm tempted to taste her skin to get a similar reaction, but I wouldn't get the giddy response this lucky pup is receiving.

"Are you lost?" Bianca smooths her palms along the dog's skinny frame, confirming the gender with a peek under its belly. "Did the big man scare you with his gun, pretty boy?"

I scowl when she glares at me. "It's for protection."

Not to mention the countless others stored around the house and barn.

"We'll talk about that later," she croons in a voice meant to soothe babies. "First, we need to name you."

A jolt electrocutes my body. "We?"

"Well, yeah. He's ours until proven otherwise."

Warmth stabs at me and spreads, expanding my chest until I'm about to burst. "You decide."

"It should be a team effort."

"Um, okay." I search my memory, thinking of something she would choose. "Spud."

"Spud?"

"Like a potato, which deserves its own food group," I recite.

"Oh, my." She blinks up at me with watery eyes. "That's perfect."

I avert my own stare before exposing more weakness. "He needs a bath."

"Did you hear that? Daddy is very thoughtful. We're gonna get you all cleaned up."

And that just about does me in. We're talking about a dog, but damn. That parental role effortlessly bestowed upon me solidifies our bond. She's taking ownership with me, practically agreeing to be a family unit.

I let my smirk finally appear. The occasion calls for it. Bianca Benson is mine, whether she realizes it yet or not.

CHAPTER FIFTEEN

Bianca

COLTON HAS A STRANGE LOOK ON HIS FACE. MAYBE he let one rip after the stress of assuming we were in trouble. I squint at him closely and purse my lips. That doesn't seem quite right.

From my perspective, he very much had things handled. The way he whipped out that gun like a Wild West duel left me breathless. It's a side of him I hadn't seen.

My gaze roves over him now. His smirk isn't ruthless or calculating. I'd almost say that he's happy. Spud chooses that moment to bump my hand, as if I could forget our new addition. His unexpected—and much needed—visit provides a welcome distraction.

I'm not an expert, but he's some sort of Shepherd mix. Many of the dogs I've rescued and adopted over the years have a similar pedigree. Unfortunately, they're the type that are commonly surrendered or abandoned. Our local shelter is stuffed full of these big babies and it stabs at me whenever I volunteer for a shift.

A pinch twists my stomach as I comb his scraggly fur. "Do you think someone is looking for him?"

Colton watches my efforts to brush Spud with my fingers. "Doubt it."

"But he's so friendly." I rub under his chin and he slumps against me. "Where's your home, sweet boy?"

"With us."

My heart stutters. I glance up at Colton to find his blue eyes already hot on mine. Gone is the smirk. The look he gives me now is a smoldering fire. I drop flat onto my butt, no longer able to hold myself in the crouched position.

Gosh, he's sexy. Almost perfect in every other way too. If Colton hadn't forced me into this situation, our situationship would probably look very different right now. But I can't get past the fact he stole my choice.

"Um..." I sever our intimate connection and the temperature immediately drops twenty degrees. It still takes my brain several seconds to recover. "Are you... uh, a dog person?"

He shrugs, scratching Spud behind his floppy ear. "Sure."

The noncommittal response reminds me that he has secrets, which leads me to reconsider the gun tucked into the back of his jeans. "Have you shot someone?"

"Once or twice."

"Did you kill them?"

His piercing gaze resembles ice when he says, "Already told you I haven't."

"But you would."

"For you." The chill thaws when his voice softens, gaining a vulnerable edge. "Does it change the way you look at me?"

It should, along with his other darker habits. I've told myself as much on many occasions. But instead, my mind conjures images of him using weapons for something other than destruction. I freeze, which has nothing to do with the mid-morning autumn breeze. What is happening to me?

Colton rumbles and I almost moan from the gravelly noise. "You like me bad, baby girl."

"I didn't say that."

That unrecognizable glint returns to his expression. "Didn't have to."

"Cocky cowboy," I mutter before refocusing on the less complicated matter in front of me. "Spud is probably hungry. There's plenty of bacon."

A yip comes from the pooch as if he can understand me. Colton grunts and gestures at the door, joining in the team spirit. The big softie even hoists me off my feet. I teeter—almost toppling into him and his addictive scent—but manage to gather my bearings. That doesn't mean my knees don't quake slightly when I lead the pack inside. Seriously, I need to get a grip.

"He also needs that bath you mentioned," I add while striding toward the kitchen.

A downward glance finds Spud too interested in sniffing every available surface to change his mind about a reunion with domestication. He won't even see the suds coming.

"There's a wash stall in the barn," Colton offers.

Which earns him a scowl over my shoulder. "He's getting bubbles in the tub."

The grump's lips twitch. "Obviously."

Sunshine streams in through the windows, painting the room in a warm glow. It displays all the effort Colton put into making this house a home. From the pictures on the walls to the restored antique furniture, I'm swaddled in cozy comfort. As I approach the knotty wood dining table and purposefully mismatching chairs, decades of unique stories speak to me.

Spud is hot on my heels the instant I pick up a strip of bacon. His butt plops on the floor, tail wagging, and tongue happily lolling out to one side. I toss a piece into the air and he catches it with ease.

"Ohhhh," I croon. "Look at you. Such a good boy."

"Lucky mutt," Colton grumbles.

"Someone is jealous," I say in the same obnoxious tone reserved for babies. "As if anyone could resist this face. Do you have an owner?"

Spud whines until I give him more bacon.

"Definitely spoiled." My smile slips into a frown. I look over at Colton parked on the top of the oversized sofa. "Should we go to the nearest town and see if anyone is missing him?"

"I thought you wanted to go riding." He motions at my outfit.

"That can wait."

"The wild goose chase can too."

"A little girl might be out there searching for her dog." There's a pleading note in my voice, which easily slips free whenever animals in need are involved.

His tattooed arms cross. "It's not safe to be out and about."

The excuse wrinkles my nose. "You were gonna trailer me to a barrel race."

"That's different."

"How?"

"It just is."

I pop out my hip, letting the brat out to fight. "Quit talking back."

A scoffed chuckle scolds me. "Real cute, Princess."

"Do you need another spanking?" My palm slaps the other in warning.

Colton stills, a visible tremble racking his limbs. Flames reignite his stare, burning the short distance between us. Our undeniable attraction thrums like a pulse. He straightens off the couch as if commanded. Static prickles my skin and I shiver. This is uncharted territory, but that doesn't scare me. Instead, awareness takes the reins and makes me bolder.

"Would you like that, bad boy?"

His throat works with a thick swallow. "Don't toy with me."

I inhale the control he just tossed away. "You're in big trouble."

A pitiful whimper snatches my focus. The heat fizzles into guilt when I notice Spud's sunken spirits. From his hanging head and hunched body, his sad eyes peek up at me. He's acting like I punished him.

"Not you, sweet angel. I was talking to Daddy. You're so good. The best dog."

Spud perks up at my upbeat voice.

"Do you want more bacon?"

His nails click on the hardwood when he begins to dance.

I gladly give him another piece to make amends. "There you go. All better."

He woofs and wanders off to scope out the rest of the joint. Meanwhile, Colton looks like a sullen gambler who didn't win the jackpot. I strut toward him, receiving a confidence boost when his desire roams over my curvy assets.

"Do you need a treat too?"

"That'd be nice." His timbre is gruff from indignation.

Without warning, I hop onto the balls of my feet to peck his cheek. "Thanks, Stalker."

He whips his face sideways to align with mine, brushing our lips together in the process. "For what?"

My shoulder hitches. "I dunno. Everything you're doing right?"

"Does that shift weight off what I've done wrong?"

The answer has the ability to change where we stand, which makes me smother it. "I'm gonna get the bath going."

"Need a hand?"

"No," I purr. "But I think you need a cold shower."

CHAPTER SIXTEEN

Cotton

BIANCA'S FINGERS SKIP ALONG THE RADIO DIALS AND knobs as if fascinated by the vintage style. "Why Fern?"

My thumb taps on the steering wheel to the catchy song that's playing, but I stop as her question registers. "She's green."

"There's gotta be more to it than that," she muses.

I avoid her stare that's burning into my profile. "It's the same color as your eyes."

"Really?" She sounds shocked at the revelation, or maybe it's that I compared the shade of her irises to a plant.

In all honesty, I haven't thought about the connection until recently. It's just one observation in a complex, complicated collection. Bianca is everywhere I go and in everything I see. A moment doesn't pass without her. My truck didn't have a name until she first looked my way.

"You shouldn't be surprised," I murmur.

She blows out a thick exhale that I feel in my chest. "I'm not. You're very… consistent."

It's a small miracle that she doesn't mock my obsession. That doesn't mean she won't eventually.

I glare at the road straight ahead. "Am I scaring you yet?"

"Hardly," she scoffs. "I might be your captive and you stalked me for years, but you've never given me a reason to fear you. Even when you pulled out that gun like it was second nature, I wasn't worried about me. You were ready to eliminate the threat. We'll circle back to that later."

My gut tightens along with my hands on the wheel. The last thing I want to do is reveal more of my dark past to her. I stay quiet, allowing her to fill the void.

"For now, you're taking me to town against your better judgment. I didn't even have to try that hard to convince you. It's worth the risk to find out if anyone is missing this cutie pie." Her fingers scratch Spud's belly while the dog sprawls across her lap like an actual sack of potatoes. "So, yeahhhh… you're a softie. Totally harmless where it counts."

That's laughable, but my expression remains flat. Her perception of me is purposefully skewed. She'd be singing a different tune if she had access to the skeletons in my closet. Instead, the lyrics of *Run It* by Jelly Roll are spilling from her lips.

I agreed to leave the property because I'm highly skilled at protecting her. What I'm capable of inflicting without remorse is deeply concerning. Or should be. If someone dares to look at her wrong, I won't hesitate to redirect their focus to my fist in their face.

Bianca would probably laugh. Her crazy streak is both terrifying and arousing. At any moment, she can decide to shut me out or agree to be mine. The waiting game is a sharpened blade ready to slice me in half.

At least my father is temporarily incapacitated. Brody texted an hour ago to tell me that Daddy Dearest was hospitalized after collapsing in public. Word spread quickly, which will require damage control in the underground circles. That takes the crew's interest off me.

With the immediate danger suspended, it should be safe to wander the streets and ask if anyone lost their dog. Not that I'm convinced Spud was let loose on accident. Bianca won't relax until we confirm that theory. But then the mutt will be officially ours and her good mood will belong to me.

Maybe I'll earn another kiss. The last one still sizzles on my skin like a brand. I imagine her choosing me and warmth spreads across my chest like the shining sun.

"What's got you smirking, Cowboy?" Bianca's sugary tone almost startles me.

The fact she's calling me out is another shock entirely. But my lips are indeed hitched upward. I pinch them together, refusing to appear weak. This woman already got me to fold multiple times today.

And she's not done. "Oh, don't stop. You're sexy when you smirk."

There's a sudden fire in my cheeks. I widen my eyes at the foreign sensation, but it's too late.

"No way! Nope, I'm not looking." She slaps a palm over her eyes. "You cannot be bashful. That's not fair."

Her dramatic reaction makes my whole face burn hotter. Dammit, what's wrong with me? I don't blush. My father would beat me bloody for less.

Meanwhile, Bianca peeks at me through her fingers. "Are you embarrassed?"

I quickly avert my stare, demanding the shameful betrayal to recede. My jaw is clenched hard enough to crush my molars.

"We don't have to talk about it." She makes the motion of zipping her lips and throwing away the key.

We sit in silence. It's instantly uncomfortable. I'd rather blush my ass off than sit and wonder what she's thinking about. The steady thump from the tires hitting pavement mirrors my pulse. Only five more minutes until we reach the tiny town of Morgan.

Bianca begins to softly hum along with the music. I can practically hear the wheels in her brain spinning. The tension crackles and I'm about to demand she breaks it.

"Have you let anyone else drive Fern?"

The question is so random that laughter rumbles up my throat. "No."

"Would you let me?"

"Yes."

She giggles. "That was easy."

"I'm a sucker."

"Not really. You brought me here against my will." Her nails tap on the door as if she's tempted to tuck and roll.

Automatic locks would come in handy right about now. "That's for your own good."

"What about you not letting me have my way with you?"

"That's for our future."

Her sigh is pleased with my answer. "Hard to argue when you're being romantic."

"Just say the word," I urge.

"Do ferns have a significant meaning? Other than matching the shade of my eyes." There's a wide smile in her voice when she bats her lashes at me.

I grunt at her antics. "Ferns symbolize new beginnings."

"Fitting," she muses.

"Hell of a coincidence."

"Yeah, I'm not sure those exist for you. Is it weird that I keep spare dog collars and food in my horse trailer?" She fiddles with the braided nylon circling Spud's neck.

"Doesn't hurt to be prepared."

"Would you take me to Montana if I asked?"

I squint at her from the corner of my eye. "What's in Montana?"

"Mountains."

"Why not Colorado or Wyoming?"

"The elevation is too high."

"Okay," I mutter.

"Excellent. Do you think this"—she flicks her wrist at the windshield to indicate our current mission—"is a wasted effort?"

"Yes."

"But you're going along with it anyway?"

"Yes."

"Why?"

"You asked me to." Much like answering this line of questioning.

"And you care about Spud." Bianca lifts her brows.

"By extension."

Her attention drifts out the window. "Do you want children, Stalker?"

I swerve, crossing into the opposite lane before correcting our course. "Shit."

"That one went too far. Noted." She crosses an imaginary item off an equally pretend list.

But that doesn't stop Bianca's nonsense from spilling free. She continues peppering me with random curiosities until I park the truck in front of a dive bar on the main drag of town. One look at the sign above the entrance has her cackling like she ate a handful of edibles.

Spud leaps upright onto all fours, obviously concerned for her well-being. His slobbery kisses just make her laugh harder. When his tail starts whipping me in the face, I take it as my cue to get out.

"Hey! Wait up." Bianca stumbles out of Fern, still giggling uncontrollably. "Don't you dare step foot in Dirty Dicks without me."

CHAPTER SEVENTEEN

Bianca

COLTON PAUSES IN FRONT OF THE HOOD, DUTIFUL AS ever regardless of my obnoxious behavior. The fit of giggles really can't be helped when faced with a tasteful delight such as Dirty Dicks. Whatever comedic genius is responsible sure knows how to make a bang.

And they chose an ideal location. There's no sign of another bar or restaurant along this short strip. That makes it the most logical place to meet locals who might recognize Spud. Laughter still tickles my throat when I smile over at Colton.

"Smart thinking, Stalker."

He flicks the brim of his baseball hat. "At your service."

"If only you were that easy," I mumble.

"You wouldn't give me the time of day if I were." His answer clocks me in the chest.

The truth stings. I push most people away. Nobody gets to see the real me unless they make the effort to climb over an impenetrable wall. Most don't bother trying. Meanwhile, Colton hops the defense mechanism like it's barely a challenge. This man is willing to do whatever it takes to reach me.

A shiver rolls through me as his stare burns into mine. Commitment has never looked sexier, especially after he exposed a bashful side. That doesn't mean I'm ready yet.

My gaze shifts over his head to the name that's proudly displayed in bold letters on the building behind him. I'm instantly derailed and losing my shit again. This bout of laughter is slightly unhinged. Gosh, maybe I'm finally cracking. But it feels good to just let it out.

Mom would be hootin' and hollerin' beside me. Thanks to her, I've seen some impressive sights in my twenty-three years. This one erects my expectations to new lengths. People must stop and stare on the regular.

My grumpy jailer isn't as amused. His expression is stony while I'm fighting to breathe. Tears are streaming freely down my cheeks at this point. I might be truly unraveling.

Spud chooses that moment to leap from the truck, landing gracefully at my feet. His wet nose boops my hand that's holding his leash before he turns in Colton's direction. With him tugging me along, we arrive on the sidewalk mostly composed.

"Woooo," I exhale and wipe under my eyes. "What a treat."

Colton's stare remains blank. "Mhmm."

"That was very refreshing after these past few months."

Those baby blues pierce into me. "Whatever you need, Princess."

I almost mewl at his gruff tone. The blush that very recently stained his scruffy cheeks replays in my mind. It makes me think of him laughing uncontrollably. That would probably really do me in. His lips press together in a firm line to extinguish the possibility.

But it still leaves me guessing. "How can you keep a straight face? You should be in stitches."

"It's a gimmick."

"A provocative one that I applaud. This tiny town looks very unassuming until bam! Dirty Dicks." I thrust my arms at the fluorescent signs flashing in the windows. "Maybe they'll offer us dinner and a show."

Fury rolls off him in jealous waves. "Better not."

"Feel free to whip out that pierced pistol in your pants and wag it in my face. I'll open wide." My lips pop in invitation.

Colton groans and hangs his head. "Dammit, woman."

"Don't act scandalized," I admonish.

"More like tortured."

Before I can respond, feminine voices from down the road cut into our conversation. Two women are chatting loudly, lost in their own world. It makes me miss Paisley. We'll definitely be coming to Dirty Dicks when she visits.

I'm deep in thought about friendship bonds when they notice us blocking their path.

The brunette gasps. "What an adorable dog."

"Such a cutie," the blonde coos.

Spud sits calmly, ready to be lavished with hugs and kisses. The women look to me for permission. Colton grunts and leans against the building, realizing this won't be a quick exchange. Meanwhile, I offer a shrug and scratch the pooch's head.

"We found him on our property earlier," I tell them. There's no mistaking the pleased rumble that rolls off Colton, but I don't let him distract me. "Figured someone in town might recognize him."

The blonde squats and extends her hand to Spud. "That's very sweet of you. Unfortunately, there are a lot of strays in these parts."

"You're from around here?" I glance between them.

"Ohhh, yeah. Born and raised. I'm Christy." The brunette points to herself before hitching a thumb at her friend. "This is Nina."

The blonde gives Spud a final pat before straightening to wiggle her fingers at me. "Hey."

"Nice to meet you. I'm Bianca and that's Colton." My head tips at where he's typing on his phone, undoubtedly updating Brody on my latest shenanigans.

Christy cups a palm around her mouth and whispers, "He's hot."

I give him a slow once-over and pretend heat doesn't pool in my belly. "Meh."

"Aren't you together?" Nina's voice is low to avoid detection.

"Not like that."

The women exchange a glance. Christy's stare shifts to feast on my grumpy jailer. An undeniable interest sparks from her and I bristle. It's such a strange reaction, catching me off guard.

I've never paid attention to how women respond to him… until now. Seeing these two drool over him and his bad boy vibes doesn't sit well. There's an uncomfortable tightening in my chest that feels all kinds of wrong. Spud bumps into my leg, knocking me from the misplaced jealous streak.

But then Nina smacks her lips. "You won't care if I buy him a drink?"

"He's off-limits," I blurt.

Christy's brow creases. "I thought he wasn't your boyfriend?"

"He's my something," I mumble. But I have no actual claim on him. "You know what? Go for it."

Nina eyes me curiously. "Are you sure?"

"Yep."

Maybe I can slip away and go… somewhere. Just for a slice of freedom. If nothing else, I'll get to see how he reacts to female admirers.

Christy smiles and moves closer to Colton. "Should we go inside?"

He looks at me. "What about Spud?"

"It's not a problem. C'mon." Nina motions us forward into Dirty Dicks.

But the instant we walk through the door, a burly man behind the bar is glaring at us. "No dogs."

My gaze barely has time to appreciate the outdated interior. The faded red carpet matches the brass fixtures and wood paneling. As I pull in a lungful of musty air, I realize everyone is looking at us. I have the urge to wave and applaud their cock-tastic name choice, but I doubt that would be well received.

Colton is deathly still next to me. Based on the tension in his stance, I'd guess he's seconds away from snapping. The man might be capable of eliminating threats, but we're the odd fucks out in this room.

My fingers touch his forearm. "Be nice."

"Not my style." The crack of his knuckles ripples across the small space like a warning bell.

"You're nice to me."

"That's not a comparison. How I treat you doesn't extend to others."

"Then be nice for me," I urge.

His blue gaze crashes into my green one. The rigid flex in his tattooed muscles slowly relaxes. I give his arm a gentle squeeze before releasing him. Next, a wide smile gets aimed at the bartender.

"We're just looking for this handsome fella's owner," I tell him.

The man's menacing stare lowers to Spud, but instantly dismisses him. "Shelter is thirty miles east. They'll take him."

I try again. "Nobody in town is looking for a lost dog?"

"Listen, lady. Strays are a dime a dozen. Don't waste your breath."

My mouth opens to argue, but Colton is on the verge of morphing into the Terminator again. Just as I'm about to tuck tail and forfeit the mission, Christy pipes up.

"Chill out, Bill. Just let folks take a peek at him."

A meaty finger stabs in Spud's direction. "He doesn't belong in here."

"It'll only be a few minutes, m'kay?" Nina flutters her lashes in a very familiar way.

"Fine. Whatever. Better remember my leniency when the next bake sale arrives."

Christy winks at him. "There will be an extra cinnamon apple with your name on it."

Bill sighs, tossing his hands in the air. I accept the invitation to enter and walk toward an empty table. Colton is stuck to my side until Christy moves in front of him. Nina follows her friend's lead and together they block his path. The two begin pawing at him like he's fair game. Regret is quick to thump my forehead. That odd sensation returns, churning my stomach until I'm queasy.

My stride is stuck in mud as I stomp over the remaining distance. There are a dozen or more people in Dirty Dicks, but none of them approach me. I should probably take the hint. Stubborn pride has me sitting down and soaking in the awkward atmosphere.

When I turn to check the women's progress, Colton's gaze is burning into me. He's not acknowledging their attempts to flatter him. It's as if we're the only ones in the room. That's extremely attractive and sucks me in.

His baseball hat is flipped backward, allowing the hunger to roam in plain sight. I shiver as the fire in his stare blazes hotter. But then his intense focus shifts over my shoulder and narrows into a glare. The change in his demeanor confuses me until the stench of boozy breath and too much cologne offends my nostrils.

"Well, hey there. Haven't seen you 'round here before." The masculine drawl demands my full concentration.

I keep my gaze straight ahead. "Not interested."

"But—"

"Do you recognize this dog?" I ask him without looking over.

"No."

"Then we have nothing to discuss."

The guy scoffs. "Should've known you'd be a prissy—"

"I fucking dare you to finish that sentence." Colton's tone is a sharpened blade ripped free from its sheath.

Smooth Talker eyes his competition before he wisely slinks off. Nina and Christy aren't throwing in the towel yet. They flank Colton in a cage of desperation. The blonde rubs her big boobs on his left side while the brunette suctions herself to his right. Spud reads the mood and leaps to his paws, ready to rescue Daddy from their clutches. But that's not necessary.

Without taking his eyes off me, Colton lifts his arms to swiftly dislodge them. Damn, that makes him even sexier. I grin when flutters swarm in my stomach.

"Sorry, girls." My tone is far from apologetic as I slide off the chair. "I changed my mind."

"Don't blame you," Nina purrs.

Meanwhile, Christy is pouting. "Will you share?"

"No," Colton barks.

The two shrug and wander away to try their luck elsewhere. Smooth Talker might do the trick. Unless that field has already been plowed. Either way, they don't seem too bent out of shape. Maybe Paisley and I can get into trouble with them soon.

For now, Colton dips his head until his exhale warms my ear. "Changed your mind about what, Princess?"

"Letting them have a go at you."

He pulls just far enough away to search my eyes. "And why's that?"

My fingers walk up the buttons of his Western shirt. "I want you for myself, Stalker."

"Only after they made you jealous."

"That was the last straw. I might've tried to prove a point, but it backfired." And that's putting it mildly.

When I step into him, his Adam's apple bobs with an audible gulp. "What does that mean for us?"

Our gazes lock and hold. Green swirls into blue while I balance on the steep cliff. This moment is weighted in heavy contemplation. I can feel the commitment bearing down on me. Once I agree, Colton will be even more relentless. That doesn't stop me from stretching my arms to loop around his neck.

Spud plops down on the floor beside our table, guarding our intimate bubble from invasion. It serves to remind me of the ties already stitching us together. We're an unbreakable bond. I just have to accept it and then…

That unknown gives me pause, but not from doubt. I've never let myself be vulnerable. Especially not after my mom died. It's scary and intimidating and exciting. Maybe I'll get everything I haven't dared to strive for. Only one way to find out.

Harsh breaths paint my mouth as I tug until our faces are inches apart. Colton trembles with restraint, waiting for me to give him a chance. I drift my nose along the slope of his. A slow inhale fills me with his addictive scent and reckless abandon. He bites his bottom lip, dragging the flesh between his teeth. I watch the seductive motion as if mesmerized.

Thunder drums in my ears when I whisper, "I'll consider it."

"Bianca," Colton groans. "Please."

"Ah, fuck it." And then I swoop in for our first kiss.

CHAPTER EIGHTEEN

Cotton

SHOCK AND RELIEF SLAM INTO ME SIMULTANEOUSLY the instant Bianca's mouth meets mine. I'm stunned into a brief stupor. My mind splits in a hundred directions before realizing this is actually happening.

After that, instinct floods in and I cinch an arm around her waist. A whimper breezes from her and she wiggles closer. My other hand lifts to cradle her jaw, fingers spreading to touch more of her. So damn soft.

I part my lips over hers on a rumbled inhale. She doesn't hesitate to sweep her tongue out to glide along mine. Satisfaction and unbridled lust saturate my tastebuds as a reward for my patience. It's intoxicating.

Molten desire pumps into my veins, making me feverish and frantic. I'm already hard for her. Pressure throbs into my dick, demanding release. Bianca mewls while bucking her hips forward. My palm kneads her ass and pulls to eliminate any remaining space. We're pressed flush without a breath between us.

I sip on her exhale while she swallows my desperation for more. A shudder rolls through me when she nibbles on my lip. That spurs me to suck on her tongue, flicking the tip like I plan to do to her clit. The throaty noises she releases encourage me to repeat the motions. In response, her nails drag along my scalp and grasp onto the short strands. I tremble from the electric sensation, which has her smiling against my mouth.

Her happiness nurtures mine. The constant chill in my bones begins to thaw just having her in my hold. It might look like just a kiss, but this is where our forever starts. I'm more than ready to make her dreams come true. All I can beg for in return is that she makes an honest man outta me.

My gentle grip on her face allows me to control our pace. She sags into me and opens wider. Heat engulfs me as I bask in her surrender. Fucking finally.

Except she only agreed to consider it. That won't do. I cling to her harder as if she'll disappear or change her mind. To prove the opposite, Bianca moans and grinds against my cock shamelessly.

But then a shrill whistle rips into our frenzy. "Hit it and don't quit it, girl."

Our surroundings return in a flash. The fire in my veins sizzles like I stepped into a cold shower. Bianca notices I've gone rigid and not just in my dick. Her lips slide from mine in a farewell that hurts on a soul-crushing level. I'd rather lie on a bed of nails than quit touching her, but we're making a scene. The silence in this bar is deafening.

She peeks up at me from under lowed lashes. "Was that too fast?"

I bark out a laugh and she blanches. "It was perfect, Princess. Just like you. But I'm not gonna maul you in a place called Dirty Dicks."

"Seems more than appropriate."

"Nobody gets to see your pleasure but me."

We have an audience, but I don't see them. Bianca fills my vision with her swollen lips and flushed skin. I drag my thumb along the curve of her mouth, traveling up to caress the red stain. When she nuzzles into me, I almost dive right back in.

But then I notice several men leering at what's mine. Awareness crawls up my neck in violent flames.

Bianca gasps. "You're blushing again."

"I forgot where we are."

Her lids droop to hood her eyes. "That good, huh?"

"Better." I kiss the tip of her nose.

Another loud moan slips from her sinful lips. "Just take my panties off already."

The fire burns hotter in my face and I dip down, pressing our foreheads together. "Gonna get me arrested, baby girl."

There's an unmistakable sparkle in her fern-colored eyes as she gazes at me. "Can't have that."

"No, I've got plans for you."

Color rises in her cheeks to match mine.

In a swift maneuver that feels practiced, I thread our fingers together and latch on tight. Spud is quick to abandon his sprawled-out position on the floor. Our dog reads our body language as if we've been a cohesive unit for years rather than hours. His protective stance aims for the exit, ready to guide us out for a hasty retreat. My free hand grabs his leash from Bianca, which gives her the freedom to give our audience a parting wave.

"Thanks for your help. There's nothing quite like a supportive community." She blows a kiss to the grabby women from earlier.

The blonde one lifts her beer. "Stick around for a drink."

"We won't bite." The brunette pats the empty stool beside her. "Not until he asks nicely."

Bianca bristles and scoots in front of me. "Maybe next time."

I duck to hide a grin, stamping a kiss onto her crown. Lilac perfumes her silky hair. A deep inhale calms me and I squeeze her palm in mine. "C'mon, we're going home."

Her sigh is dramatic, which pairs well with her flouncy stride. "He's gonna shag me rotten. Don't wait up."

A chorus of mixed messages from the patrons follow us to the curb. Two want us to stay, but the rest are a colorful variety of good riddance. Can't say I blame them. We tossed a wrench in their predictable afternoon.

I shake my head while boosting Bianca into the truck. Spud has springs on his paws, hopping in without trying. She holds her arms up while he gets comfortable, resting his head on her lap. That leaves his butt pointing at the driver's side—most definitely on purpose. Those two are already thick as thieves.

The brazen instigator is all smiles as I round the hood and get settled behind the wheel. Her joy is infectious, rushing my movements to get gone. Fern roars to life to announce our departure and I swear there's a collective exhale from Dirty Dicks.

As I'm pulling onto the road, I glance over at my princess. "Satisfied?"

"Not yet, but I'm gonna be"—she glances at my phone docked on the dash—"in seventeen minutes."

"No pressure, huh?" My foot instinctively stomps on the gas. I don't need the map to know where we're going, but it's an ingrained habit to avoid surprises.

"Based on what I've seen, you have no problems satisfying a woman." Her gaze roves over me like I'm about to be her favorite meal.

My cock throbs, already halfway hard and fully uncomfortable. "Only care about pleasing you."

"Which makes it even more likely." She takes a break from petting Spud to rub along my arm.

Desire floods into my veins in a rush that makes me dizzy. The pavement ahead seems to stretch on indefinitely. At this rate, I'll never survive the short journey. "Just for the record, I was talking about our dog."

"Our dog," Bianca echoes. "See? It sounds natural."

And it does. I didn't even realize I'd already referred to him as ours earlier.

"Does that mean you're done chasing a dead end?"

She nods, resuming the languid strokes to Spud's belly. "He's stuck with us."

My heart beats wildly. That sounds an awful lot like a commitment from her. I glance over to catch a serene grin lifting her lips.

"You're happy, Princess?"

The sigh she expels confirms as much. "Mhmm, Stalker. I'm about to get dicked really hard."

A dry chuckle loosens the pressure in my chest. "That dirty mouth of yours is something else."

"If you're a good boy, I'll let you fuck it."

I clench my eyes shut, just for a brief moment. It doesn't pause the erotic onslaught of her lowering to her knees in front of me. "Dammit, Bianca."

She giggles and bites her nail. "Is it something I said?"

"Are you actually giving me a chance or is this just about sex?"

"Both?" When I scowl, she whines and thumps her head against the seat. "Excuse me for being horny. I'm in a constant state of arousal just thinking about you splitting me in half with that monster in your pants. The anticipation is edging me to the brink. I'm tempted to climb onto your lap right now and scratch the itch." She pauses for a breath, inhaling deep. "But you're worthy of much more than a quick fuck. All those considerate gestures? Porn for my heart. You've managed to turn me on emotionally. I didn't even know that was a thing until you waltzed in and romanced me. The thought you put into every detail is very attractive. Am I making sense?"

An unfamiliar sense of calm settles over me. Is this peace? Whatever it is comprehends her meaning and fills me with comfort. I think she's going to choose me. Willingly.

Fuck, now my pulse is galloping in the opposite direction of tranquility.

Bianca clears her throat. "So, yeahhhh. I'm not planning to use you for your pierced penis."

Sweat slicks my palms and I can't get a grip on the wheel. "What are you planning?"

"I'm considering what our future might hold." Her body turns to face me. "I'll agree to date you on a trial period."

Which is more than I deserve, but less than the end goal. We'll get there. It's a big step for her.

"You've never dated anyone before. At least not seriously," I rasp.

"Ohhhhh, look who wants to rehash the past. Are we trading secrets?"

"Eventually," I mutter.

Her head bobs. "That's first date material. Gonna take me to dinner at Dirty Dicks?"

"We can do better than that." My mind whirls with possibilities as the road stretches on. "Does this mean you forgive me?"

She snorts. "For what?"

As if I'm going to list off my crimes against her. "The wrong things."

"Mostly. I'm still pissed you stole my phone."

"Brody told—"

In a freakishly fast motion, Bianca reaches over to smush a finger against my lips. "We've already been over this. Remember when I called you a twat waffle and swore to never speak to you again? Pretty sure you don't need a repeat, but I'll say it again. I don't care that my brother told you to do it. You're allowed to say no. There's always a choice. Put me first."

My gulp is thick with guilt. "I do."

The flint in her stare calls me a liar. "What if he asks you to do something like that again?"

This is a hard limit for her. It's not negotiable. If I want her to choose me, I need to do the same.

"I won't do it."

She studies me closely. "Even if it costs you the job?"

"I can always get another one of those. There's only one of you."

Her posture relaxes. "Really good answer."

"Even if Brody hates me for defying him, I won't betray you again. Unless your safety is at risk. You have my word, Princess."

Bianca's brother might've saved my life, but that life isn't worth living if she's not at my side.

"And you have my permission to protect me by any means necessary. I might even let you tie me up." She winks.

"Fuck," I grunt and push Fern for more speed.

Her fingers trace the tribal patterns on my forearm. "Don't worry about Brody. He hates everyone. If you're doing right by me, he won't exile you. That's why he hired you in the first place. Besides, we're on the run and don't need to seek shelter at the farmstead manor."

Before I can reply, an alert appears on my phone. There's movement detected at the driveway entrance. Perfect timing. Our house is just around this bend.

"Do you see that, Spud?" Bianca's voice is sweeter than her lilac perfume. "Daddy is grinning like the stars just aligned. I wonder what's waiting for us at home."

CHAPTER NINETEEN

MY JAW DROPS WHEN TWO MEN HAUL THE BIGGEST mattress I've ever seen out of the back of a moving truck. "What did you do, Colton?"

"Got you a new bed."

I gawk at the scene unfolding through the windshield. Suspicion was raised the instant we pulled up to the house a few moments ago. To see an unmarked vehicle idling in the driveway was a shock. The fact Colton didn't seem bothered in the least was a bigger one. Our safety is supposedly at risk and he's inviting randos to drop by? Well, I might've overreacted.

"But I already have a bed." And it looked brand-spankin'-new until I defiled it last night.

He kills the ignition and slips the keys into his pocket. "That one hurt your back."

"Most do. That's just the way it is." There's a crick in my left hip as we speak.

He just shakes his head. "I'll keep tossin' 'em out until we find one that doesn't. This brand is rated as the best on the market for scoliosis."

"Okay, that's super thoughtful. Cue the heart flutters and romantic orgasm, Stalker. But for the record, I'm not that much of a princess." As I sit and watch him hop out to come get me.

His long strides eat the ground, delivering him to open my door in three seconds. Colton unbuckles my belt, hoists me into his arms, and sets me on my booted feet. "You are, baby girl. That's one reason I love you."

The way he casually slips that into our conversation bobbles me. I swoon a bit, slumping against him. His blue stare smolders into mine. This man makes it easy to fall, knowing he's right there to catch me.

But I'm not there yet. Not even close. I straighten and brush imaginary dirt off my jeans. The moving men are carrying the wrapped mattress toward the porch. That gets Spud's attention.

Our dog leaps from Fern in a wide arch, landing in front of us to create a defensive wall against the intruders. Hair stands up straight on his back when he bristles. A low growl warns the guys to stop or he'll pounce.

"At ease," Colton croons.

I gawk when Spud's butt meets the gravel. "The fuck?"

He shrugs. "Figured he might respond to the command. Might try it on you later."

"Good luck with that," I scoff. But the submissive part of me is already preening.

"Don't talk back." His palm lightly connects with my ass.

"Hey!" But I wiggle for another.

"Boss?" That comes from the taller of the two currently balancing what I imagine to be a very heavy load.

My brows lift at his voiced concern. "Boss?"

"Don't recognize them from the trailer sales lot? Best of my overnight crew right there." He jogs over to them, keying in the code for the lock pad.

I shuffle after him at a slow drag. Colton is teasing me, but the urge to thump my own forehead is strong. With all that's going on, it's easy to forget he's the head of security for our family empire. Not to mention his permanent post within Benson Farmstead, which allows him to be glued to my side at all times. He's obviously in charge of many men to keep us all safe.

"Take it to our room." He instructs as I park myself beside him. "Up the stairs. Second door on the right."

"Got it, boss." They move swiftly to follow his order.

Meanwhile, I cross my arms and stay put. "*Our* room? I agreed to date you, not become a domesticated couple."

"You've also been very vocal about wanting sex, which means we're sharing a bed." The man makes it tough to argue with him.

Which is why I stand quietly as the security guys heave the discarded mattress to the truck. After rolling the door down, the swap is complete. It didn't take them longer than five minutes.

The one who spoke earlier trots back over to us. "Want us to put on the sheets and shit?"

"Like I'd let you touch my woman's bedding. Get lost." But Colton's tone isn't harsh, especially paired with him discreetly handing the guy a wad of cash.

The man dips his head before returning to his partner. They'll probably make it back to Cloverleaf Meadows just in time to start their shift chasing off danger. Busy day for all of us.

Colton watches them leave, offering a parting wave as they disappear from view. The heat of his unwavering stare returns to me. "And now, we get to break in the new one."

"Ohhhh," I sway into him. "I love the sound of that."

"Hang on." That's all the warning I get before he slings me over his shoulder.

Spud yips and races to the stairs. Colton follows, kicking the front door shut while bringing me along for the ride. I hang upside down like a sack of potatoes about to be devoured for dinner. The view of his ass from this angle is worth the head rush. Every step he climbs raises his muscular backside for my viewing pleasure.

Our dog disappears somewhere when we reach the second floor. He's probably claiming a hiding spot as his while Daddy does naughty things to Mommy. It's best Spud isn't around to see it.

As if I'm the most precious cargo, Colton gently lowers me over the threshold of our room. I stand while he moves to a pile of folded laundry on the dresser. It looks like the sheets and shit the guy mentioned. Colton clearly planned this, which injects me with another burst of affection.

With a purposeful swipe, he snatches the item on top. The fabric crinkles as he begins to stretch it across the foot of the mattress. That's my cue to quit being a worthless lump.

My fingers pause after gripping the unexpected texture.

It feels like the protective layer parents put down while their toddler is potty training. "What's this for?"

He smirks while securing the last corner. "You'll see."

The man is a mystery, but I don't question him further. We make the rest of the bed in a seamless process. It's as if we've done this countless times together on autopilot. When we're done, it's cozy and very inviting. The green comforter resembles a meadow. I'm tempted to collapse in the center like a starfish.

But then Colton is hugging me from behind. His tattooed arms hold my body tight against his. He's already hard, the long length of him pressing into my ass. A tame but purposeful nudge grinds him into me. I sag against him, a very willing victim in this moment.

His fingers pull the elastic band free from the end of my braid, loosening the plaited sections. As the long length cascades down my back, he combs through it with the utmost care. This tough guy is extremely careful with me. Prickles scroll across my scalp and I tremble against him. Colton groans low in his throat as if this simple gesture brings him great pleasure. It makes me feel cherished in return.

With that task complete, one hand roams under the hem of my shirt. A tremble rolls through me from the sensual contact. His palm is warm and large as he flattens it over my stomach.

"You're mine?"

"For now," I evade.

"Bianca," he rumbles into the crook of my neck.

I tilt my head to give him better access. "As if you'll ever let me escape."

His lips drift along my skin in a tender caress. "Never."

And I don't want him to. That's why I lift my arms as he drags the shirt up and over my head. His deft fingers glide under the band of my sports bra, tugging to free my breasts from the confines. The air is cool on my nipples and they harden into stiff peaks. After tossing the restrictive material away, Colton doesn't hesitate to cup my boobs in both hands. I spill over his palms and he groans at the sight. My chin tips to watch his face as he touches me. He ditched his hat at some point, giving me an unobstructed view. His eyes are latched onto my chest like I've hypnotized him. This is a man possessed. That knowledge sends a jolt straight to my clit and I squeeze my legs together. The motion jiggles my breasts in his grip.

Colton grunts and thumbs my nipples. "Fuck, you're perfect."

My blood heats into reckless desire. "I do have a nice rack."

"Can't wait to clamp these between my teeth."

"Yes," I whimper and thrust my chest into his grasp.

"But not yet."

"Why?" My tone is pitiful.

"Are you sensitive?" He flicks the needy tips again, which buckles my knees. There's a smile in his voice when he says, "Mhmm, very responsive."

Unmistakable warmth from down below floods my basement. I mewl at the wet sensation and clench my thighs again. "Please, Stalker."

A gruff noise rattles from him. "Look at you at my mercy. You beg very well, Princess."

"Mhmm, I'll be really good. Just take me. Please." My ass grinds into his cock. "I need you."

"How much?"

I scramble to undo my belt and show him, but he swats my hands away. "Hey! Don't stop—"

"But that's my job." His fingers replace mine, unlatching the buckle from the leather.

I squirm when he pops open the button and lowers the zipper. My jeans are snug, but the denim is no match for his insistence. He hooks the waistband of my thong with his thumbs, pulling it down along with my pants. The combination of fabric and any lingering doubt puddles at my feet.

Colton's palms travel over my freshly exposed skin, starting at my calves and coasting slowly to my ass. A low groan of approval praises me as he fists a handful of flesh. He gives my butt a light tap before stepping back to appreciate the whole view.

The fiery lust in his gaze spikes my own. A shiver skates through me from tit to toe. That slight ripple morphs into a limb-racking tremble when he rips the tucked duvet off the bed. I don't protest when he steers my movements, allowing him to spin and maneuver me to his liking. My back meets the mattress while my legs hang over the edge.

Colton follows me down, hovering over me to crash our lips together. I gasp into his mouth. His tongue lashes out to stroke mine, setting the pace and feeding the flames of my arousal. The kiss is hungry, filling me with an urgency to get him naked.

My fingers yank at his shirt and several snaps open from the force. Another pull undoes the rest. I part the material to reach the cotton layer underneath. While my lips feast on his, my hands blindly wander to reveal his abs. Colton swallows my sigh when I finally touch his bare skin and begin exploring. Toned muscles stacked on relentless determination greet me. This man is built to protect. That cranks my hunger to a new level and I need more. My nails skip along his sides, dancing over the grooves of his ribcage.

But then he jerks away from me like I stabbed him. "Fuck."

I startle at his harsh outburst until understanding cracks through the lust clouding my mind. A bratty grin taunts his scowl. "Are you ticklish, Stalker?"

A visible blush tints his cheeks.

"Stop it." I fling an arm over my eyes. "You're bashful and ticklish and I'm doomed."

"Wasn't either of those until you made me weak." His grumbly tone only adds to the undeniable appeal. There's no refusing him at this point, which has me uncovering my makeshift mask.

I lift a palm to cradle his stubbled jaw. "You're such a good boy."

His eyes burn. "Am not."

A burst of heat blasts through me, thrumming my clit. "Show me how bad you are."

With renewed purpose, Colton shrugs off his Western shirt before yanking the white tee over his head. I don't see where the clothes land. My concentration is consumed with sculpted abs and dark ink. This is the first time I'm seeing him shirtless. Had I gotten this view sooner, I might've folded faster than the laundry pile on the dresser. Saliva pools in my mouth as I picture running my tongue along every chiseled inch.

Colton's dark chuckle curls my toes, calling me out for staring. Before I can contemplate a retort, he swoops down and latches onto my nipple. The pressure arches my spine and feeds him more of me. His palm cups my other boob, the hardened point pinched between his fingers. My pussy clamps on empty space in a silent demand to be filled.

I spear my fingers into his short hair and tug lightly. It doesn't help anchor me.

There's a demand brewing inside, desperate to escape. A mewl dribbles from my parted lips as if that will push him faster. Colton relents, but only to switch sides. The hand not fondling my breast trails down my stomach and slips between my legs.

His hum of approval vibrates through my chest. "Soaked for me."

He slides a finger inside me and pumps slowly. The tempo is a tease more than anything.

I'm practically vibrating with need. My hips rock to match the maddening rhythm.

"My greedy girl." He smirks around my nipple. "Want more?"

I'm nodding against the pillow, ready to use my grip on his hair as leverage. On the next stroke, he adds a second digit and it's a snug fit. My muscles spasm at the invasion, regardless of the arousal easing his entry. A slow exhale relaxes me while he pushes deeper. I know his hands are at least double the size of mine, but I'm not a freaking virgin. Yet a twinge zaps me as I stretch to accommodate him. That slight sting only heightens the pleasure and a moan spills from me.

"Too tight," he grunts. "Gonna need to make room before you can take my cock."

My head thrashes. "It's fine. Don't make me wait."

Colton grinds his dick into me as a reminder of how big he is. "Nah, baby girl. We'll work up to it."

And then he's lowering himself onto the floor, draping my spread thighs over his shoulders. The position aligns his face with my pussy. I widen my eyes on the ceiling and fight the urge to squirm. It's impossible to stay silent.

"Umm…"

"Problem?" His hot exhale blazes across my slick flesh.

"Nobody has ever… uh, gone down there. On me, or whatever," I mumble as fire stings my cheeks. Overconfidence might be my cloak of armor, but this is uncharted territory.

"And nobody else ever will. You're." He licks the full length of my center. "All." His tongue swirls around my clit before he sucks it between his lips. "Mine." Those two talented fingers sink inside me again.

I'm already mindless against the foreign stimulation. It's a sensual onslaught. The toys I've used didn't prepare me for this. Not even close.

"Holy shit," I breathe.

Colton groans against my sex like a man feasting on his favorite meal. A glance at him confirms it. His features are slack as he gorges himself on me. My face heats again. He looks to be thoroughly enjoying himself, and he's very good at it.

My eyes roll back when he does something with his tongue and teeth. Static crackles in my veins while I buck into his mouth. It feels so freaking amazing. I had no idea what I've been missing. The few guys I've been with didn't even offer to go down on me. This man can't seem to get enough, proving he far exceeds the norm. And damn, I'm here for it.

A strangled noise escapes me as Colton increases the tempo. My clit throbs while my inner muscles clamp onto his thrusting digits. The pressure begins to pulse faster, pushing me to the peak. Tingles immediately follow. He must be able to tell, curling his fingers at a very specific angle to hit a spot I've never reached.

"Oh, oh!" I slap the sheets, gripping fistfuls in a white-knuckle grip. "Yes, there. I'm gonna—"

His lips latch onto my clit just right to shove me over the edge. The force of the orgasm shocks me. I'm suspended in a bubble of pleasure where nothing else exists except the warmth flooding me. My muscles quake as I ride his face, feeding him every drop. I'm dizzy and overwhelmed and never felt better.

Colton slows his motions while I float back to reality. He reads my body like he wrote the how-to guidebook. A languid comfort clutches me in a tight embrace. I sigh and surrender to him completely. At least for now. What he just did deserves compliance and a standing ovation.

"That was incredible," I murmur. My vision is hazy as I peek down at him.

He lifts the fingers that are wet from me to his mouth. A guttural sound expands his chest while he sucks them clean. "You taste like heaven."

I smile into the afterglow. "And what does heaven taste like?"

"Every wish coming true." The relief in his voice melts me.

And cue the flutters. I just climaxed like crazy, but this man isn't done worshipping me. He's determined to touch my soul and brand me as his. It's only then I realize Colton hasn't moved. My elbow wobbles as I prop myself upright to see him more clearly. He's staring at my vagina with shameless admiration.

"Do you like doing that?"

His eyes burn into mine. "Only to you."

I shiver at the underlying claim in his tone. "It felt really good."

"Glad I can please you." His nose drifts along my mound, inhaling me along the way. Satisfaction rumbles from him. "Been waitin' a long damn time, Princess."

My hips flex when his fingers spread my pussy lips wide open. "Wh-what are you doing?"

"Just getting started."

And then his mouth returns to my sex. I'm much more sensitive now, quickly rekindling the flames. It's too much. When I try to pull away, he bands an arm around my waist.

"I can't—" But the fierce pride in his gaze silences my protest.

It doesn't take longer than three seconds for him to be proven right. Arousal crashes over me like a torrential wave meant to pull me under. I gasp when the pressure returns stronger than before. That encourages Colton to spear me with his tongue before sizzling a path back to my clit. Those two fingers aren't done with me either. The digits push inside and then—

"Fu-uuuuuck," I cry out.

He hooks them harder into the secret place that has me seeing stars. Friction builds as he rubs me there at a frantic pace. Meanwhile, his tongue swipes at my clit relentlessly. Trembles start to rack my limbs, but soon I'm twitching everywhere. My entire body is a bundle of hypersensitive nerves ready to explode.

As I'm cresting the peak, Colton flattens a palm on my lower belly. He pushes down slightly and I go very still. An odd sensation pools underneath his hand. It's like an inflated balloon is in there and I need to get the air out. But if I do, I'm going to pee. My muscles seize. No, that can't be right.

I clench against the instinct to release the strain, not entirely comfortable with the prospective results. Colton doubles his efforts. The assault on my clit and that inner trigger force me to accept his agenda. Whatever is happening is beyond my control.

He's demanding me to submit. My pussy is desperate to obey. With a thick exhale, I let go of the resistance.

The climax bursts from me in a gush. It's too wet, but I'm unable to grasp that concept. Pleasure rips me into shreds until I'm shaking uncontrollably. My dignity isn't a match for his dedication to split me apart. It's messy and shocking, but blows my orgasmic expectations into nonexistent pieces. There's no comparison.

This intoxicating high is alluring and I allow oblivion to carry me away. I'm lost for who knows how long. Time doesn't belong in this space. Only pure, nonjudgmental bliss is invited. But eventually, a dampness under my ass drags me to the surface.

"How do you feel?" Colton's voice is distant and gentle.

"Hmmm." I wiggle to test my recovery.

That's when I recall the fabric beneath me is moist. Awareness slowly seeps in and I fling upright. The sheet is soaked.

He notices the ick cringing my features. "What's wrong?"

"Umm, there's a freaking puddle on the bed."

That smug gleam reignites in his eyes. "You're welcome."

"That"—I stab a finger at the evidence—"isn't supposed to happen while you're down there."

He scoffs. "It was very much on purpose. You squirted, baby girl."

"That's not all cum."

"It most certainly is."

"There's so much of it." A mixture of awe and horror tinge my voice.

"You were pent-up, but that won't be a problem ever again. I have an insatiable appetite and plan to eat you for every meal."

My thighs clench at his generous offer, but I'm still not over the amount of fluid I released. "How…?"

"That's for me to know. You just get to lie back and let it happen."

"It was pretty incredible," I admit wistfully.

"Want another?" He appears committed to getting me off until I'm senseless.

Which isn't happening unless he's losing it alongside me. "I'm ready for the sex."

Colton stands, but makes no move to strip off his jeans. "I want our date first."

CHAPTER TWENTY

BIANCA LOOKS READY TO THROTTLE ME. "THAT'S NOT funny, Stalker."

"Good thing I didn't tell a joke."

"We're not having this conversation again," she snaps.

"Fine by me. Are you hungry? I can grill some steaks for dinner."

"The only meat I want is yours. It's time to deliver, big boy." She makes a grabby-hands gesture at my groin.

"I'm not on the menu."

"Then I shouldn't have been either. What the fuck, Colt?"

My lips quirk. "Haven't called me that in ages."

"Don't act cute." Her finger wags at me. "You owe me a solid dicking."

"Or what?"

Bianca's nostrils flare as if fire is spewing out. "This

could be considered a betrayal. Awful soon to be going back on your word."

Laughter brews in my gut. Damn, I love when she gets riled up. This feisty version is almost as enticing as her submissive side. Eh, who am I kidding? I'm obsessed with every variation of this woman.

Which is why I still don't budge. It might piss her off, but I'm not backing down.

Unfortunately for me and my resistance, her naked body is still on full display. My gaze roams freely while I fight the instinct to claim her as mine. She's still not ready. That doesn't stop me from appreciating our progress.

There's a flush covering her chest, looping up her slender throat like a collar. The urge to place my hand there and feel her pulse leap beneath my touch inches me forward. Bianca forces out a harsh exhale, which lowers my gaze. Her tits tremble from her labored breathing. Mine races to match as I force my feet to remain planted on the floor.

My cock throbs painfully. I'll need to relieve the pressure soon or I won't be able to focus on fulfilling her needs. As if listening to my meal plan, Bianca scoots higher on the bed. That subtle shift draws my attention between her splayed legs. The delicate skin on her inner thighs is slightly chafed from my stubble. Fuck, she wears a brand from me. That plunges irrational satisfaction into my veins and fills me with the demand to take her.

The temptation is strong, especially with the taste of her pussy on my lips. I'm already craving another dose of her tangy honey. It's maddening. I snap the two hair ties on my wrist, but it only fans the flames. The sting is similar to when I lightly spank her ass.

Whatever expression Bianca catches on my face has her grinning like a pampered princess about to get her way. I'm weak and she can see straight through the cracks. She props herself against the headboard, crooking a finger at me to come-hither.

"Take off your pants, Stalker." The seductress motions to my belt buckle. "Or I'll do it for you."

I shake my head, not trusting my voice or my fraying control.

Her confidence wavers and she tucks herself into a defensive position. "Why don't you want to have sex? I thought that's why we came up here. Now you're giving me a complex."

The fact that she's hiding herself from me is a punch to the gut, but I won't be swayed. "I want to make love. You're not ready for that."

Bianca flinches and curls her body into a tighter ball. "Gosh, I feel like a sleazy asshole."

Every muscle in my body screams to shield her from the hurt I'm causing. "Furthest thing from it. You're everything to me, Princess. That's why I'm holding off on surrendering completely. I'm fucked either way, but I'd prefer if we're screwed together."

Her smile is almost shy. "That makes your kinky ultimatum sound very explicit."

"Am I worth the wait?" The vulnerable edge in my tone is reserved solely for her.

"Obviously." Bianca sighs, resting her chin on her bent knee. "Are you gonna put out after our first date?"

"If you're at least halfway in love with me."

Her eyes narrow as if she's about to argue. But then

the tension bleeds from her features. "Okay, fine. I'll stop pressuring you to have sexual intercourse."

That choice of phrasing alerts my sixth sense. I know better than to accept an easy surrender from her. "What's the catch?"

"You let me return the favor. Tit for tat and all that." Bianca swings her legs off the bed and stands to face me. "It's betrayal tax."

I get lightheaded at the fantasy alone. "You're offering to give me a blowjob?"

"I like doing it, but only to you," she repeats my words back to me.

Her toned legs stalk toward me like I'm her prey. It's a title I'll gladly boast about. My attention is riveted on the unique shape of her torso. That sharp angle on her right side digs in deeper when she swings her hips. The left juts out like a stubborn streak. I'm lured into a trance by her quirky curves. All. Fucking. Mine. It's a miracle that I stand my ground as she kneels in front of me.

"You've planned so much for me, right down to a plastic sheet to protect our new mattress." Bianca palms the bulge straining against faded denim. "You deserve a reward."

That slight friction hardens my dick into steel. I can already feel precum leaking out. There's no time to waste. My hands tremble as I go to unbuckle my belt.

She taps my fingers. "Nah-uh. That's my job."

And she doesn't hesitate to get to work. My jeans are unzipped and hanging slack around my thighs before I can argue. Not that another protest would dare to sneak past me at this point. I'm frozen, struck motionless by the sight of her tugging down my boxer briefs to gain unrestricted access to my cock. A tremor shoots through my legs and I sway slightly.

Bianca notices, lifting her attention off my jutting arousal. "Would you like to sit?"

I stare—completely dumbfounded—while she grins. Movement of any kind feels impossible. A gulp barely passes through the dryness in my throat. The sharp jerk of my head tests the limits. Bianca Benson on her knees for me is going to make me blow my load in two seconds.

"Suit yourself, Stalker." And then her thumb swipes at the pearl of liquid pooling on my pierced tip.

The contact jolts me like an electric fence. "Oh, fuck."

She trails the precum along my shaft, wrapping her dainty hand around me. "Sensitive?"

"It's been… a long while," I manage to croak.

Bianca tightens her grip and the ladder of barbells dig into me. "Nobody has ever touched you like this before, right?"

The possessiveness in her tone consumes me. "Just you, baby girl."

"That's what I thought." Her green eyes are fixated on my studded length. "Such a work of art."

I grunt while she admires my junk as if it's a statue erected in her honor. "Glad you think so."

Bianca hums, contemplating something heavy. "Do your balls tingle?"

My body goes unnaturally still, not expecting her to come up with that. "The fuck?"

"Like right before you come."

"No," I rasp.

"No?"

"Not that I recall."

"Oh." Her bottom lip pouts out. "That happens to a lot of guys in the romances I read."

"They're not real." Yet I'm still jealous of them.

She looks up at me, her gaze hooded with thick desire. The message in her unwavering stare confirms it's just us. Nothing else matters. My cock jerks in her secure hold. That prods her to stroke me from root to tip.

More precum collects, which she eagerly uses as lube. I'm slick in her fist as she rolls her wrist downward.

A breathy exhale coasts along my throbbing flesh. Bianca's eyes widen when my dick begins to drip faster. When she sticks out her tongue to taste me, my vision swims. Holy fuck. This moment will forever be carved into my brain.

"You're salty, Stalker." A rosy blush paints her cheeks and she bites her bottom lip.

My thumb tugs the tortured flesh from between her teeth. "And you're stunning."

"Just wait until my mouth is stuffed full of your cock."

"Woman," I growl.

The promise of pleasure is already squeezing me in an unforgiving hold. I need a distraction, but refuse to fill my thoughts with images other than her. While she gets intimately acquainted with my cock, I gather her hair into my fist and secure it with the elastic I've had for months. The one I just stole from her is a shiny replacement. But I'm likely to hoard them both for when situations like this arise.

"Very considerate," she croons.

As if I did that strictly for her benefit. I've been itching to bury my hands in her glossy waves. Shit, maybe I shouldn't have tied it up. But then the unobstructed view of her leaning forward to lick me corrects the upset. At least until she sucks lightly and my balls clench.

"Fuuu-ckkk." My voice rises to an embarrassing pitch.

Meanwhile, hers is a sultry purr. "What do you need?"

"Your mouth on me. Please."

"Hmmm, such a good boy."

The praise spanks me and I thrust my hips. Bianca swirls her tongue around the flared crown. Stars explode across my vision, blinding me to everything except letting go. It's too much.

"Gonna come." My eyes clench shut, trying to last longer than three pumps.

"Really?" She sounds positively delighted at the prospect.

I'm already nodding. "Almost did while I was going down on you. Don't stand a chance if you keep at it."

"Will you be able to come again?"

"Instantly," I blurt.

"That's good. I owe you two." Her lips part around my tip, opening wider to fit the metal ring that's hooked through the top.

When she tongues the underside, my mind goes blank. All I feel is her mouth on me and the pressure releasing. Years of unrequited yearning burst out of me. It's relief beyond explanation.

I clutch the back of her head. My fingers spear into her hair, yanking it free from the weak bind I attempted to fasten. A smirk pulls at my lips as I get another wish granted.

The pulsating surge seems endless. A dreamy stupor

lulls me. I might lose consciousness at some point. But then I feel it.

"Oh, fuck. My balls are tingling," I groan.

The corners of Bianca's lips tip upward, but she doesn't stop sucking. I blink through the haze. Am I still coming? It's tough to tell. There's a comforting numbness spreading throughout my entire body.

After what feels like a lifetime of bliss, she exhales and pulls away. "Hmmm, you weren't kidding."

I scoop her off the floor and into my arms, hugging her tight enough to suffocate. "Fuckin' love you."

Bianca clings onto me with the same ferocity. "The blow-job was that good, huh?"

"Better," I tell her.

My stride is wobbly as I carry her to the bed. I get myself sprawled out in the center, still cradling her flush against me. She blinks while gathering her bearings. The stunned expression is too adorable to resist.

A fresh blaze of heat rushes under my skin as our lips collide. I'm already hard again, or maybe my dick never deflated. This woman has me in a constant state of arousal. She realizes it and wiggles to break free. My grip loosens, but only enough for her to straddle my lap. There's a sparkle in her green eyes when she breaks the kiss. But that's not the plan.

Before Bianca can gain the upper hand, I spin her around and position her pussy above my mouth. Her addictive scent floods my nostrils. Arousal strokes me at a punishing pace to confirm it won't take much to get me off again.

She squeaks and bucks her hips when I tongue her clit. "What—?"

Tangy honey slides down my throat like the finest wine. "Gonna ride my face, Princess."

"Oh." And then she seems to notice what's right in front of her. "Well, this is fun."

The instant her lips wrap around my tip, I'm smacked with a grave error in judgment. Bianca's multitasking skills give her an advantage. This is just another opportunity to annihilate the competition. Her hand grabs onto my base, squeezing gently while sliding upward to form a seal with her mouth. All my blood and selfless intentions flood south. But that's not enough for her. She cups my balls in her other palm and massages them like sore muscles.

Meanwhile, I'm barely functioning. Her pussy is spread directly over me for a bottomless feast. That snaps me out of it. I ignore her tongue swirling laps around my cock and use mine on the task astride me. When I hit the spot, she jerks against me. My lips latch onto those sensitive nerves, pulling her in.

Bianca cries out, but the noise is muffled. I'm serenaded by the sweet sound of her gurgles. It spurs me faster. With the arm I have cinched around her hips, I grind her down until I'm buried alive. She's so slick for me. My mouth slides forward and back on a slippery cycle.

From there, we each find our own rhythm. She attempts to choke herself on my length while I fuck her tight cunt with my tongue. When I nudge her clit with my chin, she squirms and smothers me. I'd gladly give my last breath eating out this woman.

A groan rumbles through my chest when she drenches

me to the point of dribbling down my neck. The coarse texture from my stubble must really stimulate her. I rotate my jaw to give her more. Bianca increases the speed of her motions to chase mine. My insatiable appetite gorges on her, but I'm nearing the edge too fast. I drag a finger through her sex and trace an uncharted path to her ass. When I reach her puckered rim, I apply the slightest pressure.

Bianca squeals, turning rigid in my grip. A gush quickly follows when her climax strikes. Her hips snap, swiveling for more friction. I grunt into her pussy as she attempts to drown me. My throat works to swallow every drop.

Her heavenly flavor soaks me in satisfaction.

The intensity of her orgasm triggers my own and I bellow around a mouthful of delicious cunt. That regains Bianca's attention. Even in the throes of passion, she cares for my needs. Her mouth covers my cock just as I start to spurt. The sensation of releasing into her warmth has me jetting harder than a hose. I can't comprehend the stream when she laps me to completion. My balls might actually be empty after this.

Once I'm wrung dry, I collapse into the mattress. Bianca slumps on top of me with a sigh. The glorious view of her wet pussy remains straight ahead. I could get used to this.

As if hearing my thoughts, she pats my thigh with a sloppy palm. "We're very compatible, Stalker."

I press a kiss to her inner thigh. "Almost there, hmm?"

Bianca nods. "Don't think you're off the hook for that anal probing."

My chuckle jostles her. "Add it to the list of secrets to share."

She huffs. "That's not a secret."

"The fact you loved it might be."

"Pretty sure I can't deny that." She rolls off me in a graceful maneuver. Her stomach grumbles loudly in complaint. "Gonna need to feed me more than your semen unless you want me to waste away."

I'm on my feet in the next breath. "What're you in the mood for?"

Bianca's heated gaze tracks me while I tug on my boxers. "I believe you mentioned grilling me a steak."

CHAPTER TWENTY-ONE

Bianca

I WAKE WITH A SMILE THAT HAS LITTLE TO WITH THE sated thrum between my thighs. There's a scruffy cheek nuzzling into the curve of my neck from behind. Contentment is a lazy sigh as I snuggle against the wall of muscle. Colton's lips curve upward into my skin, revealing his own happiness.

"Mornin', baby girl." His coarse rasp tells me that he hasn't been awake for long.

"Mhmm," I murmur and press my ass into the hard ridge prodding at me. "Off to a very solid start."

We're naked in this snug embrace. It wouldn't take much more than a tilt of his pelvis to slip that pierced tip inside me. But Colton doesn't abandon his objective. The man's willpower deserves a gold medal.

My body relaxes against his. I promised not to pressure him and I have every intention of sticking to that. Besides, physical affection without the expectation of sex is very cozy.

"Our intimacy is exposed," I mumble.

A gruff chuckle puffs along the slope of my shoulder and he hugs me tighter. "How'd you sleep?"

"Like a rock. You?"

"Best night of my life." His lips drift along my skin in a silky caress. "How's your back?"

I stretch, wiggling to find any kinks. "Feels great."

"This bed might be a keeper."

The warmth of our cuddle cocoons me. "Won't hear me complain, Stalker."

And I may never leave.

Colton's right arm is slung over me while the left is tucked underneath. Tattoos decorate both, but two particular designs catch my eye.

"What's with the boot print?" I trace the tread permanently etched into his flesh.

"Got that done after you needed a boost."

A furrow creases my forehead. "When was that?"

"About three years ago," he states simply.

Faded memories whip through my mind, searching for the one he's referring to. "Wait. Are you talking about when my hip seized and I had trouble swinging a leg over Luna?"

His nod fills me with that fluttery sensation I now associate with him. "You left a mark on me."

I suck in a sharp breath. That's one of the few interactions we had before our ill-fated trip to Europe. My gaze shifts to the replica of a lasso cinched around his bicep. The meaning smacks me in the face seconds later.

"And this is from when I used you for roping practice?"

"No question about it," he chides.

But I'm stunned regardless. He's obsessed to the point

of inking these seemingly forgettable instances into his flesh. Gosh, that's incredibly sexy. Tingles spread in my lower belly as I bask in his level of devotion. If our relationship continues progressing at this pace, I'll be trading my last name for his by Monday.

"The secrets are spilling," I murmur.

"All you have to do is ask."

"Feel like it's my turn to reveal something, but you probably know—"

"Who's Scout?"

I snort at the impatience in his rough timbre. "That'd be you."

Colton goes still. "Explain."

"Well," I begin but immediately pause. "You're getting two secrets for the price of one. First, it might be somewhat of a shock to learn that I've always found you attractive."

His grunt isn't all that impressed with my confession. "Kinda figured when you propositioned me for sex on the plane."

"Hmm, yes. I'm very subtle."

"One of the many qualities I admire," he teases.

I soak in the carefree energy wafting off him. "Umm, so… yeahhhh. Scout is what I call you in my fantasies. That fictional version puts out like a wild stallion."

"Unbelievable," he grumbles.

"Yes," I breathe. "He's really something."

Colton's fingers tickle my side and I squeal. "You're such a brat. I've been jealous of myself."

Laughter and uncontrollable spasms contort me until he relents on the attack. My chest heaves while I take a moment to recover. "Silly, Stalker. If it makes you feel better,

I'd always picture you when I got myself off. Scout is the solo star in my clit closet."

That terminology almost turns his exhale into a chuckle "You won't need to rely on fake scenarios ever again."

"Thanks for that. Just these past two days, you've stuffed me full of filthy material." My hand roams along his forearm, stopping at the two hair ties on his wrist. The faded band has been there for months, but the second is new and very familiar. "Did you steal this from me yesterday?"

"They're both yours."

I blink at the different styles. "Why do you have them?"

"It's mainly a coping mechanism." Colton reaches to snap the elastic against his skin. "The guy who got me into the underground fighting scene told me to try it. Reminds me that I'm not the worthless criminal my father raised me to be. I used regular rubber bands back then."

Emotion lodges in my throat. "You used to fight?"

"Did a lot worse than that, Princess." Colton clutches onto me harder as if I'll try to escape. "But yeah, that's where I was when Brody found me."

"I didn't know that." There's a sting along the bridge of my nose. It's difficult to picture my protector in those conditions. "Do you wanna talk about it?"

"Later," he deflects.

Which is fair. The weight of his secrets far outmatches mine. But that doesn't stop me from fiddling with the coping mechanism he displays.

"Does it work?"

"Not until I tried it with one of yours." His deep inhale tells me there's more to it. "Your hair was in a braid when I first saw you. I had this unexplainable urge to take it out, let the length fly free. That was very symbolic for me. And then, as if you'd heard me, you left an elastic in the barn. It was like you were giving me permission to use it to chase off my demons. I've kept one of your hair binders on my wrist ever since. Whenever I feel the need to snap it, I'm reminded to be the man worthy of you."

Unshed tears blur my vision. There's a noticeable pitter-patter in my heart that can't be ignored. I can actually feel my guard crumbling into dust. My palm slaps my chest, making sure I'm still in one piece.

"Oh, no."

Colton's entire body goes rigid. "Was that too much?"

"If you're referring to the feelings I'm catching, then yes."

The tension seeps from him in a low rumble. "You're thinking about loving me?"

I fan my watery eyes. "Something like that."

His palm roams the expanse of my stomach, traveling upward to cradle the hand I still have resting over my heart. "Trust in me, baby girl. I want to spend my life making you happy."

"Uh-huh, that's becoming clear." I sniffle and wipe at my cheeks. "But are you happy?"

The hitch in my voice has him flipping me around to face him. "Why are you crying?"

A choked scoff dribbles from me. "I'm not."

"Did I upset you?" Those bottomless blue eyes dig deep, peeling away years of avoidance and indifference. "Tell me how to fix it."

Affection threatens to burst out of me in a rainbow of glitter and fairytales. "Could you maybe get me a tissue?"

Colton twists to grab the box on the nightstand. The

swiveled motion puts his back to me. That's when I notice another tattoo. Down the center, from nape to pelvis, is a detailed design of a crooked spine.

I sit upright to get a better look. My eyes widen at the recognizable shape. It's double curve scoliosis—the same type I suffer from.

"Is that…?" My voices fades into a tremble.

"Yours," Colton confirms. "It's from your latest X-ray."

I reach out with a shaky hand and trace the dark ink. The piece is massive, impossible to miss unless I'm under the influence of a very pierced penis. How I didn't notice yesterday is almost alarming. But now, it's captured my undivided attention.

"This is stunning," I murmur while admiring the quirky vertebrae. "You make scoliosis look very sexy, Stalker."

From over his shoulder, his gaze finds mine. "You do that all on your own. I just stole another piece of you to carry around with me."

"Why did you choose my spine?"

"Aside from the obvious, it represents strength. You don't let anything stop you. Even when you're in pain, you don't quit pushing. It's perseverance and grit, which can't be bought. Those thrive inside you. I feel that mantra in the depths of my soul."

A fresh wave of adoration for this man crashes over me, stealing my voice for a moment. "Um, wow. Your perception of me is rather badass."

His chuckle is gravelly. "That's what you are. My unbreakable princess."

"More of a stubborn brat, but I'll accept an upgrade." My mouth meets his tattooed skin, pressing kisses along the S-shaped bend. "What do you tell people when they ask? It's not easy to hide such a large dedication."

He twitches under my soft touch. "Anybody that sees me without a shirt on is a guy who knows better than to fuck with me."

"Hmm," I mumble into his shoulder blade. "Do your men know how you feel about me?"

Colton's hand rests on my thigh, carving an upward path to my ass. "You're not my dirty secret, baby girl."

"What if I never returned your affections?"

His fingers grip a fistful of my butt, squeezing gently. "I preferred not to consider such an unlikely possibility."

"Oh, my. How your cockiness has grown."

"You stroke my ego very well." He whips back around, pinning me beneath him in a fluid motion. "Are you ready to love me yet?"

Another lump tries to clog my throat. "I think so, but it's all happening so fast. It's too soon, right?"

His eyes blaze into blue flames. "You never let the rules define you. Why start now?"

As usual, the man has a good point. My lips part with the words he's been longing to hear. The rush in my pulse is ready for this step. Colton goes still above me, just waiting for the signal. But then several interruptions happen at once.

His groin pressed flush against mine sets off an internal alarm. The telltale pinch in my bladder warns me that the sheets will be soaked for an entirely different reason if I don't take care of business immediately. I wiggle while an apologetic wince creases my features.

Spud's patience chooses that moment to vacate the premises and he jumps onto the bed. He nudges me with his wet nose until I untangle myself from Colton's embrace. Before I can scoot off the mattress for double potty duty, my phone begins to rattle on the nightstand.

I grab it on my way to the bathroom, stopping short at the name flashing on the screen. A quick swipe answers before I lift it to my ear. "Hey, Dad."

"Good morning, Bee!" His tone is especially chipper for whatever time it is. "Hope I didn't wake you."

My gaze flings to the clock. "It's after eight."

"I know how you like your beauty sleep," he chuckles.

"Uh, right. I've been awake for a while." I glance at Colton lounging against the pile of pillows. The urge to snuggle against him again weakens my knees. "No worries."

"That's great to hear. We'll be there in ten minutes. Wanted to give you a heads-up."

Dread is a rock plummeting in my gut. "Ten minutes?"

"That's what the noisy map on Brody's phone says. Damn thing won't be quiet."

"My brother is with you?"

"And his lovely wife." Dad sounds entirely too pleased, still taking full credit for their union.

"Ohhh-kayyyy," I chirp. "See you then!"

My finger jabs at the red circle to end the call before he can deliver more disturbing news. I swivel my bare feet on the wood floor to face the naked man tenting the covers with his massive erection. Colton isn't bothered in the least. Meanwhile, my heart is pounding from the approach of a cockblocking stampede.

"My family is almost here."

A smirk slants his kissable lips. "And?"

I gesture wildly at our current state of undress. "We look like we've been banging all night."

"Close, but not quite." His casual indifference irks me straight to the toilet.

After relieving myself and turning on the shower, I call out to him over the stream. "I'm gonna rinse off. Feel free to put some clothes on."

But Colton's irresistible appeal fills the doorway. "Want some company?"

My mouth goes dry. There's a physical clench in my vagina that refuses to deny him. "Uhh… Spud needs to go out."

His head shakes in the negative. "There's a doggy door. It opens and closes with the tap of a button."

My jaw drops. "Since when?"

"Since I planned for this to be your safe haven. Wherever you go, there's at least one pampered pup not far behind."

I'm smacked with a lusty dose of appreciation. "Good grief, Stalker. Could you be more considerate?"

"Maybe if you let me conserve water. Not to mention that breakfast is the most important meal of the day," he recites while striding toward me. "I'll eat fast."

It takes all of two seconds for me to forget about our incoming guests. "There's no need to rush. I don't want you to get a stomach ache."

CHAPTER TWENTY-TWO

Cotton

FRESHLY SHOWERED AND STUFFED FROM BIANCA'S pussy, I swing open the front door to greet our family. I can finally claim them as mine by extension, which will be officially and legally announced when she's ready. Our hands are clasped in a secure hold to present us as a cohesive unit. She doesn't fight me or try to pull away while I usher her out onto the porch. My chest expands to the point of bursting with pride.

Brody and Dennis are perched against the railing. Paisley is poking around the property, wandering her way to the barn. There's a gooseneck trailer hitched to their truck. From the chorus of stomping hooves, I'd say there are three horses itching to be unloaded.

Bianca's cheeks are a revealing shade of red as she releases me to hug the most important men in her life. "Howdy, y'all. This is unexpected."

"You invited us," Brody drawls.

Her backpedaled stride returns her to me. "That's true, but you didn't tell me you were coming."

He points a thumb at Dennis. "Dad did."

"When you were ten minutes out," Bianca huffs.

"Paisley wanted it to be a surprise."

"The phone call was a bit of a shock." Her legs clench as if recalling what we've been busy doing since they last spoke.

"You're happy we're here?" Dennis sounds unsure.

Which has his daughter rushing to say, "Yes, of course. Welcome to… our safe house to escape the chaos." She turns to find my gaze on her. "That's a mouthful. We need to actually name this place."

I stoop down to whisper in her ear. "Kinky Ultimatum."

Her blush darkens. "No."

A soft chuckle scrapes free from the bowels of my hardened exterior. "You decide, Princess."

She taps her chin before gasping. "Keller's Keep."

Talk about perfection. I bite my bottom lip, dragging the flesh between my teeth. "Are you agreeing to stay and become a Keller?"

"That's putting several carts in front of the horse, but probably."

"Bee is safe to come home," Brody interjects. His steely gaze fastens on me. "If you want to stay out here until the smoke clears, I'll give you paid leave."

"She's not leaving without me," I inform him.

His nostrils flare. "Care to rephrase that?"

"No."

Bianca cackles. "Well, how about that? He listens to me now, big brother."

"About damn time," he boasts.

She purses her lips into a luxury bow. "You're not mad?"

"Livid, but can't fault him. Love fucks with logic."

Her jaw drops. "Are you saying I'm making him illogical?"

Brody almost grins. "Wouldn't dare."

I tug her closer to my side. "Better not."

"Oh, umm… spoiler alert." Bianca's eyes dart to the dumbfounded expressions gawking at us. She straightens her shoulders, lifting our joined palms. "In case you can't read the room, we're together now. After much begging and considerate gestures, I convinced Colton to become my boyfriend."

Brody snorts. "That's ass backward."

But Dennis is grinning broadly. "Well, it's about damn time. Marion and I had placed a bet ages ago to see how long it would take." He wags a gnarled finger at the sky. "You called it, love."

"Phew." Bianca fans her face. "It's been an emotional start to the day."

My friend studies his sister's wet hair, shifting his stare to mine that's tucked under a cowboy hat. "Did we interrupt something?"

"What?" Bianca's tone is too pitchy. "No. We were just having a slow start to the morning. Had to speed things along once we knew you were coming."

The sloppy excuse narrows Brody's eyes on me. "You're in a good mood."

"Can you blame me? The woman of my dreams just claimed me as hers." I mean, damn. It's a challenge not to toss her over my shoulder and fuck her with my tongue right now.

A loud gasp interrupts us, drawing our attention to the source. "You're willingly in a relationship with Colton? That's not the story you told me yesterday morning, Bee."

Bianca winces at Paisley's accusation. "A lot can change in twenty-four hours."

On cue, Spud trots over from his shady spot under the oak tree. He sniffs the affronted blonde and the upset immediately clears from her expression. Paisley kneels in the grass to welcome him with open arms.

"Who's this fella?" Her voice transforms into a babble for babies.

"That's Spud. He's such a good boy," Bianca replies in the same tone.

"Like a potato?"

"Mhmm, my favorite food group. Colton named him after he showed up yesterday. We went into town and asked if anyone was missing a dog, but it was a dead end. That means he's ours."

"One big happy family, hmm?" Paisley's stern focus observes me before softening on her friend.

Bianca shrugs and bumps me with her hip. "As it turns out, he's not so bad."

The blonde stands and beckons her forward. "Help me unload the horses. The men want to discuss dangerous manly things."

"Better fill me in later," Bianca murmurs from the corner of her mouth.

"No more secrets." And then I swat her ass to send her along her way.

Brody and Dennis appear flabbergasted, their heads swiveling from me to her and back again. Their astonishment is serenaded by the squeal from the rusty windmill. It takes a dozen beats of my rapid pulse for the men I admire like idols to collect themselves. The one I view as a father figure finds his voice first.

"Really didn't think I'd see the day," he murmurs.

Brody nods slowly. "She seems to actually like you."

Doubt snakes through my veins in a lethal dose. "Is that so hard to believe?"

"Yes," they say in unison.

"Thanks a lot," I grunt in response.

"It's not you," Dennis is quick to clarify. "I'm amazed to see Bianca serious about someone. That isn't a knock against you, kid. My daughter is very strong-willed. Fiercely independent."

"No man has ever been good enough," Brody adds. "But what did I tell you?"

Now they're looking at me with an openness that's tough to read. The kindness in their eyes spreads warmth through my chest. Is this acceptance? Or maybe belonging? Fuck, it feels nice. I place a palm over the soothing sensation.

But then my heart gallops faster as I admit, "Just wanna do right by her."

Dennis claps me on the shoulder. "That much is obvious. You're keeping her safe and provided a little slice of paradise. What else could she ask for?"

I blow out a harsh breath. "Freedom."

Brody grimaces. "She'd get herself into trouble with too much of that."

The accusation widens my stance. "How do you know?"

"I'm her brother," he states plainly.

"And you still treat her like a wild child."

He bristles. "Is that what she told you?"

I shrug. "It's what I've observed. Bianca isn't overly reckless or irresponsible beyond reason. If she ever decides to be, I'll be there to protect her."

"You'll follow her wherever she wants to go," Dennis says.

"Whether she likes it or not," I say.

Brody crosses his arms. "As if that's any better than fencing her in."

"There's a difference."

"Which I'm sure you've explained to her."

My jaw flexes. "We've reached an understanding."

"Okay, boys," Dennis barks. "Enough of this pissin' match. We all want what's best for Bianca. That's why we're here."

The fight drains out of me instantly. My focus shifts to where the women are leading the horses to the barn. All three are saddled, which leads me to assume Luna and Bandit will soon be too.

"What's with the cargo?" I lift my chin at the scene.

"Bianca mentioned how much fun you had on a trail ride. It's something we used to do a lot together as a family. Thought we'd join you for the day." Dennis glances toward the pastures that spread far and wide.

That comforting buzz fills me again. "Appreciate you making the drive."

He chuckles. "Don't thank me. It was overdue. I haven't spent much time away from home since Brody sent me on the road with Jimmy and that was a month ago."

The guilty party doesn't appear to be apologetic in the least. "Not a single regret."

"What about cutting off your sister from her best friend?"

Brody glares at me. "Got something to say?"

"Nah, I've made my peace with it."

"Fuck, she's turning you against me." He shakes his head.

I lean back against the house. "Gonna fire me if I choose her over you?"

"Hell no," he spits. "You're like a brother to me. If you get Bianca to marry your sorry ass, that'll make it real. Not about to stand in your way, Colt."

Dennis hoots. "That's the spirit."

Meanwhile, I'm at a loss for words. My mouth moves soundlessly as I struggle. Brody takes pity on me and changes the subject.

"Your father is still in the hospital."

I exhale the pressure in my lungs. "Any word on when he'll be released?"

"Rumor has it that his cancer has progressed to the point that he'll spend the rest of his days right where he is. We don't have proof that it's true yet," Dennis utters.

"Damn." I scrub a palm over my mouth, digesting that dark news. "I wonder how the crew is handling it."

My cousins are still involved in his shitty organization. Several others that I used to consider friends are too. Without my father around, they're left to fend for themselves. But it's not my problem.

Brody is studying me too closely. "Do you want to see him?"

"No," I say without hesitation.

"Are you sure? It might haunt you." His gaze loses focus for a moment. "That's the type of regret you can't escape."

Which undoubtedly has him thinking about his mom. Our situations couldn't be more different, though. Marion Benson was a saint. Her life ended abruptly, stolen out from under her without warning. My father deserves what's coming for him.

Not a drop of guilt sinks into my gut over that fact. Maybe I'm a horrible person. Or maybe that goes to show just how detached my father left me.

"I've said my goodbyes to him. More than once. That's all the closure I need."

Brody adjusts the brim of his hat, tugging it low to shadow his eyes. "Why is he so hell-bent on you replacing him once he's gone?"

"Not a damn clue. Maybe some strange sense of sentiment. He wants to keep his legacy alive." The disgust in my voice is evident.

But Dennis nods. "I know a thing or two about that."

"Don't compare yourself to him," I grunt.

His chuckle is dry. "We both take pride in our work and want to pass it down. That's about all we have in common. I don't blame you for putting the past to rest before truly burying it. The future you're building is where your life's purpose will be born."

"If she'll have me," I mumble.

"You're a good man, Colton. Bianca is lucky your sights are set so firmly on her. To be loved that loudly is a rare gift." Dennis ambles toward the stairs. "Enough chit-chat. I want a tour of your land."

I'm too stunned to move. Brody nudges me along. My

boots scuff across the porch as I drift in a daze of unexpected relief.

"You know I was just giving you shit."

I scoff at the humor in his tone. "Could've fooled me."

Brody hitches his shoulders, not bothered by my mood. "How long are you planning to stay here?"

"Until the threat is eliminated. My father might be on his last leg, but he's still capable of delivering trouble to our doorstep as a parting gift." More than that, I want to tell him that this is our home. There's no reason to leave unless Bianca says so.

He nods as if agreeing to those terms. "I suppose it's only been a few days."

My lips twitch. "Miss me, boss?"

"No," he's quick to grumble. "But Paisley is pissed that her friend is gone again."

"Sounds like a you problem." I have plenty of my own.

Which allows a smirk to crack through my mask of indifference. That's what Bianca does to me. And thinking about what I'll do to tame my bratty princess next is too tempting to resist.

CHAPTER TWENTY-THREE

Bianca

PRICKLES SKIP ALONG MY CROOKED SPINE. IT'S NOT the colorful leaves rustling in the trees that's awakening this sensation. The noticeable drop in temperature now that we're exposed to the autumn elements isn't responsible either. If anything, the windy chill that chases us on our ride across the open field keeps me from burning up.

I turn in the saddle to glance behind me, already knowing what I'll find. Colton is staring at me. No, that's too basic. The look he's giving me is much deeper than that simple term. It's burrowing beneath layers until I feel him promising my body filthy pleasure.

"Good grief," Paisley sighs from astride her own horse next to mine. "What did you do to that man?"

"Nothing yet." But then I study him and his unwavering intensity again. "Well, that's not entirely true."

"Duh, Bee. His smolder is hungry and you're his meal of choice. Spill."

"We've been alone for… two days." That gives me pause as my hips sway to Bandit's smooth stride. "Gosh, is that all? I'm such a hussy."

"No judgment." Her soft smile is for my brother and their fast-acting fuckery, but that's a different story.

"It's bound to happen in the forced proximity trope, right? Resisting is pointless, especially when Colton is so thoughtful. And persistent. The man is a romantic ninja. I can't anticipate his next move. Is he still back there?"

My bestie laughs into an approaching gust. "As if he'd let you out of his sight."

"I dunno," I mumble. "When we were on this trail last, he vanished without a trace only to creep up behind me. It scared me until I was pinned protectively beneath him."

Paisley nods, not disturbed in the slightest. "'Tis the season."

My blank stare has her quickly clarifying.

"It's almost Halloween. Getting chased and tackled in the middle of nowhere seems very appropriate."

"Interesting." My mind wanders to how I might return the favor. And then I consider what will happen once I catch him.

"Are you blushing?" Paisley's voice rises in volume to alert the freaking birds miles away.

I brush my cold fingers along the heated skin. "It's the breeze stinging my cheeks."

"You're serious about him." It's not a question.

Which earns her a quirked eyebrow. "Haven't I mentioned that already?"

There's awe in Paisley's slack expression. "This is incredible. I've never seen you like this."

"Okay, let's take it easy. I'm not a tourist attraction."

She makes a noise of agreement. "Freak show is more your style."

"Brat," I laugh and lightly shove her.

"See? You're talking to yourself. Totally freaky."

A wispy breath doesn't deny it. I'm more than ready to get my freak on with a certain protective grump. We'll see what tonight brings.

In the meantime, my attention wanders to where Spud is scouting the property ahead of us. It's only been a day, but he's claimed this territory as his. I love that he's ours. Animals have a way of establishing unbreakable bonds.

"How's Echo?" I reach to pet my mom's favorite horse.

"She's great. Don't change the subject," Paisley scolds.

But I veer off course again regardless. It just feels like that kind of moment. The buckskin mare belongs to my friend now. That's what Mom would've wanted.

My gaze drifts to the right. Dad is off on his own, appreciating the rural scenery. His stare is unfocused but reflective. I imagine he's picturing my mom at his side. They loved to hit the trails together. Maybe that's a ritual I can adopt with Colton.

"He learned how to ride from watching my YouTube channel. Kept it a secret," I reveal absently.

Paisley's interest burns into my profile. "I was a bit surprised he even knew how to get on."

"It turns out he was my first subscriber."

A noise of outrage fumes from her. "That's who beat me to it?"

"Guess so," I laugh. "His truck is named after the color of my eyes."

"Really?"

My gaze returns to her. "Mhmm, and he had a new bed delivered after the other one hurt my back."

"That's… very considerate."

"You should've seen the breakfast spread he cooked for me yesterday morning."

Either her stomach grumbles or there's rain on the horizon. "Was it really good?"

"Better than a personal chef." I smack my lips. "There was a no-strings massage included."

She hammers the saddle horn. "Those exist?"

"Apparently," I sigh wistfully. "And his hands are very strong. He got at the tough knots. Loosened me right up."

"Brody needs to learn a thing or two." Her eyes narrow on her husband riding beside Colton. "Such a slacker."

My humor sobers. "When we first arrived at the house, I noticed that he'd planted daisies in the flowerbeds. It's going to snow soon and they won't last, but the message was clear. He wanted to make sure a piece of her was here waiting for me."

"Oh." Paisley covers her mouth with a shaky palm. "What an incredible tribute."

"The Shasta type was her favorite. They're the standard white and yellow. I'm more partial to pink gerberas. Although, blue is starting to grow on me. There's a whole variety in the gardens."

"It didn't even occur to me when I was poking around earlier," she mumbles.

"And the list goes on. If you need to get in the front door, my birthday is the code."

Paisley grins. "Jeez, when's the wedding?"

"That's not funny. We'd already be hitched if it were up to him."

"How do you feel?"

"I can't be in love with him already," I whine. But it doesn't sound that far-fetched.

"Just follow your heart. Unless your gut makes a really solid argument against it."

Which has me asking, "Want to hear something crazy?"

"Always," she blurts.

"It's kinda hot that he's stalked me for years," I say shamelessly. "Well… only because it's him and I know he's safe."

"Right, of course."

"The slight abduction to protect me from his creepy father isn't that bad. I'm not actually his captive. He's only my jailer because I allow it." I peek over at her reaction.

My friend has a knowing look on her face. "Are you wanting me to excuse his behavior?"

"Not necessarily," I mutter.

"Do you want permission to forgive him for it?"

"Will you think badly of me if I do?"

Paisley huffs out a laugh. "Does it matter either way?"

"I guess not." A heavy exhale whisks away from me. "I'm lowkey obsessed with Colton Keller."

She holds out a palm for me to slap. "What're you gonna do about it?"

My shoulders bounce to a casual gait as I turn in the saddle again. "Hey, Stalker. When are you taking me on a date?"

His smolder blazes hotter. "Just say the word, Princess."

Brody whacks his chest. "Can you not slobber over her like a piece of meat in my presence? That's my little sister."

"She's a big girl and doesn't appreciate you trying to censor her boyfriend's desire." My tone is purposefully sweet to piss off my brother.

He pinches the bridge of his nose. "I'm ready to leave when you are, wife."

"We just got here," Paisley complains.

"And I'm being visually assaulted by these two."

"Now you know how it feels." I wag a finger between them. "Still not comfortable with this."

"But we're sisters," Paisley whines.

"That makes it tolerable."

Colton stretches to thump Brody on the arm. "Why don't you feel that way about me, *brother*?"

My bestie's eyes bug out. "Was that a playful comeback?"

"A man of many talents," I sigh.

She lowers her voice and asks, "Best you've ever had?"

"That hasn't been confirmed. He's denying me the dicking of my dreams until our love is a two-way street."

Her brows wiggle. "Oooooh, he wants to lock you down."

"Big time."

"And you're going to let him?"

My head bobs. "There's no alternative to this kinky ultimatum."

Paisley sputters. "Excuse you?"

"Ah, you missed that earlier." I wave off her shock. "Long story short, it doesn't get better than him."

"Um, okay. Should I be concerned?"

"Only for Colton and his enormous ego. I'm going to drag it out." And make him beg. Maybe toss in a spanking or two. Not that my friend needs to hear any of that. A giggle that's dipped in diabolical intentions escapes me. "But first, I'm taking you somewhere special for lunch."

CHAPTER TWENTY-FOUR

Cotton

Our second trip to Dirty Dicks is received just as poorly by the regulars holed up inside. Silence announces our entrance. It's the stagnant type that crawls across my skin and leaves a sticky residue behind. My boots scuff across the floor, dragging me to an empty spot along the wall.

That allows me to catch the array of emotions splashing over Bianca's face. From uncertainty to excitement, she can't seem to decide how to feel. But then her focus snags on a pair of shirts hanging on a flickering beer sign that proudly proclaim the name Dirty Dicks.

"Are those for sale?" She stabs a finger at the merchandise that probably hasn't been touched in months.

The grouchy bartender from yesterday nods while pouring three shots of vodka.

"We'll take them both," Paisley shouts as if someone else is about to steal the loot.

"That'll be forty bucks," the burly man drawls.

Brody coughs into his fist. "Damn rip off."

The guy stares him down. "They're in high demand."

"You can afford it." His wife holds out an open palm.

"Now you want my money." He peels a crisp fifty from his wallet.

"Gonna need more than that, husband." She wiggles her fingers.

"For what? There are only two available, which is two too many."

"We're having burger baskets for lunch." Paisley nods at a chalkboard that lists the barely legible specials.

"Delicious," he deadpans. His lack of enthusiasm hands her another fifty.

"Thanks." She smacks him with a kiss before spinning on her heel. "I'll tell him to keep the change."

Which the man in charge is all too eager to have. I didn't think the weathered local knew how to smile, but he's looking pretty pleased while passing the women their purchase. Paisley shakes out the white fabric before slipping it over her head. Bianca doesn't hesitate to do the same. Dust billows around them in a thick cloud.

My lips twitch as I watch my princess enjoy herself. She tugs at the bottom hem of her friend's top, tying the baggy material into a makeshift knot at Paisley's waist. Bianca's shirt gets the same treatment before she lifts her phone to take a selfie of their matching outfits. The duo cackle loudly at the promotional image they create, proudly displaying the Dirty Dicks logo. If the bartender cared about bringing in new customers, he'd post that picture out front. But then I'd have to threaten him with bodily harm.

"This place is a dump." Brody wrinkles his upturned nose at the stained carpet.

"Don't be a rich asshole," I complain at him in return.

"That's exactly what I am."

"Doesn't mean you need to spoil the vibe." I inhale a deep breath. The recognizable stench of grease and cheap beer permeates the air. "Our women and your dad love it."

His focus trails to where Dennis inserted himself into a cribbage competition at a corner table. "Ridiculous."

"You could join him."

My friend recoils. "What the fuck is wrong with you?"

"They're having a blast." I thrust an arm at his wife dancing circles around Bianca. "It's like Christmas in late October."

He curls his upper lip at me. "And you're a jolly fucking giant all of a sudden."

"Why wouldn't I be? What's to be upset about?"

"For starters, your father is hounding you and my sister is involved by proxy."

That flattens my mood into a scowl. "She's safe with me."

"Didn't say otherwise. Just pointing out that you're technically on the run and there's not that much to be overjoyed about."

Bianca chooses that moment to tip her head back with a giddy squeal that vibrates the walls of this dive bar. It's a different pitch than when I make her come, but my cock doesn't care. I widen my stance in an attempt to hide the evidence of her effect on me.

"Fuck," Brody spits. "You're not even bothering to hide it anymore."

"Why would I?"

What started as Bianca acknowledging feelings for me quickly became her exposing our relationship. That already had me reeling. Then she went and spelled out what's to come. Bianca might've tried to keep her voice down on the ride earlier, but I overheard every word. She's got plans for me. A smile curls my lips as I admire her posing in that unflattering Dirty Dicks tee.

Brody shakes his head. "Bianca has you wrapped around her manicured pinkie."

"And?"

His phone rings before I get a response. A glance at the screen has him muttering a curse. "I've gotta take this."

The door bangs shut behind him, signaling that I'm free to ogle his sister to my obsession's content. She must feel my stare, twisting to wink at me over her shoulder. The temptress takes it one step further and wiggles her ass in my direction. I straighten off the wall with every intention of making a scene that'll get us kicked out.

Brody storms back in like a dark cloud. "Time to leave. Now."

Paisley pouts at his demand. "But we just got here."

"Sorry, wife. Duty calls. The business needs me. You can screw off with Bianca later."

She's still glued to her friend's side. "What about the food?"

"Change it to takeout. You can eat in the truck." His authoritative tone has the bartender barking the adjustment to the cook.

Paisley is slow to approach. "We need to get the horses."

"Dammit," he groans. "I don't have time for this."

A calm washes over me, the kind that keeps my head on straight during a crisis. "How can I help?"

"There's nothing you can do." Brody tugs at his collar, slipping into professional mode. "One of our grain manufacturers had an incident at the factory. Several machines malfunctioned to the point of being out of commission for weeks. It sounds like a clusterfuck. He's our biggest feed supplier and this will cause a ripple effect if we don't get a handle on it."

"What about all the storage?" I ask. "Don't we have enough feed to last us a while?"

"That's the thing. Apparently, our stockpiles are almost depleted. There might be enough to last the weekend. We'll need to scramble to get ahold of a replacement vendor because all our normal deliveries are canceled."

"Shit." I scrub over my thick stubble. "There must be an easy solution."

"It's not your problem." He grunts and slaps my back. "Keep my sister happy. Don't give me the details on how you manage that. I'll text you later."

"We'll bring the horses home sometime this week." That generous offer spills free from Bianca as she balances a burger basket in one hand and a bag of cardboard containers in the other.

"Princess," I clip under my breath.

She blinks her long lashes at me while discreetly transferring the takeout to her friend's arm. "It's safe to make a quick stop, right?"

"I'd rather not risk it."

"But we're going to Haunted Harvest Haze. It's tradition."

Paisley gasps while Brody grunts. Even I comprehend the importance of that festival. Marion Benson and her slew of charitable foundations sponsored the annual event. This is the first time she won't be in attendance. Defeat slides my eyes shut.

Delicate fingers walk up my shirt. "We'll be extra careful, Stalker. And after Halloween, we'll hit the road for the next jackpot or rodeo. See some other sights. Avoid the trouble chasing us. Stay in hiding a bit longer."

"Fine," I grit through clenched teeth.

Brody makes the sound of a whip cracking. "Say goodbye to your balls, Colt."

My eyes don't stray from the woman who owns a lot more of me than that. "She's had them in her possession for five years."

Bianca's grin is the bratty version that brings me to my knees. "They're in very good hands."

"For fuck's sake. Why are we still here? Dad!" Brody bellows across the small space. "Haul ass."

Dennis stands, pointing at several folks around the table. "This isn't over. I want a rematch."

A guy with bushy eyebrows hoots hard enough to shake his big belly. "Just name the date, old timer."

"And don't forget your pocketbook," another taunts.

Dennis chuckles while he approaches us. "What a riot. Thanks for introducing me to this goldmine. I'll make a fortune off those fools."

Bianca kisses his cheek. "Love you."

My heart clenches. I'm desperate to hear those words from her. And more than that, the affection is so natural between them. The family bonds where I came from look very different.

Her dad loops an arm around her shoulders. "Love you, kiddo." His gaze shifts to me. "Take care of her for us."

"With my life," I vow.

"Good man." Dennis pats my back. "You've always been one of us, but it'll be nice to make it official."

Bianca is in the middle of saying goodbye to Paisley and Brody, but freezes. "Jeez, Dad. No pressure or anything."

He scoffs while backing toward the door. "It's a done deal, Bee. We all see it. Put the guy out of his misery."

After another round of hugs and a few more reminders that we'll see them soon, Bianca sends them off with a parting wave. The energy in the room crackles as we stay behind. A hot sensation prods at my back as if all eyes are on us. I turn to reclaim my position along the wall where I have a clear view of people pretending to mind their own business.

"Looks like we're alone again," Bianca purrs. It takes her three muffled steps to reach me and press herself flush against my chest. "Now what, Stalker?"

I was about to suggest we kick rocks out of here, but my dick appreciates her close proximity. "This is fine."

Her smile widens at my response. "Hungry?"

"Famished," I croak.

She snatches a French fry from the burger basket still in her grip, lifting it to my lips. "Can I feed you?"

I open my mouth and chew automatically. It tastes like nothing. My palate is very particular, preferring a specific tangy honey flavor.

"More?" She has half of a cheeseburger suspended in midair.

To appease her, I take a large bite. Bianca hums and wipes something from my chin. My appetite throbs, but from below my belt. The entire thing is choked down just to have her fussing over me. When I grab the other half to return the favor, she shakes her head.

"I'm in the mood for a different type of meat. Does this count as our date?"

My gaze swipes across the dingy interior. "You want to tell everyone I wined and dined you at Dirty Dicks?"

"It'll make a great story," she murmurs.

"I think we can find somewhere more suitable for a princess."

Bianca frowns. "But I like it here."

"You fit right in." I tug at her shirt.

"Welcome to Dirty Dicks," she breathes against my throat. "It's my honor to serve you."

I clench my hand on her hip. "Careful."

"Or what?"

My nose drifts along her temple, inhaling lilac and temptation. "I'll eat your pussy in the bathroom."

She laughs until catching the serious strain in my expression. "Very funny."

"Fuck around and find out, baby girl."

Her cheeks get pink as she rubs against my erection. "You already did that to me this morning."

"Which was hours ago," I argue.

"We're in public," she whispers.

"Try to keep your screams to a minimum."

But she's hesitating, squirming her hips to test my willpower. "You actually want to?"

"Need to," I correct. "Your pussy is the cure to calm my

chaos. I'm addicted. Completely hooked. Feed my craving, Princess."

Bianca ditches the burger basket on the nearest surface and slings her arms around my neck. "It really turns me on that you like going down on me."

"Love, not like," I rectify again. "Does that mean you'll let me do it whenever I want?"

"I'm beginning to think so."

"That's not granting me permission. You want me to beg?"

Her nose brushes over mine. "Mhmm, I love when you bend to my wild whims."

"And kneel at your feet?" My palm snakes between us to reach the exposed skin above her knee. A flip of my wrist has me slipping under her skirt to tease her inner thigh. "Did you wear this for me?"

She clamps her legs together to trap my exploring fingers. "It accentuates my assets."

"And gives me easy access." I stroke her satin flesh until she relaxes. "Put your pussy in my mouth."

Her eyelids grow heavy as her breath wheezes. "Right now?"

"Always, but that's unreasonable." Yet I look at her for confirmation.

"It's also unrealistic." But her rebuttal lacks spark. She must sense it and adds, "You can't constantly eat me out."

"Not with that attitude."

Her body sways into mine. "Why am I resisting?"

"Good question. Tell me yes," I exhale across her lips.

"Yes." Her mouth presses to mine, tongue sneaking out to lick me.

I cinch an arm around her waist and deepen the kiss for a moment. Just long enough for the steady thump of my pulse to spike into a feverish rush. She's snug against me, but yanks at my neck to eliminate any empty space. My teeth nibble at her bottom lip before sucking hard on the pouty flesh. It's a preview of what I plan on doing to her clit. Bianca mewls, grinding into me shamelessly. I squeeze a palmful of her ass. We're making a scene, but I couldn't give a single shit. The desperation simmering in my veins is what pulls us apart.

My mouth slips from hers on a harsh exhale. "Let me get your taste on my tongue, and then I'll take you on a date worthy of bragging to your friends."

"All right, Cowboy." She snatches the straw hat off my head, dropping it onto hers. The size is way too big, but damn, she's sexy while staking her claim. "Saddle up. I'm gonna ride your face."

That's what I needed to hear. I thread our fingers together and guide her to the dark alcove labeled with a wooden restroom sign. Before slipping inside, I pause at the bar.

Bianca sneaks past me and swings her hips to a sultry rhythm. I blindly reach back for my wallet and pull out a hundred-dollar bill. The barrel-chested man eyes the money I set on the counter.

"Keep everyone away from the can until we come out," I instruct.

He tucks the bill into his pocket. "You got it."

And then I follow Bianca into the single-person space. My gaze scans the chipped tiles and scuffed paint. It's not much, but better than expected. I'm pleasantly surprised it's not filthy. There's a noticeable sting of bleach in my nostrils. He must've cleaned it recently. My insatiable appetite for this woman appreciates his efforts.

Bianca backs herself into the far corner. "Paying off the employees just to get some?"

"It's a small price to get privacy. I prefer to eat my meals in peace without any interruptions."

A tremble rolls through her, hooding her gaze with lust. "It would be very unfortunate if you're forced to stop."

My knees meet the hard floor in front of her. "Don't worry, baby girl. Nothing comes between me and your pleasure."

I hike up her skirt and notice she's soaked her panties. My nose presses into the drenched lace, pulling in a lungful of her sweet arousal that's all mine. A pleased rumble rises from my expanded chest. Her smile is dipped in smug anticipation as I tug her panties to the side.

She drapes a leg over my shoulder, leaning at an angle to brace herself against the wall. The splayed position serves her cunt to me on a buffet platter. That's my greedy girl.

"This will be fast," I warn her.

Her bobbled nod jostles my hat on her head. "Just to quench your thirst."

The dryness in my throat demands to be soothed. "Yes, I'm very parched after convincing you."

And she's about to be singing my praises as a reward.

I drag my flattened tongue along her center, gathering a mouthful of her desire for me. It's potent and I'm instantly delirious. My mind goes blank of everything except drowning in her passion. Quick swipes to her clit make her shake above me. She bucks forward, seeking more.

Two fingers sink inside her clenching pussy while I roll my tongue faster. The combination increases her breathy whines into chanting pleas. Whatever reservations she has about being overheard are whisked away with every purposeful stimulation to her sex. My intention is to make her forget where we are and just let go. It doesn't take long until she's quivering and tipping toward the peak.

I growl into her slit, begging her to suffocate me. Bianca squeals while snapping her hips to an erratic pace. The loud moans spilling from her are a symphony I'll gladly conduct.

Her desperation spurs mine. Need pumps my cock in a forceful grip. Heat barrels through me and I'm seconds from coming in my pants. That's the moment she detonates, saving me from making a mess.

"Oh, fuck!" She slaps her palms on the wall.

Tremors vibrate our connection. That encourages me to suck harder on her clit. There's an unmistakable surge that I gulp down with enthusiasm. Her body goes rigid in my hold.

"Ohhhhh, shit. No, no," she yelps.

It's too late to be embarrassed. The trigger is pulled and I increase my motions to give her the strongest relief. Her screams rise in volume, almost to the point of pain. I grin into my next swipe as she twitches through the orgasm.

When Bianca's quakes subside, I sit back on my heels. The smug smirk is still painted on my wet lips. "That good, huh?"

But my cocky confidence vanishes after a glance at her face. A pinch distorts her features into obvious agony. As if that's not a big enough punch to my gut, tears are streaming down her cheeks in a flash flood.

I'm on my feet in the next instant, clutching her in my arms. "What's wrong?"

Bianca sniffles, but her expression relaxes into a slow smile. "My damn hip locked up."

"While you were coming?"

"While I was coming," she confirms. "It really warped the experience. I had to hold still and try not to aggravate the cramp. Almost like I was restrained." Her eyes light up. "Oooh, add that to our kinky ultimatum list. If I don't behave, you'll tie me to the fence post."

Unlocking that fantasy tries to distract from my concern. "Not the time, Princess. You're hurt."

"Oh, please. That was nothing. The release made it tolerable." She flutters her damp lashes.

Which does little to convince me. My hands cup her face, thumbing away the evidence of upset. "Fuck, I'm sorry."

"Don't worry, Stalker. Seriously. I still got mine." And then she's palming my dick through my jeans. "It's your turn."

But I shake my head. "Not until I'm buried nine inches deep inside your pussy."

CHAPTER TWENTY-FIVE

Bianca

"WANT ME TO STOP?" MY VOICE IS COY AND FULLY aware that I'm driving Colton to the brink.

Meanwhile, he's the one actually behind the wheel. His knuckles are white as he tries to keep Fern in the right lane on the road home. I trace the outline of his dick again. The bulge is straining through his jeans to the point of ripping seams.

Colton's gulp is audible. "Such a brat."

"That's not an answer," I murmur while skipping my fingers along his arousal.

He stretches his legs wider and pushes himself into my palm. "It's torture, but I love it coming from you."

"Are you going to come for me?"

His teeth grit. "No."

Which spurs me on. My teasing becomes more of a jerking motion.

"Not until I'm sinking slowly onto your cock after confessing my unconditional love for you?"

"Fuck."

That's all the warning I get before Colton takes a sharp and sudden turn onto our property. I crash into him along the bench seat from the abrupt swerve. The terrain in the field is bumpy, especially at the speed we're traveling. My arms pinwheel while looking for a stable surface to grab. His flexed thigh and the dashboard brace me while we travel across the grassy land.

"Where are we going?" There's a shrill edge to my voice that's totally called for.

Especially when he responds with, "You'll see."

"Is someone chasing us?" I whip my head around, but only dust trails our wild ride. "Why are you going so fast?"

"Because you're tormenting me." His guttural tone gives me pause.

"Ohhh." My heart lurches. "I'm sorry, Stalker."

"Don't apologize unless you're about to leave me hanging." And then he thrusts his hips.

My grin returns with a seductive vengeance. "Have you been a bad boy?"

"Yes."

"That's why you're getting punished." I resume my teasing strokes along his rigid shaft.

A low groan rips from him. It's the sound of a man teetering on the edge, but he won't give himself permission to release. That denial sparks an idea and I loosen my hold. His exhale sputters. Colton bangs his head against the seat, but doesn't complain otherwise.

We're jostled a bit when the truck crests a hill. The

higher vantage point allows me to see far ahead. There's a creek cutting through the valley below. I'm momentarily distracted by the sight. My gaze scans the area spread out through the windshield. This entire section is new to me.

When we're near the stream, Colton slams on the brakes. Tension radiates off him as he shifts Fern into park. Maybe I pushed him too far. That's precisely why I go still, allowing him to take the lead.

His eyes are crazed. "Tell me you love me, Princess. Please put me out of my misery."

"I love you." The concession falls freely from my up-turned lips.

But he still looks seconds away from losing his shit. "Do you mean it?"

I press a gentle kiss to his cheek. "Wouldn't say it if I didn't."

After a whoosh, the strain deflates from his posture. He slumps against me for several rapid beats of his heart. We tangle ourselves into a tight embrace. It spreads warmth through my chest, solidifying our undeniable chemistry. I rub a palm up his back and he trembles.

"Say it again," he murmurs. "Please."

"I love you, Stalker." And damn, it feels good to tell him.

He must agree. The noise that rattles from him is the sort of relief a person begs for. I cling onto him until there's nothing but love between us. We stay wrapped up like that for a minute or two.

When Colton straightens, his gaze shimmers with renewed purpose. Hinges creak as he opens his door to hop out. In a fluid motion, I'm dragged across the seat and scooped into his arms.

"Told you I'd be your first," he says while clutching me tight.

"Cocky cowboy," I quip.

But my pulse gives a giddy kick. This man is carrying me toward our happily ever after. Crisp air fills my lungs when I inhale deeply. The temperature is somewhere in the fifties, but the afternoon sun makes it feel warmer.

Water babbles in a trickle that reminds me of a white noise soundtrack. It's peaceful and soothing. My body goes lax in Colton's hold, trusting him to deliver me in one piece wherever we're going.

I'm too focused on our natural surroundings to notice what's directly in front of us. My oblivious bubble is popped when he sets me on my feet. A small building appears out of seemingly nowhere. Its rustic style resembles a farmhouse, but scaled way down.

"Is this…?" I stumble forward to peek in the curtained window. "Oh. My. Gosh. It's a she shed."

Colton unlocks the door and sweeps an arm inside. "Surprise."

The girliest squeal escapes me while I rush to enter the tiny space. What I assume started as a basic floor plan has been transformed into a cozy living space. It's decorated in shades of pink with neutral embellishments. A delicate aroma wafts from an automatic dispenser to welcome me.

This is meant to be a home not too far away from home. Just for a quick reprieve. Colton once again understood the assignment. That knowledge settles a comforting sensation over me.

I shuffle into the room for a closer look. My fingers drift along the sofa that's arranged to separate the sitting area from the kitchen. A basket of crochet supplies waits for me beside the coffee table that looks to be repurposed wooden crates. Three of the walls are covered in shiplap panels. The fourth—from one end to the other—has several firmly inlaid shelves.

That's where my attention is lured. On a ledge in the center, there's a collection of figurines. Even a single glance sparks recognition. Emotion stings my eyes, crashing over me in a weepy onslaught.

I whirl to where Colton is still standing in the doorway. His tattooed arms are stretched overhead in that effortlessly sexy pose. My mind taps out. There's a good chance drool is about to dribble down my chin. Damn, I'm a goner.

Humor gleams in his blue eyes. "Need something, baby girl?"

My vagina clenches at the suggestion in his voice. I blindly point at the couch. Colton's gaze shifts to a spot behind me. That triggers my memory and I gasp.

"You bought these"—my thumb jabs at the little statues—"at the markets in Germany."

He nods. "Whatever you touched or even showed a passing interest in. To remind you of our first trip together, before it went to shit."

The significance of that thoughtful gesture buckles my knees. I go down like a properly swooned lady. My fall is softened by the plush rug Colton chose. That reminds me of this entire place he created for me, as if the first wasn't enough.

Heavy footsteps pound in my ears. I blink at the unshed tears blurring the ceiling. Even that's pink.

My stare finds Colton's hovering over me. "I'm beginning to believe I don't deserve you."

He grunts and lowers himself to the floor, tugging me onto his lap. "Quit talking crazy."

"You started it," I blubber.

"Why are you crying?"

"Romantic orgasm." I gesture at my mess of feelings.

His lips hitch up on one side. "You love me."

"In a hopeless sort of sense," I sigh.

He brushes at a stray tear that escapes. "Welcome to the party."

My cheek nuzzles his palm. "Is this our date?"

"I had a picnic planned."

"Ohhhh, not again." I bat my lashes in a frantic flutter. "Do you smell that burning? It's my heart flutters working overtime. Have mercy, Stalker."

Colton's eyes go wide. "What do you need?"

"Those pierced nine inches you've been hoarding would be great."

Flames ignite his gaze into a panty-melting smolder. "Are you desperate for me?"

"Have I not been literally asking for it since"—I take a moment and pretend to count—"the flight to Europe?"

"I suppose we could postpone our date until after," he rasps.

My vigorous nod knocks into his dick. "You brought me here for a reason. It will be a celebration of our lovemaking."

"Are you mocking me?"

"No!" Outrage screams from my reply. "This moment is perfect. We can make it even more memorable."

"That'll mean you're mine. No going back."

My hand finds his, our fingers sliding together. "I'm ready for everything you want to give me. Strip off my Dirty Dicks top and get busy."

Colton chuckles, reaching for the knotted hem. "The sofa pulls out."

"But you better not."

In an instant, his expression flatlines. "There's something I need to tell you."

But I'm already shaking my head. "Whatever you have to say can wait. It won't change how I feel about you."

"I'm not so sure about that."

"Trust in me and the unbreakable attachment you inspired between us."

Colton's lips part, ready to argue. I fling upright and straddle him. He freezes at my unexpected shift in position. That works in my favor. With my palms cupping his face, I lean in and seal my mouth over his.

"Hey," I breathe into the kiss. "I love you, Colton. Forget the past. It doesn't matter."

Hesitation holds him hostage for a brief pause before he's surrendering to our pull. His fingers grab the bottom of both the shirt and dress I'm wearing, tugging the fabric over my head. Goose bumps spread over my skin and he's quick to smooth the shiver away. From there, we slowly peel away each other's layers until our bodies are bared.

Colton ropes his arms around my waist, palming my ass in the process. "Should we move to the couch?"

My hands anchor to his shoulders while I get myself situated astride him on the floor again. "I'm comfortable."

He groans when I drag my slick center along his studded shaft. "Won't hear me complain."

"Ribbed for my pleasure." My hips jerk at the foreign sensation.

Colton's chuckle puffs against the dip of my neck while I glide myself against the pierced ridges. "Just like that. Use me, Princess."

"Gladly," I whisper.

Our naked chests press flush, sharing the fire between us. A feverish need collects in my belly and he stokes the burn with a flex of his hips. My pussy slips along his cock in even strokes. I'm aroused and more than ready.

We stare at each other, allowing the meaning of this moment to sink in. He lifts an open palm and I align mine flat against it. His is much bigger, engulfing me like a protective shield. How symbolic.

His bottomless blue eyes with those few dark specks study me. "Are you sure?"

I nod, my forehead bumping his as I rise onto my knees. His pierced tip nudges my opening and I quiver. Our galloping hearts beat in harmony. Tingles spread from my core in eager anticipation. Just as I begin pushing him inside me, his grasp on my hips tightens.

"Bianca, wait."

My glare spits nails at him. "You must be joking."

"I can't have children."

CHAPTER TWENTY-SIX

Bianca stares at me, her jaw hanging slack. "You can't have children?"

"Well, I should probably rephrase that." My grasp on her suddenly feels fleeting. "I made sure I can't."

She absently lowers herself to perch on my thighs. "What does that mean?"

"I'm snipped."

A strangled noise squeaks out of her. "Holy shit, birth control. At least one of us is thinking about protection. Freaking dick-notized over here." She thumps her forehead. "I'm so out of practice."

Fury blazes in my chest and I make a decision right then to eliminate any other man she's been with. For now, I yank her against me. She's mine. Nobody else gets her like this ever again.

"I've got you covered, baby girl. That's not why I told you, but it serves a purpose regardless."

My cock is pissed—leaking from the tip and calling me a dick. I've been on edge for hours, which can push a man to his limit. The ache spreading from my balls tells me they're fifty shades of blue. But confessing the truth is more important than relieving the pressure.

Honestly, getting this secret off my chest is a release of its own. A slow exhale whistles through my lips and I relax against the wall holding me upright. The baggage saddled to me is heavy.

Bianca is quiet, but her thoughts are loud. "You don't want to have kids? Like never ever?"

"I didn't until I met you."

"But you'd already had the procedure," she mumbles.

An urgency rises inside me, reaching for her with both arms. "I'm going to get it reversed, but that's not a guarantee. If you decide we should try to have children, there's a chance we might have trouble getting pregnant. You deserve to know before committing to forever with me."

Her slow blinks confirm that this is a lot to process. "Why did you have a vasectomy?"

Darkness seeps into the corners of my vision. "It's not a secret that my father is a bad man. He tried his best to turn me bad too. When people didn't pay, he sent me to give them a warning. I was good at it too."

She doesn't take her eyes off me or look away. Bianca gazes at me with so much love and intensity that it's like she can see right into my soul. And for the first time, I'm not hiding it.

"Daddy Dearest thought I'd be his loyal enforcer indefinitely. Little did he realize, my spirit never completely broke.

That type of violence didn't sit well with me. Once I'd saved enough money, I left and never looked back."

"I'm really glad you did," she whispers.

Which urges me to go on. "I didn't have much of a childhood. No fun or games unless it served the crew. No warmth or affection either. My mom ran off when I was three, leaving me to become one of the men she hated. The world I was raised in trained me to be cold and detached. Those aren't behavioral traits I wanted forced onto me, but that was out of my control. Once I had the freedom to choose my own fate, I decided to sever the possibility of continuing my father's line."

Her eyes are glassy when I'm done. "Gosh, I can't imagine what you've been through."

My palms drift along her sides, still clutching tight. "Please don't try. It'll give you nightmares."

"And yet you're the sweetest man."

I grunt. "Don't lie."

"You're very sweet to me," she insists. "After I got past the stalking and abduction, I saw your true intentions. It's quite special to be loved so loudly."

That gives me pause. "Your dad said something similar to me."

"That means you should probably listen." Bianca recovers with a roll of her shoulders. "For the record, the thought of having kids isn't even on my radar."

"But it might be someday."

She shrugs. "And we'll deal with it then."

I eye her closely. "You're not upset?"

"Why would I be? That's a decision you made before we met. It was important to you. I respect that. We're a team now. Whatever challenges we face, we'll conquer them together."

I crush her against me. "Fuck, I love you."

"Love you too." Her fingers drift along the tattoo decorating my spine. "Guess we're both a bit crooked."

"That's not funny." But I'm fighting a grin.

"Eh, I was trying to lighten the mood. The fact you're a reformed bad boy is very sexy." She taps her chin. "Maybe that's why you love my explicit versions of torture."

I cup the back of her neck and haul her in for a punishing kiss. "Why are you so chill about this?"

She scoffs as if affronted. "I don't let anything stop me, right? That includes your snipped baby maker. You're stuck with me."

My forehead nudges hers. "What did I do to deserve you?"

"Do I need to count the ways?" Bianca gestures around the shed, stopping at the trinkets from Germany. "You've already done so much for me in a very short amount of time. If we're meant to have children, we'll have them. It's a worry for the future. As for right now, I'd appreciate you following through with the lovemaking."

Just for that entitled sass, I harness her hips in a secure hold over my cock and thrust hard. Bianca coughs out a gasp. Her nails dig into my arms, trying to get a grip. A satisfying throb pulses through me at finally feeling her snug pussy stretching around me. I'm barely halfway in, but pressure already cradles my balls. She's tight but wet. We'll go slow.

I bite her upturned jaw. "Too much?"

"Yes," she chokes.

My steely grip locks her in place. "But you're gonna take every inch like a spoiled brat."

"Uh-huh, I want it all."

"It's yours."

Determination crosses her face and she sinks lower onto my length. A shiver pebbles her skin, arrowing my focus to her breasts. I swoop down to suck a hardened nipple into my mouth. She pushes her chest at me, shoving my dick deeper in the process.

"Almost there," she breathes.

One hand unclamps from her waist to trail between her legs. Slippery arousal coats my fingers. She's fucking drenched for me. That squeezes my cock in a smug fist and I smirk around a mouthful of tit.

I glide my thumb to her clit, which jolts her against me. We snap together like two halves just waiting to be made whole. A simultaneous sigh escapes us as our desire is joined.

Her pussy clenches in greeting and I grunt at the friction. Warmth rushes under my skin to match the heat wafting off her. My cock jerks, most likely releasing a squirt of precum as a preview of what's to come.

Bianca wiggles to test the fullness. Her breath hitches at the sensation she discovers. "Ohhhhh, that Reverse Prince Albert should be crowned as king."

After a parting swipe, I unlatch from her nipple and lick a path to her collarbone. My thumb is still strumming her clit as she adjusts. A soft whimper dribbles from her parted lips, but she's smiling.

"Princess approved?"

"Yes," she breathes. "Riding bareback has a whole new meaning."

A noise of contentment from me is quick to agree. The hand not tucked into her sex roams along her side, drifting to support her upper back. While my mouth travels along her soft skin, I inhale lilac and unbridled passion.

Bianca's head tips back, giving me access to her throat. "Your pierced penis is incredible."

My lips stamp a grin into her neck. "Just for you, baby girl."

In a cautious motion, she glides up my length to the tip. She circles her pelvis and takes my full length back in. That kicks off a gentle tempo. With each rise and fall, the valve on my control weakens. My thumb strokes her clit faster to even the score.

She mewls and grinds into me. "Are you close?"

I nod against my better judgment. "Don't have a chance of lasting long after all that teasing."

"Still on edge?"

"Hangin' by a thread," I rasp.

Bianca flexes her inner muscles into a vise. "I was originally planning to keep you there. Stretch this until you begged for relief."

My teeth clack against the force of lust burning in my veins. "Never want you to stop."

"Mhmm," she purrs. "That's why we're going to race instead. Let's see who can get the other off first."

Her ass slams down to drive home her purpose. Our contact becomes electric, crackling need in a frantic jolt. I'm desperate to come, but not without her. My fingers work over her clit in rapid swipes. Bianca clings onto me and pumps her hips harder. Whenever our hips meet, I'm shoved closer to the tipping point. A glaze brightens her green depths when we lock eyes. Our bodies slap together like hoofbeats pounding toward the finish line. Tingles spread across my lower back in a warning. Her smile is blissed out, hinting she's almost there. It spurs my efforts to trigger her orgasm into a blur.

Just as my balls are drawing up, Bianca's pussy clamps me in a persuasive hold. I'm powerless to stop the surge from bursting free. My muscles seize while she cries out, quaking against me. Fuck, we find relief together. That allows me to surrender to the heat crashing over me.

Our combined pleasure heightens the climax, drawing it out for what feels like hours. Her spasms milk every drop from me. Affection hums from every movement as we regain clarity. I can't remember ever being this content. My chest presses flush against hers while the ripples fade.

Bianca's damp forehead caresses mine. "Damn, Stalker. If that's how you make love, sign me up for life."

I wrap her in a fierce hug. "You're not going anywhere."

Her nails drag through my sweaty hair. "Wasn't planning on it."

In a smooth upheaval, I flip her onto her back. My thighs keep hers spread and the tilted angle gives me a perfect view of her cunt. The combination of our cum is messy, but I've never seen a more glorious sight. It steals my breath for a moment.

"Ummm…" Bianca squirms under my invasive focus, squirting out a blob of our blended release.

I'm quick to scoop up the excess and push it back inside her. "Fuck, look at you."

She's gone still. Her wide stare is frozen on me. "What're you doing?"

"You ruined me all those years ago and we're finally even." I swipe through our cum again. "I'm appreciating the evidence."

"Oh, stop. You're too obsessed." But she's laughing.

My fingers smear through the slickness that's coating her. "I left a stain. You're never getting rid of me now."

"There's no going back," she agrees.

That calms my primal urges. "Are you sore?"

"Not yet."

I lower myself on top of her. "Again?"

She nods against me. "I've got nowhere else to be."

"Damn straight, Princess. This pussy is mine."

Bianca sneaks an arm between our pressed bodies to grasp my cock. "And this studded shaft is meant to bring me pleasure. Only me."

"That's right." Satisfaction rumbles from me. "Now put me where I belong."

Bianca uses her grip on my dick to steer me forward. The moment I thrust inside, we expel a mutual groan. It's one of the many sounds to signal the start of our forever.

CHAPTER TWENTY-SEVEN

"WORTH THE WAIT," I SIGH AND COLLAPSE FLAT ON my back. "Consider me sated."

The prediction that this man fucks like a maniac on a mission was spot on.

After the second round, Colton swept me off the floor and brought me outside. We screwed against the side of the shed. The truck was next. After that, he spread a blanket on the ground and shagged me like a retro rug.

My muscles are pleasantly tender as I sprawl out right where he laid me. I can barely lift my arm to cup his stubbled jaw. "Love you, Stalker."

"Fuck, I love you." Colton presses kisses over most of my face before rolling to the side.

His woodsy scent lingers, most likely imbedded into my pores. A slow inhale grants me a lungful of him and our combined essence. It's the smell of satisfaction.

I squint up at the fluffy clouds while lounging like a

thoroughly pounded fence post. The sun is still high in the sky, but definitely tipping toward the west. It'd be safe to estimate we've been at it for hours.

"I lost count, but you made me come more than I thought was possible for one afternoon." My grumpy jailer is a giver and I'm here for it.

He smirks. "Eleven times. You're welcome."

"Why am I not surprised you kept track?" I tap his damp chest. "How many for you?"

"Four."

"Is that a record?"

Colton grunts. "By a long shot."

"Could you go again?"

The pause that follows is thicker than his dick. "I need a few minutes."

"The fiend has met his match," I sigh.

"And he released all his pent-up energy."

"Not to mention semen." I cringe while pressing my legs together.

He threads our fingers together and squeezes gently. "Don't move."

"Not sure I could if I tried." I remain immobile while he props himself onto an elbow. "You wrecked me."

Blue eyes flicker into flames and rove over my naked-ness. "That was the plan."

And Colton Keller is nothing if not determined to make me his in every conceivable way.

That's precisely why I stay put as demanded while he ventures off to who knows where. My thoughts drift in what remains of my afterglow. It still seems strange how quickly our relationship shifted. I went from trying to avoid him by any means necessary to wanting him beside me at all times. The latter is much more pleasurable. Not a single regret rises either.

But the pop of a cork shatters the quiet contemplation.

I struggle to sit up and see Colton pouring champagne into two flutes. "Oh, my. You know how to treat a lady."

"I'm going to spoil you rotten, Princess." He reclaims his spot beside me.

"Already have." I accept the glass he extends to me, giggling when the bubbles tickle my nose. "What are we drinking to?"

"Us." His gaze burns into mine.

"Mhmm, our first date is a banger so far. That sex marathon deserves to be celebrated."

We clink in unison. Colton downs his contents in a single gulp. I'm a bit more reserved in my consumption, sipping on it while watching him exchange the empty glass for something else. An oversized pillow is wedged underneath my back. The softness is very inviting and distracting.

"May I?" There's suddenly a wet cloth suspended in midair over my vagina.

I choke on my champagne. "Umm…"

"Relax and let me take care of you."

Well, when he puts it that way. I recline against the pillow and spread my legs in invitation. He proceeds to clean me, just a gentle swipe at first. It's warm but my sensitive flesh has been put through the ringer. A hiss scrapes up my throat.

Colton's motions halt immediately. "Too much?"

"Just sore." I guzzle more bubbly. "Out of practice, remember?"

He drops a kiss to my bent knee. "That won't be a problem ever again."

I sigh in agreement. "You've broken me in like a docile filly."

"Hardly." But there's a smile in his voice.

Once I'm wiped down, Colton tosses the rag aside. A chill settles over me in the absence of the heat. I shiver, just noticing the sweat drying on my body. He immediately drapes a long-sleeve flannel over my shoulders to chase off the cold.

Warmth swaddles me and I exhale. The large size hangs off my smaller frame. Based on the rumble coming off Colton, this must be his shirt. It's cozy and toasty and doused in his cologne. I never want to take it off.

"Didn't think you could get any hotter, but you in my clothes is the ultimate fantasy."

I bury my nose in the soft fabric. "Yeah?"

"I'm even willing to cover your naked curves to get the full impact." He finishes snapping the front shut. "Damn, you're sexy."

"Thank you. For everything." I burrow deeper into the bundle of comfort. Safety and contentment swaddle me as well.

But then he whips out one of my favorite snacks. "Hungry?"

My jaw drops at the same time my stomach growls. "I could eat."

Colton opens the bag of Ruffles and container of Top the Tater. With the practiced precision of a lifelong Minnesotan, he dips a chip to coat it with the ideal amount of seasoned sour cream. My mouth waters as he holds the goodness aloft to feed me.

I moan while chewing. "Damn, that hits the spot. You're very prepared."

"To handle your needs," he finishes.

Instinct has me parting my lips to accept another dipped chip. "My stalker boyfriend is such a planner."

Colton tips his head, watching me devour the food. "Boyfriend, huh?"

"Isn't that what you are?" I shrug into the bulk of my borrowed shirt.

"It'll do for now."

I snag the Ruffles and serve him a perfect bite. He accepts it without hesitation, but I don't miss the cringe tightening his features. It reminds me of the elaborate breakfast he made to solely appease my tastes.

"What's your favorite thing to eat?"

"Your pussy." His gaze dips between my legs as if searching for his next meal.

I nudge his shoulder. "Real food, Stalker."

The hunger leeches out of his expression. "Protein."

Which this snack most certainly isn't. "More for me."

"It's all for you, Princess."

My bottom lip juts out. "But I want to spoil you too."

"Kiss me."

I do instantly. My mouth smiles against his. When I pull away, my grin is left behind on him.

"Love me," he murmurs.

My hand reaches for his and rests it over my heart. The wild thump greets his touch. I'd never felt such a giddy hitch in my pulse until him.

He must sense it too. His posture is relaxed as he leans into my personal space. There's a flicker of unease in his eyes when he stares deep into mine.

"Stay with me."

My nose brushes against his. "I'm not going anywhere."

His exhale blows a tangled section of my hair. "You want to go back to Cloverleaf Meadows."

Confusion works my mouth soundlessly for a few beats. "Are you worried it isn't safe?"

"That's not the issue." His gaze abandons mine, roaming across the open field surrounding us. "I'd foolishly hoped you'd think of this as your home."

"Keller's Keep is our home," I insist. "Our secret hideout. But Benson Farmstead is still my home too."

"Right." The happiness that has been building inside him instantly snuffs out.

"What is it?"

"I feel like you're actually mine here. In Cloverleaf Meadows, I have to share you." That rare vulnerable edge returns to his voice, slicing me where it hurts.

"Hey." I brush the crumbs from my hands and cup his face. "You're mine, Colton Keller. I'll shout it from the middle of Main Street if you'd like."

His cheeks get pink and I bite back a whimper. "You'd publicly claim me?"

"Haven't I already?"

The steely clench of his jaw suggests I didn't do a good enough job of it. "You're never open about your relationships. I don't want to make you uncomfortable."

"My relationships?" I snort. "There haven't been any."

His stare penetrates mine again, peeling at the defensive layers that trap secrets. "Why is that?"

"Umm…" It's a question I've often asked myself, but the answer is finally clear. "Nobody was good enough until you swooped in and snatched me. Normal guys can't compete with this." A sweep of my arm motions from the custom she shed to the sprawling acres we're parked on, pausing at his truck that's named after my eye color, and ending on our celebration picnic. "I needed an obsessed, morally gray bodyguard armed to protect me. One who's fluent in the arts of abduction and stalking. He also must be extremely thoughtful and pierced for my pleasure. Oh, and taught himself how to ride a horse. You know, the full package. It's a rare find."

A pleased noise escapes him. "When you put it that way, it sounds like I was delivered from your wish list directly to your doorstep."

"It's beginning to seem that way, hmm?" I press a soft kiss to his lips. "We're in this together. It doesn't matter where we are."

"There's nothing to worry about." The words might be more for him than me.

But it reminds me of why he stashed me out here in the first place. "What's the latest with your father?"

Colton's features lose any semblance of joy. "He's in the hospital."

My chest tightens. "Do you want to see him?"

"No." The answer is harsh and final.

"I don't blame you after what you shared earlier." Saliva sticks in my throat like glue. "And that seemed like a censored version."

A sharp dip of his chin is confirmation. "Which is why there isn't a single part of me that wants to see him."

"Then you won't. We'll stay far away from that part of town."

"We?"

"Are you planning to ditch me?"

The fire in his eyes is answer enough. "I love that you're counting us as a cohesive unit that doesn't split."

My snort is very eloquent. "It's cute that you pretend it hasn't been this way for years. You'd be tracking my movements with or without my permission. I'm just finally catching on."

"And that doesn't bother you?"

"Meh." I take another leisurely glance at our slice of paradise. "It's serving me well."

Before he can answer, a recognizable jingling enters our solitude. It gets louder as our scent is detected. Spud appears at the top of the hill, running full speed toward us.

"Awww, he found us."

Colton puffs up with pride. "Trained him well."

Our dog collides into us in a flurry of sloppy kisses and tail whips.

"Did Daddy let you out? I don't even know where the button is." My sing-song tone makes me sound just as clueless.

"Daddy takes care of everything, but he'll show Mommy if she asks."

"Nooooo!" I clap my hands over my ears. "You can't do the baby voice!"

Which only encourages him. "Did you hear that,

Spuddy Bud? I think Mommy is about to let me eat her for dinner. You better go chase a squirrel."

My feet kick to pair with my giggles. "Stop, please. That's too adorable. I can't have another romantic orgasm this soon."

His chuckle bumps our bodies together. "Wanna bet?"

I'm already shaking my head vehemently. "Absolutely not. I don't stand a chance."

"What if I told you that I bought us Halloween costumes for the Haunted Harvest Haze?"

My upturned palm meets my forehead. "That'll do it."

Colton catches me when I slump against him. "You're the reason my past has a purpose. I'm trained to protect you and the future we're building."

"That puts a positive spin on it."

"Just like you do for me, Princess." His lips dust my forehead, branding me with his declaration. "You're my bright side."

CHAPTER TWENTY-EIGHT

Cotton

TWO DAYS LATER, WE ARRIVE IN CLOVERLEAF Meadows with a trailer full of horses and irrational desire thrumming between us. The latter might be one-sided. Bianca appears content in her bubble of chaos as I test every traffic law along the way. I'm ravenous for her. Constantly.

My palm squeezes her thigh for the tenth time in as many minutes. She doesn't stop crocheting while smiling over at me. Whatever she's making has her full attention until we're pulling into Benson Farmstead.

It doesn't take long for us to unload the horses and detach the trailer. Spud makes friends with his numerous siblings. Their chorus of barks trail us around the compound as we search for Bianca's family.

"Guess they're busy," she sighs.

My eyes cast around the quiet stables. "It's the middle of the workday."

Her gaze narrows on me. "Are you still getting paid to watch me?"

"I don't prefer to think about my job like that."

Bianca leans close. "Now that we're doing it? Mhmm, seems like a Human Resources nightmare."

"My position is head of security for the company. It's very broad and includes many duties. I just happen to spend most of my hours stuck to your ass like those jeans."

She spanks herself. "Can't say I blame you. And for the record, I'm not complaining. Let's go."

"Where to?" But I'm already following her to Fern.

"Camp Cloverleaf."

That stops me short. "No."

She whirls like a ballerina, but her glare belongs in a cage match. "Yes."

"It's not safe," I argue.

Her scoff calls me an idiot. "Seriously, Stalker? It's a therapeutic establishment for children. Do you honestly think someone is going to attack me while I'm surrounded by families?"

"Already happened."

I'd always considered it a low threat level until her last shift. The woman that confronted her in the barn remains a mystery, which marks the spot as dangerous. That's one reason I made the decision to whisk her away to the other house. Unfortunately, Bianca doesn't share the same concern.

Her hands park on her hips. "I love you, but I'm not a pushover. Either take me or I'll go alone."

That's how I find myself scouring the outdoor portion of the camp fifteen minutes later. My focus rakes over crowded paths and tables that are set between the corrals.

There are too many people. Any number of them could be on my father's payroll. This heavy sense of dread sits in my stomach like a cinderblock. It overshadows the insatiable urge to be buried in her pussy.

"Relax. It's just for a quick visit," Bianca assures me.

Which turns into an hour faster than my continuous scan of the area can track. She fusses over every kid and animal she comes across. We don't make it a single step without her finding a reason to stop. It's obvious she's adored by this community, but it only takes one individual to change that.

Bianca slides her hand into mine, which eases an ounce of the pressure off my chest. "Are you okay?"

"I will be once we leave."

Her compassion melts into a frown. "What happened to looking on the bright side?"

My stoic mask doesn't slip. "That's easier to do when we're in a secure location."

She studies my expression. "You haven't smiled since we arrived back in town."

"Those are few, far between, and reserved for you during happy circumstances." Which doesn't describe this congested setting.

Her mouth stoops lower. "Did your father get released from the hospital?"

"Not that I know of."

"Then what are you so worried about?"

"He's still alive," I deadpan. "That makes me uneasy."

"I suppose that's… fair. Do you think he's that determined to get at you?"

My gut tightens. "I'm not sure what he's capable of in his condition. The promise of death might make him desperate."

"What does he want from you?"

That's the million-dollar question. "At this point, it's tough to say. Respect? Loyalty? Some bizarre, misguided sense of passing the torch?"

She snorts. "He's delulu."

"Which is what scares me."

"We'll deal with whatever he tries to toss at us. But until then, try to relax. Nothing is amiss," she insists.

Another glance across the picturesque grounds proves her words. It's quiet and peaceful. There aren't any obvious suspects lurking in the shadows under the colorful trees. Nobody is watching us.

"Oh, look. It's the happy couple."

I turn to the masculine voice, pushing Bianca behind me. My fight reflexes calm at the sight of Byron and his daughter approaching. Ronnie rushes straight at Bianca, cinching her legs in a fierce hug. There's a desperation in the child's grip.

"Have you seen my new mommy?"

Bianca blinks at the little girl before lifting her gaze to her cousin. "Are you seeing someone?"

"Uh, no." Byron scrubs the back of his neck. "She's talking about the redhead in leather."

"My new mommy is a superhero," Ronnie breathes.

Her father looks pained. "What have I said about calling her that?"

His daughter huffs. "She's gonna love me once I find her. It's the longest game of hide and seek ever."

Byron looks to us for help. "I'm not sure what to do. Ronnie has built this woman up to be Taylor Swift, but I'm no Travis Kelce."

Bianca rolls her lips between her teeth to stifle a laugh. "Mhmm, I can see that. No offense, cuz." Her gaze returns to Ronnie. "Superheroes are really busy fighting crime. If that woman we saw is a superhero, you might not see her for a long while. Especially if she's locked up. Fingers crossed."

The little girl gasps. "You think she's captured in a super tall tower? What if she's cursed and sleeping? Or chained to dragons that breathe fire?"

I rock on my heels, trying to follow the swerve in storyline. But I'm not one to judge.

"We can only hope she's locked up tight," Bianca mumbles. She's holding a mean—and rightful—grudge.

"Daddy!" Ronnie appears horrified as tears collect in her eyes. "You gotta save her!"

Byron pinches the bridge of his nose. "Thanks a lot, Bee."

"You're welcome. My bill will be in the mail." Bianca tips toward her cousin and whispers, "But seriously, maybe mention this strange attachment to the therapists here. It's not a good one for her to have. They might have some advice."

"She's met with every single specialist and hasn't clicked with one. I've reached out to countless other clinics. The waitlists for kids' mental health services are months long. There's a counselor at school, but the sessions with her are very minimal."

Bianca winces. "Is there anything I can do?"

"Hunt down this enchantress and get her to undo the spell. I've been tangled in trouble since she vanished without a trace."

Brooding silence is my preferred status unless in the comfort of my inner circle, but this situation calls for reinforcements. "If she's affiliated with my father, you don't want her anywhere near you. Just forget about her."

Ronnie's bottom lip wobbles. "But I'm gonna love her forever."

Her dad exhales. The sound is weary to match the dark circles under his eyes. "You don't even know her name, cupcake."

"I don't care!" And then she runs away.

Byron immediately follows, calling her name. Two staff members give chase as well. The three adults catch up to the little girl at the playground.

"Breaks my heart." Bianca is rubbing her chest. "I think Byron needs help with her."

"Do you wanna go over there?" My skills in the child department are zero, but I'll tag along regardless.

"No, I mean in general. It's gotten more challenging as Ronnie gets older. He might be struggling to adapt to her recent changes in attitude."

I scratch at my stubble. "Sounds slightly familiar in a completely different scenario if the roles were reversed."

She pins me with a narrowed stare. "What're you trying to say?"

"Gotcha." I lasso an arm around her waist and crush her to me.

"In spite of your outrageous demands."

My palm cups her cheek. "See? You get it."

"That was a stretch."

"Wasn't sure what else to say." The heat rising in my face could be caused by the wind. "Empathy doesn't exist where I come from."

She bumps her forehead on my chest. "Gosh, I'm so

sorry. You're listening to me prattle on about small problems when you were raised in horrific conditions."

"Princess," I chide and her gaze lifts to mine. "Don't apologize. That's not what I need from you. Just be patient with me in these types of situations where you're expecting sensitivity."

Her caring gaze assesses mine. "Who's been taking care of you this whole time?"

"Doesn't matter. I ended up exactly where I wanted to be." My shrug pretends to be casual and carefree.

Bianca loops her arms around my shoulders. "Allow me to fill the position."

"It's yours whether you want it or not," I chuckle softly.

"You're a great man, Colton Keller."

Warmth travels through my veins, bending me to her every whim. "And Byron seems like a good dad. Better than most. And if he needs support, your family won't hesitate to stand beside him."

She nods, a soft smile returning to her beautiful features. "We stick together."

"It's incredible to watch."

Her brows pucker at my solemn tone. "You're one of us, Stalker. My dad and Brody have made that clear for years."

I tug her tighter against me. "What about you?"

Bianca laughs, peppering kisses along my jaw. "I took more convincing, but I'm sold."

That odd, uplifting sensation spreads through me when she peers up at me. It's as if I truly belong. "Are we done here?"

She bites her bottom lip. "Is there somewhere else you need to be?"

"Inside you," I murmur against her mouth.

Her grin caresses mine. "What a coincidence. That's exactly where I want you."

"We're very compatible."

Bianca threads her fingers through mine, tugging us toward the exit. "Mhmm, and you don't think you're in touch with other people's emotions."

"Just yours, baby girl."

We're in a crowded area full of recognizable gossips, but she doesn't hesitate to initiate another public display. I bask in her joy when she glues herself to my side. Mutual affection pulses between us. It's a connection I didn't understand until meeting Bianca.

My much taller height towers over hers, but I bend to kiss her forehead. "I know what love feels like because of you."

CHAPTER TWENTY-NINE

Bianca

WAKE EARLY THE NEXT MORNING—FULL OF ENERGY and anticipation. A sideways glance confirms that Colton is still asleep. It's rare to see him at rest. After rolling to my side, I watch him in the muted sunlight streaking through the curtains.

A slow smile curls my lips as his chest rises and falls at a lazy pace. My extremely considerate boyfriend is constantly surprising me with thoughtful gestures. I recently discovered an important date he's been keeping a secret and I'm ready to celebrate it.

In a sly motion, I duck under the blanket and kneel between Colton's spread thighs. It's dark but my eyes are on the prize. My fingers peel his boxer briefs down until his pierced penis is set free. He's already hard, which makes my job easier.

A salty burst of precum greets me on the first lick. I swirl my tongue around his flared crown that's bejeweled like the king he is. His cock jerks and he groans, but that's the extent of his response. Maybe he's dreaming about me. That has me grinning on the initial descent.

My mouth stretches around his length as I retreat and swallow him to the root again. I wrap my fingers around his base while setting a steady rhythm. Other than a few strangled sounds, Colton doesn't stir. For a guy who's constantly alert and aware of his surroundings, he sleeps like a statue. It takes me fondling his balls to rouse him. His body turns into stone as awareness surfaces.

"Princess?" His groggy voice is extra deep.

I spit out his dick and rip the covers off us. "Were you expecting someone else?"

A drowsy smirk humors my attitude. From hooded eyes, he feasts on the sight of me in a black lace bra and matching thong. "Nah, just love it when you're feisty."

My grip on his dick tightens, earning me a grunt. "Happy birthday."

He goes still. "How'd you find out?"

"Your driver's license." My bland tone suggests he should thump his forehead.

"Wasn't keepin' it from you. Nobody has ever cared enough to ask."

For probably the hundredth time, I have the urge to smack his father with a riding crop. "That's painful history, Stalker. We're moving forward. Birthdays matter from now on. Any other occasion you want to celebrate does too."

The cocky smirk returns as he tucks his arms behind his head. "Is this my present?"

"One of them."

"Must've been on the nice list this year."

I wag a finger that's not idly stroking his cock. "This is the day before Halloween. Not Christmas."

Colton thrusts into my grip. "Trick or treat, baby girl?"

"That's up to you. Where do you want to come?"

His focus scatters like a kid in a candy store.

I decide to take it easy on him. After ditching my bra, I squeeze my boobs between my arms. "Tits?"

His breathing accelerates as a practiced shimmy removes my thong.

My hips tilt forward. "Pussy?"

There's a demanding throb in his dick. But I'm not done.

A smack from my lips is next. "Mouth?"

Colton's gaze shifts rapidly between the choices.

Just for fun, I end on a seductive wiggle. "Or maybe…?"

He's practically drooling as I trail off on the last option. "Or what?"

"I'm willing to consider anal, birthday boy."

His eyes bulge. "Your father is somewhere in this massive house."

"Which is why I'm very proud of you for sneaking in here last night. I can't believe he tried to separate us." My plans almost needed an overhaul, but Colton couldn't stay away.

"I just needed to sleep with you in my arms," he murmurs. "It didn't go any further."

"Until now," I purr. "You're about to hit a home run. Maybe even slide into the back door."

He shakes his head. "If I'm going to take your ass, I want you to be comfortable. That includes screaming your pleasure for me."

"Rain check on that." I roll my wrist, stroking him from

root to tip. "What'll it be, Cowboy? Should I finish blowing your birthday candle?"

A tremor flexes his muscles. "I'm conflicted."

"Too many choices?"

"This is your father's house," he reiterates.

I glower while continuing to pump his shaft. Colton's respect for my dad under his roof is admirable, but I'm a big girl and have my own wing in this mansion. I also have every intention of gifting him an orgasm one way or another.

"Maybe this will sweeten the deal." I grab the sealed container on the nightstand and open the lid. "It's a little early for cake, but I know how much you love breakfast in bed."

His gaze tracks my movements as I paint my breasts in frosting. It's creamy and thick, forming a tempting layer. I lick the excess off my fingers and moan. The sugar mixes with his salty flavor lingering on my tongue.

"Want a taste?" After scooting forward on my knees, I thrust my chest at him in invitation.

Colton gulps, but makes no move to feast on me.

Realization rises like the sun. "Oh, gosh. You don't like chocolate."

His wince confirms my suspicion. "I haven't had it since I was a kid."

"How is that possible?"

"It wasn't served to me like this."

"Does that mean—?"

I don't get to finish the question before he's lunging upright and latching onto my nipple. His tongue swipes out, lapping at the frosting in greedy strokes. He palms my ass while I cradle the back of his head. In a joint effort, we adjust our position to align his cock with my entrance. A harsh thrust pushes him deep, stretching my inner muscles in a delicious ache.

"Good choice, Stalker."

Colton grunts against my cleavage. He's about halfway done cleaning off the frosting. I consider slathering more on, but then he shoves the rest of his length inside my pussy. The friction from his Jacob's Ladder strikes just right. Need already coils tight in my core after I complete two quick plunges. A loud whimper spills from my parted lips, ready to demand more.

"Fuck," he mutters. "You're too irresistible."

I'm hoisted into his arms on the next thrust. It's incredibly sexy how easily he holds my weight. After kicking off his boxers, he carries me to the bathroom. We're still connected and don't break stride. Not even when he reaches into the shower to turn on the spray.

I kiss the scruffy column of his throat. "Are you calling me dirty?"

"More like loud." A swift kick to the door slams it shut. "Now you're free to holler my name."

My back meets the cold tile as warm water rains down on us. Colton's tempo turns frantic, slapping our wet skin together. It's the sound of a rough pounding and I'm gladly taking it.

We work in tandem to chase relief. He pumps his hips while I clamp my inner muscles to the same beat. Our bodies are already in harmony, knowing exactly what buttons to push. Steam billows around us to create an intimate shield. It's just us. Forever.

A slippery finger traces along the crack of my ass. "Still interested?"

I chew on my inner cheek while rocking against the slight tease. He's toyed with me back there before. It felt good. Great even. That's why I find myself nodding along to the fast pace he's set.

But Colton is gentle as his digit breaches my bottom. Pressure is quick to accompany the foreign sensation. Between his studded shaft and this new fullness, I'm barreling toward an explosive climax.

Our combined passion echoes in the small space. My labored breaths puff against his cheek. He buries his face in the crook of my craned neck. Abrasive stubble sends prickles across my skin, heightening the stimulation. A purposeful arch of my hips sends him deeper in both holes. I tremble from the impact.

"Damn, Princess. I can feel us." He swivels his finger, pushing against the thin barrier between my ass and vagina. "You take me so well."

When he rubs that sensitive spot, stars burst in my vision. I don't even see the release coming. Pleasure sweeps in and takes control. Every part of me is throbbing to a feverish pulse. It's solid and comforting and causes me to babble incoherently.

Colton jerks against me, stumbling in rhythm. The intensity of my orgasm must trigger his. After a final thrust, he bellows and stills. Small tremors ripple through him. Warmth floods me from the inside out. It's overwhelming but soothing.

There's a buzzing in my ears as I regain possession of my faculties. Colton is slumped forward, caging me against the wall. Our harsh breathing is drowned out by the stream. I slide my eyes shut and float.

Seconds or minutes pass before he straightens. A slow blink reunites our gazes. Matching grins soon follow.

Colton rests his forehead on mine. "Have I told you I love you?"

"Not yet this morning," I tease. "Happy birthday."

His lips caress mine. "Thanks to you, this will be the first one worth remembering."

CHAPTER THIRTY

Cotton

AFTER WE RINSE OFF AND GET DRESSED, BIANCA TUGS me downstairs for whatever she's planned next. If it's anything like her first surprise, I'm in for a treat. My dick twitches in my jeans. Damn thing is never satisfied.

Which is a direct extension of my obsession for this woman. She pulls me around a corner and I willingly follow like a trained pet. Another hurried yank from her makes me wince. The shirt I chose is the softest I own, but it's still agitating my skin.

Bianca glances at me. "Are you sad?"

I force my expression into a neutral mask. "This is my excited face. It's rusty."

Her snort calls bullshit. "We can't stay in my room all day, Stalker. I'll do you dirty again soon."

My cock gives another giddy throb. Meanwhile, there's an irritation blazing across my chest that won't be concealed for much longer. My face is flushed and I'm starting to get hot. That can be easily written off as a lingering effect from the shower. Abnormal bumps appearing on my body are harder to explain. It's a miracle she hasn't noticed yet. The burn is beginning to creep higher without remorse. Too bad turtlenecks aren't my style.

Brody is in the kitchen when we enter. My friend barely looks up from whatever he's reading on his iPad. I'm about to exhale the breath burning in my lungs when his eyes flick over to me.

"What's wrong with you?"

"Fuck off," I grunt. Now isn't the time for pleasantries.

Bianca agrees and swats his arm. "Don't be an ass. It's his birthday."

Brody studies me like a problem to solve. "Did you eat chocolate?"

Heat blisters my skin in confirmation, but I don't verbally reply.

The peppy party planner scoffs at her brother. "Yes, I let him have dessert for breakfast. His protein diet will survive. It was just a little bit."

He huffs right back at her. "That's more than enough to cause a reaction. Right, Colt?"

Bianca whirls to face me. Her flawless beauty is scrunched in scrutiny as she gives me a slow once-over. My hand lifts to cover the evidence she doesn't know to look for. The hives are peeking out of my collar at this point.

Sunlight from the nearest window glints off her dark hair as she comes up empty. "What's he talking about?"

Words fail me. My tongue might be swelling, but that's unrelated to the chocolate. I don't want to disappoint her, which is how I got myself into this itchy mess.

"He's allergic," Brody drawls to burst my discretion.

Bianca slaps her palms to her cheeks. "Holy shit! I'm taking you to the hospital."

"No," I bark.

She barely blinks at my harsh retort. "Just let me find my keys."

My gentle grip hooks her elbow before she starts the search for her purse. "I'm fine."

Her gaze is frantic when it collides with mine. "How can you say that? You're having an allergic reaction!"

"It's just a rash," I pacify. "More of a nuisance than anything. My throat doesn't close or anything."

The tight pucker of her lips isn't convinced. "Let me see."

Hesitation turns my muscles into lead. "I'd rather not show you."

Bianca's sharp intelligence zeroes in on the palm still resting on my neck. She circles my wrist and plucks off the makeshift bandage. Without even looking, I know the exposed skin is red and bumpy. Her horrified gasp confirms it.

Tears flood her eyes, gutting me with a dull knife. "You're not fine."

"This is just temporary. It'll clear up by tomorrow."

"How far does it spread?"

My jaw clamps shut, grinding the truth into dust.

Her watery gaze narrows and she yanks my shirt up. Another strangled noise rips from her. "What the fuck, Colton? It's all over!

"Barely a flesh wound," I mutter.

But her stricken expression pinches tighter. "Why did you let me feed you chocolate?"

"Is that a serious question?"

"But you're suffering."

I grip her chin in a gentle hold, tilting until our lips brush. "Haven't you learned by now? I'll do anything for you."

A red hue flushes her face to match mine. "Still should've stopped me."

I chuckle, but it lacks humor. "Just for the record, I'd slurp chocolate off your tits even if it killed me."

Brody gags. "There goes my morning."

We don't acknowledge his exit from the kitchen. Bianca is too focused on my condition. A stray droplet trickles down her cheek and I thumb it away. The sight of her misplaced guilt is twenty times worse than the allergic reaction.

"Please don't cry," I rasp.

But another tear escapes. "I did this to you."

"No, I did this to myself. It was my choice. I'd make the same one in a heartbeat."

"That's harmful for your health," she scolds.

Real laughter spews from my throat. "Good one, baby girl. Love is what's keepin' me alive. If I have to suffer a rash to make you smile, it's a small price to pay."

Her bottom lip wobbles. "I don't deserve you."

A reflexive motion drags her against my chest. The close contact singes my flesh, but the desperation to comfort her takes precedence. It's a pain I'll gladly endure just to hold her.

Bianca must feel the flames wafting from my upper body. Delicate fingers peel the cotton from my burning skin with the upmost care. I can't stifle a hiss.

"Sorry," she whimpers while tugging the fabric over my head. "You're burning up."

"Part of the reaction."

Her palm shakes on the way to covering her gaping mouth. "Is there medication you can take?"

I shrug. "When this happened before, ice and aloe vera did the trick."

She's already rushing toward the freezer, dumping cubes into a bowl. Her free hand grabs a wrapped gift from the table before snatching a green bottle from the cabinet. A jerk of her chin suggests I haul ass to the front door.

My feet remain firmly planted. "Let me help you carry stuff."

Bianca recovers from her upset. The concern is replaced with a scowl as if I personally offended her bubble of chaos. "Outside, Stalker."

I'm nothing if not willing to fulfill her desires. We step onto the porch between the two stone pillars that stretch to the roof. Benson Farmstead is a work of rustic art. My gaze appreciates the sprawling view of sun-dappled pastures and fallen leaves. Spud is playing tag with the other dogs while I'm herded to an oversized deck chair. The cushion cradles my ass, which thankfully isn't inflicted with this awful itching. It's too quiet as I stare at the pups across the manicured lawn. A glance at Bianca finds her frozen and gawking at my back.

My smirk is rewarded with a glare. "How's it look?"

"Like you were attacked by a hive of rabid bees."

"Do bees contract rabies?"

She dumps the contents from her arms onto the lounger beside me. "Not the point."

"Just tryin' to make conversation."

"We can talk about how I ruined your birthday," she mutters.

"Princess," I chide. "That's the opposite of what you did."

Her eyes roll. "Let me find you a mirror and see what you think."

"C'mere." I tug her in front of me, caging her curves between my splayed thighs. "Believe it or not, just celebrating the fact that it's my birthday is more than anyone has done for me since I can remember."

Her slim shoulders hunch. "But I wanted it to be special."

"Trust me when I tell you that it is. We'll never forget the day I had an allergic reaction after licking chocolate off your breasts."

Bianca stifles a laugh between her pressed lips. "I suppose. Are you able to open your present?"

As if she even needs to ask. I've been staring longingly at the wrapped box since she set it down next to us. Birthdays weren't acknowledged growing up. Christmas was a date to earn our keep by stealing from others. We never received a gift. That means I'd pop every blister on my palms to see what she got me.

I tear through the paper slowly, wanting to savor the moment. Bianca is jittery as I take my time. When I lift the lid, all the air whooshes from my lungs. Anything my wildest dreams dare to conjure can never compete with this.

The agony stabbing into my flesh is instantly forgotten. My fingers tremble as I unfold the crocheted blanket. It spills over in a woolly cascade. The size is massive—big enough to fit two of me.

There's a quake in my voice when I ask, "Did you make this?"

Bianca quirks a brow. "Is that a serious question?"

I'd laugh at her regurgitating my earlier quip, but I'm too emotional. My vision is blurry. The sting at the bridge of my nose is foreign and uncomfortable. A lump expands in my throat until it's hard to swallow.

"Incredible," I manage to croak.

"Oh, no. Don't you dare." She fans my eyes. "You cannot cry."

I sniff in vain, mostly for her benefit. "Can't help it. This is the nicest thing anyone has ever done for me."

"Don't let my brother hear you say that."

"He'll get over it." I fondle the soft texture that's priceless. "I'll cherish this forever, Princess."

Bianca kisses my quivering lips. "The color is for your eyes. A blue that sparkles if you're willing to look close enough. There are a few dark flecks that speak of your past, but the light inside you conquered it. That goodness stretches far and wide like the ocean. The depths are bottomless but safe. I feel protected in those turbulent waters."

Fuck. I choke on a sob. Only this woman can bring me to tears.

The fight for composure is a battle I've never fought, but I come out victorious. "Is that how you see me?"

She nods. "You're always there when I need you. Reliable. Steady. Endless."

Fire reignites in my eyes. "Is this real?"

"Yes, my love. My stalker," she blubbers and dips to press our foreheads together.

"Love you," I whisper into her mouth. "Ruining me all over again."

"Ditto," she sighs. "Okay, you need relief." Before my dick can perk up, she grabs the aloe vera. Two squirts fill her palm with a green blob. I suck in a breath when the cooling sensation touches my chest.

Her glistening eyes search mine as she rubs my shoulders. "Okay?"

"Perfection," I groan.

"When I planned to spoil you, this wasn't what I had in mind."

Another low sound slips from my parted lips. "I'm not complaining."

"Are you enjoying this?" Bianca spreads the aloe across my chest.

I shudder under her caress. "Your hands on me are a gift I'm grateful to receive."

"Seems you're easy to please too."

My head hangs forward, totally lax. "Did you actually have an agenda for today?"

"Mhmm," she hums while massaging my back. "After an actual breakfast, I thought we could stroll along Main Street. I wanted to show off my first boyfriend to the masses. Spread the news like wildfire. After that, we would've swung by the fairgrounds. The food trucks for Haunted Harvest Haze are already lined up. One of them serves a meat tornado. If that doesn't satisfy your protein diet, I'm not sure what will."

"Your pussy," I mumble as she slathers me in another cool layer of goo.

"Nope, you're cut off."

I straighten into a ramrod post. "Excuse you?"

Her pert nose tips skyward. "Only rest and relaxation until you recover."

My palms roam the long length of her legs, gripping tight when I reach her ass. "I beg to differ."

"Oh," she laughs. "You'll be begging all right."

"Tell me more," I rumble.

"You're gonna sit here in the shade like a pampered king while I go ride my horses."

"Do I get to watch?"

"If you behave."

"Will you let your hair down?" I tug at the end of her braid.

"If you ask nicely."

"Please," I blurt automatically.

Bianca wipes the excess moisture from her palms along my arms. "You're lucky it's your birthday."

"And tomorrow, we can do everything else you had in mind. It'll still be there. By then, I'll be good as new."

"Along with matching Halloween costumes."

My smirk rises for the occasion. "Something like that."

CHAPTER THIRTY-ONE

Bianca

TRUE TO MY INITIAL ITINERARY FOR COLTON'S birthday, we find ourselves at the Shetland County fairgrounds on Halloween. Haunted Harvest Haze is in full swing. The smell of pumpkin spice and fried food on a stick hangs in the air. Kids are racing around with their faces painted in a variety of recognizable designs. It's total chaos, which is my happy place.

Colton hasn't fussed about our social outing. For once, he appears to be at ease in a crowd. That has me thinking about his relaxed stride as we puttered down Main Street earlier.

"You're different," I observe while we walk past the corn maze.

A downward sweep showcases his entirely black outfit including the Stetson on his head. "Sure about that? I'm a shadow blending into the background. You don't see me there protecting you."

Meanwhile, I'm wearing a bright green dress that sticks out like a pageant queen in a parade. "The princess and her stalker."

"Clever, huh?" My grumpy jailer winks.

The carefree, flirtatious action stuns me momentarily. It was shocking enough that he wanted us to make a scene throughout town. Our couple costume, which probably doesn't make sense to many, put me in a very cozy mood. I've been snuggling against him all day and people have stopped to stare.

Lynn Ellen Paige—the biggest gossip in Cloverleaf Meadows—chooses that moment to strut by us. I wiggle my fingers in greeting before lifting onto the tips of my cowboy boots to kiss Colton's cheek. He wraps one arm around my waist, bracing the other behind my shoulders, and lowers me into a romantic dip. Our lips brush in a chaste peck before he flings me back to my feet. Giddy flutters swarm my entire system, but I still hear when the rumor hound gasps at our display. She quickly skitters off like a cockroach to spread the news.

I nudge him with my elbow. "Are you enjoying the attention?"

He nods and puffs out his chest. "We're making a very public announcement. You willingly claimed me as yours for the entire town to see."

Warmth spreads through me. "I'm proud to show you off, but I couldn't care less who notices. You're meant to be beside me. That's the way it should always be."

His chin tucks, trying to mask the bashful redness coloring his face. "Means the world, baby girl."

"Been waiting for that, hmm?"

He reaches for my hand, threading our fingers together with a gentle squeeze. "Feels like I can finally breathe."

My bottom lip gets tortured between my teeth as I consider bursting the bubble. "What happened to staying under the radar?"

"You're safe with me."

I study his casual gait and sunny expression. This man is completely unbothered.

"There's more to it," I prod.

"Just choosing to take it all in," he sighs.

It's a positive view from him. One I can effortlessly share in this festive atmosphere. Haunted Harvest Haze is another event that was very near to my mother's heart. Her memory lingers in every cheerful laugh that dances on the autumn breeze. But that doesn't explain Colton's sudden change in attitude.

I want to drop it. Probably should. But there's an itch under my skin that demands I unsaddle this secret.

"What's the latest with your father?"

He doesn't falter. If anything, his posture broadens. "Had a stroke yesterday. He's catatonic."

Air gets caught in my throat and I cough. Welp, that'll do it. He's nonchalant and unapologetic. That's the biggest "fuck you" he can offer to James Keller. It's not the reaction I'd have about my dad, but our childhoods couldn't be more opposite. Colton's past has obviously weighed him down and this update has significantly lightened his load. I can't fault him for celebrating.

That's why I find myself directing us to a certain food truck. "Can I interest you in a meat tornado?"

"Fuuuuuuck," he groans. "I love you."

My hip bumps into his. "Love you right back."

We approach the vehicle to order. Grease and smoky flavors waft from inside the small kitchen. Colton greedily accepts the turkey leg that's wrapped in thin layers of chicken and beef, which is magically held together by strips of bacon.

I stare at the creation in awe. "Good luck eating that."

"It's remarkable." He kisses the protein overload before taking a massive bite.

"About to get jealous," I mutter.

"Want some?" Colton offers me the mangled meat tornado that's now dripping in juices.

"Um, no. That's all yours, Stalker."

He shrugs and resumes devouring his meal. I guide us in the direction of the darkened bleachers that surround the riding arena. The horse show ended hours ago, leaving that portion of the grounds quiet.

But before we can leave the carnival section, Brody and Paisley cross onto our path. Or that's who they are on an average day. Halloween changes everyone, even my grouchy brother.

Laughter folds me in half. "I can't believe what I'm seeing."

My bestie smooths a palm down her fluffy pink costume. "You like?"

"Is it Christmas?" I cackle. "This is the gift I never asked for, but really needed."

Brody scowls, obviously not impressed with his matching pony onesie.

"How—?" My question is a sputter. "Oh, gosh. I'm speechless."

"He lost a bet," Paisley answers.

I wipe under my eyes, fighting for composure. "And what was that?"

The blush on her cheeks punches me with regret. "You don't wanna know."

An exaggerated retching sound agrees. "Please forget I asked."

Paisley's smile is coy. "You two have caused quite the stir."

"Us?" I snort. "That's hilarious."

She lifts her brows. "Costumes and jokes aside, your names are spilling from every mouth we walk by."

I glance at Colton, but he's too busy eating and making Brody envious. "They've never seen me in a relationship."

My friend hums. "And Benson fodder fills the cup to the brim. You'll be the talk of the town for months."

"Good," I chirp.

Paisley's jaw drops. "You don't care?"

"I do care. That's why I'm glad they're witnessing our fairytale."

Her expression melts into goo. "I'm really happy for you, Bee."

"Thanks. It feels really good to be loved like this."

"You deserve it," she exhales. "Okay, soak in the romance. We're doing another lap. Have to get the most out of this reward before he retaliates."

My brother grunts, but follows his wife like a dutiful husband in the doghouse.

I turn to Colton after they blend into the crowd. "Well, that was—"

The words die on my tongue. Desire burns his gaze into

a hypnotic smolder. I feel the heat in my veins, pumping hotter with each second. Saliva sticks in my throat and I gulp. My grumpy jailer looks positively feral.

"You fed me, but I'm still famished."

The lust in Colton's gravelly tone makes me shiver. "What're you craving next?"

He puts his cowboy hat on my head, sending a fresh wave of whispers through the gossip mill. But it's the skull mask he pulls over his face that captivates me.

"Run, Princess. Try to hide from your stalker."

Liquid heat collects in my lower belly, swirling to gather in my knees that threaten to buckle. "You're kinda scary."

"Does it turn you on?" His voice dips lower.

"Yes," I gasp.

Colton juts his chin. "Show me how much."

My legs quake as I begin backing away from him. "Do I get a head start?"

"Sure, but it doesn't matter. I'm gonna catch you."

That's all I need to hear. I whirl around and take off. People are everywhere, but not clustered close enough to conceal me. My boots kick up dust as I dodge a couple by the corn booth. The concern in their eyes slows me down a notch.

I can't move too fast or it'll raise alarm. The best strategy is to weave and swerve to get Colton off my tail. A quick glance over my shoulder reveals him staring directly at me over the throng. Damn him and his vertical advantage.

A stampede drums in my ears while I duck behind a bouncy house. The leafy obstacles and thick trunks of the woods call to me. It could be the escape I need.

My determination pounds against the turf, but heavy

footsteps chase me. I'm almost to the isolation of the bleachers when thick arms cinch my middle. A pitiful wail strips me of my dignity as I'm taken to the ground. His hat pinwheels off my head, wisely choosing to abandon this battle. If only we were all so lucky.

"Mother trucker," I spit as my spine hits the dirt.

Colton pins me beneath him, his bulk pressing against me like prison bars. "Did you even try, Princess?"

Rather than answer, I struggle under his immovable force. "Why are you so heavy?"

His creepy skeleton mask hovers over me. "Blame the chocolate."

My eyes roll as I force my muscles to go slack. "You're back to normal. Don't drag it out."

He doesn't answer. Not directly. After a few tense seconds, hunger rumbles off his chest like the main course is served.

"What do you want?" My voice is too breathy.

Colton swoops down until our lips touch. "Everything."

CHAPTER THIRTY-TWO

Cotton

I CAUGHT BIANCA BENSON.

Damn, that's some unbelievable shit.

A chuckle sets itself loose as I watch my rodeo princess wrap the third barrel and race for home. Bandit's mane whips into the wind from their speed. Much to my pleasure, Bianca's hair is wild and free as well.

What a ride this has been. After Haunted Harvest Haze, we hit the road. It's been three weeks of traveling to different Midwestern cities for the last horse shows of the season. Once the ground freezes, it's over until spring.

This is the final competition Bianca entered and she just won. It's only fitting that she chose to end the year on Minnesota soil.

I whistle as her time is displayed on the screen. "That's my girl!"

Her eyes connect with mine and she blows me a kiss. I pretend to catch it, a total fool for this woman. Every cowboy drooling on the fence wishes they were me. But she's all mine.

The arena lights make her and Bandit glow like the stars they are before the champions disappear through the gate. Spud barks as I lead us toward them. Even in the shadows, I see Bianca's smile stretch. I open my arms and she leaps from the saddle, giggling as I spin us around.

She kisses my waiting lips. "Not bad, huh?"

"Flawless as always." When she grimaces, I lower her slowly. "Dizzy?"

"No." Bianca rubs her chest and makes a pained noise. "There's this strange burning sensation. It's been happening on and off."

I blink at her. "Heartburn?"

She scoffs and removes the reins from Bandit's neck. "I don't have heartburn."

"Sounds like it." My palm finds the small of her back as we begin walking to the trailer. "It can develop later in life."

Bianca gasps, giving me an elbow to the side. "I'm twenty-three years young, sir. That's not later in life."

I chuckle while darkness swallows our forms. "There are some antacids in the truck."

"Prepared as always, even though I don't need them."

"Sure," I drawl. "Or maybe give 'em a try. Might feel better."

She sighs, tipping her head against my arm. "Have I thanked you for hauling me around?"

"Almost constantly."

Her eyes roll. "Well, it means a lot. I haven't done this since Mom passed."

An ache stabs behind my sternum. "I'm sorry she can't be here with you."

Bianca sniffs, nodding slowly. "I like to think she sent you in her place. To take care of me."

"Damn, Princess." I clear my throat, trying not to get choked up. "That's really special. I won't let either of you down."

"Colt."

I turn toward the voice. It's difficult to see clearly without the floodlights, but there's no mistaking my cousin. It's a shock to see him, especially here. Maybe my father left some final wishes before he died. Unlike the thoughts of Marion, the memory of James Keller does nothing for me.

Bianca tugs on my shirt. "Who is that?"

"It's okay. He's family." I lift my chin at him in greeting. "This is a surprise, Walker."

"Would've done this sooner, but you're tough to track down."

Which leads me to believe he's got business to discuss. "Is there something I can do for you?"

My cousin squares his shoulders. Two others are behind him, but they're too far away to identify. Whatever this is requires reinforcements. Fucking awesome.

"Stay out of our way," Walker demands.

I almost laugh. What a joke. "Don't gotta worry about me. I'm out of the game and plan to keep it that way."

"Wish I could trust you. Unfortunately, the old man said otherwise."

For fuck's sake. My father is still pulling strings, even from the grave. "I want nothing to do with the crew. It's all yours."

Walker rubs his nose. "Doesn't work that way and you know it. There was a vote. Even though you abandoned us, the majority is still loyal to you. They want you in charge."

"Not happening."

"That's what I said." His eyes have a crazed gleam and I can tell that he's on something.

"Let's agree to go our separate ways."

"Not good enough." And then Walker pulls out a gun, aiming it directly at me. "Need you out of the picture. Permanently."

CHAPTER THIRTY-THREE

I MUST BE HALLUCINATING. IT'S THIS AWFUL FIRE crawling up my esophagus that's causing me to see things. That's the only explanation for why this guy—Walker— is pointing a gun at Colton. Spud's growl snaps me from the ignorant illusion, revealing this is actually happening.

Colton lifts his open palms. "Put the gun down, Walker."

The guy huffs a laugh. "Nice try, but you don't get to tell me what to do."

"Are you going to shoot me?"

Walker nods. "If I kill you, I'll get promoted. You're in my way and it's up to me to remove you from the equation. Simple as that. It's nothing personal."

This can't be real. My eyes are burning, but I'm too afraid to blink. A lone tear leaks out as I listen to Colton try to reason with his cousin. He lowered his guard after his father died. The threat was eliminated. We've been driving across state lines without a care, feeling secure in our safety.

That's why he's unarmed and a defenseless target. Even if he had a weapon, it's three against one.

"Colton," I whimper.

"It's okay." His voice is soft but firm. "Get away from here. Go to the trailer."

"And leave you alone? No way."

Walker's menacing glare pins onto me. "That's right, sweetheart. Stay where I can see you."

"Don't talk to her," Colton snaps.

His cousin chuckles, but the tone is mean. "You're not in the position to be giving orders, Colt. I'd shut the fuck up before I aim a little higher. That rich bitch behind you will be splattered in your brain matter."

"You're high and not thinking straight. Put the gun down. Let's talk about this."

"Quit telling me what to do." Walker stabs the space between them with his pistol. "It's time for me to take charge. Maybe I'll earn myself a slice of expensive pussy pie."

Nausea curdles in my belly. "Should I scream?"

"No," Colton clips. "Just get to the trailer."

"I'm not leaving you," I reiterate.

"Dammit, Princess. Please."

Walker tips his head back and howls. "The great Colton Keller is begging a woman to listen. How the mighty have fallen."

"You don't want to do this, cousin. We're family."

A disbelieving snort spits from him. "Is that why you left us all behind? It only got worse in your absence. Uncle James blamed us after you cut ties. You were playing house with Bianca Benson while we were getting tortured."

"Nobody forced you to stay," Colton tries.

"Nah, fuck that. I'd never abandon my family." His hand holding the weapon shakes slightly. "That's the worst part. The crew would welcome you back without hesitation."

Walker does something to the gun that makes it click. Somebody must've heard that. I lick my dry lips and glance around. There are people nearby, but not close enough. Why did we park so far in the back? Fuck privacy. I need someone to walk past us.

That's when a twig snaps. Spud lunges forward with animal instincts, barking loudly into the darkness. In the next instant, a shot is fired. It's loud and startling, filling the air with gunpowder. The ringing in my ears doesn't drown out Colton's grunt. I stare through watery eyes as he crumples to his knees.

My boots skid on the grass as I leap into action. The rawness hacking at my throat tells me that I'm screaming, but I can't hear over the devastation of him collapsing. I'm there just in time to catch him folding onto the ground.

A feminine screech stabs into the carnage. "What the hell, Walker? You weren't really supposed to shoot him!"

"Finger slipped. Let's go."

A woman shoulders past him, coming into view. "I'm not leaving him."

"Traitor!" he roars. "I won't forget this."

If Walker and whoever else is involved disappear, I don't notice. My focus is solely on Colton gasping for breath. I cradle his head in my lap and try to make him comfortable. Tears are streaming down my face, blurring my vision.

"T-tell me w-what to do." My uneven exhales spew fog into the cooling night.

He just stares at me, blindly searching for my hand. "Love you, Bianca."

"No," I blubber. "Don't start with that. It sounds like goodbye."

"I'm hit," he rasps. "Too much blood."

My movements are frantic as I pat his shirt, hunting for the spot. The fabric covering the left side of his abdomen is completely saturated already. Warm and sticky and gushing out. I can tell my hands are coated.

"Shit, shit," I chant. "Need to call someone."

The woman from before kneels on Colton's opposite side. "Ambulance is on the way. We need to put pressure on the wound."

I lift my gaze to her, just long enough for recognition to strike. "You."

The redhead villainess shrugs. "I'm not that bad."

As if I can trust her. I don't even know her name, but now isn't the time for proper introductions. She rests both palms over Colton's torso and he groans.

"You're hurting him!" I yell.

"Saving him," she corrects. "Keep him conscious. Just talk to him. It'll help."

Too many thoughts rush through my mind. I stare at this man who's my everything, never feeling so helpless. His hat fell off in the fall, allowing me to rake my fingers through his hair. I'm caking the strands with blood, but I doubt he'll care.

"Hey, Stalker. You're going to be okay."

His lashes flutter, staying closed for long seconds. When Colton's eyes find mine again, they're unfocused.

"Kiss me," he breathes.

I lean forward to gently seal our lips together. The motion shoots a fresh burst of flames into my chest. My swallow is thick and useless against the onslaught. The foreign sensation seems cruel at a time like this. My heart is already burning without adding in acid reflux.

"Thank you for agreeing to be mine," he murmurs. "Even if just for a little while."

My palms shake as I cup his cheeks. "I love you so much, Colton. Please stay with me."

He nuzzles into my touch, but doesn't move otherwise. "Loving you has been my greatest honor."

"There's no quitting, right? I chose you and you're stuck with me. Forever."

His eyelids droop, barely open. "Don't… worry about… me, baby girl. You're gonna… be fine."

"Fight," I beg. "Just hold on."

"Tryin' my… best." But his breathing is getting more shallow.

"Colton!" I wail. "You gave me your word. You can't betray me."

"We're losing him," the stranger on my right says.

"No, that's not possible." But I watch in horror as his eyes slide shut and remain that way. A broken sob rips from my throat. "Colton, wake up."

"His pulse is weak," she warns.

Another jab of heartburn blasts through me. I take a moment to consider the sudden onset. A faded memory clicks, one my mom used to share with us. It's unlikely the cause for me. I haven't experienced other symptoms. But if it gives him a reason to fight, I'll use that to my advantage.

My hand grabs his to rest on my stomach. "I can't do

this without you. Please, Colton. Fight. For us. We need you."

The woman across from me makes a strangled noise. "You're pregnant?"

I don't answer her. All of my concentration is centered on keeping Colton alive. "Wake up. Please, please. You can't leave us. Don't you dare try. We're in this together. You're saddled in secrets with me, Stalker."

But he doesn't hear me. His skin is clammy and cold when I check his temperature. I try to snap the elastic band around his wrist, but the damn thing breaks. As if that's not some kind of omen. My chest is caving in. There's a cinch tightening around my ribs, pulling harder until I'm heaving. Fuck, I can't breathe.

The wail of sirens cracks into the dismal outlook. Red and blue lights soon follow. A team of medical professionals spills onto the scene. I'm nudged away from Colton as they take control of the situation. Numbness spreads, leaving me empty. The life is draining out of me too.

Once he'd loaded onto a gurney and lifted into the back of the ambulance, a paramedic motions me forward. My mind is blank. All I can do is stare.

"Go," the redhead tells me. "I'll handle things here. You'll owe me one."

My head is bobbing robotically, willing to do whatever she says if it means going with him. No matter where that road leads.

CHAPTER THIRTY-FOUR

Bianca

MY KNEE BOUNCES TO THE ERRATIC BEAT OF MY impatience. It's been hours since I've seen Colton. The paramedics managed to stabilize him in the ambulance, but he lost a lot of blood. They couldn't tell me how bad his injury was. Not until he had surgery. Last I heard, he's still in the operating room.

I stand and begin pacing again. There's little else I can do. Dad, Brody and Paisley are on their way but it's a haul up to northern Minnesota. People stop to stare at the gore splattered on my clothes. Those stains belong to Colton and I'm not washing him off. A harsh glare burns my weary eyes. It's too white in this hospital. Sterile like a fresh start that mocks me. All I want is the life we were already building.

Another jab punches the hollow ache in my chest. I feel gutted. The stench of bleach and antiseptic burns my nose. At least they have a readily available pharmacy. With quaking fingers, I pop two antacids in my mouth and chew.

"Are those safe for the baby?"

My boots squeak on the tile floor when I whirl to confront the redhead. "I'm not pregnant."

She saunters over, all leather and cautionary tales. "Sure about that?"

I chomp on my bottom lip. "No."

"Had a hunch this was a new development." She tosses a box at me. "Go squeeze the lemon."

I wrinkle my nose. "Pass."

"What else are you gonna do? Drive yourself crazy waiting. Might as well get answers."

Which reminds me. "Who are you?"

Her smile is sharp like a dagger. "Been wondering how long it would take. I'm Frankie. We're gonna be the best of friends."

I snort. "Doubt it. Have you fucked my boyfriend?"

She hisses and claws at the air. "Such a brat. You can relax, Bee. Colton and I go way back, but not like that."

The use of my nickname is almost as irritating as the old lady gawking at the blood on my face. "Give me that."

I take the pregnancy test to the nearest private bathroom, which isn't too far from the waiting area. A quick glance at the directions is plenty. The process is simple enough. After doing my business, the wait begins. It almost pains me to wash my hands, but I'm not that desperate to keep every drop of Colton on me.

My gaze purposefully avoids the test until a solid five minutes pass. Just to be extra sure. The sinking in my stomach is unexpected. We weren't planning it. The odds spoke for themselves. There's nothing to be upset about. I nod just for the sake of acceptance. This is probably for the best.

But disappointment follows me back to Frankie. I plop onto the empty seat next to her. "Negative."

"Let me see." She opens her palm.

"We're not at that level."

Her fingers wiggle. "Just give me your pee stick. Consider it a second opinion."

"Gross, but whatever." I whip the test out of my back pocket.

Frankie peers at the little window closely. "Bitch, that's positive."

"It's not." Didn't she hear me the first time?

"The second line is faint, but it's there." She taps a pointy nail at the evidence.

I blink, squinting hard. Shock freezes me. She's right.

"Holy shit," I exhale.

The grin she gives me is actually genuine. "Congrats, mama."

But the truth hasn't sunk in. "I'm pregnant?"

"You're pregnant."

I cradle my forehead as too many thoughts bounce around. "I'm not sure what to say."

"Didn't you have a feeling?"

"Well, yeah. Kind of. But it was more of a stretch. Something for Colton to grab onto."

Frankie's brows lift. "Are you happy?"

My reaction is cut short. The doctor that was on scene at Colton's arrival appears from behind the illusive double doors. I'm on my feet and hoofing it toward him. He's wearing a pair of navy scrubs. The color hides any evidence of blood, which I'm thankful for.

"Mrs. Keller," the middle-aged man greets. "I'm Dr.

Trustworth, one of the emergency surgeons on staff here at Cook County Regional."

I paste on a waxy smile to cover my lie. "How is he?"

"Your husband is very lucky," Dr. Trustworth begins. "It was a fairly clean shot. From what I imagine was close range, the bullet could've done a lot more damage. Mostly muscle and tissue was impacted. His spleen was barely nicked, but still required immediate repair to stop internal bleeding. The impact almost got to his pancreas, which would've put him in much worse shape. It's a blessing that his lung didn't get hit or collapse under the pressure. The fact he can breathe on his own will greatly reduce his recovery time."

Relief whooshes from me and I almost collapse. "Can I see him?"

The doctor nods. "His surgery was a success. He's resting now. You can sit beside him. He'll probably be comforted by your presence."

"Make sure to tell him the good news." Frankie makes a large bubble over her flat stomach.

Dr. Trustworth clucks his tongue. "That can probably wait until tomorrow. He doesn't need added stress."

Which is exactly what I'm afraid of. A baby he purposefully tried to prevent might not be a welcome announcement. In the heat of a tragic moment is one thing, which didn't make a difference. The ambulance and paramedics are what saved him.

But the woman who has a secret history with Colton scoffs, waving off the doctor's advice. "Oh, I'm sure he'll want to hear this immediately."

An audible gulp betrays my nerves. If only I could share Frankie's confidence.

CHAPTER THIRTY-FIVE

Cotton

'M DRAGGED INTO CONSCIOUSNESS THROUGH A LONG, dark tunnel. My brain feels like a soggy sponge that can't grasp more water. Awareness fades in and out. Several bright lights are flashed in my eyes before I'm pulled under again. Urgent whispers try to tickle my ears, but I can't comprehend the words.

It's a tender squeeze against my palm that finally yanks me free of the void. My vision swims when I manage to stay lucid for more than five seconds. Bianca is at my bedside. Her fern-green eyes are fastened onto my battle against lethargy. The eager gleam in her gaze rouses me like a shock to my system.

But my smile still feels sluggish. "Hey, Princess."

She immediately bursts into tears. "Y-you're awake."

"Why are you crying?" My throat is a coarse strip of sandpaper.

Her hand shakes when she offers me a spoonful of ice chips. "I've been so worried."

Bricks weigh my limbs down onto the mattress, but I manage to turn slightly to see her clearer. The blanket she crocheted for me is sprawled over my immobile form to deliver another dose of comfort. A new hair tie is snug around my wrist to offset the hospital bracelet. I could almost be convinced this is my happy place. Damn, these drugs are potent.

My thoughts struggle to stay on track, drifting in several directions. But the woman beside me is an anchor.

I squeeze her palm. "Should've known I could never leave you."

Bianca rests her forehead on my arm. A choked sob rattles her frame. I try to move my left arm to the back of her head, but there are too many tubes attached.

"Look at me," I rasp.

Watery misery instantly collides with my effort to concentrate. "I love you, Stalker."

"Fuck, baby girl. C'mere." I try to beckon her into the fold, but it's a weak attempt.

She straightens, but doesn't move. A stubborn pout sticks out her bottom lip. "Can't. You're hurt."

"Just a scratch," I scoff.

As if to contradict me, there's a knock on the door. A man in hospital scrubs pokes his head in. He gives me a warm grin as if we're friends.

"Ah-ha, the rumors are true. I heard you returned to the land of the living. I'm sure your wife is relieved." His gaze moves to the woman beside me as if there was any doubt who falsified this claim.

"My wife," I croon at Bianca.

"Oh, ummm… about that." Her face is the color of a tomato.

"She hasn't left your room. You're in very good care, Mr. Keller." The man pats his chest. "My name is Dr. Trustworth. I had the honor of stitching you up. Good to see you awake and alert."

"Thanks, Doc." But my focus hasn't strayed from Bianca.

She wrinkles her nose, glancing down at her outfit that's covered in my blood. "I should probably shower."

"You should probably kiss me."

Her eyes skitter off mine to peek at the doctor still hovering. "I don't want to dislodge anything. Besides, I haven't brushed my teeth."

"Do you honestly think I care about your breath right now? You're more beautiful than ever, Mrs. Keller. Get over here." After a jerk of my head, she humors me with a soft peck.

Dr. What's-His-Face hums. "Yes, she's positively glowing. That happens to expectant mothers."

There's a screech in my tired brain. "Care to repeat that?"

His jaw drops. "Please don't tell me I spilled the beans."

Bianca is hanging her head, muttering under her breath about letting the cat out of the bag.

"Princess?" I clench her hand tight in mine. "Are you…?"

"I should probably take another test," she mumbles.

"Allow me to order that for you. It's the least I can do." The doctor gets typing on his tablet. "In the meantime, I want to know how you're feeling, Colton."

It's difficult to move on from the idea that Bianca could be pregnant with our baby. But if answering a few questions gets me alone with her sooner, I'll pay the tax. I don't look away from my wife—legal or not.

"My cousin shot me in the gut. How do you think that feels?"

I'm actually numb from whatever drugs they're giving me. Except for my heart. That beats like a herd of wild horses for the woman next to me.

"At least he missed your vital organs," Dr. Lingering Too Long muses.

"Silver linings do exist," I grumble.

"Speaking of," a woman I haven't seen since she was a girl strolls into the room. "My brother is being hounded by the cops. I'm sure he'll be caught in no time."

My mouth moves soundlessly for several seconds. "Frankie?"

"Oh, good. The reunion I've been waiting for," Bianca complains. But then she steels her spine. "Wait, you're his cousin?"

I glance between the two women, landing on Bianca. "Who did you think she was?"

Her arm flings accusingly at Frankie. "She's the ex-lover who tracked me down at the camp."

"Oh, boy." The doctor squirms as if uncomfortable. "Maybe I should give you some privacy."

I offer him a shooing motion. "That'd be grand."

He excuses himself as Frankie slinks deeper into the room. She parks herself against the wall. A silent conversation passes between her and my soon-to-be wife. It's tense and uncomfortable, prickling across my skin like a challenge.

"What're you doing here, Frankie?"

"Helped saved your life." She inspects her black nails.

"Walker went back on his word. You're going to protect me if he ever comes looking."

My mind spins. "I feel like I'm missing something."

"Just keep me safe if my brother weasels his way out of trouble." Frankie shifts her focus to stare at Bianca. "Did you tell him about the bun in your oven?"

"No," she bites back. "Dr. Trustworth did the honors."

"What a thunder stealer," Frankie huffs.

Even my brain fog can connect the dots. "You're pregnant, Princess?"

She cringes. "Maybe?"

"Did you show him the test?" Frankie taps her boot on the floor.

"Do I need to show you the exit?"

My cousin lifts her palms in surrender. "Hint taken. Just don't forget our deal."

Which is one more thing I'll need to ask about. But for now, I'm focusing on a potential miracle. The door clicks shut with Frankie's retreat. It's just the two of us again. My heart thumps faster, trying to catch hers.

"How is this possible?" I use every ounce of weakened strength to reach Bianca's torso.

She stands to make it easier for me. Her palm lays flat over mine. "Super sperm?"

Emotion wells inside of me like an overflowing river in spring. "We're having a baby?"

"Would that make you happy?"

The hesitation in her voice furrows my brow. "Are you seriously questioning it?"

"We didn't plan this."

"Doesn't mean I wasn't hoping for it to happen with every far-fetched wish I could muster."

Bianca sniffles, her eyes getting glassy again. "You mean it?"

"I can't wait to watch you grow," I murmur to her stomach. My gaze finds hers already on mine. "How did you know?"

"The heartburn," she explains. "My mom always told us she only had it while pregnant. It's what prompted her to take a test. While you were fighting for your life, the story clicked and it felt right. I wasn't sure it could be true, but I guess she passed that down to me."

My eyes burn with unshed tears. "Our baby is in there?"

"Yes," she confirms.

"And you're going to marry me?"

She laughs. "Eventually."

"How about now? I bet there's a pastor or preacher in the chapel."

"We're not getting married in a hospital."

When she puts it that way, I can understand her resistance. "That's fair. Climb up here and ride my face to celebrate our engagement."

Bianca's ass remains firmly planted on the chair. "I don't recall you asking for my hand, Stalker."

"You're the one who skipped all the paperwork to pronounce us husband and wife."

"For good reason," she counters. "They're sticklers for the rules around here."

That sends my thoughts on a tangent. "Have you seen my jeans?"

Bianca points to a bag on the floor. "Not sure they're salvageable. I'll try to get the blood out."

But I couldn't care less about keeping them as a souvenir. "Can you check the front pocket?"

"Sure," she mumbles and begins searching. Her whole body turns to stone when she finds what I'm looking for.

"Maybe it's too soon, but I've been waiting years to get my ring on your finger." I open my palm for the velvet box.

Bianca drops it like a hot potato. "How long have you been carrying this around?"

"Longer than I should admit." I flip open the lid, flooding the drab room with radiance. My hand beckons for her left one. "Remember that I'm laid up after having surgery. Can't get down on one knee, but getting shot deserves several sympathy points."

"As if I'd say no," she blubbers. "You got me more daisies."

I pluck the diamond ring from the velvet pillow. "Do I even need to ask?"

Her wet lashes bat at my confidence. "I think you should."

"Bianca Jane Benson," I breathe. "You're the love of my life. I knew it from the first moment I saw you. Will you make me the happiest man to walk this earth and agree to be my wife?"

She's already nodding, fresh tears streaking down her cheeks.

"Tell me what I need to hear, Princess."

"Yes!" Her voice is rubbed raw. "Yes, yes, yes. I can't wait to marry you."

"That's my girl." I tug her closer and slide the ring on her finger. "Now you're really never getting rid of me."

"Gonna hold you to that." Bianca gingerly sits on the edge of my bed, mindful of the tubes and wires snaking from my body. Her diamonds sparkle when she wiggles her hand. "Well done, Stalker. This is stunning."

We study the brilliance for a moment. A three-carat canary solitaire is surrounded by dozens of smaller pink diamonds in a halo formation. The design replicates her favorite flower. Six platinum daisies join together to make the band, each with a stud in the center.

"My wife better kiss me again." I lift my chin.

She obliges, even adding a glide from her tongue. "My husband better get well soon so I can do a lot more than that."

"Sit on my face," I demand. It's been a full day without her pussy in my mouth and I'm starving.

Bianca snorts a laugh. "Absolutely not. I'll get kicked out and that's not going to end well for either of us."

I grunt. "Have they said how long I'm stuck in here?"

"Maybe a week? They tossed a ton of info at me." She fans her eyes. "This has been a very emotional twenty-four hours."

"And we're stronger because of it." My mouth slides against hers for a brief kiss. But then I'm reminded of something. "What about your back?"

She gives me a quizzical look. "What about it?"

"Can you handle the toll that pregnancy demands from your body? We need to talk to your orthopedist."

Her blink is slow. "You're worried about my scoliosis?"

"Yes."

"You're in the hospital after almost dying."

"I'm fine." But sleep is threatening to yank me under again.

"Massive understatement, Stalker."

Dizziness makes the room spin and I grip onto her tighter. "Tell me you'll make an appointment."

She waves me off. "Don't fret. Mom made sure to ask all the right questions when I was first diagnosed. I should have no issue carrying a baby to full term."

"That's my girl." I lift her wrist to my lips, kissing her smooth skin. The motion is dipped in molasses. "Can you sleep with me? I'm getting drowsy."

Bianca brushes her lips across my cheek. "I'll be here when you wake up."

"Promise?"

She nods against me. "No quit. Even when I smell like a dumpster fire."

"You're perfect," I mumble.

"That's the drugs taking," Bianca teases. "If you need me, I'll be in my bubble of chaos."

"You have all your stuff?" My words are starting to slur.

"Mhmm, Paisley brought me everything I need. Clothes too. Now that you woke up, I'm going to shower and change."

"Paisley is here?"

She nods. "Dad and Brody too. They'd love to see you when you're ready. Tomorrow or the next day, they'll take the trailer and horses back to Keller's Keep. That's where we'll stay until you've completely recovered."

I fight the exhaustion for another moment. "They drove all this way for me?"

"Of course," she scoffs. "We're family."

And with that knowledge, I allow myself to drift off with a smile on my face.

CHAPTER THIRTY-SIX

Bianca

THE HOSPITAL MANAGED TO FORCE COLTON TO STAY a full week. One more day and he would've started climbing the walls. His recovery has been quite impressive to watch. He frequently gave his fiancée credit for encouraging him to heal faster. Our life together is ready to continue—full speed ahead—just beyond the sterile walls.

As promised, I didn't leave Colton's side. That includes now as I settle behind the wheel to drive us home. Fern starts with a loud roar, more than ready for the journey.

"Be gentle with her. She's old." He pats the dashboard lovingly.

I glance at him in the passenger seat as I pull from the lot. If we never return, it'll be too soon. "How does it feel to sit over there?"

"Not a bad view." Colton's blue stare feasts on me

while he sprawls out like a lion about to be fed a massive, juicy steak.

"Don't even think about it," I chide.

"Oh-ho," he chuckles. "I'm definitely thinking about it. That's all I've thought about since you agreed to be my wife."

The sparkles on my ring finger distract me momentarily. "You're still recovering. No strenuous activity until you're healed."

He scoffs. "I'm better than ever. About to be a wedded man. But first, we need to consummate our engagement."

Laughter bubbles from me as warmth begins to spread through my lower belly. "I think that only counts for marriage."

"Not in my book," he rasps. "Pull over, Princess."

"No way," I giggle.

"There's nothing but empty space." He motions to the rolling meadows on both sides of the road. "Just park behind a tree."

"We'll be home soon."

"C'mon, baby mama." He slides a palm along my thigh, traveling upward to cup my pussy. "You want Daddy's dick. I'll make you scream like a brat. Unless you're in the mood to be my good girl."

The heat in my core burns hotter. My eyelids slide to half mast instantly. Sex hasn't been an option since his surgery, but we've passed the time teasing each other. I'd been tempted more than once to actually ride his face. The filthy things that spill from this irresistible man make for top tier dirty talk. My pregnancy hormones don't stand a chance.

That's why I scour the landscape for a decent spot to conceal our salacious act. Fern bounces across the uneven ground when I turn into a random field. There's a grove of tall oaks to shield us from the nonexistent traffic. I pull into a small clearing and shift into park, killing the engine.

Colton is already stripping. I'm stunned immobile as tanned muscle and masculine energy are unleashed. Drool puddles in my mouth, threatening to drip off my chin. A hungry moan spills free when he releases his cock.

Metal gleams from his crown and shaft. I had the honor of reinserting his piercings after his catheter was removed. That was a real test to my resolve. How easy it would've been to slip him into my mouth for a quick blowjob.

But then my attention shifts. The skin on his left side is still mottled in bruises. A patch of gauze covers his wound, but I'm intimately aware of what that close call looks like. Hesitation must reflect on my face.

"Don't," he scolds. "I'm fine. Definitely had worse. This is barely a scratch in comparison."

Salvia sticks to my throat at the horrible images assaulting me. "I don't see how that's possible."

"It's better that you don't. Just focus on the fact that I'm very much alive and desperate for you."

My bottom lip gets tortured between my teeth. "You should be resting."

"There's plenty of time for that after. I've been trapped in a bed for a week. Let me have my way with you for a few minutes. Then I'll go back to being your patient."

"Promise we'll go slow?" I'm not sure why I bother trying to deny him.

"Sure, if that's what you need to hear. In return, I need you to take off your dress," Colton commands.

My fluid motion obeys him without hesitation, leaving me in a satin bra and thong. My fingers hook into the flimsy elastic waistband and yank the barrier free. I'm about to straddle his lap, but he shakes his head.

"Not in the cab. I can't get at the right angle. Get your ass in the bed, baby mama."

"And what angle is that?" But I'm already hopping out to get in the back of the truck.

The weather tries to intimidate me, but we're protected from the worst of the elements. A nip bites my cheeks as I skip to meet Colton. His chiseled bulk doesn't appear to be impacted by the chill in the slightest. His injury isn't slowing him down either. There's a pearly droplet escaping his tip that whisks my mind from the cold.

"Gotta take you from behind," he murmurs in a husky tone.

My steps falter before I climb onto the lowered tailgate. "That doesn't sound like taking it easy."

Colton smirks. "I read it's the most pleasurable position for a pregnant woman."

"How do you know that?"

"Read an article. Figured we should prove if that's fact or fiction." It casually rolls off his tongue as if he's discussing lunch plans.

"When?"

Colton chuckles and strokes a palm over his dick. "Had a lot of free time on my hands recently. Wasn't allowed to do what I actually wanted."

"You chose to read about pregnancy?"

"And what to expect for our baby."

"Oh, Stalker." Emotion blurs my vision. I could write it off as another hormonal side effect, but the guy across from me is responsible. "That's really sweet."

My heart melts, chasing off the cool breeze. Any lingering doubt floats away too. The afternoon sun makes the late November weather somewhat tolerable. I'm suddenly feverish, squirming to be filled.

His arm ropes my middle and pulls me in. "C'mere, Princess. Let me show you what I learned."

Once I'm standing in front of him, his fingers unclasp my bra and toss the cups away. Frigid air hardens my nipples. It's a small miracle the winter frost hasn't struck yet. That doesn't mean it's comfortable to be naked outside.

"Brrrrr." My teeth chatter for exaggerated impact.

"I'll keep you warm. Turn around. Get on your knees. Hands on the truck."

My palms flatten on the rear windows, leaving a mark to remember this risky tryst. Colton's desire blankets my back and I press flush against him. Our combined body heat does its job. All I can think about now is getting him inside me.

His cock glides through my slick center. The loop from his Reverse Prince Albert strokes me from ass to clit. I tremble in his hold, ready for more.

"Soaked for me," he groans.

"Need you," I mumble and tip my head back.

His lips coast along the curve of my throat as his dick begins sinking in. That initial stretch spears me with a delicious ache. My toes curl against the cold metal, trying to get a grip. I shiver as the emptiness gives way to the pressure of being complete. A mutual sigh slips from us once we're fully joined.

"Missed you," he rasps while picking up a slow rhythm.

"So very much," I whine.

Colton glides his hips forward, giving me his entire length in a single thrust. Stars burst behind my eyes. There are already tingles building into an inferno. This man knows how to play my body like a seductive melody. I sway into him, surrendering to the pleasure he gladly offers.

"How does it feel?" He grinds into me tenderly before pulling almost all the way out, only to repeat the motion. "Better than normal?"

Friction burns hot in my pussy, getting me to the edge with each pierced entry. "I think so."

His tsk blows across my ear. "We can do better than that."

Colton plucks my nipples. The peaks are extra sensitive and I cry out. If his intention is to make me spontaneously combust, he's damn close to completing the task. I dig my nails into the truck to get a grasp. My arms have the consistency of cooked noodles and don't support my weight.

Not that it matters. He's owning my movements, taking full advantage when I sag onto my elbows. Colton grunts and I immediately straighten. A glance over my shoulder reveals a wince cinching his features.

"Stop," I breathe. "You're hurting yourself."

"Fuck no," he grunts.

"Lie down right now or you're cut off until next year." Authority clangs in my tone.

It's a demand he listens to. After pulling out, he gingerly lowers himself flat onto the bed of the truck. The lazy movements are probably more for my benefit. I straddle him and ease myself down onto his cock. Mutual desire instantly rebounds when our gazes lock along with our bodies.

The shift in position gets him deeper. I can feel him everywhere. Especially as I begin to shatter and he fills in the cracks. With tame thrusts from below, Colton's cock sends my mind reeling. Our combined lust crackles like sparks as we chase relief. The soft clap of skin joining is drowned out by the insistent throbbing. It's frantic and demanding, sizzling between us in fiery waves.

One arm cradles my waist while he spreads the other palm on my abdomen. "Whose baby is in your belly?"

"Ours," I gasp. "You're always inside me now."

Tremors quake from him in response. The jerky motion shoves him impossibly deeper. I moan loudly, no longer caring if we're caught.

"Tell me again," he demands.

"Gonna be a daddy, Stalker." I rest my hand over his. "There's a part of you growing in me. Soon enough, I'll be big and round with our baby. Everyone will know you did this to me."

His muscles jerk against mine, revealing the end is near. "Fuck, Princess."

That's another new development. Colton is obsessed with the fact that he got me pregnant. It drives him wild and I can only imagine his reaction once I'm showing.

His dick thickens, forcing me to stretch wider. That slight pinch pushes me over. Tingles burst into a hot surge that floods me with pleasure. Colton bellows and tugs me over him, tucking his face against my neck. His release spurts from him in three uneven jolts. My arms wobble, threatening to collapse under the pressure. I don't want to put too much weight on him.

Colton maneuvers us so that my torso is mostly plastered to his right side. While riding the high, he drags his palms over my crooked spine. Gentle strokes guide me through the climax. I'm floating in euphoric bliss, lost to everything except the man holding me against him.

"Okay," Colton exhales across my bare shoulder. "Now we can go home."

CHAPTER THIRTY-SEVEN

Cotton

Bianca might be in the driver's seat, but I still rush around the hood to open her door. My fiancée beams at me and opens her arms, allowing me to hug her. But when I try to scoop her off the seat, she yelps and pulls away. The look she gives me is a harsh scold.

"No lifting," Bianca chides.

"Princess." I tug her forward. The sutures in my side tug from the movement, but I'm not letting it stop me.

"Nope." She slinks out on her own, much to my displeasure.

"Have it your way, but I have a surprise for you," I whisper against her puckered lips.

After a gentle kiss, she sighs with a smile. "Why am I not the least bit shocked?"

"This is kind of a big one."

Suspicion pinches her features. "What did you do, Stalker?"

"Don't give him all the credit." Frankie appears from behind the house. "It was more of a group effort."

"That's what happens when the hospital won't release me for a week."

"Could've been a lot longer," my cousin quips. "I've been keeping the place running for you."

"Appreciate it. Good to have you on our side."

Her glare is sharp as she jabs a finger at me. "That could've been a lot sooner. Walker was right that you abandoned us. My brother is a lost cause—and arrested, by the way—but I would've left with you."

I wince. "You were just a kid."

"But haven't been for years." She exhales and waves at the dirt we're airing. "Didn't mean to dampen the mood. That's a discussion for another day."

Which is when we realize that Bianca is quiet beside me. Her eyes are wide and pinned on Frankie's dress. She opens and closes her mouth several times without uttering a word. After another muted round, the cat releases her tongue.

"What are you wearing?"

My cousin does a slow spin. "You like it?"

"It's pink," Bianca deadpans. To say it's the complete opposite of Frankie's whole vibe is an understatement. But I have to admit, she's rocking it.

"And it has pockets." Her hands disappear into the folds. "Paisley found them online. The super fast shipping was key."

"Ooooh, good timing." The blonde strolls up to our small gathering.

Bianca sputters at the sight of her friend wearing an identical dress. "What's going on?"

Rather than answer, Paisley winks at me. "We're ready when you are."

Frankie and her link arms before retreating their steps. Bianca watches them until they disappear from sight. When her eyes swivel to me, the green is warm with affection.

"We're having an engagement party?"

I cough into my fist. "Well, shit. Didn't even consider that."

She spins on her heel and begins stomping across the driveway. Spud bursts free from the barn, immediately followed by the rest of Bianca's dogs. Her hasty stride stops abruptly. When she realizes each one of them has a black or pink bow tie attached to their collar, her forehead creases in the middle. But the pieces truly click together once she looks back at me.

I finish tightening the silk tie around my throat. "Thought we might get married, baby mama."

Her eyes expand into saucers again. "Today?"

My fingers tug at the cuffs of my black dress shirt. "Right now is good for me."

"But…" Bianca glances down at her dress, just realizing I told her to change into the white one after our pitstop earlier. "Holy shit, you're like next-level sneaky."

"As if you expected anything else."

Her jaw is still slack. "You want to get married?"

"If you're willing," I reply. "If not, we'll call it an elopement."

"Who's officiating?"

"Is that a yes? I asked your father and he granted me permission." My smirk is a slow grower, blooming into a full grin.

My beautiful bride shrugs, getting with the program. "Why not? Seems as good a time as any."

I chuckle and offer her my crooked elbow. "That's my girl."

"Soon to be your wife." She tips her face toward mine for a kiss.

My mouth glosses over hers. "Can't wait to be your husband."

"Hey, now," Brody cuts in. "Save that for my cue."

Bianca stumbles into me at the sound of her brother's voice from our makeshift altar. My best friend stands proudly under the wooden arch that's covered in daisies. The rest of our guests—which looks to be only Dennis, Paisley, and Frankie—stand to one side of the shriveled flower gardens. Fresh blooms will appear in spring, but that's not what catches my focus. Cousin Byron and his younger brother are noticeably absent, along with little Ronnie. Jimmy didn't make the cut.

"You got Brody to officiate?"

"He owed me one for almost ruining everything with you." I brush the backs of my knuckles along her cheek.

"Consider me impressed," she exhales as we walk down the petal-strewn aisle.

"Before we get started," Brody says and gives us a stern glare. "I don't want to hear any sexy shit, okay?"

My bride snorts. "No promises."

"You're just encouraging her," I tell him.

He pinches the bridge of his nose. "Why did I agree to this?"

"Just stand there and look pretty, husband. It's mostly for tradition." Paisley pretends to take a picture of him.

"Let's get this over with. Who wants to go first?"

Bianca gasps. "I didn't write any vows."

"Just tell me you love me," I prompt.

"I do," she replies obediently.

"One down," Brody spouts. "Your turn, Colt."

My bride glares at her brother before refocusing on me. "I love you, Colton Maxwell Keller. My love came on fast, but it will burn forever. We're already a family and I'm looking forward to expanding it until your heart is bursting. Thank you for choosing me. For stalking me." That draws a few chuckles from the assembled crowd. "For abducting me and protecting me. For turning this house into a home. For being my safe space. The list is endless. I understand what it means to be cherished because of you. In return, you deserve to be satisfied and fulfilled in every aspect. That's my goal in this marriage. You might have the advantage of loving me for longer, but I'll make it my mission to prove we're evenly matched. Maybe I'll even gain the upper hand. Especially in the bedroom."

"You're done," Brody breaks in. "Feel free to drown him in smutty mush on your own time. Got anything short and sweet to say, Colt?"

"Don't appreciate you interrupting her."

"Complain to the boss. Oh, wait." He flips me off. "I don't care. Spill your guts or let me wrap this up."

Bianca leans toward me and hitches a thumb at her brother. "Big mistake hiring this guy, huh?"

I chuckle, holding her hands in mine. "That's just one thing I love about you, Bianca Jane. You don't hesitate to speak your mind. While our relationship started off slightly unconventional, we've grown a bond that others can only dream of. You're everything to me and I'll spend every breath in my lungs proving it to you. What began as an obsession has formed into a love so strong I can't describe it. You give love a definition. It's always been you, Princess."

"That wasn't bad. Okay, time to exchange rings. You've already got yours, Bee." Brody glances at her rock before nudging me. "Nice work, brother."

I smirk at the compliment while whipping out a set of matching wedding bands. "Don't forget about these."

Bianca whimpers. "I didn't get you a ring either."

"Been there," Paisley laughs.

"Comments from the peanut gallery aren't appreciated." But Brody winks at his wife like a total sap.

I pass Bianca my thick band before hovering her much smaller version over her finger. "Do you accept this ring as a token of my unconditional love for you?"

Tears glitter in her eyes as she nods. "I do." After a deep breath, she holds mine out and repeats the words. "Do you accept this ring as a token of my unconditional love for you?"

"I do."

The weight of the platinum band gliding over my knuckle is long overdue. I fist my hand, making sure this moment is real. Bianca lifts my fingers and presses a kiss just above my ring.

"Allow me to introduce the happy couple," Brody shouts. "Congratulations, Mr. and Mrs. Keller. You may now kiss the bride."

And I don't hesitate to do so. Bianca is tucked against me in the next breath. Our lips brush softly before letting instinct open us wider. The following exhale is shared into our first kiss as husband and wife. Heat stings my eyes and I clench them shut, treasuring this moment for another beat.

When I pull away, Bianca has a smile waiting for me. "Love you, husband."

"Love you, wife." My palm lowers to her stomach. "This baby and any others you bless me with will be swaddled in nothing but pure love."

I sweep Bianca into a tight embrace, leading her from the altar to the podium that holds our marriage license. She doesn't question my methods of obtaining it. Her signature is scrawled next to mine. It's official.

Something loosens in my chest. It feels old and rusty and long forgotten. A soothing warmth fills its space. I laugh for what feels like the first time.

Bianca cups my cheeks, dragging my face down to hers. "Love looks good on you."

"It's only possible because of you, my love." I kiss her passionately, getting lost in her addictive hold on me for several moments.

A throat clears nearby. Frankie is there, not so patiently waiting for us to finish. "Not to barge in, but time is of the essence. I need a place to crash. Your house is about to become the honeymoon suite and I'm not dealing with that."

"You can stay with us."

Frankie whirls to face Byron who appeared out of seemingly nowhere. Her eyes narrow. "Do I know you?"

"No, but you're about to get a thorough introduction." But first he tips his hat at us. "Congrats on getting hitched. Sorry we're late. Chance had trouble at the auction barn." Then his gaze returns to Frankie. "Now, where was I? You've been haunting my dreams, darlin.'"

She's already shaking her head. "Definitely have the wrong—"

"Daddy!" Ronnie is running full speed toward us, but her eyes are fixed on my cousin.

"This is gonna hurt." Frankie braces for impact.

Byron grunts. "She's harmless."

"But I'm not."

And with that, I take my bride away from their drama. We don't need it on our wedding day.

"Where to, groomy?" Bianca gazes up at me with so much affection I can feel it pumping in my veins.

I drop my forehead to rest onto hers. "You choose. It's best when you follow your heart."

"Let's get saddled in secrets and ride off into the sunset. That's how the most unforgettable happily ever afters begin." She threads her fingers through mine, tugging me toward the house.

I hold my ground. "You're going the wrong way."

My wife laughs when I nod toward the barn. "Did you think that I'd actually let you get on a horse in your condition? Straight to bed for you."

"But—"

Her finger smooshes against my lips to silence my rebuttal. "There are countless interpretations of riding off into the sunset. We're going to take a more unexpected route until you're fully healed."

"Our story definitely follows along with that," I'm quick to agree.

Bianca twirls in my arms, a carefree giggle escaping her. "Prove it, Stalker."

EPILOGUE

Bianca

One week later…

"**I**S THERE ANYTHING YOU CAN'T DO?" MY AWE SWIVELS between Colton and the golden turkey he's about to try pulling from the oven. "Other than lift that yourself."

"I can handle it." He frowns when I nudge him out of the way.

"Nope, doctor's orders. I got her in there. That's how she's getting out." I breathe through my mouth while hefting the sizable load onto the cooktop.

"Thanks, Princess." My husband doesn't look too pleased with me still babying him. "But don't give me too much praise yet. We gotta check if she's moist."

I gag, slapping a palm over my mouth. "That's such a gross word."

He furrows his brows. "But we want our turkey to be moist."

Spud and our six other dogs woof from the hallway in agreement.

"No, please stop."

After setting the heavy load onto the cooktop, Colton's head tilts at me. "How about juicy?"

"Better." But I'm still gulping down excessive amounts of saliva.

My husband lifts his shoulders. "Either way, we don't want it dry."

It doesn't make a difference to me. I don't want to tell him, but the smell of cooked meat is making me nauseous. Everyone else will gladly devour the bird. Bile rises up my throat at the thought and I choke it down. Colton notices, rubbing my back in soothing circles.

"You okay?"

"Mhmm," I mumble. "Just taking it all in."

But he's not convinced. His gaze searches for any sign of upset. "Do you need to rest?"

That earns him a gentle swat from the dish towel. A giggle distracts from my queasy stomach. "Quit fussing over me and worry about your feast."

"Need help carving?" Brody's offer comes from the living room where he's lounging unapologetically.

"As if you're getting off your butt," I sass.

"One of us needs to lend a hand. I'd hate to see you break a nail."

My tongue sticks out at him even though he can't see me. "It doesn't count if you don't mean it."

"Come give me a push and I'll be right there. Your sofa is too comfortable." His broad bulk slouches lower into the cushions.

"Gonna need a forklift to remove you." I imitate the beeping of the heavy machinery.

"We're good," Colton tells Brody to end the debate.

My brother gives a thumbs-up before returning his focus to the football game. Dad sits beside him on the left and Paisley flanks his right. It's a beautiful image—one I capture with a quick photo. I'm starting to clutter our walls with framed memories. The only person missing is Mom.

Well, that's not entirely true. Our cousins couldn't make it. Chance's response didn't surprise me, but Byron and Frankie were another story. When I asked the grumpy single dad what the deal was, he said something about a flight risk and hung up. Less mouths for us to feed.

Colton groans, which clenches my vagina walls in eager acceptance. At least until the thick aroma of steamy poultry assaults my nostrils. Another smooth slice cuts deeper into the roasted turkey, boosting his joy higher.

"Look at that, Princess." Pride shines in his voice. "Extra juicy."

The urge to hurl lurches me forward. "Umm, that's… great. Almost ready to serve? I'll pour the drinks."

Bottles of wine and sparkling apple juice get gripped in my whitened knuckles as I try to get ahold of myself. The gurgles in my gut slowly fade when I get space from the smelly scene. After the glasses are full, I toss a few ginger mints into my mouth. The taste settles my sickness immediately. I dare to inhale, discovering I can breathe without the threat of vomiting.

Relief has me grinning at my husband, but then I'm struck by a very intense craving. His tattooed arms flex from the force of slicing and plating. Sweat glistens on his forehead, sparking a fever in my lower belly. A soft whimper dribbles free as he gets started on scooping the mashed potatoes. I blindly reach out for support, curling my fingers around the top of a chair. Damn, he's sexy.

I glance over my shoulder. The three on the couch are still distracted by the football game. Maybe I can steal Colton away for a halftime show of our own. There hasn't been nearly enough sex in our marriage and I'm ready to fix that.

Our honeymoon officially starts after Christmas. We decided to wait until after the holiday season. Colton lightly suggested we could host Thanksgiving a few days late due to the recent upheavals in our routines. In that same speech, my overly considerate husband made sure to spell out that he'd handle all the preparations. I'm barely pregnant, but he's already acting like I should constantly have my feet up. Right now, I'd love to be folded like laundry with my ankles at my ears while he—

A soft touch to my shoulder rouses me from the filthy fantasy that doesn't belong in this setting. "Are you feeling well? You're really flushed, Bee."

I swipe at my chin, not bothering to peek over at Paisley. "Super hungry."

Brody lumbers over with the grace of a buffalo. "Good thing we're ready to eat."

"I think you should all leave," I mumble under my breath.

Dad balks. "What?"

The shock in his voice slaps the hussy trying to invade me. "Please take a seat."

He chuckles. "That's not what I heard the first time. Shoot, gotta get my ears checked."

A fire spreads across my face as I dash into the kitchen, grabbing the beans and salad. Colton follows with the rest. I claim the chair next to him, snagging his hand in mine.

"What a spread!" Dad rubs his hands together before patting his stomach. "We're eating well tonight."

Colton nods, a hint of a smile lifting his lips. "Thanks for coming to our home. It means a lot. Can't properly describe how much."

Brody lifts his drink toward him. "Nowhere else we'd rather be, brother."

My husband sits at the head of our table, surrounded by family and love. There's an unmistakable sheen in his eyes as he looks at our circle gathered to celebrate. Nobody else notices, but I rarely miss a thing these days when it comes to this man.

Colton is finally getting the life he deserves and we're just getting started.

Colton

One month later…

"Bianca," I rasp while bucking my hips. "Please."

But she wags her finger. "Not yet."

The buzzing starts again. It sends an electric spark along my spine and I arch against the invisible binds. A frustrated grunt voices my complaint, but the woman spread in front of me only smiles.

My gaze feasts on Bianca stuffing her cunt full of

silicone cock. She hasn't allowed me to touch her in at least five minutes. The last contact we exchanged was a quick swipe of her tongue along my Jacob's Ladder. I'm allowed to watch, but I can't join in. Not until she gives me permission.

Pregnancy hormones have her constantly ravenous. It's made our honeymoon extremely pleasurable for both of us. Bianca is sentimental at heart, much like me. It was an easy decision to redo her dream vacation and return to Europe. We haven't made it much farther than our bedroom in this Paris suite that overlooks the Pont de Arts bridge.

My wife has decided to recreate the scene where I overheard her masturbating. In this version, I'm in a chair at the foot of the bed with a direct view of her actions.

The pink vibrator I bought thrusts in and out of her pussy in a languid pace meant to seduce. My cock weeps in desperation. Her performance could get me off in one stroke if she allowed me to touch myself. But that's against the rules.

Bianca loves to push me to the limit. I beg for relief that she refuses to grant. Her teasing edges me to the point of madness. We've expanded our sexual horizons together and I'm appreciating our joint effort.

These power dynamics she plays get me hard instantly. Toss in the fact Bianca has become more adventurous and I'm blowing my load constantly. The wood creaks beneath me as I rock frantically with her rhythm. It does little to ease the pressure in my balls. She pushes the dildo deeper into her pussy, moaning loudly as the toy hits the spot. My dick throbs in complaint, but I don't move my hands from their grip on the armrests.

Bianca rocks her hips. The motion grants me a

shameless glance at her bottom. We've been prepping her ass for anal. The plug I sunk into her tight hole earlier is taunting me. There's a distinct clench in my balls. I clamp my jaw shut before a curse can spill free.

My wife thrusts the vibrator in deep. "Where do you wanna come, Stalker?"

"Don't care." My voice is rushed. Urgent. It matches the rapid pace of my pulse.

Bianca tsks. "That's not a very good answer. You're a bad boy."

"No," I blurt. "Please let me come."

Her cunt squeezes the silicone as if wishing for my cock. "Tell me where."

My wild gaze rakes over the three options. Her tits are too sensitive. It honestly doesn't matter since I'm seconds away from exploding. But I can't deny my desire for the untraveled.

"Your ass."

She grins. "That's my good boy."

I tremble from the praise. "Now?"

Her scoff scolds me. "Try again."

"Can I please fuck your ass?"

Bianca squirms on the mattress. "Will you be gentle?"

I chomp on my bottom lip, knowing what she needs to hear. "No."

"You always give me what I need," she croons.

My legs shake when I stand, daring to break the restraints. "Are you ready for me, Princess?"

She nods and grinds against the bed. "Claim my ass as yours. I need to feel you there."

Renewed conviction ripples through me. That's all I

needed to hear. My fingers pull the toy from her ass. The progress we've made gapes at me while I lube my girth. There's a pulse in my balls that warns me this won't take long.

I flip her onto her hands and knees, which grants me an impressed moan. The vibrator is still shoved to the hilt in her cunt. Its low thrum spurs me onward. My thumbs trace the slit of her center, dipping into her stretched pussy around the silicone. Her gasp is surprised but pleased.

A wiggle shoves the digits deeper. "Do you like that?"

"Mhmm," she moans into the pillow.

"Maybe you'll take me and a toy at the same time."

"Yes," she agrees automatically.

"Now who's being good?"

Bianca rocks her hips. "Don't test my patience. Give me that pierced penis."

I glide my thumbs out, drifting to pry her ass cheeks apart. "Tell me if it hurts."

Her untamed hair whips in denial. "Quit stalling."

With that shove, I align my dick at her puckered entrance. Bianca slips a hand between her thighs to work her clit. It might be my imagination, but vibrations from the dildo already stimulate me. My balls tighten to the point of no return.

I'm barely hanging on. A shiver quakes from her as I push inside her untried hole. Her snug rim suckles my tip. That's all it takes. My hips flex with the first burst. Bianca cries out, going rigid against me. That triggers two more spurts to unleash into her ass.

Spots dance in my eyes as we surrender to the pleasure.

Her spasms drain me of every drop. I come until my teeth are numb. But at some point, my exhausted cock slips out.

"Put the plug back in," she whines. "I don't want any leaking out."

"Fuuuuuuck, baby mama. What're you doing to me?" But I'm all too eager to trap my release inside her.

Bianca rolls onto her back once I'm done. The grin she gives me is too innocent. "Everything you've been missing, Stalker."

Bianca

One year later…

Colton's voice drifts down the hallway as I climb the stairs to our daughter's bedroom. My heart flutters at the familiar words from *If You Give a Mouse a Cookie*. A trail of dogs leads me in the right direction. Not a single one of them bothers to lift their heads.

I'm sure my husband is aware of me leaning in the doorway, but he doesn't stop reading. Our baby girl is cradled in the crook of his arm to best see the book. As if she's able to comprehend more than his gentle tone at five months old. She also appears to be snoozing. But it's always the thought that counts.

A smile curls my lips while he reveals the mouse's mischievous behavior. He's very animated. Not to mention dedicated. This sweet man never got bedtime stories. Marion Maxine doesn't go a day without at least five.

Her daddy has been reading to her since I first found out I was pregnant.

That unmistakable ache sears my chest whenever I think of his childhood. Colton doesn't let his past define him. He's determined to be the best husband and father in spite of it. I couldn't have asked for a better partner to share this life with.

After finishing the last page, Colton sets the book on the shelf. Another one was probably planned until I arrived. I slipped out of the house earlier without telling him where I was going. He's not quite as capable of stalking me while on baby duty. The tracker on my phone reveals my location, but I'm sure he's been itching to ask.

"Where has Mommy been?" Colton coos the question to conceal his actual concern.

"Finally got a tattoo."

His eyes snap to mine. "Without me?"

"That was the whole point." I sashay toward him, swinging my hips with extra flounce. "It's a surprise."

Silence wedges between us when I extend my arm for his inspection. Even in the low lighting of the nursery, my fresh ink is visible beneath the clear bandage. His handwriting circles my wrist.

"I choose you," he reads.

My other palm cups his jaw, tilting until our gazes reconnection. "And I choose you too. Always."

Colton's bottom lip trembles. He bites down on the middle, but there's no trapping the emotion. "You put me on your flawless skin?"

"Permanently and long overdue," I breathe. "Wanted to do it much sooner, but pregnant women aren't supposed to get tattoos. I've been trying to schedule an appointment for months. It's difficult to sneak out unnoticed around here."

"For my sanity." He nuzzles against my hand, pressing a kiss to the center. "I need you with me."

"Ditto, baby daddy. But you managed to get me a push present without my knowledge."

Colton smirks at the daisy pendant hanging around my neck. The center holds a large ruby—Marion's birthstone. Our baby girl and my mom were both born in July, which makes his gift even more special.

"I'm very good at what I do," he rasps.

"Oh, I'm well aware. It's one of the many reasons I love you."

A pleased rumble rolls off his chest, competing with our daughter's snores. "Love you."

"I think Daddy deserves a reward." My thumb pushes in and out of his mouth.

When he begins to suck, my breasts swell. The heat flooding them warns me that I'm seconds from spilling over. It's been hours since Marion has drank.

"Let me nurse her, and then I'll feed you."

Colton rises from the rocking chair, passing over our bundle of joy. "I've worked up quite an appetite in your absence."

"Wait your turn." I grin against his lips before sitting down.

A quick flick unsnaps my shirt. Marion sighs and begins rooting around. Even deep in slumber, instinct has her latching on. I sigh as the pressure instantly recedes.

Colton fidgets in my peripheral. "Is it weird that I like to watch?"

My laugh is soundless. "Why would you stop now?"

"You get me." His mouth peppers kisses on my upturned

forehead while his palm drifts over our baby's downy hair. "Such a miracle."

I hum a peaceful tune. "Wouldn't be here without you, Stalker."

The smile he grants me is big and full and unapologetic. "Your husband is a very patient man."

My nod is grateful. "Thanks for choosing me."

Colton's fingers gently brush over my tattoo. "Might not seem like it, but you chose me first. For both of us."

I wink at him. "Just needed a little bit of convincing along the way."

THE END!

But not really. I have a few extra scenes that you can read for free. Get them HERE!

I bet you can guess who's next in the Cloverleaf Meadows series. If not, this snippet from Frankie's point of view should give you a big hint. :)

My eyes narrow to expose thinly veiled annoyance. I can't believe I'm having this conversation. The boss better keep his word and give me a raise.

Bianca returns my glare, as if this spoiled brat has anything to complain about. Her attitude has been nothing but a headache. What my cousin sees in her is far beyond my comprehension.

I shrug, rolling her hostility off my shoulders. "You'll want to hear what I have to say."

The youngest Benson snorts like a champion mare asked to breed with a Shetland pony. "I don't see how that's possible."

"A little birdie told us that you're having trouble leaving town on your own. We can help you escape."

"Ohhhh," Bianca laughs. "The cowboy criminals want to make me disappear. Convenient."

"Is that what you're calling us?" I flip my hair at the endearing title, trying it on for size. "I'll have shirts made."

"That'll have you dressed more appropriately at a family-friendly facility." Her gaze scours over me in distain, as if I'm manure stuck to the sole of her expensive boots.

It doesn't bother me that much. I'm used to this judgment from the likes of her. "Bitchy, huh? Makes sense."

"Excuse me?" Bianca bristles and straightens her short stature.

"Don't get your thong in a twist," I huff. "That's just what Colton sees in you."

"Guess he has a type," she launches in return.

And the friendly portion of our chat is over.

Fire licks at my skin, preparing to deliver a real message. Talk is too cheap for this rich princess. A single step slices the distance between us in half. I wonder how hard she'll cry if I just pull her hair a little bit. The visual almost makes me smile.

But then a blur of motion is launching at me. I don't have time to react. Fuck, I'm caught off-guard. That never happens. It allowed Bianca's reinforcements to pummel me. She deserves more credit, but I won't be the one to admit that.

My body flexes into a weapon as I assess the situation. Except this attack feels… gentle? That can't be right. A glance down steals the breath from my lungs.

There's a small child attached to my legs. I think she's hugging me. My eyes widen while I slowly lift my hands. Shit, am I surrendering? My pulse is galloping too fast. It feels like I've been compromised.

I've stared down the barrel of a gun more times than I care to count but never flinched. An unexpected embrace from this little girl is what's going to do me in. Instinct tells me to push her away, but that seems unnecessarily cruel. Even for me. I'm at a total loss, which suspends me in a trap I can't escape.

Another person arrives on the scene, but I can't look away from this tiny human. She's staring at me with such adoration. The happiness shining off her is brighter than the sun. It's unsettling but pleasant. Warmth threatens to cradle my frozen heart.

Her pretty face nuzzles my leather pants. "She's a superhero, Daddy."

Daddy? Her father must be nearby. Why isn't he detaching

her from me? I'm a stranger, not to mention extremely dangerous.

In my peripheral, I watch a very tall man look me over. "She's something."

What the fuck is happening?

The little girl clings to me like we're family. Or maybe that's from whatever she ate last. There's a sticky residue on her cheeks and fingers. That's going to leave a stain.

Which must not be permanent enough damage for this small child. She blinks at me, revealing her genuine soul and intentions. "Will you be my mommy?"

Something strange happens to my stomach. Almost like it flips over onto itself. I might be sick. She's asking me to be her mommy. Is this a joke? Maybe I'm being tested. I definitely can't hang around for what comes next.

With more care than I've ever freely given, I pluck the kid off me. A squeak from my biker boots announces my retreat. Dammit, I'm never one to flee.

Forget the raise. The boss can find someone else to handle that level of dirty work.

Are we excited for the next couple in this small town standalone series? *Tangled in Trouble* is coming soon and you can preorder it HERE!

Have you read *Buckled in Barbwire?* This is Paisley and Brody's story. Check out this excerpt to get a feel for their enemies-to-lovers, marriage of convenience romance.

Paisley

I angle my screen higher, but Bandit's large head is still cut off. The palomino stands patiently while I attempt to fit us in the frame for a picture. No such luck. As it turns out, I haven't perfected the skill of snapping a selfie with a horse. Bianca will appreciate an update regardless.

"You're off to a productive start. Why am I not surprised?"

A gasp rips from me as I whirl to confront the gruff voice. My phone almost drops into a pile of manure from the abrupt motion, but I barely notice the bobble. Not while Brody Benson is leaning on the paddock gate, glaring at me. I gulp at the sudden dryness in my throat.

"Um, hi. I didn't see you there."

"Wonder why," he deadpans. "Is this what I can expect from your work ethic?"

I blink at the snark in his tone. "Is everything okay?"

"You tell me."

"I'm fine. You're the one…" I trail off and gesture at his surly expression.

Brody's scowl deepens into a sharp point that punctures my confidence. "This is what you get for slacking off while on the clock."

I'm shocked silent by his obvious irritation. "Slacking off?"

"What would you call it?"

"I'm doing my job."

"You're not getting paid to be a photographer."

The smile I give him is honey slathered on a thorn bush. "It won't break the bank if I take a quick pic. Bianca approves of my methods. You can trust me too."

"I'd rather eat horseshit."

In a fluid motion, he hops the fence and lands in the dirt. The loss of the barrier between us feels detrimental. I'm an open target as he stalks toward me. Brody's stride is a lethal prowl, like a predator hunting the stench of weakness. Nerves punch my stomach the closer he gets. We've only been alone on one other occasion and that didn't end well.

But that previous stumble doesn't register in this moment. I'm too preoccupied by his steady approach, and the fantasy he represents. It's no secret I've always been attracted to cowboys. Brody turns that general interest into a specific point.

The shade from his straw hat does little to conceal his devastating features. I almost choke on my tongue. My ovaries are singing hallelujah and ready to spit out eggs like a firing squad, which is wrong on so many levels.

But damn, he's sexy. Such a manly man. The complete opposite of those sorry excuses for masculinity who parade around rodeo chutes after just sprouting their first chest hair. Don't even get me started on his Wranglers. Brody is distinguished and chiseled and striking and… I'm staring. He notices my blatant ogling, which sets fire to my cheeks.

"Aren't you hot?" I blurt.

His eyes smolder into green flames. "Excuse me?"

"I'm hot just looking at you."

"And now you're hitting on me," he mutters under his breath. "This just keeps getting better."

"What? No." My cackle is shrill. "You're wearing long sleeves and it's almost ninety degrees. I'd be sweltering in that shirt."

"My clothes aren't your business, but your poor work ethic is mine."

I recoil from the hostile barb. "Are you upset about something?"

His penetrating glare is beginning to give me a complex. "What was your first clue?"

"Your sister assured me that we"—I point from his chest to mine—"won't have any problems."

"She isn't here to keep that promise. You let her run off."

Static crackles in the air, raising the hair on my arms. "I didn't *let* her do anything. Bianca is in control of her own destiny. I just offered to help so the decision to leave wouldn't weigh on her."

He snorts. "Must be nice."

"Maybe you're the one who needs a vacation," I hint.

Which is the wrong suggestion to offer. There's blistering fury in Brody's stare, ready to be unleashed. "Listen, Twinkles—"

"Twinkles?"

"You're so"—he waves a hand at my rhinestone belt and bling jeans—"sparkly."

"Should I take that as a compliment?"

"Absolutely not. You're too much."

I blink at the attitude he's flinging my way. "Too much?"

"Are you going to question everything I say?"

"Can you blame me when you're making ridiculous

statements that I don't comprehend? I'm beginning to feel like this is an interrogation."

He grins but the expression is cold and detached. "Glad we're finally on the same page."

Read *Buckled in Barbwire* today!

I have several broody, overly protective heroes in my back-list. Check out Ridge from *Score on You* as he obsesses over the shy girl he moves in next door.

Ridge

As a former professional athlete, I know how it feels to be put on a pedestal. Fans still flock to me when I'm out in public. Those years in the league also taught me what it feels like to be put on the spot and handle the stress that accompanies such a bright spotlight.

I was always able to manage the chaos in a packed arena. Block out the noise to get the win. Nothing could shake me. Past tense.

As it turns out, silence from Calliope Porter is what tests my limits. This timid woman snatches every ounce of composure I possess just by giving me her attention.

The quiet yawns and stretches, then demands a snack after such a lengthy nap. My jaw itches and I scrub at the stubble there. I need to say something. She just stumbled upon me painting her front door. This was her idea. Kind of. But that's not the point. As the trespasser, it's my responsibility to explain myself.

My tongue swells to the point where speech is impossible. Only a muffled grunt is audible from me. *Real fucking eloquent.* I clear my throat and try again.

"Hey, Callie." My palm lifts to wave at her as if that small gesture will ease the tension. "As you can see, I went ahead and took care of the update you suggested. Now you don't have to get your hands dirty. Not that it would be a bad thing if you did. It wasn't my intention to cross a line. I just wanted to handle the project for you. Consider it a housewarming gift. A personal touch from me to you."

That's not grounds for calling the cops or anything. I tuck my chin and fire off a round of foul expletives aimed directly at my mouth. The fact I'm stumbling over my words like a toddler in ice skates isn't doing me any favors. As if agreeing, Callie's lips twitch in what I trick myself into believing is amusement. At least I'm useful for something.

The affirmation—self-proclaimed or not—loosens the strain in my lungs, allowing me to breathe freely. "I meant to have this done before you got home."

A crease appears between her brows. She still doesn't speak, which is a stark contrast to the girl who has been rambling to me over text messages longer than my dick. This timid version can barely look me in the eye. It seems her fondness for conversation is reserved for our text thread. That's just fine. I'm the one who sprung this unannounced visit on her.

"This isn't how I planned for us to officially meet," I rush to explain. "But here we are. I saw you leave and figured the time was right. It was meant to be a surprise. Guess I took longer than necessary to finish."

Callie peers around me to inspect my artistic ability. The hint of a smile from earlier expands into a full grin.

I follow her line of sight to stop myself from gawking.

The effort is commendable, but worthless. My focus returns to her within seconds. "Do you like it?"

A soft hum is paired with a nod.

"If the shade isn't right—"

"No!" She startles at her own voice. "It's perfect."

And just like that, I feel ten feet tall and capable of anything. "Good. That's, uh… really good." I scrub at the prickles spreading across the back of my neck. "I'm glad."

"Thank you," Callie murmurs. She dips her face, but there's no hiding the smile that's likely to spark a heatwave. Or the way she bites her bottom lip.

It's no wonder that I find myself staring at her. Shamelessly. But I quickly recall how our exchange began. Those handful of utterances she gave me are a big step. I won't test my luck.

"Um. Is there anything else I can do for you? While I'm here, I mean?" The initial deed is done, but I'll gladly stick around for more.

Red splotches appear on her cheeks. Before my mind can take a dirty turn trying to picture what's causing that blush, she shakes her head.

I shove my hands in my pockets and prepare to leave. "Well, I did what I came to do. I'll be next door if you need me."

Callie peeks at me from beneath her lowered lashes. "Bye, Ridge."

My foot catches in the grass and I barely keep myself upright. Damn, I've been waiting a long time to hear that. What I've been imagining doesn't come close to

the real deal. My name from her lips is a burst of sweet-
ness wrapped in sinful delight. I'm already addicted and
thinking of ways to have her call out to me on repeat.

Read *Score on You* today!

ACKNOWLEDGEMENTS

Howdy! If you've made it this far, I'm crossing my fingers that you enjoyed Colton and Bianca. Thanks for picking Saddled in Secrets to read. My goal is to provide you with the story you were hoping to find when choosing it. I hope I've given you that. These two are quite a wild ride!

Can you feel my gratitude extending your way? I'm forever grateful to my readers for allowing me to keep following my author dreams. I couldn't do this without you. And this cowboy era I'm currently in is super fun. I can't wait to give you more! Get ready to giddy up.

To my husband—the grump to my sunshine. We're living a romance novel every single day and I'm so thankful you're mine. Thanks for showing me what true love feels like. Our kiddos are the best too. I'm such an emotional wreck thinking about how blessed we are. Love you so much!

To my work wife—the responsible voice to rein in my chaos. Our opposites attract in the best ways. I'm not sure what I did without you, but we'll never be a part ever again. Endless nachos and Reels.

I also need to give endless snuggles to Shain, Kate, Allison, Renee, Jackie, and Jodie for all you do. This author gig is a lonely business, but I'm very fortunate to have incredible friends. You give me pep talks when I need them most and make every day brighter.

Thanks to Alex with Infinite Well for editing my words to make them sparkle. Leticia's Editing Service is a must for cleaning up after me and my lingering typos. I appreciate you always squeezing me in! And to Bryanna for being such an awesome alpha. This book wouldn't be what it is without you.

Major thanks to Candi Kane PR for always rockin' the promo for my books. Your services and friendship are invaluable. I appreciate you so much!

The beautiful interiors of my books are thanks to Stacey and Champagne Book Design. She always wows me and makes each one unique. You're stuck with me!

All the love to Harloe's Hotties—my reader group. These are my people. My safe space. The reason I'm excited to write books and yap about them. Why I want to continue striving to improve. I'm so thankful for your support. I couldn't do this without my tribe! Same goes for my review crew, influencers, bookstagrammers, betas, and YOU for picking up this book. You're all the reason I get to continue doing this job. Keep reading for me!

Cheers to book baby number twenty-four. WOW! If you loved Saddled in Secrets, and want to do me a small favor, please consider leaving a review. Even one sentence helps new readers find my books.

Thanks for everything, and until next time.

Happy trails!

xx

Harloe

ABOUT THE AUTHOR

Harloe Rae is a *USA Today* & Amazon Top 5 best-selling author. Her passion for writing and reading has taken on a whole new meaning. Each day is an unforgettable adventure.

She's a Minnesota gal with a serious addiction to romance. There's nothing quite like an epic happily ever after. When she's not buried in the writing cave, Harloe can be found hanging with her hubby and kiddos. If the weather permits, she loves being lakeside or out in the country with her horses.

Broody heroes are Harloe's favorite to write. Her romances are swoony and emotional with plenty of heat. All of her books are available on Amazon and Kindle Unlimited.

Stay in the know by subscribing to her newsletter at
http://bit.ly/HarloesList

Join her reader group, Harloe's Hotties, at
www.facebook.com/groups/harloehotties

Check out her site at www.harloerae.com

9 781960 561213